VOLUME 37

OFFICAL SKETCHBOOK OF
JACOB HENRY KIMBALL

JAKE LOVES AMY

IF FOUND UNATTENDED,
PLEASE RETURN TO
POTTERY NIEDERBIPP

Becoming Isaac
The Next Potter of Niederbipp

First printing, September 2010

Published by
Abendmahl Press
P.O. Box 581083
Salt Lake City, Utah 84158-1083

ISBN 978-0-615-39870-9

Artwork by Ben Behunin and Erin Berrett
Photography of pottery sequence by Al Thelin
Designed by Ben Behunin and Bert Compton
Layout by Bert Compton- Compton Design Studio

BECOMING ISAAC

THE NEXT POTTER OF NIEDERBIPP

VOLUME THREE IN A SERIES

BY

BEN BEHUNIN

REMEMBER, DISCOVER, BECOME

TO LYNNETTE –
AND ALL THOSE WHO
HAVE SHARED THE JOYS
OF NIEDERBIPP.

BEHOLD,
AS THE CLAY IS
IN THE POTTER'S HAND,
SO ARE YE IN
MINE HAND.
JEREMIAH 18:6

DISCLAIMER

YOU MAY THINK YOU KNOW THE PEOPLE IN THIS BOOK, BUT UNLESS YOU'VE BEEN TO NIEDERBIPP, ANY SIMILARITIES TO THE PEOPLE YOU KNOW IS MERELY WISHFUL THINKING.

PRELUDE

I have put off writing this prelude—wondering what more I could say. Though this is the first part of this book, it is the last piece I will write in this series. It seems strange to be here, looking back at all I have learned from Isaac and the people of Niederbipp over the last twelve years. This has been a very interesting journey for me. It has been a journey of faith and sacrifice, and ultimately, a journey of understanding. As I have received emails, letters and phone calls from friends and strangers alike over the past eighteen months, thanking me for my books, I have begun to understand what these books and this series is all about. It's about light and truth and faith, and at the end of the day, it's about LOVE.

It has been more than twelve years since Isaac first began speaking to me. At the time, I was a struggling potter, a newlywed, and a student. I didn't know why he came to me. I was busy and though the things he was telling me were meaningful and instructive, they were also inconvenient. From early on, I knew I was supposed to write a book about them, but I was doubtful and stubborn. Over the past twelve years, I have learned that it requires either insight or hindsight to understand the reasons for trials in our lives. In 2004, at age thirty, I was diagnosed with arthritis in my hands. That's bad for anybody, but for me, a potter, it was humbling and often overwhelming. In hindsight, my trial was a blessing. It encouraged the changes that have led me to this point in my life. It encouraged me to finally listen, to believe, to do.

I am still a potter—supporting my family by making mud pies. But life often has an interesting way of molding you into something more than what is comfortable. It is difficult for me to consider myself a writer because all that I have written was given to me. I feel no ownership of it. Instead, a strong sense of stewardship has pushed me forward with eagerness to do what the universe wants to do.

As I finish this series, I am weighed down by a heavy sense of responsibility I feel to those who have joined me on this journey. You, too, have fallen in love with the people of Niederbipp. You, too, have sat at Isaac's wheel and learned from him. In many ways, you have drunk his tea and learned to love those whom he loved. I promise to not disappoint you with this book.

There are things I have learned from each of the books—things that have humbled me, strengthened me, and made me open my mind and heart to truth. But this third book is different. Becoming Isaac has taught me with greater clarity and insight, the love that God has for each of his children. I hope it will do the same for you. There is much about this book that I love and would like to claim as my own, but as I said before, it is not mine. With humility and reverence, I give this offering back to the universe which gave it to me, and hope you, too, will find all the Joy that its pages contain.

May your journey to Niederbipp be filled with the brightest of joys. I hope our paths will cross someday. I'll bring the tea if you bring the pastries.

Cheers to the Journey!
Ben Behunin

TABLE OF CONTENTS

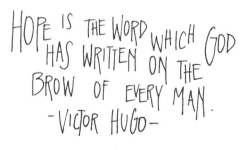

HOPE IS THE WORD WHICH GOD HAS WRITTEN ON THE BROW OF EVERY MAN.
-VICTOR HUGO-

THE PLACE OF TEARS

BEAUTIFUL LIGHT IS BORN OF DARKNESS, SO THE FAITH THAT SPRINGS FROM
CONFLICT IS OFTEN THE STRONGEST AND THE BEST.
—R. TURNBULL—

The June sun was warm on Jake and Amy's backs as they faced the river. They'd discovered the old weeping willow together just a week before when they'd come looking for it after discovering a drawing of the tree in Isaac's sketchbook. He'd called it "The Crying Place", but the well-worn path suggested it was not his alone.

There was a reverence that accompanied this place—something they both felt and acknowledged without words being exchanged. Though they'd had no problems finding things to talk about on their way here, the sight of the tree when they rounded the river bend put an end to their conversation. They'd paused for just a moment to look at the majestic tree before continuing on. It was only then that they began to feel the weight of the burdens they carried.

In Jake's backpack, next to a water bottle and a couple of sandwiches, there was a book, held together with a wide rubber band. In Amy's hand was a white envelope, the first letter she'd ever received from her father in her twenty-two years.

There was history at this tree, history that few people knew. Isaac's sketchbooks had opened that history to them—opened their minds to the tragic ruin of Isaac's family. The story had torn at their hearts, but from all they'd learned, all they'd gleaned from their reading and from the stories the town had shared with them, they had to believe Thomas' words were correct—that out of sorrow and humility, great things often come to pass. Somehow, from the shadows of tragedy, hope had risen from the ashes, inspiring not only Isaac himself, but an entire generation of Niederbippians. As they neared this place of hope and sorrow, they were both filled with peace, knowing they had come to the right place.

Jake pulled back the veil of long, straggly branches that reached nearly to the earth, allowing Amy to pass through into the dark green shadows of the tree's canopy. Though it was still before noon, the low light made it feel much later. Light reflected off the river's rippled surface and danced magically in the branches high above their heads. They watched this light in silence for a long moment, mesmerized by the singular glory and beauty of this place.

The path ended at the two low branches that ran parallel to the low grassy embankment, just inches from the river's edge. Jake dropped his bag from his shoulder, leaning it against the trunk of the tree before offering Amy his hand. She smiled softly as she took it, stepping onto the flat rocks that formed stairs to the tree's natural bench. The bark was soft here, worn smooth by unknown numbers of visitors. After Amy had taken her seat, Jake climbed up beside her. He watched as Amy traced each expertly carved letter on the big branch in front of them with her index finger:

Be still, and know that I am God.

The smooth and polished letters silently suggested that she had not been the first to do so.

She took a deep breath, exhaling slowly before she turned to face him. She smiled weakly as she stared into Jake's eyes. He responded by leaning toward her and kissing her softly.

"I never could have imagined being here," she said, lifting her head to look at the dancing lights above them. "I'm so glad I didn't take that job back in Springfield. Thank you for making me face my fears."

"I'm the one that should be thanking you."

"For what?" She looked surprised.

Jake shook his head. "For saving my life … for giving me a chance to start over … for loving me and opening my eyes to all the reasons I need to be here. Amy, you saved me from myself. You made me stop and think about what I really want out of life."

She turned and faced the river, running her fingers over the envelope she had in her hands. Jake watched her curiously. She looked unsettled— uncertain.

"What are you thinking," he finally asked after a long silence.

"I'm afraid," she said, turning again to face him. She smiled, but there were tears in her eyes.

Jake looked at her, surprised at first, but then nodded knowingly. "You're afraid of truth."

"How did you know?"

"Because two weeks ago I faced the same dilemma, remember? The details were a bit different … my truth was in a book I didn't want to open. Yours … yours is in an envelope that's just a few inches away from a watery grave."

"How did you know I was thinking about that?"

Jake shrugged, looking away. "Takes one to know one, I guess."

Amy looked back at the envelope. "So what should I do?"

"Well, you can toss it in if you want, but your mom said there's a letter in there for me too. I … I hope there's a lot of good stuff in there for you, but I guess I'm hoping there's something in there for me—granting me permission to marry you."

Amy smiled. "Do you want to open it?" she asked, extending the envelope to him.

He looked at her for a long moment. "Do you really want me to? This is the first letter you've ever received from your dad," he reminded her.

"I'm sure," she said, thrusting the envelope toward him.

He took the envelope in his hands and examined it. In the upper left-hand corner was the logo for the Clarkston Mansion Bed and Breakfast, a stylized line drawing of the mansion itself printed in silver ink. He rubbed his fingers absent mindedly over the embossed texture, his own fears giving him an unsettled feeling.

"What are you waiting for?" she asked, watching him stall.

Jake forced a smile. "I just realized I hold in my hand something that will affect the rest of my life—*our life*—if your father gives his blessing for us to marry. And if it doesn't, it will influence where we choose to spend Christmas for the next thirty-to-forty years. It just seems like a lot of big things pivot on whatever is in here. Maybe we should just throw it in the river," he said, pretending to launch it into the drink.

Amy started laughing, but quickly reached for the envelope. She tore open one end and pulled the paper from it, exposing three letters folded separately. She handed Jake one of the letters that had his name printed on the outside. Then, looking up at him, she unfolded the thickest of the letters. There, hanging from the upper left-hand corner with a silver paper clip was a familiar piece of paper.

Jake glanced at it before turning to face Amy with wide eyes. "Where in the world did he get that?"

Amy shook her head, looking as surprised as Jake. The paper had been ripped from her sketchbook just a week earlier. There in Amy's own hand was the note she had written and floated down the river in a plastic bottle.

Help me.

I'm stranded on an island with a handsome potter and we have nothing to eat but sunflower bread and nothing to do but throw rocks in the river and kiss. He's getting better at both, but he still needs some practice.

If you find this note, know that I am happy on my island. I'm in love.

Amy Eckstein

Jake slid over next to her so their shoulders touched. "I can't believe this. I never, in a million years could have imagined that your Dad would have found that. How do you think he got this?"

Amy shrugged, looking at the note in complete disbelief. "I know my dad grew up here, but I never ..." She shook her head.

"What are you thinking?"

She stared at the letter, shaking her head again. "I … I got that job selling makeup just by Daddy calling Mr. Schatz. Maybe he's better connected here than I realized."

"Maybe it says something more about it in the letter," Jake said, nudging her to continue.

Amy nodded, folding the note over to expose her father's words, loosely scrawled on Clarkston Mansion Bed and Breakfast stationery in blue ink. The words were big and bold, filling the page. She looked up at Jake and smiled weakly before reading the letter aloud.

CLARKSTON MANSION BED & BREAKFAST
MIDBURY, IN.

AMY,

IT IS NOW 3 A.M. AND I AM TIRED OF STRUGGLING TO FIND THE RIGHT WORDS, SO I AM JUST GOING TO TELL YOU HOW I FEEL SO I CAN FINALLY GET SOME REST. I CAME HERE THIS WEEKEND INTOXICATED WITH ANGER AND FRUSTRATION. I BELIEVED, AND STILL MAINTAIN THAT YOU ARE WASTING YOUR LIFE AND BEV AND JERRY'S HOSPITALITY WITH YOUR SILLY DREAM TO BE AN ARTIST.

WHEN MY OLD FRIEND, PATRICK SCHNEIDER, CALLED LAST WEEK TO ME TO TELL ME ABOUT A LETTER HIS DOG HAD FOUND IN THE RIVER, I REALLY LOST IT. WE HAD JUST RETURNED FROM THE BUS STATION WHERE WE ANTICIPATED WE WOULD PICK YOU UP. WHEN YOU WEREN'T ON THAT BUS, YOUR MOTHER WAS CONVINCED THAT YOU HAD BEEN DRUGGED AND WERE LYING IN DITCH SOMEWHERE—DEAD.

BEV PUT YOUR MOTHER'S MIND AT EASE AS TO YOUR SAFETY, BUT YOUR IRRESPONSIBILITY AND LACK OF COMMUNICATION HAS BEEN DISAPPOINTING TO BOTH OF US. WE CAME HERE DETERMINED TO TAKE YOU HOME WITH US, BUT THE EVENTS OF THE LAST 24 HOURS, OUR INVESTIGATION, AND THIS EVENING AT THE RESTAURANT

HAVE MADE ME REALIZE THAT *I* REALLY DON'T KNOW
YOU. SOMEHOW, OVER THE PAST FEW YEARS, YOU HAVE
BECOME AN ARTIST DESPITE MY BEST EFFORTS TO PUSH
YOU IN MORE PRACTICAL DIRECTIONS.

   I WISH YOU WOULD RECOGNIZE THE
IMPRACTICALITY OF YOUR CHOSEN COURSE, BUT *I* SEE
THAT ARGUING WITH YOU HAS PROBABLY ONLY PUSHED
YOU FURTHER AWAY FROM MY DESIRES. YOU HAVE
ALWAYS HAD A MIND OF YOUR OWN, AND A STUBBORN
ONE AT THAT.

   AS *I* HAVE REPLAYED IN MY MIND THE EVENTS OF
THIS EVENING, *I* HAVE BECOME INCREASINGLY ANGRY
ABOUT THIS SITUATION. YOU AND YOUR BOYFRIEND
PUT ME IN A VERY AWKWARD AND UNCOMFORTABLE
POSITION AT THE RESTAURANT. *I* HAVE NEVER BEEN SO
HUMILIATED. *I* HOPE THAT ONE DAY YOU WILL HAVE A
DAUGHTER WHO IS AS UNGRATEFUL, DISRESPECTFUL AND
IMPRACTICAL AS YOU ARE.

   I DON'T EXPECT THAT JAKE WILL EVER BE ABLE TO
PROVIDE YOU WITH THE LUXURIES YOU HAVE ENJOYED
IN MY HOME OR WHILE YOU WERE BEING SUPPORTED
BY MY POCKETBOOK. *I* HAVE PROVIDED YOU WITH AN
EXPENSIVE EDUCATION. *I* HAVE TRIED TO PROVIDE

YOU WITH A MIND FOR BUSINESS. *I* HOPE YOU WILL
USE THESE THINGS *I* GAVE YOU TO FIGURE YOUR LIFE
OUT. *I* STILL FEEL LIKE YOU ARE DOOMING YOURSELF
TO A LIFE OF POVERTY, BUT *I* SEE NOW THAT ALL THE
ADVICE *I* HAVE TRIED TO GIVE YOU OVER THE YEARS
HAS BEEN WASTED ON YOU.

   WE CAME HERE TO TAKE YOU HOME, BUT WE ARE
LEAVING IN THE MORNING WITHOUT YOU. *I* SEE THAT
THIS BACKWARDS TOWN IS MORE OF A HOME TO YOU
THAN IT EVER WAS TO ME. IF YOU COME TO YOUR
SENSES AND CHANGE YOUR MIND, WE WILL BE BACK
IN A FEW WEEKS. *I* TOLD YOUR MOTHER IT WAS A
WASTE OF TIME, BUT WE WILL BE SPENDING A WEEK

AT A MARRIAGE RETREAT. IF YOU WOULD LIKE TO GO
HOME WITH US AT THAT TIME, I MAY STILL BE ABLE TO
PULL SOME STRINGS AND GET YOU THAT JOB WITH MY
FRIEND AT THE ADVERTISING FIRM.

AMY, I OBVIOUSLY DON'T KNOW JAKE, BUT
IT IS ABUNDANTLY CLEAR TO ME THAT HIS LACK
OF CONNECTIONS AND WEALTH WILL OFFER YOU NO
ADVANTAGE IN THE LIFE YOU HAVE CHOSEN. I HAVE
OBVIOUSLY FAILED TO CONVINCE YOU OF THE FOLLY
OF YOUR ASPIRATIONS, BUT FOR THE RECORD, I
THINK YOU ARE FOOLISH TO MARRY SOMEONE YOU JUST
BARELY MET.

AS I HAVE WITH EACH OF YOUR BROTHERS WHEN
THEY MARRIED, I AM GIVING YOU AN ADVANCE ON
YOUR INHERITANCE. ENCLOSED YOU WILL FIND A
CHECK. BASED ON YOUR REBELLIOUS NATURE, I AM
HESITANT TO LEAVE YOU WITH THIS MUCH MONEY, BUT
YOUR MOTHER INSISTS THAT IT IS ONLY FAIR. YOUR
BROTHERS HAVE USED THEIR FUNDS TO BEGIN THEIR
BUSINESSES. I TRUST YOU WILL DO SOMETHING MORE
PRACTICAL WITH THIS MONEY THAN SPENDING IT ON
MAKEUP AND PAINT.

  -DAD

Amy turned the letter over as if she was looking for more, but there
was none to be found. On the back side, however, attached with the same
paper clip that held her own note in place, was a check. She separated it
from the other papers and turned it over. Jake leaned in, resting his chin
on her shoulder. His eyes widened when he saw the amount—twenty-five
thousand dollars!

He drew back so he could look at Amy. Tears were flowing down her
cheeks. "What are you thinking?" he asked.

She shook her head as her tears flowed more heavily.

He rested his hand on her back, trying to comfort her, but entirely unsure of what to say. Outside of his acquisition of The Pottery and the apartment, no one had ever offered him anything like this. There had never been any hope of an inheritance from his family. His mother's cancer had depleted all of her savings, and her life insurance policy had been cancelled after her first bout with cancer. He found himself feeling once again like the poor orphan that he was. Twenty-five thousand dollars was more than he hoped to make that year. Heck, it was almost more than the total amount of money he had earned in his entire life. He tried to imagine what was going through her head. Was she overwhelmed with her father's generosity? Was she calculating how far that would go to provide her with art supplies?

He was pulled from his thoughts as she handed him the letter. Then, without another word, she took the check in her fingers and ripped it up over and over again before tossing the confetti into the river. Jake followed the paper with his eyes as it floated on the surface of the green water until it drifted outside of the tree's canopy and beyond his field of view.

"All I hoped for was an apology for the way he treated me last night," Amy said, shaking her head. "He couldn't do it. He never has. This might be the closest he ever got, but he has never apologized to me for the way he's treated me more like property than his daughter—than his own flesh and blood."

Jake looked down at the letter she'd just read, skimming over it, looking for an apology. But she was right—there was none. He really hadn't even gotten close to admitting wrongdoing or apologizing for the hurtful things he'd said.

His reading was interrupted by her laughter. He looked up, surprised by her change in emotion, but it was short-lived.

"There is no such thing as free money with my dad," she said, turning away from the river to look at him. "He claims my brothers' successes as his own because he gave them the money to get started. Call me proud, but if I am going to make it, I want to make it on my own—or not at all."

Jake nodded thoughtfully. "I guess you can understand now how I feel about receiving a free studio and apartment?"

She turned to face him, looking surprised.

"You're right Amy. There is no such thing as free money, or a free studio and apartment. Everything we are given comes with expectations. I guess it's comes down to whether we are willing to accept whatever baggage comes with the *gift*."

After a long silence, she spoke. "So, after meeting my parents, are you willing to accept me with all the baggage that comes with me?"

Jake nodded in response to the loaded question. He felt no reason to hide his feelings. There was no need for secrets any longer. He put his hand on top of hers and squeezed it softly. "Amy, I love you. I'd want to marry you even if you came with a mountain of baggage and your parents were trolls."

She smiled. "Trolls might be easier to live with."

"But we don't have to live with them. We don't even have to visit them if we don't want to. I never considered the lack of a car to be an advantage, but it gives us a legitimate excuse."

She laughed, reaching for her father's letter. "It's so strange to think I spent eighteen years in my father's home and he doesn't even know me—doesn't even know that I don't wear makeup?"

"Why don't you just rip it up and send it down river?"

She held the letter in her hands as if she were about to do just that, but she hesitated.

Jake watched expectantly, but when her tears began again, he took the letter from her, dropping it on the ground behind them before taking her in his arms the best he could as they balanced awkwardly on the limb. She cried for a long time, while her father's unkind and thoughtless words from the night before ran through his head. His letter had done nothing to quell the pain his words had inflicted—only added to the sorrow and hurt. The only letter she had ever received from her father was a total flop. It had explained the reason for their visit, but there was only justification for his actions and blame for his own discomfort where a simple apology would have made all the difference in the world. As he held her in his arms, Jake was surprised by his own emotions. They were not manifested in the same way as Amy's. They were much more subtle but nonetheless real. Envy. Jealousy.

Why did he feel this way? He held in his arms the blubbering fruits of that tree, and yet there was still envy for what she had. Maybe her father was a troll or at the very least—a jerk, but she *had* a father. Jake knew his emotions were irrational and ridiculous, but they still stung. He had never really known his own father, and the memories that remained of him were dark and painful. He had never  received a letter—not even a birthday card from the man who'd given him his name. The feelings were confusing and draining. There were already too many unanswered questions. It made his head hurt to think about them. But Amy's letter had opened an old wound—one he had long tried to ignore. He had no father—and what was worse— he had no answers.

FOLLOW YOUR BLISS AND THE UNIVERSE WILL OPEN DOORS FOR YOU WHERE THERE WERE ONLY WALLS.
- JOSEPH CAMPBELL -

SONG OF THE RIVER

ADVERSITY MAKES MEN, AND PROSPERITY MAKES MONSTERS.
—VICTOR HUGO—

Amy stopped crying after several minutes and dried her tears. "I have already given my dad too many of my best days. I'm not going to give him any more," she said resolutely. "We still have a couple of letters to open. There has to be something good in my mom's at least."

Jake nodded, turning to pick up the remaining letters from the clump of tall grass where they had fallen. Jake's name was written on the top letter, scrawled in Doug's handwriting. He offered Amy the other letter as he unfolded the single piece of paper and began to read.

CLARKSTON MANSION BED & BREAKFAST
NEDERODT, PA.

JAKE,

YOU DID NOT DIRECTLY ASK FOR MY
PERMISSION TO MARRY MY DAUGHTER, BUT
IT WAS MADE CLEAR TO US TONIGHT THAT THAT
IS YOUR INTENT. AFTER DEALING WITH HER
DEFIANT BEHAVIOR FOR THE PAST SEVERAL
YEARS, I DON'T KNOW IF THE PERMISSION IS
MINE TO GRANT, BUT IF IT IS, I OFFER YOU
MY BLESSINGS. I WILL WARN YOU, HOWEVER,
THAT SHE IS STRONG-HEADED AND OBSTINATE.
IF YOU ARE WILLING TO ACCEPT HER AS SHE
IS, THEN I WISH YOU WELL.

- DOUG ECKSTEIN

Jake looked up from the letter, smiling broadly. "Well, all things considered, I'd say that was pretty positive," he said sarcastically.

Amy exhaled as if she'd been holding her breath. "Funny that he didn't even mention my name, referring to me only as 'my daughter.' I guess I shouldn't be surprised after his letter to me."

Jake pointed to the letter. "He did offer his blessings. That's better than a curse."

She shook her head, looking down at the last letter which she held tightly in her hands as if she was clinging to the end of a rope. "Would you mind reading this," she asked, handing him the crumpled letter. She turned and put her elbows on the limb in front of her, resting her chin in her hands and looking out at the water. She looked tired and emotionally drained.

Jake unfolded the letter and began to read.

Dear Amy,

After trying to help your father edit his first few letters to you, he asked me to leave him alone. I have no idea what the outcome will be. I am sorry if it is less than you hoped it would be. I am sorry for this trip. I am sorry for the way we embarrassed you in front of your friends. I am sorry I didn't stand up for you. I am sorry for spying on you and Jake.

It is hard for me to believe my baby girl is now a woman. You are beautiful and talented and amazing. I have always admired your strength and ambition. Regardless of what we have said and the paths we have encouraged you to follow, you have always been one who has marched to the beat of a different drummer. In so many ways, the paths we have chosen have been wrong for you. You have proven that fact time and again. It has been a struggle for all of us, but from what we learned today and experienced this evening at the restaurant, I know we have no reason to worry about you. You have found love. You have found direction. You have discovered your passions and you are pursuing them, independent of us.

I know you will not understand this for many years, but it's not easy to watch your little girl grow up. It's even more difficult to realize that you don't need me any more. Your father and I have no idea how our genes could ever have produced a person as creative as you. There must be something special that accompanies the generation-skipping Eckstein red hair. You have been an inspiration to me since you were a child. I will never forget how long you always took to walk home from school, even though it was only a few blocks away. There was never a flower you didn't notice or an insect that was left unexamined.

As we spent time talking with your dad's old friends today, our questions were met with mixed reactions. It was no surprise to me to hear that you have already broken many hearts in the short time you have been here. Several of the young men we interviewed had nothing good to say about Jake. It was apparent to me long before your father clued in that their disdain for Jake was more a result of their jealousy than it was out of anything substantial. Many others defended you both. It

seems the whole town has been watching you. Many of the old folks who recognized your dad as we walked through town stopped us to say how delighted they have been as they've watched your friendship and love grow.

I am happy for you, Amy. Though our exposure to Jake has been very limited, I am impressed with him. As I watched him defend you and your honor tonight, I realized I could not imagine a better person for you. I have missed out on this—watching you fall in love—and I'm afraid our actions this weekend will only serve to alienate you further. Jerry and Bev made it clear tonight that you are in love—that you both love

each other. When they mentioned Jake's intention to marry you, my first thought was that you are too young to make such a decision. But you're an adult now, and already 2 years older than I was when your father and I ran away and got married. You have a better head on your shoulders at 22 than I did at 40.

I think your father has forgotten our humble beginnings. We met when your father's student loans made him worth more dead than alive. I reminded him tonight of the first time I took him home to meet my parents. That visit went very poorly. Because of my wealthy upbringing, my father accused your dad of being a treasure hunter. He responded by lashing out, insulting your grandfather as coarsely as he could before leaving with me. We decided to elope that night and we just kept on driving, getting married by a county judge just outside of St. Lewis, Missouri. We planned to honeymoon in California, but your father's old car started having problems when we reached Denver. Instead, we spent a week in Vail with his second cousin and his family while our car was being repaired. We returned back to school – poorer than we were before, but happier than I ever remember being. Your brother Robert was born a year later.

Over time, your father and I were able to mend fences with your grandparents. You kids were a great bargaining chip in that respect. It became increasingly easy to visit them as our financial status grew, but even then, your father was often intimidated by the money and position my parents maintained. As I have replayed in my mind the events of this evening, I realize we have become the monsters we once accused your grandparents of being.

Amy, I am ashamed of the way we treated you tonight. We wasted the whole weekend-being more concerned about what others think about you and Jake than taking the time to get to know him and you better. I am sorry. We are bad spies and even worse parents.

CLARKSTON MANSION BED & BREAKFAST
NIEDERBIPP, PA

I am grateful for Bev and Jerry and the love they have always had for you.

I was angry and worried when you weren't on that bus last Sunday, but I understand why you stayed. You have always loved Niederbipp. I see now that you need to be here. I hope that in time you will forgive us. Our desires have been good even though our methods have obviously failed miserably. I hope that time will bring healing and forgiveness.

I don't know if it counts for anything at this point, but I love you and sincerely wish you all the best. You are my only daughter and I have looked forward to your wedding ever since you were a child. I know our tastes have not been the same for many years, but if you will allow me, I want to offer my help with any preparations.

I love you, Amy, and I am very proud of the woman you have become - in spite of us. Please call me at least once a week to let me know how you are doing.

Love, Mom

Jake looked up to find Amy smiling through her tears. He was surprised she had any tears left, but her smile seemed to indicate emotions vastly different from those following her father's letter. This letter was different. It was more humane, more sensitive, more understanding, more … like Amy. He was grateful that Amy was more like her mother in temperament. He wasn't sure how or if things would ever become better with her dad—the chasm seeming so wide and deep. As Jake watched her trying to compose herself, he realized her father clueless about his own daughter and the amazing person she was.

Jake put his hand on her shoulder and she responded by embracing him again.

"Thank you," she whispered in his ear.

"For what?"

"For being here. I couldn't have done this alone."

Jake laughed softly.

"What?" she said, pulling back to look in his face.

"I was just thinking—if it hadn't been for me and that note we sent down the river, you wouldn't have all this drama in your life."

She laughed, shaking her head. "Who would have thought love would be so difficult. Jake, this had to happen sometime. My father never would have allowed me to get away with something so contrary to his wishes without a fight. I'm just really grateful for your help."

"Amy," Jake said softly, "I love you. You said something last week that I've been thinking about ever since. They are the only parents you have, and although they're only going to be in-laws for me, that's the closest thing I have to family."

She smiled and hugged him again. "I need to walk," she said after a moment. "My legs have fallen asleep."

Jake jumped down from the limb. He stood behind her as she draped her arm over his shoulder and fell back against his chest as he lifted her legs off the limb. It was the first time he'd ever held her like this. His left arm protested at the scar, but he ignored the dull pain, enjoying the moment of holding the girl he knew he was going to marry. Reluctantly, he set her feet on the ground, but held onto to her waist as her legs and feet regained feeling.

More than an hour had past since they'd arrived here, and the magical light that had danced in the branches above their heads had changed with the flight of the sun. Only a few glimmering sunbeams illuminated the branches where hundreds had danced before, but the peace that embraced this place remained.

"I'm glad we came here," she whispered over the song of the river.

Jake nodded, letting her go and stooping over to pick up the letters that had scattered on the soft ground. She watched him as he shuffled the pages back together. He looked up to find her smiling.

"What are you thinking?" he asked.

"I was just thinking about Isaac and the history he had here."

"What about it?"

She sat down on the ground next to him. "This was a place of sorrow, but also of hope. I was just wondering if he ever imagined us—if he ever had a dream about us like he said he did about you in the dedication of your new book."

Jake smiled at her. "I hope he did. I … I'd like to imagine that wherever he is, he's rooting for us."

He stood and offered Amy his hand. "What do you want to do with these," he asked.

She pulled her mother's letter from the stack. Jake pulled his letter from her father. "I don't think I ever want to read that one again," she said, nodding to the remaining letter. Litterbugs have always bothered me, but …"

Jake nodded, walking to the edge of the water. He stooped over and was about to lay it on the surface when a dark object caught his attention on the trunk of the tree just inches away. He turned his head to see that the dark object was actually a hole in the trunk. Without a word, he slipped the letter into the hole until it disappeared into the darkness. Then he took Amy's hand as they walked out of the shadows of the old willow and into the light of the summer sun.

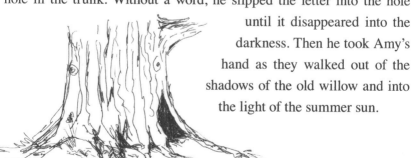

FROMAGE BON VIVANTS

MONEY IS NOT REQUIRED TO BUY ONE NECESSITY OF THE SOUL.
—HENRY DAVID THOREAU—

A hh, the potter and the barber's niece, I presume."

Jake and Amy looked at each other, then back at the man on the trail in front of them. He was dressed in a pair of sage-colored, corduroy knickers with red argyle socks and hiking boots that covered all but the smallest band of his hairy legs. His white blouse was embroidered with bright flowers around the neck and collar. He looked entirely out of place—like a Swiss yodeler who had gone out for a hike in the Alps and wound up on the flat trail that followed the Allegheny River instead.

Amy squeezed Jake's hand until he turned again to find her smiling.

The stranger continued toward them. Around his neck he wore a camera, and his right hand held a long walking stick adorned with dozens of colorful, metallic pendants.

"Good afternoon," said the man, as he came to a stop. He pulled a white handkerchief from his back pocket and mopped the sweat from his long, white mustache and rosy cheeks before smiling at them again. "Lovely day for a walk, but I'm afraid I didn't plan for the heat."

Jake nodded, extending his hand. "I'm Jake Kimball, and this is Amy Eckstein."

The man nodded to Amy as he took Jake's hand. "It's a real pleasure to meet you, Jake and to see you again, Amy."

"Have we met before?" asked Amy, looking confused.

The man nodded. "Yes, but it's been the better part of fifteen years. You were just knee high to a grasshopper  the last time I saw you. I wouldn't have recognized you if it weren't for your red hair. Your father and I have done a lot of business together over the years."

The timing of this revelation was not great, and Jake watched as Amy bristled slightly.

"I am Eric Schmelding," he continued. "I just got back in town on Wednesday. I understand I would have met you earlier today if my jetlag hadn't got the best of me. I'm just coming from the church now. Thomas said I might run into you."

Jake stole a glance at Amy, wondering if this man might be Mr. Allan's long lost brother or maybe a cousin to the Mancinis, but Amy's face registered the same confusion he felt.

"So, Jake, tell me how things are going. I was in the Himalayas when I received word of Isaac's passing. He was a good man—one-of-a-kind—salt of the earth. I was looking forward to showing him the pictures of my travels. He was always so anxious to see and hear about the places I've been."

This information piqued Jake's interest, as images of high mountain peaks ran through his mind. "Did you make it to Tibet?" he asked.

"Yes, I spent more than a month there this time before working my way through Nepal and Rajasthan. I captured some amazing images," he said, patting his camera softly with his hand. I look forward to showing them off."

Suddenly, Jake clued in to who this man was. "Hey, you're the guy that gives slide shows from places around the world!"

"Well, I used to, but for the past several years I've gone digital. It makes it easier than a slide show. You've heard about me?"

"Yeah, Sandy told me about how you inspired her and her fiancé to plan their honeymoon to Norway."

"Is that right?"

"That's what she told me. She said you do your presentations a lot during the summer. She said you've been all over the world."

Eric stood a little taller and nodded proudly. "I've been to all seven continents, but only 173 countries. I'm hoping to get to them all before I die."

"How many more do you have? I didn't know there were more than 173," responded Amy.

"It depends on who you ask, but the UN currently recognizes 195. When I started my travels there were only 190." He held out his walking stick. "I've collected pendants from lots of those countries. It's been quite an adventure."

"Do you go just to take pictures?" Amy asked.

Eric laughed. "No. Most people think it's about the pictures, and I suppose it is—to an extent—but it never started out that way. I'm more of a collector, really."

"What do you collect?" asked Jake.

Eric smiled broadly and mopped his brow with his handkerchief again. "We all have to have our passions. Mine just happens to be cheese."

"Cheese?" Jake and Amy asked in unison.

Eric blushed slightly, but then stood tall, resting his hand on his belt like he was a famous explorer posing for a photo. "Yes, well, it may seem odd to you, but there is a small, unique band of globetrotters like myself whose travel is governed by our appetite for the world's rarest and finest cheeses. We call ourselves *Fromage bon vivants.*

Jake and Amy looked at each other, unsure if they should believe this strange man.

"But … isn't it kind of hard to collect something that you eat?" asked Jake.

"That, my boy, is the very reason my hobby is so difficult. I have found that just when I obtain a decent specimen for my collection, I'm sorely tempted to consume it. It requires an enormous amount of discipline. I am fortunate to have been able, over the course of my travels, to acquire some wonderful friends whose cheesemaking abilities can keep up with my infatuations."

Jake nodded. "So, what do you do with the cheese when you discover it?"

"It depends a great deal on the cheese. Of course I always consume some, but a true *Fromage bon vivant* must also collect, catalog and warehouse his cheeses. I maintain a rather extensive and elite assembly in my cheese cache."

"So, you travel the world collecting cheese that you don't really eat?" asked Amy, trying hard to understand this man's unusual ambitions.

"The word 'eat' seems so raucous, so … unrefined when applied to cheese. We *Fromage bon vivants* like to refer to it as '*nosh.*' We eat it, but not like a teenager might consume a cheeseburger. A *nosh* is really more of a graceful dance. As with wine tasting, in order for one to fully appreciate the properties of a cheese, one must *see, sniff and savor.*"

"I see," said Amy, lying the best she could. She tried to imagine what he was talking about, but was sure she had no real idea.

"Yes, well, I'm afraid it's a bit of a bore for most folks. I come from a long family line of *Fromage bon vivants,* but I'm the only one in my generation who developed the necessary passion to pursue it. It makes for a rather chaotic life of travel and adventure."

"Then why do it?" asked Jake.

"Passion! As misguided as it may seem to some, I believe passion is the only reason to do anything in this life. In my case, I am fortunate that one passion supports another. I might have had to give up my passion for cheese if I hadn't discovered photography, and that would have been a tragedy. I was born a *Fromage bon vivant* and I'm certain I would have perished long ago if I had been unable to pursue my God-given talents."

"Do you mind if I ask you a personal question?" asked Amy.

"Not at all."

"How do you support yourself financially? All that travel and collecting rare cheeses can't be cheap."

"No, you're right, its not. But I have found that my rare talent is in high demand. I run my grandfather's old watch shop on Hauptstrasse during the tourist season. That takes care of my living expenses for most of the year. My travel is generally paid for by independent cheesemakers who seek the internationally acclaimed stamp of approval from the *Society of Fromage bon vivants*. In the evenings, I'm a busker. If all things work out as I plan, I stay a couple of dollars ahead of my needs until I return home.

"A *busker*?" Jake asked, looking confused.

"Yes—a performer—of sorts. I share Power Point presentations of my pictures. People are always interested in the world beyond their own village, though few of us venture far—and even fewer return with the tales to tell. It's difficult for many Americans to understand that most people around the world have never been more than fifty miles from their homes. I show them pictures of the other side of the world, and they offer me a place to sleep and food to eat. Some of my oldest and finest cheeses have come as gifts from families and individuals who have become my friends as I sat by their fires and told tales of people and places in exotic lands."

Jake smiled. He liked this guy, even if he was a bit eccentric. "So, what brings you down to the river?" he asked

Eric closed his eyes tightly and looked directly at the sun. "I was hoping to get back in sync with the rhythms of this place." He put his hand into the pocket of his knickers and pulled out a red bandana. He unfolded it slowly to reveal a handful of small, ivory-colored cubes. "Six-year-old yak cheese from Tibet," he said with a wink. "I ... I'll share with you if you'd like to try."

Jake looked at Amy before reaching in to take one. She followed, also taking one. Jake was about to pop it in his mouth when Eric spoke. "There are a few important things to fully appreciating a six-year-old yak cheese. Remember to *see, sniff and savor.*" With that, he lifted one of the morsels above his head, held securely between his thumb and forefinger, until it blocked out the sun, causing the nugget to glow like the moon.

Jake and Amy smiled at each other as they watched the man handle his cheese as if it were the finest of jewels.

"Next, comes the sniff." He placed the morsel in his palm before curling his fingers gently around it. He lifted his hand to his large nose before closing his eyes and inhaling deeply. "Can you smell it?" he asked.

Jake and Amy quickly responded by mimicking his actions, taking deep breaths. The scent of the small morsel was earthy and strong, but pleasing.

"Do you smell the sage?" Eric asked, his eyes still closed as if he were shutting down all of his senses that might interfere with his sense of smell.

"A little I guess," responded Amy. "What else do you smell?"

Eric took another great whiff of the cheese, filling his cheeks with air. He moved the air around in his mouth as if he was swishing and gargling water. Then he exhaled slowly. With his eyes still closed, he began to speak. "I smell the fullness of the wind as it flies down the rocky canyon walls. I smell the scent of crystal blue water that comes only from the runoff of ancient glaciers. I smell grass. I … I hear the sound of bells and I can see hundreds of colorful prayer flags fluttering in the same alpine breeze that tickles my neck and mustache. In the distance—maybe in the next valley over—I hear the chant of Buddhist monks as it echoes off the canyon walls."

He opened his eyes and looked at them, blinking as though he'd just been startled awake from a long nap.

"Now, for the nosh. Pinch it softly between your front teeth and inhale deeply, filling your lungs with the aura of the cheese. Then you can let your tongue take over."

They watched as he performed the ritual in the way he'd just described. Then they did the same, watching each other as they chewed—trying not to chew at all, but rather nosh like they were pros. By the time he swallowed, Jake knew for sure he had never chewed any single bit of food for anywhere as long. But he also knew he would never be able to look at a yak the same way.

"That, my young friends, is one of the finest yak cheeses I have ever experienced."

"Me too," said Jake.

Amy nodded. "Are all yak cheeses pretty similar?"

Eric smiled as he curled the ends of his mustache with his fingers. "That's a bit like asking if all cow cheeses are the same. No," he said, shaking his head, "there are thousands of yak herds in the Himalayas, each one producing milk that is as unique as the blades of grass they eat. Each valley has its own water source and each cheesemaker, his own recipes—many of which have been passed down from generation to generation. To taste a cheese like this is to taste history and place and culture, no pun intended."

"Do you feel the same way about all cheeses?" asked Jake.

Eric shook his head, looking disgusted. "Some cheeses are made without soul. Some, I am told, are even made without milk—modern day concoctions of recycled cardboard and soybean derivatives. Good cheese takes time and passion and work. It requires understanding and patience. I guess that is where people like me come in—people who have exercised our talents to be able to weed out the imposters and give our approval to those cheesemakers who have earned the world's respect."

Jake nodded, considering his own passions for clay and good pottery. He knew he didn't entirely understand Eric, but he figured he probably understood him better than most.

"So, when are you giving your next presentation?" asked Amy, interrupting his thoughts.

"The Mayor just asked me about that an hour ago. We are planning for next Sunday night if the weather cooperates. Do you think you would like to come? I'll be showing my latest pictures from Nepal, Tibet and Rajasthan."

Amy looked at Jake.

"Yeah. But is it going to make my wanderlust flare up? I've been a bit of a globetrotter myself," Jake said, squeezing Amy's hand, "but I recently made a commitment to put down some roots."

Eric smiled, nodding. "Good for you. Love is a beautiful thing. I often wonder where I'd be if I'd paid more attention to my heart than I did to my travels. I can't tell you how my presentation will affect you. My intention is never to encourage world travel, but it is often a result."

"So, why *do* you give the presentations?" asked Amy.

"To share the stories that I witness in my travels. All of us have a story to tell. I justify my travels and my obsession with cheese because of the stories I get to share and hear from others along my journey. It gives meaning and substance to my life—filling the void that might have been filled with family had my path taken me down that road."

He nodded before glancing up at the sun again. "I don't mean to be rude, but I've been trying to catch a glimpse of a rather rare species of carp for several years now. Their mating season only runs one week a year and I fear I've nearly missed it. I hope you don't mind if I catch up with you later."

"Not at all," said Jake. "We'll see you next Sunday."

They shook hands, and Jake and Amy watched as the strange man hurried up the meandering path, disappearing down the steep banks where the river and the rocks mingled at the water's edge.

IF YOU WILL MAKE LISTENING AND OBSERVATION YOUR OCCUPATION YOU WILL GAIN MUCH MORE THAN YOU CAN BY TALK.
- ROBERT BADEN- POWELL —

SHARING CHICKENS

LIFE IS REALLY SIMPLE, BUT WE INSIST ON MAKING IT COMPLICATED.
—CONFUCIUS—

B y the time Jake and Amy left Gloria and Joseph's home that evening, the morning's tears were all but forgotten. All four of them had huddled in the small kitchen, preparing their meal. The feeling of belonging to a family that Jake had experienced in their home before was stronger than ever. Gloria and Joseph embraced Amy with love and affection, as they had done with him from the very beginning. The stories and laughter they shared with each other was healing and enlightening, scattering any remnants of sorrow like the sun burning off the morning fog.

It was after eleven when Jake and Amy finally emerged with both their bellies and their hearts filled. Jake took Amy's hand as they walked out onto Hauptstrasse in silence. The street was still, but a charming glow from the street lamps illuminated their path, casting long shadows.

"Thank you," Amy said when they reached her door.

"For what?"

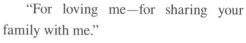

"For loving me—for sharing your family with me."

Jake looked at her, surprised. But then he understood. "Mi pollo es tu pollo," he said as he embraced her.

"What?" she asked, laughing and pulling back to look at him.

"Oh, just something my roommate used to always tell the girl he ended up marrying."

"What does it mean?"

"I think it means, my chicken is your chicken."

She laughed out loud. "Jake, you really know how to get to a girl."

"I always thought it was funny too, but it seemed to work for him. They've been married for more than a year."

"Well, maybe that's one of the secrets to a happy marriage."

"Sharing your chicken?" he asked with a grin across his face.

"And everything else," she said hugging him tighter. "Thank you for sharing your day with me, for crying with me and loving me and letting me share the good things in your life. I'm sorry that sharing my family with you was not anywhere near as much fun as Gloria and Joseph were tonight."

"Oh, it's not that bad. I love Bev and Jerry, and even Mr. Allan is starting to grow on me."

Amy laughed again. "I just wish my parents could be as happy for me as Gloria and Joseph are for you."

Jake hugged her again. He wanted to tell her everything would work out—that her parents would change, open their eyes and realize what a wonderful, amazing, beautiful woman they had as a daughter. But memories of her father's letter held him back. He knew the change that Amy desired in her father might never come. He might never open his eyes to the truth of who his only daughter was and the person she'd become while he'd been too busy with his own life to notice. The thought of it was depressing. Doug was not his father, but he hoped with time, Doug would be his friend. But even that seemed like a hope that would likely not happen until the very distant future. It was hard to think of friendship with this man when even civility seemed like a foreign concept. Still, as Jake held the cranky man's only daughter in his arms, he hoped beyond hope that there would come a time when there could be peace—and maybe even friendship between them.

"What are you thinking?" asked Amy.

"That I love you," Jake fibbed, knowing that sharing his real thoughts, in this case, would only re-ignite the sorrow she'd felt earlier.

She squeezed him tighter and he leaned his face down to kiss her. It was a long kiss—longer than it had ever been before. He didn't know for sure, and he didn't want to ask, but he thought he was probably getting much better at this kissing thing than he'd been that night in the graveyard. In many ways, it seemed like it had been months since that night. So much had happened—so much had changed. Change. *Change.* Jake pulled back, giving Amy another hug. "I'd better go," he said.

She looked at him and nodded with disappointment in her eyes.

"I think the tiles for Sam's floor will be ready to glaze tomorrow. Do you think you can help me?"

"Jake, you know you need my help. Besides, I want my share of the bread. What time should I be there?"

"If we get started early, we might still be able to go on that scooter ride in the hills that I've been promising you."

"Oh, yeah. Should I come at eight?"

"Sure," he said, giving her another hug before letting her go.

"I love you," she said when he reached the bottom stair.

He turned to look at her. "I know, and I love you back."

As he walked back to his apartment, his mind was once again filled with excitement. So many nights before he'd walked this way with his mind filled with thoughts of Amy. Tonight was different. Change was on his mind, inspired in part by his own change of heart. If *he* could change—if he could put away his pride and allow himself to be shaped by the universe that seemed so eager to make him into something better than what he naturally was, maybe change could come to Doug as well. He considered the events that created the catalyst for these changes. It was Amy who had started it—leaving him sitting on the church steps to consider how his actions were affecting others. But it was the accident, his time in the hospital and the truth he learned while he was there that had wrought the change in his heart and mind.

As Jake considered these things, he thought about the events of the previous evening. Doug had been a real jerk, but if things had *really* gone down as Thomas reported, Doug had received his own giant slice of humble pie. Jake wondered if it would be enough to bring about any *real* change. His letter certainly lacked humility and understanding— there was no *real* apology for the way he'd treated his daughter. But for the first time in his life, he'd done something different—he'd written a letter—he'd reached out. And even though the attempt was lame and produced only more sorrow, it was still an attempt.

Jake climbed the stairs to his apartment and switched on the kitchen light, illuminating the pots that filled the shelves and lined the walls. He had done this very thing a hundred times before, but tonight was different. His thoughts had opened his mind to new ideas. As he looked at them now, the faces of hundreds of flawed pots looked back at him. These were the mistakes of the past—each one flawed, but kept to preserve the lessons learned, so those who followed might not have to make the same mistakes.

Jake sat down at the table considering Doug's relationship with his wife and daughter. His family had been hurt by his inability to see and hear and understand. Surely, Jake thought to himself, there had to be a better way. He could learn from Doug—what not to do. But as his thoughts continued to wander, Jake wondered if Doug could learn from himself—from his own mistakes. He knew he

was in no position to encourage or even suggest such a notion to Doug, but as he stared at the pots—at nearly three hundred year's worth of mistakes and lessons, he had to hope.

He turned off the light and went to bed, but after nearly an hour of tossing and turning, he wandered back into the kitchen. He pulled the green pitcher from the overhead shelf and set it on the table. After removing the rolled-up paper from inside, he sat down on the bench under the window and re-read Isaac's note from so many years ago.

When he looked up again, with tears in his eyes, he saw the painting Amy had left here when he was in the hospital. Maybe her father needed something like this—some loving reminder of who he was and the love available to him if he would just let it in.

November 12, 1972

— Don't be discouraged by failure. It can be a positive experience. Failure is, in a sense, the highway to success, inasmuch as every discovery of what is false leads us to seek earnestly after what is true, and every fresh experience points out some form of error which we shall afterwards carefully avoid. —— John Keats

I found this quote tonight in my reading and thought it applied well to the pots on the shelf.

SCHNECKEN

THERE ARE ONLY TWO FORCES IN THE WORLD, THE SWORD AND THE SPIRIT.
IN THE LONG RUN THE SWORD WILL ALWAYS BE CONQUERED BY THE SPIRIT.
—NAPOLEON BONAPARTE—

Jake was just finishing unloading the tiles from the kiln when Amy arrived shortly after eight with her easel on her back and a bag from Sam's bakery. She kissed him before setting the easel under the back window.

"I told Sam we were glazing his tiles today and he gave us four Schnecken."

"Can you eat that?" Jake asked, having never heard the name before.

"That's exactly what I said. I guess it means 'snail' in German. They look delicious."

Jake looked at her incredulously. "Snails for breakfast?"

She laughed. "No, we're safe. Sam said only the French eat snails for breakfast. These are just giant cinnamon rolls."

Jake handed her a mug of tea and they took their breakfast out in the courtyard, sitting on the old stone bench at the base of the chestnut tree.

"How'd ya sleep," Amy asked, trying to tame a rooster tail on the back of Jake's head.

"Not very well."

"How come?"

"I was thinking about your dad."

"Don't tell me you're losing sleep over my dad, too."

"You didn't sleep well either?"

"I slept just fine, thanks to you and Gloria and Joseph. I guess happy thoughts crowded out the sad ones."

Jake nodded.

"So, what were you thinking about?"

"Change—the possibility that he could change."

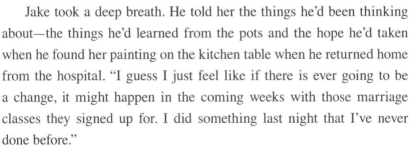

Amy smiled, but shook her head. "I've been hoping and praying for that for a long time. Nothing ever seems to change with my dad, at least not for the better."

Jake took a deep breath. He told her the things he'd been thinking about—the things he'd learned from the pots and the hope he'd taken when he found her painting on the kitchen table when he returned home from the hospital. "I guess I just feel like if there is ever going to be a change, it might happen in the coming weeks with those marriage classes they signed up for. I did something last night that I've never done before."

"What?"

"I prayed for the father of the girl I love."

Amy smiled, but looked away quickly.

"I know he was a jerk to both of us Amy, and a whole bunch of other people too, but in my heart, I find myself hoping … I don't know … hoping he can change, I guess.

She nodded slowly, thoughtfully.

"I don't think I would have given him much thought if I'd met him a month ago."

"So why do you care now?"

"You mean besides the fact that he's the father of the girl I hope to spend the rest of my life with?"

Amy nodded again, but didn't look at him.

"I guess I've just been thinking a lot about change—mostly about my own change—thinking how grateful I am for you and Thomas and Gloria who loved me enough to believe I could change and helped me open my eyes to the truth. I'm afraid to say that might never have happened if I hadn't had that accident, and if you hadn't given me the best reason to change."

She sat up and turned to look at him. "Remind me what I did?"

"You loved me, Amy, and your love made me want to be a better man. I guess I wonder if your dad might be the same way."

"Jake, you and my father have nothing in common."

"Except for that we are both fools—full of pride and stubbornness—*and* that we both have been given a gift we don't deserve."

"Oh, really? What's that?"

"Women who love us in spite of our flaws."

"Are you trying to make me feel guilty for being mad at my dad?"

"No, I'm not. I'm sure you have more reason to be mad at your dad than I could ever imagine. It's hard to love a porcupine, especially a two-hundred-pound mutant porcupine that has at least twice as many needles and likes to throw his weight and ego around. I don't have any answers, and I'm sure it's not our job to fix him, but I guess I just find myself being hopeful that he has at least one awesome change inside of him, somewhere.

"I don't know," she said, after a long moment of silence. "Sometimes I wonder if he is even human—he seems so cold-blooded. I'm not sure if he's capable of feeling or understanding the way his actions make others feel."

"Okay, so he's obviously broken. I know I don't know his history, but what if there was something that could fix that … whatever it is that's broken."

She turned to face him. "Jake, I've tried to imagine all sorts of fixes. The father of one of my girlfriend's once wrote him a prescription for an enema."

DR. ROBERT ADAMS

FOR DOUG ECKSTEIN
ONE ENEMA
APPLY DAILY

℞

Jake laughed. "How'd that go over?"

"Are you kidding? I never actually gave it to him. I'm sure he wouldn't have found it as funny as my brothers and I did."

"Amy, I really don't know if there is an answer, but if there is, I guess I just have to believe the universe can make it happen for him the same way it happened to me."

"Jake, you needed an oil change. My dad, he needs a complete overhaul!"

He laughed and stood, pulling her up with him. "I know you've been thinking about this stuff for years. I guess I just want you to know that I'm thinking about it too. Like I said before, I don't think it's our job to fix him, but I don't think praying for him could ever hurt."

Amy nodded. "Thank you. It will be nice to have someone to share that hope with. I'm sure my brothers gave up on him a long time ago."

"Do you think it's just us then?"

"No. I'm not sure if my mom prays about it, but I'm sure she still holds out hope. I know she loves him, even though he makes it so hard most of the time. I've been thinking a lot about that old photo Mr. Allan gave me last week—that one of my parents in Vail."

"What about it?"

"That was taken while they were on their honeymoon. They looked so happy. I wish that could happen again—that they could find a way to make their marriage and their life happy again."

They went back into the studio and unfolded the paper patterns they'd created for the mosaic for Sam's floor. Soon, all the tiles were laid out on the floor in the correct order. Only three of them had cracked in the firing, but considering that the tiles were part of a mosaic, the cracks made little difference. While Amy drew the designs on the white tile with pencil, Jake pulled out all of the glaze buckets. Then he began tracing Amy's pencil sketches with wax resist, applied with a very thin paint brush and a steady hand. Amy was done with the sketch long before Jake could finish the tracing, so he handed her a mug full of green glaze and a handful of different paintbrushes.

"This is the darkest of the three green glazes," he said. "I'll leave it up to you to decide were it needs to go."

She nodded, but looked uncertain.

Jake watched her out of the corner of his eye as she approached the first tree. She dipped a brush in the mug and pulled it out, covered in glaze. Then she bent over and began filling the space between the wax lines with the green glaze. The porous, bisque-fired tiles sucked up the moisture quickly, and before Amy could respond, the brush's hair was stuck to the tile with drying glaze.

She looked up, looking surprised. "What just happened?"

Jake laughed. "I guess this is a little different from oil paint. You have to move faster. The tiles soak up the moisture really fast."

"You think?" Amy asked, pulling the brush free of the dried glaze. "This is going to take forever."

Jake stopped what he was doing and stooped down next to her. "Try this one," he said, handing her a fat round brush with very fine hair.

She laughed. "That's a makeup brush for applying blush."

"Well now it's a glaze brush. It will hold more glaze and help you spread it more evenly."

She looked doubtful, but after she tried it the first time, she looked up, surprised. "Look at you, Mr. Smarty Pants. Maybe you could get my old job at the makeup counter."

"Thanks, I'll remember that if things don't work out here."

They laughed together as they worked. Jake was finished with the wax resist before Amy was finished with the dark green. He joined her in the glazing, squatting over the tiles with a mug full of black glaze. This, he began applying with one of the few tools he'd brought with him from school—a bulb syringe.

"Wait, that was supposed to be black," Amy said, looking distressed.

"It is black."

"Are you sure? It looks red."

"It is red, but it becomes black in the firing. It's full of red iron oxide and some cobalt that will fire to a nice matte black."

"How do you know what color it's going to be?"

"You just have to know. You get used to it. Just wait till we start with the yellow. It looks pink before it's fired. The copper red is pale green and the cobalt blue is gray."

Amy started laughing. "How do you possibly keep it straight?"

"You have to trust what's written on the side of the bucket, but you also have get to know your materials. It's got to be like what you do."

"No, I don't think so. If I ever bought a tube of yellow paint and pink came out, I'd either know I was going color blind or that someone messed up at the factory."

"Okay, but color aside, you have to know what colors require a couple of coats to have the right thickness."

She laughed. "Jake, my paints are all mixed in giant batches and they all have the same consistency. Oh, and I'd never let my brushes get to such a sad state as these."

Jake shook his head, smiling. "Remind me again why you get so much more for a painting than I do for my bowls. You don't make your canvas or even your paints and you can whip one of those up in a couple of hours. I just don't get it."

"Yeah, I was just thinking how grateful I am that I chose an art with some consistency. Not to rub it in, but the only things I've ever over-fired are a couple batches of cookies."

They laughed again, their banter and laughter making the time and work pass quickly. By the time the church bell tolled twelve, the tiles had all been glazed and loaded back in the kiln for the glaze firing.

"Do you mind if I do a little more work before we leave?" Jake asked as they enjoyed their second Schnecken of the day.

"What do you need to do?"

"I wanted to get those sink basins made for the Parkins. I promised them I'd get them done before the first of July."

"How long will it take?"

"Maybe an hour. Why?"

"I was just thinking I could do a painting."

"Are you asking me to be your model?"

She set up her easel as Jake descended into clay cellar for the first time in two weeks. His left arm protested as he wedged the clay, but he persevered, kneading each of the eight balls until they were round and ready for the wheel. He gathered up his tools and refilled the water in the old, cracked batter bowl that sat on the wheel. Then he sat down to get to work. He looked up to find Amy's attention focused on the still life she had set up on the old, dusty stool—a teapot with two mugs. He wanted to watch her, wanted to stand behind her and watch her skillfully render what she saw in front of her, but he pushed that aside and got to work.

He was just finishing the first big sink when Amy noticed.

"Oh my gosh! How did you do that?"

Jake looked over the lip of the basin, smiling. "Hey, I'm a potter. That's what I do."

"Well, can you make another one?"

"I hope so. I plan to make seven more." He lifted the basin from the wheel head by the wooden bat underneath it and sat it on the table. Then he placed a new bat on the wheel before throwing the big ball of clay forcefully onto the center of the bat. As the wheel began to spin, Amy stepped away from her easel and took a seat on one of the other stools near the wheel.

Jake smiled at her as he centered the clay between his hands, forcing it to rise tall in a cone-shape before forcing it back down to form a flattened dome, perfectly centered. Amy did not return the smile, having fallen into a trancelike state, seemingly oblivious to her surroundings. Jake pushed his fist into the center of the clay as the wheel continued to turn. After the floor of the bowl was made, the dome began to take shape, rising slowly in a blur of creative motion. Then, with a kidney-shaped, wooden rib, he pushed against the inside wall of the vessel, slowing forcing it take on a more graceful shape with each rotation. Finally, he formed the lip of the bowl by laying the rib against it and flattening it out.

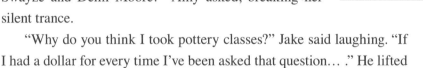

"Did you ever see that movie with Patrick Swayze and Demi Moore?" Amy asked, breaking her silent trance.

"Why do you think I took pottery classes?" Jake said laughing. "If I had a dollar for every time I've been asked that question... ." He lifted the bowl from the wheel, setting it next to the first.

"How's your arm?"

Jake rubbed his goopy hand over the crescent-shaped scar. "It's still kind of sore."

"Are you sure you should be doing this?" she asked, looking concerned.

"Sandy said I'd be okay in two weeks. I guess I'm a day early, but I gotta get these done."

"Do you care if I watch you work?"

"No. That's fine. You've never worked with clay, have you?"

"No. It's really amazing to watch you work."

"Do you want to try it?"

"Yeah, but can I watch you do it a couple more times? I think I'd make a fool of myself if I just sat down and tried."

"Probably about like me trying to paint a picture." He put another bat on the wheel head and began again as Amy watched his every move. When he started the fourth bowl, she moved her stool closer to him so she could get a better view of his hands. By the time he'd finished the fifth bowl, she'd scooped up a handful of slip from the splash pan and was playing with it.

Jake was working on the final bowl when she asked if she could touch the clay. He agreed and they sat side by side as the clay wound its way through their fingers and tools.

"I can't believe I've never done this before," she said.

"Do you mean pottery, or this?"

"Both, I guess," she said, laughing.

He smiled, brushing his face on her hair and inhaling deeply. "I love the smell of your hair."

"Yeah, I get that a lot."

They laughed together as they finished the final bowl. Then he moved it to the table to dry with the others. When he returned to his stool, she had scooped together another handful of the buff-colored slip and was playing with it. "This is the coolest feeling ever," she said.

Jake watched her for a moment before taking hold of her slip-covered hands, letting his fingers play with hers. "You're right," he said, smiling. "We just need the jukebox to start playing "Unchained Melody.""

"I wonder if the Righteous Brothers ever knew their song would be associated with one of the most romantic movie scenes in history."

"I don't know," said Jake, "but you've got a little clay on your nose."

"I do?"

"Yeah, right there," he said, touching the end of her freckled nose with his clay covered finger, smearing slip all over it."

She immediately started laughing. "I guess I walked right into that one, didn't I."

"Yeah, that's one of the oldest in the potter's book of tricks," he said, laughing.

"Uh, huh," she said, grabbing hold of his apron and pulling his face next to hers until their noses touched. "Then write this down as one of the newest tricks in that book. It's called The Eskimo Potter's Kiss." She closed her eyes like she was about to kiss him, but as soon as he followed, she began rubbing her clay covered nose all over his face. He tried to pull away, but she had a tight grip on his apron, pulling his face closer until he stopped resisting and let her retaliate as they laughed together.

"Hey, have you guys ever seen the scene from 'Ghost.'"

They looked up, surprised to see Molly at the back door with a small bundle in her arms, laughing.

"Jake was just teaching me how to make pots," Amy said, laughing hysterically.

"I was hoping that was the case. This is a Christian community. What happens behind closed doors is your own business, but when the back door is open, well ..." She couldn't continue, except with laughter. "Congratulations, Jake. It looks like you've made a quick study of that kissing stuff," Molly managed to say before she burst into laughter again.

"What are you doing here," Jake said, getting to his feet and wiping his hands and face on his apron. "The Pottery is closed today."

"Yeah, I can see that," she said, falling again into a fit of laughter. "I wish I had a camera. I just thought I'd take Zane out for a walk and give Mrs. Yoder a break. I thought you two would be off on some fun adventure on your day off."

"We had to get some work done first," Jake explained. "We were just getting ready to leave actually."

"Yeah, that's what it looked like," Molly teased.

"So how are things at home," Amy asked as she stood at the sink and washed the clay from her hands and face. "Are you getting any sleep?"

"Yeah, Mrs. Yoder has been really helpful. She's given me a lot of time to rest."

"How long is she going to stay?" asked Amy.

"She said she'd be here until I didn't need her anymore. I'm not sure what that means exactly, but she's an amazing cook. I'm learning a lot from her."

"How's Zane?" Jake asked, stepping closer to take a look at the sleeping child.

"It's been a long time since I've been around a baby, but he's really a good boy. He's a great sleeper— in fact, it seems that's all he wants to do."

"Yeah, that's what Kai said. I guess we'll have to put off the tree fort for another summer," teased Jake.

Molly turned the baby's head away from her shoulder. He was swaddled tightly in a blue blanket that covered all of his body except his face. He whimpered and opened his eyes for a moment before settling into his new position and falling back to sleep. "Mrs. Yoder said it's good for babies to be exposed to the sun, but then she made sure his whole body was covered before I took him out. There's so much to learn. We read a bunch of books before he arrived, but when you have an actual baby to deal with, sometimes the theory seems a little impractical." She smiled down at her son before turning back to look at them. Jake and Amy both stood close, watching the sleeping child. "So, where are you guys going?"

"Jake's taking me up into the hills on a scooter ride."

"That sounds like fun. Where?"

"I was up on an old farm road a couple of weeks ago. I'm not sure, exactly … west of here."

"Then I won't keep you. I just saw your door open and thought I'd say hi. Mrs. Yoder has been asking about you."

"About me?" asked Amy.

"No, about you, Jake."

"Why? What kind of questions?"

"Just questions—you know—where you're from, what kind of training you've had, what kind of potter and person you are. She also seems interested in your relationship with Amy."

"Why?" asked Jake.

"I don't really know. She's talked a couple of times about the fire they had at the workshop and the way Isaac helped her family rebuild. She says she's glad you're here—that Isaac's shop is still open. I wouldn't be surprised if she dropped in sometime. Anyway, I better get back. Kai needs some help with orders. I just wanted to check and see if you'd seen that movie." She winked at Jake and turned to leave. "You guys have fun. Drop by later, if you want. Mrs. Yoder makes some great desserts."

THERE IS NO SITUATION THAT IS NOT TRANSFORMABLE
THERE IS NO PERSON WHO IS HOPELESS.
THERE IS NO SET OF CIRCUMSTANCES
THAT CANNOT BE TURNED ABOUT BY
ORDINARY HUMAN BEINGS
AND THEIR NATURAL CAPACITY
FOR LOVE OF THE DEEPEST SORT.
        - ARCHBISHOP DESMOND TUTU -

ZOOM, ZOOM, ZOOM

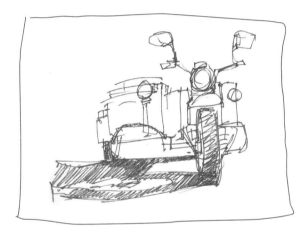

WHEN YOU EXAMINE THE LIVES OF THE MOST INFLUENTIAL PEOPLE WHO
HAVE EVER WALKED AMONG US, YOU DISCOVER ONE THREAD THAT WINDS
THROUGH THEM ALL. THEY HAVE BEEN ALIGNED FIRST WITH THEIR SPIRITUAL
NATURE AND ONLY THEN WITH THEIR PHYSICAL SELVES.
—ALBERT EINSTEIN—

With two people sharing the saddle, the scooter was much slower as it climbed the hills than when Jake had come here alone, but he hardly noticed, distracted by the comfort of Amy's grip around his belly. They passed a tractor bailing alfalfa, and Amy waved to the man in the driver's seat. The day was warm and humid, but the rush of wind and the frequent patches of shade that intruded into the old road made it feel cooler. Jake smiled as he caught their reflection in the rearview mirror. He'd taken the old goggles and given Amy the bubble-head helmet to help keep her hair from turning into a snarled mess. Still, a couple dozen red whispies escaped in the wind.

Soon, they were parked in the shade of a tall tree next to the old split-log bench where Jake had taken his lunch weeks before when he'd escaped from Niederbipp. They laid out the quilt on the tall grass and enjoyed a picnic of peanut butter and honey sandwiches. They chatted as they reveled in the beauty of this place, looking out on the three valleys they could see from this vantage point. Amy set up her easel as Jake turned to his new sketchbook, inspiring the conversation to turn to Isaac and his unfinished bench at the cemetery.

Feeling a little guilty for his delay in getting started on the bench, he decided the first entry in the book would be a new sketch of it. When Jake mentioned his ambitions, Amy stopped her painting to kneel next to him and add her input.

"I'd really like it if you did the drawing for this," he told her, offering her the book and pen.

"Jake, this is your story—its your book," she protested. "I agree you could use some help with your sketching," she said with a smile, "but this isn't my sketchbook."

Jake returned the smile, ignoring the not-so-subtle dig to his drawing skills. "Amy, you are a huge part of my story. My chicken is your chicken, remember? If this book is to be passed along with the others, I want future generations to know that you are an important part of my life."

"But ..."

He smiled and pushed the book toward her, ending the protest. With Amy working as scribe, the sketch took on a dimension that his previous attempt lacked. When she returned to her painting, Jake recorded in words some of the things they'd learned from Isaac's sketchbooks. As he remembered these things, he shared his thoughts with Amy, expressing again the gratitude he had for her and the patience and love she had given him. In turn, she responded by opening her thoughts to Jake.

"I don't know how to say this, but I wanted to thank you for respecting me."

Jake looked up from the quilt where he'd been sitting, looking confused. "What do you mean?"

She looked him in the eyes and smiled. "Jake, I told you this before—that night up at Taufer's Pond, but I've dated a lot of different guys over the years."

Jake nodded, wondering where she was heading with this.

"I've dated some good guys and some real toads, but none of them have respected me the way you have. Some of those toads tried to kiss me on the first date and then never spoke to me again when I turned them down. Maybe I'm a prude, but I've always felt like dating was about getting to know the other person rather than getting it on."

"How do you know it's not just because I don't know how to get it on?"

Amy shook her head, smiling. "Jake, I know you're a little slow sometimes, but you're far from stupid."

"Thanks," Jake said sarcastically.

"I just want to say thanks for not pushing the physical stuff—for romancing me for me and not for what you think you can get from me."

"You're welcome. Thanks for respecting yourself and me enough not to throw yourself at me or make me feel uncomfortable. That impressed me from the very beginning."

"What do you mean?"

"I don't know, just the way you carry yourself, the way you dress, the way you act. From the first time I met you I knew you were someone who knows who you are."

"What does that mean?"

"Take the way you dress for example."

"Yes?" she said, raising her eyebrows.

"I don't want you to get mad by me bringing her up, but it was very difficult for me to be around Alice because of the way she dresses. I've never been concerned about that with you."

She looked confused.

"Amy, when I'm with you, I get to see *you*. I … I'm not worried about where to look. The way you dress has made me respect you, because I know you respect yourself. I'm completely attracted to you, not just physically, but mentally and spiritually and intellectually. I've never been comfortable around girls who … I don't know … who like to let it all hang out, for lack of a better way of saying it. I've never felt comfortable enough to even talk to a girl like that, but I can't imagine we'd have much to talk about. I don't know anything about skin creams and moisturizers and I've never been to a tanning salon. I don't know. I know it's a huge generalization, but it seems to me that girls who have more skin showing than they have covered, are usually pretty shallow."

"It's really refreshing to hear you say that. I thought all guys liked to look at girls who dress that way."

"Oh, I'm sure there are plenty of guys that do, but I wouldn't want any of them dating my sister—if I had a sister. I remember talking to my roommates about this one night. We all agreed that it was a lot easier getting to know a girl if she actually wore clothes that covered her body. It's hard to concentrate on figuring out who a person is if the only thing you see is skin or if their body language is louder than the words that come out of their mouth."

"So, are you honestly telling me that you're not attracted to Alice."

Jake shook his head, knowing she had him trapped. "Amy, Alice is a beautiful girl, physically, but I'd never want to date her. She's aggressive and manipulative and … ughhh." He shook his head, wishing this had never come up, but he knew he was in too deep to leave it alone.

"Amy, I'm sure there are lots of guys who are attracted to girls like

Alice, but I've never been one of those guys. I could never imagine myself being married to girl like her."

"Why not?"

He looked thoughtful as he considered his response. "I'm sure this probably sounds strange coming from me—a guy who never kissed a girl before you, but I guess I just feel like physical intimacy is pretty special." He let out a long breath. "This is hard to talk about. I've never had such an open conversation about it with anyone, and I've *never* talked about this kind of stuff with a girl."

"But you are attracted to me, right?"

"Amy," he said, shaking his head, trying not to laugh at how awkward he felt. "I've never been more attracted to anyone. You are the most beautiful person I've ever known. Its hard for me to walk away from you at night … I … I look forward to sharing a more intimate relationship with you, but …"

"But what?"

"But for the time being, you're not my wife, Amy. You haven't given me the green light and I respect you all the more for it. Even when we are married, I won't treat you like you belong to me. I may be romantically backward in a lot of different ways, but I never want the kind of relationship my parents had. I was too young to remember, but my mom sometimes talked about my dad treating her like she was his property—to do with as he pleased.

"I'm excited to spend the rest of my life with you, but I would never want you to feel like my love for you is only skin deep. Separating my physical attraction to you from all the other ways I'm attracted to you has made me realize how much I love you—how much I want to spend the rest of my life next to you. Like I told you the other night at the hospital, I'm looking forward to the time when I don't have to drop you off at Bev and Jerry's. I look forward to holding you in my arms all night, but I'm afraid that if I think too much about that future time, whenever it is, I'll miss out on all the amazing things that are happening between us every day."

"Jake, what planet are you from?"

He shook his head. "I'm really sorry, Amy. I'm obviously not very good at explaining this," he said, looking away.

JAKE'S PLANET

She left her paints and sat down on the blanket next to him. He didn't look at her. "Jake," she said, resting her hand on his arm, "you misunderstood me."

"I did?" he asked, turning to look at her, warily.

"Yeah, I only asked what planet you came from because I'm sure there are millions of women who would like to meet a guy like you."

Jake smiled and reached out to embrace her.

"Thank you," Amy whispered. "Thank you for loving me enough to fall in love with all of me."

"You're welcome," he responded. "And thank you for respecting yourself enough to demand my respect ... for making me want to love everything about you."

THE WHOLE PACKAGE

A BASKET OF ROCKS

MUTUAL RESPECT, WHEN COUPLED WITH FAITH, ENDOWED WITH GRACE
AND UNSELFISHLY NURTURED BETWEEN TWO PEOPLE WHO LOVE EACH
OTHER, HAS THE UNIQUE ABILITY TO MAKE LOVE BLOSSOM AND GROW
EXPONENTIALLY MORE POWERFUL.
—BEN BEHUNIN—

ver the next few days, as Jake and Amy spent time working
together, the magic of the conversation they'd shared on that
hill-top sanctuary was repeated many times, each subsequent
conversation becoming easier and more comfortable as they discussed
their truest feelings. Their words inspired more than their hearts and
minds—it inspired their work. On Tuesday, Amy finished three nice
paintings in The Pottery while Jake trimmed the sinks, fired the kiln and

made three dozen mugs. They worked together again on Wednesday, making the tiles for Isaac's bench.

As Jake carved Isaac's words and mottos into the clay, he recognized how the old potter, though dead and gone, continued to shape lives from the grave, namely his. Not a week had passed without someone repeating Isaac's mantra—*Joy, in all its glory, can only be obtained through unselfishness.* As he flipped through his sketchbook, reading the notes he'd made since his arrival in Niederbipp, he stumbled upon the entry he'd made after Brian's visit and the message Isaac had shared with him as they sat on the back of the broken-down Porsche—*My greatest wish is that you will come to know the love of God.*

CARVING TOOLS

Jake read to Amy the entries he'd made as he discovered each of the earlier potter's benches at the cemetery and the thoughtful messages that had been preserved in clay for future generations to discover. *"Sweet is the peace the gospel brings,"* from Zebulon's bench. *"Rob not God, the source of all good gifts,"* from

Abraham's. Then there was Joseph's bench, decorated by his son, Alvin, the potter who was known for his tiles. That bench, even though it had been damaged by vandals and thieves, displayed some great words of truth and faith and love. The thoughts he'd recorded were comforting as he read them now, but they also left him burdened. He felt the weight of the responsibility he had to memorialize in clay, a man who had shaped the lives of several decades' worth of Niederbippians. Still, he felt compelled to move forward, not wanting to put it off any longer. He was grateful to have Amy around, not only for the talents she brought to the project and her companionship in the studio, but also because she took it upon herself to help the customers who wandered into the shop, affording Jake the time he needed to concentrate on his carving.

After much thought and discussion, it was decided that Isaac's mantra about joy would be the best choice for the words that would encircle the edge of the bench. As Jake carved these words into the clay, he reflected on the powerful truth the statement contained. Joy had come into *his* life only when he had given up his selfish desires. It had been difficult to do so—difficult to allow his faith to overcome his ego—difficult to give up the life he had without knowing for sure what would come. But something *had* come, and as he considered all that had changed—all that was better—his only regret about the decision he'd made was that he hadn't made it sooner. As he looked at Amy, his emotions spilled over. When he'd arrived here, less than two months ago, the love of a woman was the last thing on his mind. He was independent, free of all responsibilities and obligations. He was his own man. But now, as he looked at her, looked at his work, the shop, and considered the friends he'd made here and the influence they'd had on him, he couldn't deny that though his life had become much more complicated, it had also become much more full and rich and wonderful. Finishing the carving of the final word, "unselfishness", he felt Amy's hand on his shoulder and looked up into her face. If she were the only gift that had come into his life because of the change he'd made, it would have been worth it. But as he stood, taking her in his arms, he knew the gifts the universe had offered him were infinite. In that moment, he knew he, himself, was his only limitation, his only obstacle in receiving all that the heavens and the earth had to offer him. In that moment, there was no question in his mind—he knew he, himself, was where he was supposed to be.

Their hug was interrupted by the sound of bells on the front door and they turned to see David and Nancy Garber, the owners of Robintinos, climbing the steps to the showroom. Nancy carried a basket on her arm. They'd already stopped by earlier in the week to check on Amy's progress with the paintings they'd commissioned. They'd selected four paintings at that time and made arrangements to return once they were framed.

"It looks like you've been busy," said Nancy, setting the basket down on the counter.

Jake and Amy went into the showroom to greet them. "I would have finished more," Amy said, "but the framing took a little longer than I hoped. I should have a few more finished by next week."

"Oh, they're wonderful," Nancy said, standing under Amy's newest painting, a still life of the old cash register. "Can we have this one too?"

"Uh, sure," said Amy, glancing at Jake.

"This one is new too," David said, pointing to a still life of a dozen clay-covered pottery tools with a bright silver spoon tangled in the mess.

"Yeah, I did that one yesterday."

"Does it have a title?" asked David.

"I call it "Tools of the Trade."

"Oh, I love it," said Nancy. "We've got to have that one too."

Jake and Amy pulled six paintings from the walls, being careful not to smear the oil paint that was still wet, laying them cautiously on the front counter."

"What's this?" asked Amy, pointing to the unusual willow basket. It was stacked full of smooth, colorful river rocks ranging from the size of a walnut to the size of an apple.

"Oh, I almost forgot," said Nancy. "I know we've monopolized your time this past week, but we were talking last night and were hoping you might be willing to do a special commission."

Amy picked up a rock, turning it over in her hand. "What did you have in mind?"

"We'd want this to be bigger than the others," said David, "probably about twenty by thirty to fit over our mantel. Do you paint that big?"

"Yeah, it's been a while, but I think I could do that. What do you want me to paint?"

The couple looked at each other, before David spoke again. "We hope it's not below you, but we were hoping you might use these rocks and the basket to make up a composition."

"We would leave the layout completely up to you," added Nancy. "We don't even pretend to be artists and we don't want to step on your toes. These rocks have a personal meaning to us. We are so happy with everything you've painted so far that I know we'll be happy with anything you come up with."

Amy nodded. "I think this would be a fun challenge, but I'm not really sure how to price it."

"We'll pay you whatever you'd like," said David. "Our thirtieth anniversary is the first of July. We would like to give it to ourselves to mark the milestone. If you don't mind, we could just settle up with you when you're done."

"Sure," said Amy, putting the rock back in the basket.

"Can we treat you kids to lunch again?" Nancy asked.

Jake laughed. "I actually still owe you for dinner for four last Saturday night."

"Well, how about if we make a trade?" said Nancy.

"Sure, what do you want?"

"I've had my eye on that black-and-white bowl in the front window."

"It's yours," said Jake, walking to the window. "What else would you like?"

"We'd like you to help us carry these paintings down to the restaurant so we can feed you," said David.

Jake smiled, handing Nancy the bowl. "You've got a deal."

EVERY MAN MUST DECIDE WHETHER HE WILL WALK IN THE LIGHT OF CREATIVE ALTRUISM OR IN THE DARKNESS OF DESTRUCTIVE SELFISHNESS.
— MARTIN LUTHER KING JR —

HOPE REVEALED

HE THAT CANNOT FORGIVE OTHERS, BREAKS THE BRIDGE OVER WHICH HE
HIMSELF MUST PASS IF HE WOULD EVER REACH HEAVEN; FOR EVERYONE HAS
NEED TO BE FORGIVEN.
—GEORGE HERBERT—

The kiln was finally ready to unload at noon on Saturday, though the tiles were still too hot to touch without gloves. As Jake carefully unloaded them, placing them in the clay boxes from the cellar, Amy sanded the greenware tiles for Isaac's bench. By two, the kiln had been emptied and Isaac's tiles loaded into the kiln along with the eight big basins and the mugs Jake had made earlier in the week. Because of the thickness of the basins, Jake decided it would be a good idea to let the kiln candle over the weekend to force out the remaining moisture.

Plans for the installation of the mosaic floor had been made on Thursday morning when Jake stopped by to pick up some bread from Sam. The news that the tiles were cooling in the kiln caused Sam to rally his employees into singing a shortened and rather off-beat rendition of the "Hallelujah Chorus." Sam agreed to pick up the mortar and grout at the hardware store, along with any other supplies, and be ready to get started as soon as the bakery closed at three on Saturday afternoon.

Amy offered to help with the installation, but Jake was dubious that there would be enough room to maneuver in the relatively confined area. So, instead, she offered to keep The Pottery open for the steady stream of tourists while she worked on the Garbers' commission.

It took three trips for Jake to carry each of the heavy boxes full of tiles to the bakery. Sam met him at the door of the bakery with the final load, locking it after he entered.

"Are you ready to get started?" asked Jake, as he set the box down next to the others.

"Almost. I'm hungry. Why don't we eat something first?"

Jake nodded, following Sam to the back room. He had already eaten lunch with Amy and wanted to get started with the floor so they could do something fun that evening, but he knew he couldn't turn down a man who had kept him fed since he'd arrived here. A dozen assorted pastries sat on the table with a gallon of chocolate milk and couple of chipped mugs.

"Help yourself," Sam said, taking a seat on one of the two chairs. "I assume you like chocolate milk."

"Who doesn't?" Jake asked

Sam nodded, filling both mugs. He passed one to Jake

before lifting his own mug. "Cheers to a job well done," he said, clinking the side of Jake's mug.

"Don't you think we should wait until we're done before we do this?"

"What, and miss out on an extra mug of chocolate milk?" He winked before putting the mug to his lips and tilting his head back, quickly emptying its contents. "I'm proud of you Jake and I'm glad you decided to stick around so I wouldn't have to send my posse to break your knees." He laughed, slapping Jake on the back, causing him to spill some of his chocolate milk.

"I'm sorry it took so long for me to get started, but I'm glad I waited. Amy was a big help. She's an amazing artist. I'm sure you'll be happy with what we did."

"I'm sure I will," he said, filling his own mug again.

An awkward silence fell between them, and Jake found himself wishing they were working on the mosaic. He picked up a pastry, but as he bit into it, he noticed something in Sam's face that he hadn't noticed before— sadness in his eyes. He'd always seemed so jolly, so exuberant, that this hint of sadness surprised him. He tried to think of his interactions with this man—all of  them had been positive, all of them happy, all of them … except one. As he strained his mind, trying to recollect that instance, Jake remembered the feeling of tension he felt when the old man spoke of his son during his last visit to this back room. He looked again at the family picture on the wall. He'd only glanced at it before, but as he looked closer now, a few things surprised him. The most obvious of which was that the boy who stood next to the baker and his wife looked much younger than his two sisters, maybe even fifteen years younger. He was also surprised to see that Sam and his wife hadn't aged much since that time, suggesting to Jake that the photo was much newer than he'd originally guessed.

"Are you ready to get started?" asked Sam, untying the strings of his apron.

Jake nodded and followed him back to the front of the store.

"I had Bill bring the tools and stuff up here before he left," Sam said, pointing to a couple of five-gallon buckets and an assortment of tools. Jake opened the bag of powdered mortar and dumped half of it into an empty bucket while Sam swept the bare cement floor where the tiles would go. With an old broomstick, Jake stirred the powder, while Sam slowly added water until it was the consistency of thick frosting.

Then Jake unloaded the boxes of tile, laying them out on the tiled floor under the display cases to keep them out of the way until they needed them. Sam tried to help at first, but because he didn't know the pattern, he stepped back and watched as the design came together around the centerpiece Isaac had made.

"What do you think?" Jake asked, as he slid the final piece into place.

"It's much better than I hoped."

"Me too," said Jake, getting to his feet to admire the work. "We better get started. I'm meeting Amy later."

They decided it would make the most sense to lay the tiles by the door first and work backward into the shop. So while Jake spread the mortar on the cement floor with an ancient-looking trowel, Sam gathered up the tiles that would form the first row. This system worked well until they came to the small tiles surrounding Isaac's centerpiece. Then the work became much slower and more tedious.

"How is your family?" Jake asked, trying to make small talk to lighten the mood of concentration that their project had taken on.

Sam took a deep breath and looked away. He was silent for a long awkward moment before taking another deep breath and exhaling noisily through his nose. "It's a mess, if you must know." The silence had been awkward, but the answer made it even more so.

"Is there anything I can do?"

Sam shook his head, looking sadder than ever. "Not unless you have a miracle in your pocket."

Jake laughed uncomfortably. "I wish I did. What's going on?"

Sam rolled over on his rear and began rubbing his knees. "Jake, I really don't want to talk about this. I'll just say that my family is a mess and leave it at that, if that's okay with you."

"Sure," said Jake, a little taken aback. "I'm sorry I brought it up. It seems like that's going around."

Sam laughed, putting an end to the awkward tension. "Yeah, I guess you and Amy have had some family drama lately."

"Yeah, we have. I meant to thank you for coming out to the restaurant the other night. It meant a lot to both of us to have your support.

"You're welcome. How'd things work out?"

"I'm not sure they have yet. I guess it's a lot to ask for things to be better after so many years of unhappiness and contention."

"Amy's mom is a real saint to have stuck it out as long as she has."

"That's right, didn't Amy's dad date your daughter."

"Yep," Sam said, looking disgusted. "You know, it's like we used to say, 'some people are alive only because it's illegal to kill them.' "

Jake laughed out loud.

"Before Saturday night, it had been nearly forty years since I'd seen Doug Eckstein, and I still wanted to take him out to the woodshed and … well …"

"But he comes to town at least once a year. How have you missed him?"

"I'm not sure how we've missed each other— it's a small enough town, but I don't think he'd ever come looking for me. I usually post a wanted sign with an old picture of him that says, 'wanted dead or alive' every time I hear he's in town." Sam laughed, shaking his head.

"He was that bad?"

"Jake, Doug Eckstein has been a bully since the day he was born. Then he grew up to be a jerk. I can't tell you how great it was to see you take him on the other night."

"I just walked away," Jake said, shaking his head. "I've thought of a hundred things I wished I would have said since then."

"Nope, you did just what you should have. You set him straight and you walked away. You never would have won an argument with him if you'd stayed. You did the right thing. He would have fought with you, but he couldn't do much to a bunch of old geezers who have more dirt on him than you can shake a stick at. It was good therapy actually. I never would have guessed Hildegard had that kind of gumption, speaking of sticks."

Jake laughed again, imagining Hildegard threatening Doug with her cane. "So, are your family's problems better or worse than Amy's?"

"It all depends on who you ask."

Jake raised his eyebrows and nodded, curious, but not wanting to pry. "Hand me that piece over there," he said, pointing to a tile with a tree glazed on it.

Sam handed him the tile. "Ya know Jake, I'm pretty sure nobody ever gets married and plans on having problems, but they always come along. Most of them work themselves out in a week or two, but some problems never heal. Some of them fester and grow and turn into monsters."

Jake nodded. "I think I know what you mean. I grew up with a mixed bag too."

"Maybe we all do, but when you get to be my age, you start thinking about those monsters a lot more, wishing you would have tamed them when they were smaller. I guess I figured things would get better when the kids moved away and got married, but they didn't. They just set up camps on opposite ends of the country."

"What about your son? Didn't you say he lives in Pittsburgh?"

"Yep. Less than an hour away and I haven't seen or heard from him in over eight years. I heard he even has a couple of kids, but I've never met them. My wife was invited to the wedding, but I wasn't."

"Sam ... ," Jake said, but his thoughts failed him. This was obviously a tender subject. He knew it was none of his business, and yet he felt compelled to continue talking. "You might have heard that Amy and I are planning on getting married."

Sam nodded and smiled.

"So, what advice would you give to a guy like me who's just getting ready to jump into a barrel of monsters?"

Sam laughed and put his hand on Jake's shoulder. "Jake, there are at least a million things that I wish I'd done differently. I guess I shouldn't be surprised that my kids don't like me, I didn't like my dad much either."

"Why's that?"

"He was cranky and I never really knew him until I was about fifteen—until I was working here as his apprentice."

"Why was he cranky?"

"Probably for the same reason I am. He got up every morning at four to make bread. By the time we got home from school and finished our homework, he was ready to go to bed so he could start again the next day. He never took a vacation. He never had fun. He never had time to do much of anything with us. And what did I do? After spending my childhood swearing I'd never be a baker, I did the exact same thing. I worked too much, I yelled at my kids too much, and I raised three monsters who feel the same way about me as I did about my old man."

"So why did you go to work for him?"

"I didn't have much of a choice back then. The war had just ended and I didn't have any money to go to school, and my folks needed someone to take over the family business. I guess you could say I was 'guilted' into it. My dad died when I was only twenty-two, just as I was beginning to understand him. I had to keep the bakery going to support my sisters and my mom. When mom died, twelve years later, I thought about closing up and leaving town, but by then my wife and I had two little girls to feed and clothe, so we stayed."

"But don't you like what you do?"

"I've learned to love it, but it never would have been my first choice. I'm not a morning person. After almost sixty years of getting up at four in the morning, I still cringe every time my alarm goes off."

"And your son followed in your footsteps?"

"Hah, if you can call it that," he said, biting the side of his cheek. "He's baking bread for the devil."

Jake laughed, but as he looked up from the tiles, he saw that Sam was serious. "What do you mean?"

"He works for Wünder Bread, down in the corporate office in Pittsburgh."

"So, what's wrong with …"

"Jake, you've been in town long enough—you've eaten my bread long enough to know Wünder Bread is not bread. Its clouds with a crust—and the worst crust I've ever seen. In my youth, there was a saying, 'the whiter your bread, the sooner you're dead.' There's nothing in that stuff that's even remotely good for you. He sold his soul to the devil and now he's his baker." Sam shook his head, but didn't say anything more.

"I think it's interesting that your son would choose to make a living in the bread business, even after growing up with a father who was a baker. Maybe this town just isn't big enough for two Gottlieb bakers."

"Jake, he wanted this, and I was ready to give it all to him, but then he just disappeared one day, without even saying goodbye. He just walked away from a three-hundred-year-old family business."

"What happened?"

"I wish I knew. He was here one day and gone the next. We tracked him down in Pittsburgh, but …" Sam shook his head.

"But what?" Jake asked after a long silence.

"I messed up!" Sam said loudly. "I really messed up. After we hadn't seen him in a month, I found out where he was living and parked my butt in front of his apartment until he came home. I was so mad for the way he'd deserted us that I let him have it. After I slapped him across the face, I called him a bunch of horrible names and tossed him an ugly and hateful letter I'd written in my anger, telling him that he was expected home as soon as he was ready to act like an adult and apologize. That was the last time I saw him. That's the picture I have in my head when I think of him, sitting on the stairs, holding that blasted letter and bleeding from his nose from the blow I gave him. I messed up, Jake. I sowed the wind and now I am reaping the whirlwind." He took a deep breath, shaking his head.

Jake looked up from his work to see tears. In the time since he'd arrived in Niederbipp, he'd witnessed more tears and shed more of his own than he had during the rest of his life combined, but there was something different about these tears. These tears were heavy, filled with guilt and regret and great sorrow. Somehow, Jake could tell these were tears that had been cried before—that they were tortured tears—tears that climbed back up as soon as they had fallen, becoming more painful each time they rained down again.

As he watched Sam cry, he was struck by a very heavy and dark feeling that came to roost on his heart. It was a similar feeling to what he'd felt Sunday at The Crying Place with Amy. What if his own father were out there, somewhere, feeling this same thing—ashamed of what he'd done—wondering what had become of his estranged son and wife? It had been easier to think his father was dead than to consider he might feel the same way as Sam. John Henry Kimball, the man who'd given Jake two of his names might be out there somewhere feeling very much like this baker.

Jake had looked for his father a couple of times when he was at Hudson University. A Google search produced dozens of people by the same name, but none of them shared his father's birth date or anything familiar, and he'd given up his search before it really even started, acknowledging that it was easier to believe his father was dead. And there was a part of him that *wanted* his old man to be dead. Death was easier than carrying the burden of anger that he'd had from time to time when he was younger, feeling unloved, abandoned, unwanted. Even in recent years he'd wondered how any man could leave his own son and walk away forever. Jake felt sick as he looked at Sam and realized that here was a man who had done that very thing. The circumstances were different, but the outcome was the same. And yet Jake loved this man. Sam had fed him, encouraged him and had chosen him to replace his best friend in The Pottery. He struggled to understand how someone who'd shown him so much kindness could be capable of the actions he'd just confessed.

As Jake's emotions stirred inside his soul, his body did something completely involuntarily—he reached out and placed his shaking hand on Sam's arm. This wasn't his father, and he wasn't Sam's son, but something magical happened at the very moment he touched the old man's wrinkled hand—something so powerful that it burst upon them both like a clap of thunder. In that moment, the darkness they both felt was shattered by a feeling of warmth and light. In that moment, *there was hope!*

HE WHO WANTS TO DO GOOD
KNOCKS AT THE GATE;
HE WHO LOVES FINDS THE DOOR OPEN.
—RABINDRANATH TAGORE—

MAN-HEAVEN

ANYTHING YOU CANNOT RELINQUISH WHEN IT HAS OUTLIVED ITS
USEFULNESS, POSSESSES YOU, AND IN THIS MATERIALISTIC AGE, A GREAT
MANY OF US ARE POSSESSED BY OUR POSSESSIONS.
—PEACE PILGRIM—

am, you've got to fix this. You have to make this better," Jake
said passionately.

Sam smiled weakly. "Jake, I don't know what else I
can do. I have no excuse for the way I treated my son, but
something deep inside me wonders if there's not something else—some
other reason he stays away."

"What do you mean?"

Sam shook his head. "He once told his mother that we're better off without him. I'm not sure what that means. When there's no communication for so long, your mind begins to wrestle with every possible idea. It's probably just me wishing … just feeling guilty and hoping that maybe … that maybe I'm not the only reason he stays away."

"Does your wife still have contact with him?"

"I'm not sure. We stopped talking about him a few years ago because it always ended in a fight. This hasn't been easy on either of us. She's not the reason my son left, but she feels the sorrow and loss all the same. The burden of the truth that I hurt my family and haven't been able to do a thing to fix it in eight long years has been a heavy stone to carry. That stunt I pulled so many years ago has cost me what was left of my relationships with all my children. It had never been strong before, but that one event put an end to what little I had."

Jake shook his head in disbelief. "I don't get it, Sam. How can you be such a cool guy to me and everyone else and have your kids … well, have your kids …"

"Hate me?" Sam said, finishing his sentence.

"Is that what you think it is?"

"I don't know. I was never very close to the girls. I didn't know how to be a father. By the time I figured it out, the girls were pretty much grown. Matthew was a surprise. He came along sixteen years after we thought we were done. His name means God's gift. I was forty-six years old when he was born and I was finally ready to be a dad. Unlike his sisters, he loved the bakery. He was always under my feet—always asking questions—always wanting to help. I hoped he'd take over the family business."

"Even after you didn't want to?"

"I know … believe me, I know. I have often wondered if he left because I pushed him too hard." He shook his head. "Jake, I didn't understand it when my father began dragging me to work with him, but what man doesn't hope his son will follow in his footsteps?

"When Matt began showing an interest in taking over, I began making plans for my future. I was planning on sticking around long enough for him to learn the ropes, then spending my Golden Years trying to be a better grandfather than I was a father. Now, I'll never have that chance."

"There has to be something you can do."

 "If you can figure it out, let me know, but for the past eight years I've written at least one letter a month and I have a box full of unopened letters to show for all my efforts. I can't tell you how many times my hopes have been dashed when one more letter arrives with 'return to sender' scrawled across it. All those letters, all that time and pain and sorrow—it hasn't done a bit of good."

Jake swallowed, feeling this man's pain, but also remembering his own at never having received correspondence of any kind from his father. "Do you really feel that way—that no good has come from it?"

Sam looked thoughtful and didn't answer for a long moment. "No, I guess I don't. I'd like to think I'm a better man for writing them. It's forced me to look at myself and change, but those letters have also left me broken-hearted. The door is still locked and it seems there is nothing I can do to get in."

"So what would you do if you had a chance to talk to your son … what would you say?"

Sam paused. "I've rehearsed that in my mind a million times, but I don't know if it's right."

Jake looked up, distracted by the shadow that had fallen across his work. He turned to see Amy at the bakery's glass doors.

"I'll let her in," said Sam, as he rolled onto his knees and struggled to get up.

He was just about to step on the new tiles when Jake yelled, "STOP!" fearing he'd ruin the work they'd just completed.

Amy laughed and motioned that she would go around to the back door.

Sam disappeared to let her in.

"Well, it looks like this is taking a bit longer than you boys thought," Amy said with sass in her words that made Jake smile. "Remind me, Sam, how many years of bread this is worth?"

"Three."

"I thought it was four," Jake said, brandishing his trowel, but his smile betrayed him.

"I think we've already eaten a years' worth, Jake."

"Thank you, Amy for keeping him honest. I also understand you deserve a lot of the credit for this design. Thank you, it's totally awesome."

"You're welcome. I figured if I'm going to benefit from this trade, I needed to do my part. Besides, Jake really needed help." She lowered her voice slightly, but still loud enough for Jake to hear. "Have you *seen* his drawings?"

Jake smiled as he dipped his hand in the water bucket before flicking it at Amy.

"Hey, I'm getting hungry," said Sam, breaking up the fight before it had a chance to start. "Do you kids want some dinner?"

"What have you got?" asked Amy.

"Pastries and chocolate milk."

She laughed. "Sounds like dinner in man-heaven."

"So you'll join us?" asked Sam.

"What the heck. It looks like you guys could use some help."

The conversation was much lighter after Amy arrived. Jake sensed that Sam was grateful for the change, but he wondered what Sam might have told him, what more he might have shared if they hadn't been interrupted. But Jake couldn't deny that he, too, was grateful for the change in mood.

Darkness fell as they continued to work on the floor, making slow but steady progress. Finally, just before midnight, the last piece was set in its place. Jake stood slowly, trying to make his knees work. His fingertips were raw from the mortar. They carried the tools and buckets into the back room where Amy took it upon her self to clean the tools while Jake carefully washed the rogue mortar from his hands and forearms.

As she was scrubbing the oldest of the trowels with a big yellow tile sponge, she noticed that the old wooden handle had something written on it. At first she thought it was just the brand name of the tool, but as the mortar fell away, she was surprised to see her own last name carved into the polished handle—G. M. ECKSTEIN.

"Sam, where did you get this tool?"

He looked up from the bucket he'd been scrubbing. "Oh, my wife found it at a garage sale a hundred years ago."

"Were there any other tools?"

"Yeah, a whole box of them," he said, nodding to a long, dusty wooden toolbox on the opposite counter. "She thought they'd look cute hanging in our kitchen. I didn't agree so I snuck them out of the house and put them down in the cellar. Why do you ask?"

Amy handed him the trowel, pointing to the name on the handle, before turning her attention to the tool box. With the sponge, she wiped away years of dust to reveal the Eckstein name on the corner of the open box. She reached in and pulled out a rusty piece of metal that looked similar to a boomerang. She set it aside, picking up an old hand drill followed by a few very rusty drill bits. Two smaller trowels of different shapes came next, each covered in dust and cobwebs and a rusty patina. There was a strange-looking hammer, a half-dozen chisels and a tarnished wood-something that looked like a top with dirty string wound loosely around it. She set these all aside and picked up a handful of crudely-shaped, rusty nails that were scattered on the bottom of the box.

"Your name is on this one too," Jake said, pulling the hammer from the jumbled pile.

"I don't know much about tools," said Sam, but these look like the tools of a stonemason, which is kind of ironic. Did you know your name means 'cornerstone?' "

"Yeah, Thomas just told us last week. Are these tools for sale?"

"No, but you can have them if you promise to never let my wife know I gave them to you. She's probably forgotten about them by now, but you never know."

"Thanks, Sam."

"Sure. What are you going to do with them?"

"I thought I'd use them for props for a painting, or maybe just put down in the Pottery's cellar," she said, smiling at Jake like a little girl who'd just brought home a stray cat.

"Do you know who G.M. Eckstein is?" asked Jake.

"No, but I happen to have recently acquired a book that might help me figure it out," she said with a wink.

A SLIVER OF HOPE

HUMANITY IS NEVER SO BEAUTIFUL AS WHEN PRAYING FOR FORGIVENESS,
OR ELSE FORGIVING ANOTHER.
—JEAN PAUL RICHTER—

ince the first time he'd heard them, Jake had been charmed by
the sound of the church bells. But as he pulled his pillow over
his head, trying to drown out their morning peal, he realized
the charm also came with some inconveniences. He was tired
and sore from having spent the better part of eight hours on his knees,
working on Sam's floor. As he pulled his fisted hands from under his

pillow, he could feel they were swollen and blistered. In the eight years since he'd been making pottery, his hands had become strong and his skin, thick, protecting them from blisters except for the occasions when his hands were forced to conform to the shape of a tool or handle that he did not normally use. The old trowel and the lime from the mortar had done a number on his hands, and he found himself wishing he'd used gloves.

A big part of him wished he could sleep in—he would have had he been back in Albany at school, but he'd so enjoyed the various Sunday sermons since he'd arrived that he put his excuses aside and pulled himself out of bed to shower and shave. As he hurried down the stairs, he remembered the old Bible he'd planned to bring but forgotten so many times before and he ran into the studio to grab Isaac's old copy from the shelf above the wedging table. As he ran back out, he nearly stepped on a piece of paper lying just inside the threshold. He picked it up, turning it over to find his name scrawled over the top of a hand-written grocery list.

As he hurried across the courtyard, he unfolded the paper to find a note written on the back side.

Jake,

I am sorry we missed you. You don't know me, but I've heard a little bit about you from my mother, Mary Smith. My wife and I are in town for the weekend and we hoped we might be able to speak to you while we're here. Please give me a call on my cell phone. Cell service is patchy, but leave a message and let me know when or if that might be possible. Isaac was a dear friend of mine. We look forward to meeting you.

Charlie Smith
215-582-9282

Jake had never heard of Charlie Smith, and he searched his memory for a Mary Smith but couldn't think of anyone he'd met with that name either. He folded the note and slid it into the Bible as he hurried up the hill to the church

As promised, Amy was sitting near the front, next to Bev and Jerry. Jake squeezed through the crowded center aisle and sat down next to her, greeting them all with a smile.

Jake's attention was drawn to the woman at the organ as it had been every Sunday since he'd first watched her donning her platform shoes. As he watched her now, he realized there was something different about her this week—she was smiling. The music she played was something he'd heard just the week before as the congregation had sung together "There Is Sunshine In My Soul Today", but Jake was surprised by how animated she was. The smile remained as her playing continued.

Jake looked around at the congregation. The Sunday morning chatter seemed louder than normal and Jake wondered why. Amy seemed to notice as well, and they both turned toward the back door where the chatter seemed to be focused around a young couple who were slowly making their way down the center aisle, their way clogged by dozens of people swarming them with words of congratulations that bounced off the chapel's stone walls. Thomas stood behind the crowd with a smile on his face, slowly nudging them forward while encouraging folks to take their seats.

As the crowd slowly dispersed, Thomas escorted the couple to the front row and invited them to take a seat. Then he walked to the lectern to begin the meeting.

"There truly is sunshine in our souls today!" said Thomas, beaming, once the prelude had ended. "This spring and summer have marked the return of many who have wandered from Niederbipp. I had the choicest of meetings last night with a young couple who stopped by to visit family. Many of you will remember Charlie Smith as the rabble rousing teenager who … well … kept us up at night with worry."

The congregation chuckled and Jake watched out of the corner of his eye as Beverly nodded her head. The name sounded vaguely familiar, but he couldn't remember why.

"None of us had seen Charlie in nearly a decade before Isaac Bingham's funeral a few months ago. At that time, I learned that Charlie was engaged to be married, but as we visited, I also learned that this son of Niederbipp has seen many wonderful changes in the past few years. I invited him to share those experiences with our congregation if he ever passed through town. This last week, Charlie and his wife Jodi were married in Philadelphia where he's been working for the past seven years as a youth counselor at an inner-city juvenile detention center. Jodi, his new bride, happens to be one of the directors of that center." There was a rush of hushed voices that filled the chapel as Thomas gave pause for his words to sink in.

"I was planning on giving the sermon today, but when I visited last night with Charlie and Jodi, I knew I needed to step aside and give Charlie the opportunity to stand at this pulpit for the first time and share with all of us the things he's learned."

Thomas looked at his watch. "I know we normally begin with a hymn, but we're a little late in getting started, so, if you don't mind, Mary, I think we ought to allow the mood you have set with your rousing prelude to be the only introduction to your son's sermon."

Mary nodded, smiling proudly.

"My friends of Niederbipp, I give you Charlie Smith." Thomas extended his hands, inviting Charlie to come forward. Then Thomas walked away, taking Charlie's seat next to Jodi.

Charlie stood at the lectern dressed in a white dress shirt and khaki cargo pants. His hair was combed back and secured in a short pony tail with a red rubber band. He smiled at the congregation, revealing a deep scar in his cheek, but before he could begin talking, his smile faded and his shoulders slumped, turning to a look of great humility.

"If anyone would have told me ten years ago that I would be standing at the front of the Niederbipp chapel to tell my story, I would have laughed in his face. But here I stand, humbled by the path my life has taken, humbled by the grace of God and the love of one of His servants. I have no doubt that most of you were surprised to see me at Isaac's funeral. Those of you who weren't surprised probably didn't recognize me. When I received the call from the Mayor, inviting me to be one of Isaac's pallbearers, I wept for the next three days, and a day has not passed since then that I have not been brought to tears by the memory of a man who loved me with the greatest compassion and understanding that I have ever known." He shook his head, obviously trying to fight back the tears.

"I know this is not a funeral. I know Isaac is dead and buried, but I also know that I cannot share my message of redemption with you today without referring to the man who taught me more than any other what my God must be like. It is because of him that I am alive today. His actions—the sermons he taught me by example—those have remained with me over the last decade and pricked my heart until I had the courage and humility to change.

"My story in Niederbipp began when I was four years old. My mother brought me here after reading a travel brochure she picked up somewhere. I have learned over the years that many of you took care of us, providing work for my mom and direction and distractions for me. I became friends with your kids and grandkids. As I got older, you hired me to do odd jobs to keep me out of trouble, but trouble eventually found me. It seems I was born with a chip on my shoulder, and that chip grew every day until it nearly ruined me.

"Before Isaac's funeral, many of you had not seen me for more than eight years." He gripped the edges of the pulpit with his hands, looking down. There was a long pause before he spoke again, and when he did, his voice was shaky. "I can't go any further without apologizing to you for the person I was back then. I am certain there was never a time in the past eight years when I was missed, even by my own mother. I was ignorant and selfish and rude, and I doubt there was anyone here who wasn't negatively affected by my actions or attitudes. I am certain that as I stand before you now, even after your warm greetings, that there is in your hearts, some feeling of pain or disappointment that remains from the person I was. I am truly sorry. With all my heart, I am sorry for the trouble and pain I caused you. I have spent the last eight years trying to make up for the foolishness of my youth."

He unbuttoned a sleeve and rolled it up to reveal his forearm, heavily covered in colorful tattoos. "Though I have tried with all my heart to rectify my wrongs, I will always be left with physical reminders of my own stupidity. I was a thief and a liar and a rotten kid. I have done all I could to repent and restore what I took from you. It was difficult at first to see so much of my paycheck going to pay for the things I lifted from your shops and your homes, but as I worked with the boys and young men at the detention center, I realized I could not teach them to be just and honest men if I had not done all I could to become one myself.

"I have struggled for years to remember even my slightest infractions against you, wanting so badly to become the man ..." He trailed off, struggling to contain his emotions. "... I wanted so badly to become the man Isaac knew I could be. He had more faith in me than I've ever had in myself. He loved me unconditionally. He picked me up when I fell and set me on a new course that has changed my life and given me a desire to spend it helping others do the same.

"Over the years, many of you have received letters from me. Some of them contained money for what I knew I owed you, but all of them contained apologies for the way I treated the trust and friendship you offered me. With each letter I wrote, with each payment I sent, I felt the burdens of my heart lighten—I felt a load lifted—just as Isaac told me I would. But even as the burden lightened, the feelings of unworthiness

I felt about returning home remained." He took a deep breath before looking up with resolution in his eyes.

"And then one day, three months ago, I got a phone call from Mayor Jim. He told me about Isaac's passing and the request he'd left for his funeral proceedings, inviting me to be a pallbearer. Even in death, he was teaching me—forgiving me. This potter who had reshaped my soul after the mess I'd made of it, gave me the greatest gifts I have ever known. He changed my course from the fast track to hell to a course of enlightenment. He forgave me, and even at the very end, his invitation to carry his broken-down body encouraged me to forgive myself.

"When someone's path is as crooked as mine was, it requires a lot of straightening." He reached in his back pocket and pulled out a piece of paper from his wallet, unfolding it and lifting it for the congregation to see. Even from where Jake sat, he could see it was worn and tattered. Only a few words were written on it.

"Shortly after I left, I received this letter from Isaac. It simply reads, "Charlie, remember the slivers. I want to help. Let me show you how." Enclosed in this letter was a silver needle that I've long since lost, but this simple message gave me a lot to think about.

"You see, when I was about seven years old, I talked Isaac into helping me build a tree house down by the river. I took him for a walk to show him the perfect tree, and on the way home we stopped by the hardware store to price out the materials. I remember hoping that Isaac would buy all the stuff we needed. Instead, he bought five dollars' worth of nails. Then we went back to the pottery shop and we drew up our plans. I was so excited to get started, but he reminded me that we didn't have any lumber. He put the bag of nails in front of me and told me that he would trade me a nail for every piece of useable wood I brought to

the pottery shop. I began scrounging for wood that afternoon. As I looked around town, I discovered that lots of people had small pieces of lumber around their houses that they were happy to give to a kid with ambition. I also found some wood on the banks of the river, and finally the man at the sawmill gave me a bunch of warped lumber in exchange for sweeping the floor at the mill. In the matter of a week, I'd collected an impressive pile of assorted lumber and earned every one of Isaac's nails.

That Saturday afternoon, Isaac helped me load all my lumber into his big, old wagon along with a ladder and a couple of hammers and saws, and we pulled it all down to the river to begin our work. Over the next several days, our tree house came together. In the process, I accumulated a couple of deep slivers in the palms of my tender hands. They were painful at first, but I didn't want to slow our progress by telling Isaac. It seems silly now, but I figured all I needed was a couple of good Band-Aids and everything would be better."

Several people in the congregation laughed softly.

"By the time the tree house was built, my slivers had been festering for several days under the warmth of the Band-Aids. As we pulled the wagon back to the shop, the bandages fell away from my hands and Isaac noticed the infected wounds. When we got back to The Pottery, he insisted that I wash my hands with soap and water so he could see the extent of my wounds.

"I watched as he heated a needle in the flame of a candle. Then he invited me to take a seat on the stool in front of him so he could remove the slivers. I wanted nothing to do with that needle. I begged and pleaded and insisted that I just needed more Band-Aids—that everything would be better if I could just cover it up. In response to my pleadings, Isaac's voice became soft as he explained the potential serious effects of leaving the slivers in. Still, I refused. I was scared of the pain. He seemed to sense my fear and assured me that the pain of the needle would be tiny compared with the pain of a major infection. But I continued to resist. It wasn't until he threatened me with the potential need of amputation—if the infection were to spread—that I finally agreed to sit down.

Charlie's smiled broadly. "In the years since that time, I have learned the meaning of "potential," but at that time I was very scared. I don't remember the words he spoke to me as he worked, but I do remember the calm they brought me. He was kind and gentle and before I knew what had happened, the slivers were gone, along with the infection. He washed my hands again with warm water and dried them before applying a healing balm.

"After reading Isaac's letter and thinking about the slivers of my youth, I'll admit I was confused, wondering how that simple lesson from my childhood could apply to the mess I'd gotten myself into."

He paused, panning the congregation as if he were taking them all in. "There is a big part of me that wants to confess all the sins of my younger years, but when Isaac offered to help me the night I left, he was very clear when he asked me to keep my stupidity and selfishness— as well as his generosity—secret. I will tell you in broad terms that the last act of stupidity that I performed here  in Niederbipp was illegal and had it not been for Isaac stepping in, I'd probably still be behind bars and innocent people would still be hurting. The gift he gave me was a chance to change my life, but it was not until he sent me his old copy of "Les Misérables" and I read the story of Jean Valjean that I really began to understand the responsibility that came with the gift he'd given me.

"That was the first book I ever read cover-to-cover. I was never much of a student. In my grade-school years, I spent a lot of time being tutored by a mortal angel, Gloria, who tried to help me—tried to save me from my ignorance. Though I loved the time I spent with her, the influence of the world pulled harder in other directions, each decision becoming increasingly worse. After nearly flunking out of high school, I moved to Warren and landed a job as a janitor at the bus station where

I was introduced to drugs and alcohol by travelers and locals and my roommates. I made a lot of really stupid decisions over the next few years. One night, after a few beers with my friends, we went out looking for trouble at the Bungee Bipp. One bad decision led to a dozen others, and to make a long story short, I made a decision that night that altered the course of my life forever.

"Twenty-four hours later, I found myself on the streets of Philadelphia—a small-town rebel in a big world, with more sobriety forced upon me than I'd ever known. When I left Nierdebipp, Isaac gave us … gave me fifty dollars and the name of a friend of his at the YMCA. I took shelter there. I was desperate, and humbled. When Isaac's package arrived, his copy of "Les Miserables" and a letter informing me of the enormous cost of my actions, I began to realize, probably for the first time, the pain and trouble that my selfish choices had caused others.

"In that sad and desperate state of mind, I began reading that great book. As a child, I'd attended services here each Sunday, sitting on the front row so my mother could keep an eye on me while she played the organ. But it wasn't until reading "Les Misérables" that I began to understand the need we all have for a God. Isaac's friend who'd given me shelter at the Y acquainted me with other great books, and in my misery, I began looking for sources of hope. It was during those weeks that I *really* became a Christian and began a new journey on a different path. Isaac's letters encouraged me on my way—encouraged me to allow a God much bigger than myself to remove the slivers in my hands and soul and move forward. I got a job and began repaying Isaac for the money he'd spent to right my wrong, knowing it would take me a lifetime to repay both him and all of you. A councilor at the Y helped me apply for grants, and I got into school, hoping to do something more with my life.

"School was tough, but whenever I became discouraged, I would remember the responsibility I'd been given to not only change my life, but also the lives of others. With the debt I owed a very generous potter always in the back of my mind, my life took on a focus it had never had before. I worked full-time, went to school full-time and stayed up late, studying—each month, managing to send some money back to Isaac to pay my debt.

"I graduated three years later at the top of my class, but I knew I had more to learn. I knew that my learning needed to put me in a position where I had more to offer, more to give to the world. While many of my peers went on to other jobs and positions, I knew my path would be different. I knew I needed to work with kids—young people like myself who'd chosen their paths poorly and needed a friend to help them see a better way. As I began counseling kids, I realized that the methods and the protocols I'd learned in school were often insufficient to inspire long-term change. In those cases, I drew upon the education I'd received from Isaac—the mercy, the love, the compassion, and the responsibility and accountability we all have to our world. Over and over again, I have shared the story of my slivers. Over and over again, I have seen kids change as they recognize the possibility of hope. Over and over again, I have watched as kids respond positively to love in ways infinitely more powerful than they've ever responded to fear.

"Every time I watch a kid change, I remember the debt Isaac paid for me. He purchased my freedom with money, but it was his love …" Charlie paused to wipe his eyes. "… it was his love that made me want to believe in a physician that can cure all the world's pain and sorrow. It is because of the love of that wonderful man that I am here today.

"I have learned in these past eight years that there is a big difference between covering a sliver with a Band-Aid and taking the sliver out. I have learned that for most slivers, we are incapable of removing them ourselves. I have witnessed the change that comes into people's lives when they learn that only the hands which have been pierced with nails are sensitive enough to remove the slivers from our hands … and souls and apply the healing balm we all need."

He took a deep breath, looking at his mother and then at his wife. "It is because of love that I am alive. It is because of love that my life has meaning and direction and hope. I stand before you all today knowing in my heart that I have done all that I can to restore what I have taken—to repay the debts I have acquired. I know that it may take many more years for you to trust me, but in the meantime, I ask you to do something I cannot do for myself—I ask you to forgive me."

Charlie's words faded off, but he stood where he was as if he was hoping for an answer.

Amy squeezed Jake's hand as they watched an old woman across the aisle rise from her seat. A man stood, several rows behind her and began clapping, putting an end to the awkward silence. At first, the sound of clapping seemed entirely out of place, but as others stood and joined the man in the ovation, an other-worldly feeling of happiness filled the chapel with a spirit of joy. Men and women wiped tears from their eyes as they felt that joy, but applause continued for several minutes and seemed to be accompanied by the clapping of a thousand angels joining in from the heavens.

Jake and Amy had joined the congregation in the united assent, and even though they had never met Charlie Smith, the electric feeling pulsing through the crowd was powerful and meaningful and drew them in with its infectious enthusiasm. Charlie's tears flowed as he braced himself against the lectern. When his wife walked to him and embraced him, the congregation erupted again in applause. This continued until Mary took her seat on the organ's bench and began playing a familiar tune. Without prompting, the congregation remained standing where they were and sang the words together.

Amazing Grace, how sweet the sound,
That saved a wretch like me.
I once was lost but now am found,
Was blind, but now I see.
T'was Grace that taught my heart to fear.
And Grace, my fears relieved.

How precious did that Grace appear
The hour I first believed.

Through many dangers, toils and snares
I have already come;
'Tis Grace that brought me safe thus far
And Grace will lead me home.

The Lord has promised good to me.
His word my hope secures.
He will my shield and portion be,
As long as life endures.

Yea, when this flesh and heart shall fail,
And mortal life shall cease,
I shall possess within the veil,
A life of joy and peace.

When we've been here ten thousand years
Bright shining as the sun.
We've no less days to sing God's praise
Than when we've first begun. [1]

Jake and Amy were unfamiliar with the words after the first verse, so they listened as the older folks in the congregation raised their voices for the following verses. Before the song was over, there was not a dry eye to be found in the chapel. Jake put his arm around Amy and she looked up at him, tears streaming down her freckled cheeks.

"There's hope," she whispered softly. And Jake knew she wasn't talking about hope in some obscure, general term. He felt it too. There was hope. There was hope for Amy and her parents. There was hope for Sam and his son. And somewhere out there, there was hope for Jake and the father who'd forgotten him.

[1] John Newton, 1779

TREASURES

DARKNESS CANNOT DRIVE OUT DARKNESS; ONLY LIGHT CAN DO THAT.
HATE CANNOT DRIVE OUT HATE; ONLY LOVE CAN DO THAT.
—MARTIN LUTHER KING, JR.—

"We've missed seeing you two this week," said a familiar male voice from behind them.

Jake and Amy turned around to see Joseph and Gloria, their faces still damp with tears. "Sorry, we've missed seeing you too," said Jake, reaching over the pew to hug them both. Amy did the same. "We've been busy working on Sam's floor," Jake said. "I'm sorry we haven't even stopped by."

Gloria smiled softly. "It's okay. It just warms our hearts to see the two of you. Have you set a date yet?"

Jake squirmed, looking at Amy. "No, not yet, but you'll be the first to know."

Gloria and Joseph smiled approvingly.

"So did you meet Charlie and Jodi last night?" asked Gloria.

"No, we were working over at the bakery until after midnight. Why?" asked Jake.

"Oh, we ran into them last night at Mancini's. When they left, they said they wanted to stop by and meet you," explained Gloria.

"No, I ..." But at that moment Jake remembered the note he'd found on the floor of The Pottery just an hour before. He picked up the Bible from the bench and flipped through it until he came to the note. "I knew his name sounded familiar," Jake said, shaking his head, feeling dumb. "I found this on the floor this morning. We must have missed it last night when we dropped the tools off at the shop," he said, looking at Amy.

She looked over his shoulder, reading the note.

"Would you like us to introduce you?" Gloria asked, nodding to Charlie and Jodi, in the center of a large and noisy crowd.

"Sure, but maybe after the crowd dies down," said Jake.

While they waited, Jake and Amy told them about their week—the tiles, Amy's paintings and the scooter ride to the hills. Gloria and Joseph told them about the commotion on Hauptstrasse with Mona's Antique Shoppe making way for The Lamar Mancini International Museum of Pudding Molds. The sign had already been hung and most of the antiques had been moved out. They laughed together as Gloria spoke of a single protester picketing outside the new museum with a hand-written sign that read, "My brother is an alien" on one side and "Avoid the curse, boycott the museum!" on the other. They explained that Roberta gave up and went home when she realized her sign and protest were only serving to draw more attention to the museum.

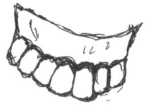

"Well, what a delightful surprise."

The four of them turned to see Mr. Allan smiling with a new set of teeth. Jake stood and shook his hand, inviting him to sit with them while they waited. Before he sat down, he produced a gift for each of them from the many pockets in his three-piece, brown polyester, pin-stripe suit—four rocks of various sizes and colors—each one of them declared to be "one of his favorites."

In an unusually lucid way, Mr. Allan spoke of his own feelings of hope that the sermon had inspired—that his children might find a way to forgive him for his neglect. As he spoke, his eyes looked sad and tired, and Jake was struck with the sense of loneliness that surrounded him. He felt sorry for the old man in the same way he'd felt sorry for Sam and the chasm between him and his son. Though the details of each man's pain were different, the loneliness and regret were similar. He thought it strange that so many people he knew, including himself, were dealing with the pain and sorrow of familial relations. In some ways, it made Jake feel better to know that he wasn't the only one struggling to find understanding and meaning in these relationships. But another part of him wondered if there weren't an answer somewhere, somehow.

He could hear the conversation continue around him, but his mind was distracted, searching for answers and understanding. His attention was pulled toward the front of the church where people continued to hug Charlie. There was something powerful—something magical taking place there. The only things Jake knew about Charlie were what he'd learned from his message of tragedy and grace. But as Jake watched the emotion of the offender as he was embraced by the offended, Jake felt that this outpouring of love and acceptance was perhaps an equally powerful sermon on grace—an assembly where the fruits of repentance were embraced by the fruits of forgiveness.

"Jake, are you listening?" Amy asked, touching his knee and pulling him away from his thoughts.

"What ... no ... sorry, what?" he stammered.

"Mr. Allan was talking about commissioning you to make him something."

"I'm sorry," he repeated, turning to face Mr. Allan.

"I know I shouldn't be talking about business on the Sabbath, but I don't know when I'll be back in town, and I've been wanting to place an order since you visited me out at my place."

"Sure. What did you have in mind?"

"Journey Jars. I have some gifts to give. I need five of them with two lids each and eleven with just one lid apiece."

"Uh, sure, but I've never made them. Do you know what you want?"

"Yes, I want five Journey Jars with two lids each and eleven with just one lid apiece," Mr. Allan repeated, a little louder this time.

Jake smiled, looking up into Gloria and Joseph's faces. They nodded, returning the smile. "So, should I just make them however I want?"

"Aren't you a potter?"

"Yes, but I just wondered if you had any specific requests."

"Yes, I do. Make them really pretty, and I want each one to be different."

"What about color?" asked Jake, still unsure.

"Color would be nice. Why don't you surprise me."

"Okay, but how big?"

Mr. Allan pulled a small rock from his chest pocket. "I want something this big to be able to fit inside.

"Okay, when do you need them?"

"My birthday is on the Fourth of July. My kids are probably coming. I want to give them each one of your jars."

Jake did the math quickly in his head. He had less than two weeks. "That might be pushing it, especially since I'm not really sure what I am doing."

"Well, do what you can." He reached into his pocket again, then looked from left to right before slipping Jake a small roll of bills.

"Keep it a secret." He stood, patting the few strands of hair on the top of his head that he'd combed over from his left side. "I need to be on my way, but before I go, I'd like to give each of you one of my treasures."

Jake was about to remind Mr. Allan that he'd already given them some of his treasures, but Gloria put her hand on Jake's shoulder, putting an end to his protest before it even began. Jake turned to see she was smiling and shaking her head. They each received another one of Mr. Allan's treasures, more pretty rocks, and waved goodbye to the old man as he made his way to the chapel doors.

"We've learned that when an older person wants to give you something, its best not to protest," said Gloria.

Joseph nodded. "I think most people in town probably have a sizeable rock collection from Mr. Allan's gifts. The last time his son, Paul, was in town, he asked us to accept anything his dad offered us with a smile, and throw it away if we didn't want it. We haven't been out to his place in a while, but his whole house used to be filled with *pretty* rocks. Paul said he and his siblings hoped their father could get rid of some of the junk before he died so it wouldn't be such a chore to clean out the house."

"But you know why he shares them, don't you?" Amy asked, looking concerned.

Gloria nodded. "Isaac gave us a Journey Jar, too. We often recycle Mr. Allan's *treasures* in our arrangements by filling the bottoms of vases with them. I've kept one of the bigger ones on the counter at the shop for several years to help me remember to treat everyone with kindness."

Jake shook his head, smiling. "I can't imagine you ever having trouble treating people with kindness."

"See! It works." Gloria said with a wink.

"So, you guys know Mr. Allan's kids?" Jake asked.

"Sure, Gloria did the flowers for all of their weddings," said Joseph.

"Do you still have contact with them?" asked Amy.

"Every once in a while. They haven't been here for a long time. Cindy calls every few years to check in and catch up."

"Where are they?" asked Jake.

Gloria looked at Joseph. "Let's see … last I heard, Karl was in California, Paul is in Colorado, Cindy is in Boston and Robert is in …"

"Isn't Robert in Tennessee?" asked Joseph.

"No, I think he moved to Virginia," Gloria replied.

Jake nodded, looking disappointed.

"Why do you ask?" said Joseph.

"I … I guess they're probably not coming for Mr. Allan's birthday then."

Gloria shook her head. "I doubt it. He's been hoping they'd come for a long time, but they never do. The last time I spoke to Cindy, she said she'd like to come back, but everybody has been busy with their own lives and kids."

"When was the last time they were here?" asked Jake.

Gloria and Joseph looked at each other. "Do you mean all together?" asked Joseph.

"Yeah."

"Probably not since their mother's funeral," said Gloria.

"Didn't Mr. Allan tell us that was nearly twenty years ago?" Jake asked, turning to Amy.

"Yeah, I think so. What are you thinking?" asked Amy

Jake grinned. "What if we threw Mr. Allan a birthday party?" He looked at Gloria and Joseph. "Do you think they would come?"

"That's less than two weeks away, Jake, and that's a long way to travel for some of them. You might be able to get a couple of them. Cindy would probably come, but the boys … I'm not so sure," said Gloria. "They haven't had anything to do with their dad in years. It's sad. I know he's missed them, but I guess life goes on. Unfortunately, family sometimes becomes an inconvenience for people. Niederbipp isn't exactly the crossroad to anywhere."

Jake nodded, looking disappointed.

"Maybe we could figure out a way to get Cindy to come," suggested Amy. "She's the closest. Maybe she'd make the trip if she got a ticket in the mail. Mr. Allan said he had money. Maybe we could help him buy her a ticket."

Gloria smiled. "Well, it wouldn't hurt to ask. I could call Cindy later this afternoon. I haven't spoken to her for a long time. It would be nice to catch up."

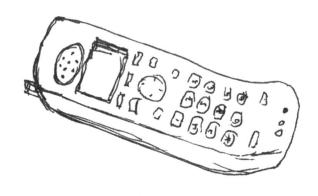

OF LIFE'S TWO CHIEF PRIZES,
BEAUTY AND TRUTH,
I FIND THE FIRST IN A LOVING
HEART, AND THE SECOND, IN A
LABORER'S HAND.
—KAHLIL GIBRAN—

REDEMPTION

AS FAR AS WE CAN DISCERN, THE SOLE PURPOSE OF HUMAN EXISTENCE IS TO
KINDLE A LIGHT IN THE DARKNESS OF MERE BEING.
—CARL JUNG—

So this is the potter who never sleeps?" said a voice from behind them.

Jake and Amy turned to see Charlie and his wife, Jodi.

Gloria and Joseph moved forward to embrace the couple before turning back to Jake and Amy to make introductions.

Charlie reached out his hand to Jake, shaking it vigorously before doing the same to Amy's. "We camped out behind The Pottery last night, hoping to catch you."

"We waited the better part of two hours before we gave up and wrote you a note," added Jodi, smiling.

Jake pulled the note from his Bible. "Yeah, sorry, we were working on a project over at the bakery last night. I didn't get home until after midnight. I just found your note before church started."

The last stragglers brushed past them, patting Charlie on the shoulder again as they made their way out into the bright day, leaving just the six of them in the chapel.

"We'd better be going too," said Gloria. "Charlie told us he was anxious to talk to you and I've got a phone call to make."

"And I have date with my pillow," added Joseph. "There's nothing like a Sunday nap. It was great to see you Charlie, and to meet your beautiful wife. Please let us know next time you'll be in town and we'll have you both to dinner."

"Thank you, we will," said Charlie with a grin that pulled on the deep scar on his cheek. He turned to Jake and Amy. "I can't tell you how happy I was to hear that they were able to find a new potter to take Isaac's place. Like I said this morning, I'm alive today because of the things Isaac taught me." He took a deep breath and turned to look at his wife who moved closer to him, wrapping her arms around his middle as she slid under his arm. "I've done most of what I knew I needed to do this weekend, but there's still a couple of things. I ... if it's not a major inconvenience, would you mind if I spent a few minutes in The Pottery.

"Not at all. We were just on our way there. Amy made some peppermint tea yesterday and we have some day-old pastries."

As they walked down Hinterstrasse together, Charlie talked about his memories of the town. He'd left right after high school to go to Warren, so it had been more than twelve years since he'd walked along this way and his words were filled with nostalgia and emotion as he spoke of people and events and recollections.

"My bum is still sore from sitting on that bench," Jodi said, pointing to the old, stone bench under the chestnut tree as they entered the courtyard behind The Pottery. "I'd heard Charlie's stories before, but hearing them again here, where they actually took place, gave me a different perspective. Isaac must have been an amazing man."

"He was," Jake, Amy and Charlie said in unison, as if it had been practiced.

They smiled together as Jake unlocked The Pottery's back door and pushed it open for his guests to enter. Charlie took three steps inside before closing his eyes and inhaling deeply through his nose.

"It smells exactly the same as I remember," he said, turning to Jodi. "Do you smell that scent of mildew?"

"That would probably be the clay in the cellar," suggested Jake. "It's always stronger when the back door has been closed for a while."

Charlie nodded, but his attention had clearly been drawn away by something else—the mugs on the overhead beam.

"It's still here," he whispered, his voice choked with emotion. He turned to Jake. "I can't believe its still here. It's been at least twelve years since I drank my last tea with Isaac, but he left my mug hanging on the same nail all that time."

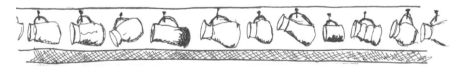

"It looks like it has *at least* twelve years worth of dust on it," said Jodi, standing next to him, looking up at the ceiling as if they were stargazing.

Jake left them alone, returning a minute later with Sam's day-old pastries to find Charlie unhitching his dusty mug from the beam. He cradled it in his hands like it was a kitten as he walked to the sink to rinse it off.

Amy pulled three house mugs from the rack above the sink while Jake brought in the glass jar filled with amber liquid from the back steps where it had been sitting in the sun.

"I've felt like I've been swept away in a dream all weekend," Jodi said as she watched Jake fill the mugs. "This is the tea you told me about, right?" she asked, turning to Charlie.

He nodded, too emotional to speak.

"Charlie has told me so much about the time he spent here with Isaac. He said this tea is magic."

"It's true," said Jake. "I didn't understand it at first, but I think I do now. It opens hearts to truth."

Jodi smiled. "Have you considered selling the recipe? I'm sure there would be a huge market for tea with that kind of a result."

Jake smiled, but shook his head. "I'm afraid I'd lose my soul if I ever tried to sell this recipe. It's not mine to sell, and I've been told it's kind of a package deal. The tea never leaves the shop. You're welcome to as much of it as you would like while you're here, but you can't take it with you."

Charlie took a sip before sitting down on a stool, lost in a world of nostalgia. "Thank you for keeping this place the same as it always was," he said softly, his emotions still close to the surface. "I can almost see Isaac sitting there at the wheel, throwing pots."

"It sounds like you spent a lot of time here," said Jake

"I did—more when I was in grade school. My Mom was his cleaning woman for a while when we first moved here."

"She was?" asked Jake.

Charlie nodded. "I'm not sure how long that lasted, but it was long enough for me to figure out that I liked it here. Isaac always had tea for me and mom, and he'd often have a couple of Sam's pastries hiding somewhere. We ate dinner with him from time to time, too. He was always trying to help me, always trying to keep me out of trouble, but he did it in ways that made things fun."

"Like what?" asked Amy.

"Well, take that tree house I mentioned at church. I know he could have bought the supplies we needed, but he turned it into a game for me. He taught me to find creative solutions to my problems. I don't think I realized how valuable that lesson was until I was on the streets of Philly. He was always doing stuff like that—making me stretch a little further and think a little bigger. I think I would have done better if I'd allowed my life to be sculpted more by him and less by my anger and negative emotions."

Jake leaned against the wedging table as the girls sat down on the other stools. "What does that mean exactly?" he asked.

"Oh, I was the classic story of a boy growing up with a father who was absent and indifferent."

Jake looked at Amy and then back at Charlie. "I grew up the same way. When did your dad leave?"

"As soon as he knew he was responsible." Charlie said sarcastically. "My parents were never married. They met in New Haven, Connecticut, where my mom was waiting tables and my dad was going to school at Yale. I really only know what my mom told me about him. He was a blue-blood boy with charm to match his money,  and he tricked my mom into believing he loved her. He was a gentleman in the beginning, but one night he took her too a party where the alcohol ran rich and his chivalry wore thin.

"When she found out she was pregnant, he tried to talk her into having an abortion, but when she refused, he stopped talking to her. I didn't know much about him until I was old enough to start asking questions. I was curious, so I started writing him letters when I was about ten. After I'd written a dozen or so, I finally got one back from him telling me that my mother was a whore and that he didn't want anything to do with me. I think that's really where my anger began. I read that letter over and over again and each time I did, my anger grew."

Jodi put her hand on his back, patting him softly. "Charlie still gets upset when he hears stories of paternal abandonment. Unfortunately, that's probably the cause of better than ninety percent of the issues we see in our program. There are some kids that make it through life pretty well without a dad, as long as their moms are strong and involved, but for most kids—boys especially—not having a father around makes things really tough. It's hard to stop that cycle once it gets going. Some of the kids in our program are the third generation which is suffering because of the choices made by their fathers and grandfathers. We spend a lot of time dealing with anger associated with abandonment."

Charlie nodded. "I know we can't save all the kids who come through our center, but, like I said earlier, I knew after reading "Les Miserablés" that I had a responsibility to change, and once I'd begun, I realized I needed to help others."

"I've been curious about that," said Jake.

"What part?" asked Charlie.

"I recently read a note," Jake said, walking to the front desk where Isaac's Volume 36 was stowed. He returned with a wrinkled blue envelope and handed it to Charlie. "Some of the things I heard you say have me wondering if you might know something about this."

Charlie ran his fingers over the words written on the envelope— Isaac the beloved Potter of Niederbipp. "Where did you get this?" he asked, looking surprised.

"It was given to me in a stack of letters that were left on Isaac's grave on Memorial Day."

"This is my mom's handwriting!"

Jake nodded softly. "I wondered if it might be. I read that letter a few weeks ago when I was in the … when I was trying to figure out where I belong. I probably read that letter a dozen times. I guess you could say it kind of opened my mind and heart to the truth of this place. Since I got here, I've had lots of people dropping by to tell me their stories, but there was something about that letter that made me … I don't know, I guess it opened my mind to the idea that me being here wasn't an accident or a coincidence."

Charlie opened the envelope and pulled out the two pieces of blue paper.

"What does it say, Charlie?" Jodi asked, leaning closer. Amy did the same.

Charlie took a deep breath before beginning to read the letter aloud.

Dear Isaac,

So many days have passed since that dreadful night. I have wanted so many times to write you, to thank you for what you did for my son. Your kindness to him at a time when he least deserved it meant the world to him, and to me. I tried so hard to raise him so he wouldn't be like his father, but Charlie always had to choose his own way. I know you wanted your generous gift of compassion to be kept a secret, but I wish I could have done something to repay you, to thank you before you passed away. Charlie told me I could never tell a soul what you did for him. I have kept my promise, but my inability to express my gratitude for what you did for my only son has caused me so much anguish and heartache. My tears of appreciation have stained my pillow over the past eight years. Your kindness, your love, your generosity have inspired me to be a better person, a better mother. You have inspired me to reach out to others, to find secret ways to give, to love and to serve. You have restored my faith in the innate goodness of mankind. You have given me hope when hope was gone. You brought my

son home to me and gave him his life back. He has honored your gift. He has become a man of integrity. He has become a man like you. I am proud to be his mother. I am proud that he is working hard to continue the legacy you have given him. I thank the heavens for you and the change you wrought in him. Thank you for caring, for loving in a way no other man ever did for my son. You broke through his thick head and gave him confidence to know he could change and become a better man.

We attended your funeral and wept together. Even in death, your generosity, your expectation of goodness in others was evident. Your request for Charlie to be a pallbearer brought many to tears, but to none more than him. Your ability to forgive, to find goodness in the weakest of souls has inspired many. How I wish I could have shared this with you before you were gone. My tears continue to stain my pillow and my prayers are full of gratitude to God who allowed you, a potter and molder of clay to have the ability to shape the life of my son. Your funeral taught me that many share my admiration and gratitude for the life you have lived and shared with each of us. I pray that these words may somehow find you, that you may know of my love and appreciation for you. I pray that I may live my life in a way that will enable me to tell you these things myself, to thank you for all you have done. I will love you forever for what you have done for me and my family.

With all the sincerity of my heart, Thank you.

MS

He choked through many of the words and by the time he finished, all four of them had tears in their eyes.

"Charlie," Jake said, "I know Isaac asked you not to talk about whatever happened eight years ago, but I was hoping you could tell me. I … I need to know. I feel like whatever happened … that it might have affected a lot of people's lives. It seems like maybe … Amy and I have been trying to piece things together and it feels like, I don't know … it just feels like you have some answers that we can't get anywhere else."

Charlie nodded, looking very sober.

Jodi wove her fingers into his, leaning against him. "That's one of the reasons why we waited for you last night," she said, looking at Jake. "He's been talking about this for the last two years."

"About what?" asked Jake

Charlie slid his hand into his pocket on the side of his cargo pants and removed a small white envelope, handing it to Jake.

"What's this?" asked Jake

"It's my final payment. It took me eight years, but I finally feel like I am free. Go ahead and open it."

Jake tore the end off of the envelope and reached his fingers inside, pulling out a folded piece of paper. He unfolded it and read it before looking up, his face full of confusion. "What's this for?"

"When I heard that you had taken over for Isaac, I knew my last payment needed to be to you."

"But this is … I don't understand."

Amy looked up at the paper in Jake's hand. It was a cashier's check, written to Jake Kimball for $4,325.00. She looked at Jake and then back at Charlie and Jodi, a look of wonder on her face.

"Jake, just over eight years ago, I did something really stupid that resulted in a workshop being burned to the ground."

Jake nodded. "Was it the Yoders'?"

"You know the story?" Charlie asked, looking surprised.

"No, not really. I met the Yoders a few weeks ago. They made some cabinets for some friends of ours, and we met when we were picking them up. Mr. Yoder mentioned that he had Isaac to thank for helping them rebuild after a fire eight years ago. I guess that's what got me wondering if your story might tie in. How did it happen?"

Charlie shook his head, looking down at his hands. "I got phone a call from an old friend one Friday night. He'd just graduated from college and wanted to hang out, so I invited a couple of girls I knew and we met at the Bungee Bipp. In the spirit of celebration, I brought along a case of beer." He shook his head. "If we'd stayed sober, that evening might have ended a lot differently, but …" He trailed off.

"How did you end up at the Yoders?" asked Jake.

Charlie shook his head. "We all jumped in the girls' car and headed up to Warren to see a movie, but the girl who was driving hit a pothole and we ended up with a flat tire. We knew we'd be in trouble if the sheriff found us drunk on the highway, so we kept driving until we found a place to pull off the road where we could fix it. That just happened to be the parking lot in front of the Yoders' workshop. We wanted to be heroes, but half the tools we needed were missing from the car's toolbox. After struggling with the tire for several minutes, I decided to break a small window next to the workshop door and let myself in. We never meant to do any harm, we were just too drunk to be thinking clearly." He paused, his eyes glazed over as he stared into his mug.

"So, how did the fire get started?" Jake asked

"A kerosene lamp! You probably know that Amish don't use electricity—except for the generators they use for their power tools."

Jake and Amy nodded.

"Well, it was dark inside, so I lit the lamp and found the tools I needed. We fixed the tire and my buddy and I went back inside to return the tools. We were on our way back out when I tripped and dropped the lamp, sending kerosene and flames all over the floor. We freaked out. We tried to put it out, but the flame was so hot and spread so quickly that we knew we had to get out." He rubbed the scar on his cheek. "The smoke came so fast and strong that I lost my bearings and went down. If it hadn't been for my buddy, I would have died that night. He picked me up and carried me out.

"I guess it was too much adventure in one night for the girls. They waited until they saw us come out, and then they took off without us. I remember feeling so helpless. There was no telephone and we were several miles from the nearest firehouse. My buddy and I watched as the flames climbed higher and higher, knowing our lives would never be the same. We made a decision that night that I have regretted a thousand times. We ran away and left the building to burn."

"Where did you go?" asked Jake.

"We ran back to my buddy's car back at the Bungee Bipp, hiding in the ditch whenever we saw headlights approaching. We were scared we'd get caught—scared we'd spend our life in jail. It was truly an accident, but the police already had a file on me and I knew how bad it looked. I knew there was no way I was going to be able to walk away if they found out it was me.

"It was only five miles back to the car, but the distance gave us both a lot of time to think. We were both twenty-two years old. My buddy had big plans for his future. I didn't have any plans, but I knew I didn't want to go to jail.

"When we got to the car, we drove south, not wanting to drive past the fire. We were dirty and tired and scared. The reality of what we'd done began to hit us. For the past eight years I have been haunted by the image of my friend, sobbing at the wheel, as he drove. I knew all his dreams would be different and I knew much of it was my fault. Hanging out with me had gotten him into trouble in high school, but this was different. We weren't kids anymore.

"So, what did you do?" asked Amy with a furrowed brow.

"Well, we were planning on picking up my buddy's things and getting out of Dodge, but when we drove onto Hinterstrasse and found Isaac's light on, we decided we could use some advice from a sober head. I'm sure he knew we were in trouble when he saw us, but he took us into his kitchen and fixed us some tea while we cleaned up. He waited for us to talk, which came out in a mixture of words and sobs as we described the events of the night and begged for his help. I knew Isaac was angry and disappointed with us, but I watched as his anger melted away, turning into mercy as he cried with us. Then he got down to business.

"I was surprised to find out that Isaac knew my track record, even the trouble I'd gotten myself into in the four years since I'd been gone. He knew that I'd go to jail for what had happened. He told me that if I went to jail, I'd be a marked man for the rest of my life, making it even more difficult for me to become an honest man. My buddy didn't have a record, but Isaac explained that if justice were to flex its muscles, we'd both suffer and lose opportunities to improve our lives. So that night, he offered us a generous deal that we couldn't refuse. I would be sent to stay with Isaac's friend in Philly and my buddy would go to Pittsburgh were he had connections. Isaac would speak to his friend, John Yoder, explain the situation, and pay whatever was needed to replace the tools and the workshop. We would both get jobs and pay back the loan over time. It has taken me eight years, Jake, but this is my final payment. There was a time when I believed I would feel free once this payment was made, but I know the debt I owe to Isaac will go on forever. He changed my life that night and every day since then. His compassion and mercy has encouraged me to be a better man. Some things can be repaid, but many other things never can."

"So, he just showed up with a bunch of money and the Yoders just let it go?" Amy asked, incredulously.

"I don't know exactly how it all went down. Isaac told me he rode his scooter out to the Yoders' workshop the next morning. The building was a total loss, but folks from the Amish community were already there, helping them clean up. He wrote and told me that he pulled Mr. Yoder aside, told him the whole story and asked him to forgive us, offering to pay whatever was needed to build a better shop than what they had before.

I received regular updates from Isaac over the next few weeks. The Amish community came together the next Saturday to do a barn raising on a much smaller scale, putting up a new workshop in six hours. New equipment and tools came in a few days later and the Yoders were back in business before two weeks had passed."

"Did they have fire insurance?" Amy asked.

"The Amish usually don't believe in insurance, as I found out, at least not the way we think of it. They usually invest in their communities and they support each other. I've learned a lot about the Amish people over the last eight years."

"They're the best cooks in the world," said Jodi. "Our center is just a few blocks from the Reading Terminal Market in Philly. Charlie introduced me to his Amish friends who run one of the diners there and I've gained ten pounds."

"It was worth every buttery pound," Charlie said, patting his wife's knee.

Jake looked down at the cashier's check. "Charlie, I can't accept this. *I* didn't give you the money."

"I know, Jake, but I can't write a check to someone who's dead and I wouldn't be able to live with myself if I kept it. I know it's not mine. I don't care what you do with it. Maybe you could fix up the shop or buy some clay."

"How much did you end up paying back?" asked Jake.

"It was a lot of money. To be honest, I'd rather not say. It was more money than I've ever made in one year. I knew the fire was mostly my fault, so even though my friend agreed to split the cost with me, I insisted on paying for most of it. He finished paying his portion off a few years ago."

"Can I ask you about that?" said Jake.

"What do you want to know?"

"I want to know about your friend. I was wondering …"

"We agreed not to talk about it," Charlie said, cutting Jake off. "The issue was resolved eight years ago and we decided it would be better if we never …"

"But what if it's not resolved?" Jake asked, cutting Charlie off this time. "What if people are still suffering? What if the slivers are still buried deep?"

Charlie shook his head. "I'm not sure what you're talking about."

Jake pointed to the letter written on blue paper. "Charlie, your mom was able to move on because she had information. You obviously talked to her at some point in the past eight years and helped her understand why you disappeared. But knowing that you were asked, I'm willing to bet there was one pallbearer missing from Isaac's funeral."

Charlie looked surprised. Then tears swelled his eyes again. "How did you know?"

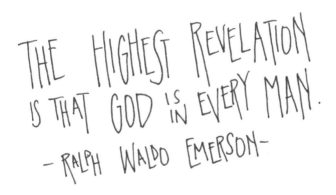

THE HIGHEST REVELATION IS THAT GOD IS IN EVERY MAN.
— RALPH WALDO EMERSON —

THE TRUTH ABOUT BAND-AIDS

"SOMETIMES THE QUESTIONS ARE COMPLICATED AND
THE ANSWERS ARE SIMPLE."
—DR SEUSS—

hat can you tell me about Matthew Gottlieb," Jake asked. "I talked to Sam last night and he said he hadn't seen his son in eight years. As you've told us your story, I've found myself wondering if there wasn't a connection—eight years, Pittsburgh. Was he the friend that was with you that night?"

Charlie looked at Jake, then Amy, then his wife. "I was asked not to talk about this."

"By whom?" Jake asked.

"By Isaac and … by Matt."

Jake nodded. "Then I'll tell you what I know. I know Sam has been broken-hearted about his son for the past eight years. I know he stopped talking to his wife about it because it has been so painful. I know he has written Matthew a shoe box full of letters that have all been returned, unopened. I know Sam hates himself for the way he treated his only son, and I know he'd do anything to be able to talk to him about it—to be able to apologize and have a relationship with him again."

"I thought Sam was still upset with Matt."

"He probably is, but it's a lot more than that. Charlie, he's been in limbo for the past eight years. He's tried to reach out—tried to fix things, but he's failed repeatedly."

"You didn't tell me about this," Amy said.

"I know. I was going to tell you about it today. We were talking about this just before you got there last night."

Amy nodded. "I never would have guessed Sam could have so much pain in his heart." She looked thoughtful for a moment, then she spoke again, softly. "Isn't it strange that so many people we know are going through this? Mr. Allan and his kids, me and my parents, you and your dad, and now Sam and his son. I'm starting to wonder if this kind of pain and frustration are an unavoidable part of being human."

"We see it every day," Jodi said. "Every parent messes up their kids and every child hurts their parents. I used to wonder why we have families at all if they cause so much carnage. There was a time in my life that I swore off marriage and having kids because I didn't want to mess up another generation."

Amy smiled. "So what changed?"

"Hope … and love." Jodi said, resolutely. "I began to hope that it would be different for me—that I could do better than my parents had done. I know that's probably pride talking, but isn't that the wish of everyone who has kids— that perpetual hope that we can learn from the past—from the mistakes we see all around us—from the mistakes we watched our parents make? Doesn't everyone want to be better than the generation before them?"

Amy nodded.

"Then we fall in love and have a family of our own and the messes begin. The problem is," she said with a little laugh, "is that no one ever gets exactly the same problems as the generation before. No matter how hard we try to prepare for our future, the world is always changing. The problems are always new, and *no one* gets through life without messing up theirs and the next generation."

"That's encouraging," Amy said sarcastically. "I'm glad we'll be in good company."

"If it weren't for that crazy thing called love …" Charlie said, shaking his head as he put his arm around Jodi. "Maybe there was something sweet enough in the forbidden fruit that Adam and Eve ate in the Garden of Eden that helped them realize the toil of life was worth it if there was the hope of love. Sometimes I wonder if love isn't God's way of perpetuating the human race so we can all learn life's pleasures and joys by overcoming the repressing burdens of selfishness."

There was a long silence as they digested Charlie's words.

"So, do you still have contact with Matt?" Jake asked.

"Sure. We email each other several times a month and talk every so often."

"Does he talk about his dad?"

"Rarely. It's still kind of a sore subject for him. You might have heard about the incident that took place right after we left."

"Do you mean when Sam slapped him in the face?"

"What?!" exclaimed Amy.

"Yeah. Sam was angry that his son left without any explanation and for some reason he … he hit him."

"He broke Matt's nose," Charlie added. "Of course I wasn't there—I didn't see what happened, but that's what Matt told me. I think that slap must have been more like a punch."

"Sam didn't tell me that," said Jake. "He said he slapped him."

"I can't believe Sam is even capable of slapping someone. He's always so nice to everyone."

"He wasn't always that way," said Charlie. "He was pretty rough on Matt growing up."

"Really?" asked Jake. "He didn't say anything about that either."

"I'm sure its not anything he's proud of. It never is," said Charlie.

"That's another thing we see all the time," added Jodi. "Parents are often in denial about the way they treat their kids. Nobody is born a delinquent and we are all products of our environment. Kids are influenced by all sort of things—friends, the media, video games, but nothing affects a kid's inclination towards violence as much as the way they are treated by their parents."

"I never had an old man to slap me around," said Charlie, "so when I first started working at the center, I didn't understand the deep scars that many kids have from being kicked around by the people who are supposed to love them the most. Sam was never a very patient person, but from what little I've heard, I gather his father was worse. I know that doesn't justify his actions, but it helps me understand a little better the conditioning he had that led him to do what he did."

"So, do you think there is any hope for Sam and Matt?" Jake asked.

Charlie shrugged. "It depends. It won't be easy. There is a lot of pain—a lot of old hurt. I don't doubt that Sam has changed a lot, but that is of little consolation to Matt who still bears the physical and emotional scars from the way his father treated him all those years. I understand Matt's point of view. Why would he want to come back to this? Why would he want to expose his kids to the same pain and sorrow he knew?"

"I think I understand some of that pain, at least the emotional pain," Jake said, "but that can't be a very easy burden for Matt to carry."

"I'm sure its not, but some people have a hard time letting go. The emotional scars of abuse usually run very deep. Some people can ignore them for a while, but unless those scars are allowed to heal ... unfortunately, the pain remains," explained Charlie.

"I get that," said Jake, "but how does anyone heal? How do we ever get over the pain?"

Charlie looked into his mug for a long moment before responding. "I'm a professional counselor, Jake. There are lots of ways I've learned to answer that question, and many of them work to a degree, but ..." He looked at his wife. "But the truth is, most of the things I learned in school aren't much different from a Band-Aid. Don't get me wrong, Band-Aids and counseling can help with a lot of things, but for the deepest wounds, a Band-Aid usually only covers up an infected gash. Some people, when they can't see the gash, think they're healed and can go for years without problems surfacing again. But infection—the pains of the past—fester if they're not taken care of. It boils down to the fact that, just as a wound won't heal with a sliver in it, a soul can't heal until it receives the correct treatment.

"Our prisons are full of people who have spent their lives self-medicating themselves, trying to dull the pain in their hearts. Politicians and organizations have been fighting the war on drugs for years, but I'm not sure we've made much progress. We can't fight fear with fear. We can't scare people into sobriety. We can't force them to walk the line. The only answer is love."

"It's crazy sometimes when you think about it," Jodi said, piping in. "People spend billions of dollars in this country every year trying to make themselves feel better. We try diets and the latest antidepressants. We go to counselors. We have plastic surgery. We divorce the people we once loved because they just don't make us happy anymore. We do a lot of hard things in an effort to avoid giving in to the reality that all we need is love." She laughed and shook her head. "The funny thing is— love is free. The only currency exchanged in the transaction of love—is love. Everything else is a counterfeit."

Jake nodded, looking very thoughtful. "I don't doubt what you're saying is true, but it kind of seems over-simplistic. How does it apply in this case—I mean with Sam and Matt? How do things ever change if one person spends years apologizing and the apology is never accepted?"

Charlie smiled. "That's a good point. They don't change because love hits the dam of pain and pride."

"Are you saying Matt's issue is pride?" asked Jake.

Charlie shrugged. "I can't say for sure. He never mentioned to me that Sam has been writing him letters. That actually surprises me. Charlie is a pretty level-headed guy, but … giving up pride is a big sacrifice for most of us.

"What do you mean?" asked Amy.

He nodded slowly, thoughtfully. "I guess it all comes back to what I said this morning about the slivers. Most of us know when we have a sliver in our life that is keeping us from healing, at least in our subconscious minds, but as I said before, our natural inclination is to cover it up and forget about it rather than deal with it. Most of us require a humbling experience before we're willing to admit we need help. The more I observe people, the more I realize most of us are broken souls who are blinded by our own brokenness."

"That sounds familiar," said Jake.

"Doesn't it? I guess I should have admitted earlier that we know a little bit more about you than we've let on. Joseph and Gloria told us a little about you last night. They said you spent some time in the hospital recently."

Jake smiled at Amy and then turned back to Charlie. "It's a small town. Yeah, I guess you could say I had some slivers removed."

"Some big ones," Amy said with a wink.

"We've all got 'em," Jodi said. "None of us get through life without picking up at least a few."

"And that's really where we focus with our program at the center," Charlie added. "Jodi and I have spent a lot of time talking about this with some of the other counselors over the past couple of years, and we've made some changes to our approach. We are a state institution so we had to be careful in the beginning about how we approach things, but taking our lead from Alcoholics Anonymous, we began introducing the **IT'S ALL ABOUT LOVE** kids to the possibility of there being a higher power. Of course, we have kids in our programs from all different backgrounds— Christians, Jews, Muslims, and many with no religious background at all. We have to steer away from any one religious dogma, but there is still plenty of room to wrestle with the spiritually of life. Jodi and I are Christians, but our counselors are a mixed bag.

"In the process of working things out, we've found that there is far more that unites us than divides us. And we focus on the shared belief that there is a higher power who loves us and desires that we find joy in this life. As it turns out, love is the best medicine we've ever found. The program is still new and always developing as we learn more, but kids are responding to love in ways they never have with threats and fear tactics. Having been where these kids are helps me reach them. For many years, I hated my tattoos, but they've opened many doors for me. When I sit down with a kid who refuses to talk, I roll up my sleeves and tell him stories about a kid I know who wanted to put Band-Aids on a sliver. It is easy for me to love them when I remember they aren't much different than I was at their age."

"We try to teach the kids that they can change the course of their lives if they can learn to let go of the slivers, if they can allow whatever higher power they believe in to remove the slivers from their hands and souls," Jodi added.

"It sounds like a great program. I'd like to make a donation." Jake said, trying to hand Charlie his cashier's check.

"No, Jake. I appreciate it, but I can't accept that. I owe it to Isaac, and since you've taken his place, I owe it to you."

"Charlie, I can't take your money. I'm sure Isaac would be proud of you and what you're doing. I'm sure he would be happy to know this money is going to the center."

"I hope he is proud of me, but I can't take it, Jake. Isaac has already shaped our program in ways that money never could. I'm sure you'll find a use for that," he said pointing to the check.

Jake looked down at the check, shaking his head. "So, what can we do about Matt?"

"I don't know. It's hard to help people with their slivers if they don't want your help. I knew he had a hard time with Sam, but I didn't know how bad it was."

"Do you know where he lives?"

"Yeah, I mean I have his address. Why?"

"I don't know what I can do, but listening to Sam talk last night—I just feel like there has to be something."

"We'll be going through Pittsburgh on our way home, won't we?" Jodi asked.

"Yeah, we will," said Charlie.

"We could look him up."

"I don't know. I haven't seen him in eight years."

"It might be a good place to start," Jake said, looking hopeful. "When are you planning on leaving?"

"Tomorrow night. I had one more thing to take care of before we leave town. We'll probably take off right after dinner. Why? Do you want a ride to Pittsburgh?"

"No," Jake said, laughing. "But I think I might have an idea."

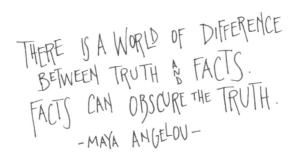

THERE IS A WORLD OF DIFFERENCE BETWEEN TRUTH & FACTS. FACTS CAN OBSCURE THE TRUTH.
—MAYA ANGELOU—

AMISH CHICKEN

ALL MANKIND IS DIVIDED INTO THREE CLASSES: THOSE THAT ARE
IMMOVABLE, THOSE THAT ARE MOVABLE, AND THOSE THAT MOVE.
—BENJAMIN FRANKLIN—

ake and Amy spent the afternoon with Kai and Molly and Baby
Zane. After her ten-day visit to help with the baby, Mrs. Yoder
had gone home to be with her family but not before she filled the
fridge with gallons of homemade chicken noodle soup. She'd also
made four loaves of homemade bread, and the apartment was
still perfumed with the scent of baking.

"You guys have got to try this soup," Kai said, pulling them into the
kitchen. "I'm sure you've never seen such thick noodles. They're like five
times thicker than the noodles we sell."

"Kai, that's for you and Molly. We're not going to eat your food," said Jake.

"Dude, you have to eat some with us. We have enough to last all week. I love it, but I want to eat something else and I don't want to waste it. She made enough to feed the whole Amish community. She said she didn't know how to make a smaller batch. We sent half of it home with her in her jam jars and we still have more than we can eat." He pulled the fridge door open to show all the containers filled with the beautiful soup. "She had her sons bring in a couple of baskets full of vegetables they grew in their own garden and three Amish chickens too."

"Okay," Jake relented, "but its only because I've never tasted an Amish chicken."

It was really too hot for soup in the middle of June in Pennsylvania, but friendly conversation made the heat bearable as they gathered around the small table in the kitchen while Baby Zane slept. When Jake asked Molly what she knew about Matthew Gottlieb, she blushed before explaining that he'd been her first crush. Nothing had ever come of it, he being five years older than she. She told them that he was handsome and friendly, but other than that, Molly was of little help. When Zane woke up, Jake and Amy took turns holding him until his cries made it clear they didn't have what he needed. They made plans to meet at Eric Schmelding's presentation before excusing themselves so Molly could nurse the baby in peace.

"I wonder if Thomas knows anything about Matthew." Jake mused as they descended Kai and Molly's stairs.

"I bet he would," Amy said. "He spends a lot of time with Sam and has probably been around long enough to remember when Matthew was born. There's one way to find out."

They stopped by Jake's apartment to pick up his sketchbook and then made their way back to the churchyard and Thomas' little house on the side. The Dutch door was open on the top to let in the air. Their

AMISH CHICKEN

knock was met by the sound of a thud and then Thomas came into view, straightening his disheveled hair.

"I'm sorry, did we wake you up?" Amy asked.

"Uh, no I was just reading and I must have dozed off. What are you two up to?"

"We had some questions, but we could come back later if now isn't a good time," said Jake.

"No, come in, but you'll have to excuse the mess. I never have visitors, and suddenly I get two handsome couples in one weekend. It might be the kick start I need to clean up around here. Come in."

Jake and Amy opened the lower half of the split door and walked inside, following Thomas into the bright room at the end of the tiled hallway. Bookshelves lined the walls, filled to overflowing with books, reminding them both of Isaac's shelves full of pots and Mr. Allan's shelves full of jars. Thomas straightened the pillows on the sofa, sending a shower of dust into the light that streamed in through the windows.

"Please, have a seat," Thomas said, offering them the flowered, plush sofa that looked like a relic of the sixties. They sank into the couch as Thomas pulled up an old wooden chair and sat in front of them. "What can I do for you?"

Jake looked at Amy and then back at Thomas. "We were wondering if you might be able to tell us what you know about Matthew Gottlieb."

Thomas raised his eyebrows. "Pfff. That's a name I haven't heard for a while. Who have you been talking to?"

"Sam told me a little bit about him yesterday when I was working on his floor, but he didn't say too much about him."

"No, I suppose he wouldn't. That's been a pretty sore subject for Sam for many years."

"Do you know why Matthew left?" Jake asked, testing the waters, not knowing how much he should say.

"Not exactly, but I wish he were around so I wouldn't have to get up so early," Thomas said, laughing.

127

"What do you mean?" asked Amy.

"When Matthew went away to school, Sam asked me to start helping out at he bakery more. Sam always hoped his son would come home when he was done with college and take over. I was more than ready to step down when he came home, but he was only here for about two weeks or so before he disappeared. I think that was pretty tough on Sam. He was upset for a long time."

"Did Sam ever tell you why Matthew left?" asked Jake

"No, he never did. I don't think he really knows."

Jake nodded thoughtfully, considering his next question, trying to make sure he didn't reveal anything he surmised had been kept quiet for many years. "What kind of a relationship did Sam have with his son?"

Thomas shrugged. "For the most part, I think it was fairly normal. Sam was never a very patient person. I know his girls never really had much to do with their dad. When Matthew came along, Sam was overjoyed to have someone to carry on the family name. He had Isaac make him a couple of mugs, one that read, "Prez" and another one for Matthew that read "Vice". He used to save pastries for Matthew and they'd sit in the back room and drink chocolate milk after the bakery closed for the day. They did that for years. I always thought they had a great relationship, but …"

"But what?" Jake asked.

Thomas shook his head. "Oh, nothing."

Amy looked at Jake, then back to Thomas. "Thomas, are you aware of Sam ever being violent toward his kids?"

He looked away as the color faded from his face.

"Thomas?" Jake said after a long pause.

"He's changed a lot in the past few years, but … why are you bringing this up? This stuff is really old. I'm sure that part of him hasn't come out in over ten years. I haven't seen it in a lot longer than that."

"What did you see?"

Thomas bit his lip and shook his head. "I don't really want to talk about it. It makes me sad to even think about it."

"Thomas, I … we … we're trying to help. Sam told me last night about some of the things that happened years ago, but I feel like there's got to be more. I don't know how, but there's something about this that makes me want to help, if I can."

"Jake, that's noble of you, but what makes you think you can do anything? Sam hasn't spoken to his son in … I don't know how long."

"Eight years, Thomas. It's been eight years. Before I got started yesterday, Sam took me into the back room and sat me down at an old table and poured me a mugful of chocolate milk. Whatever happened all those years ago, he's still hurting. I'm convinced he's still dreaming of the time he can sit down with his son and share a mug of chocolate milk and eat day-old pastries with him."

Thomas nodded. "He always keeps chocolate milk in the fridge and Matthew's mug on the shelf." He took a deep breath. "I  know Sam has a lot of regrets. He rarely talks about it, but I've found him weeping many times over the years."

"So, what did you see, Thomas?"

He shook his head. "You're not going to give up, are you?"

"No, I can't. I'm in too far to give up. I still feel like there's hope."

Thomas took a deep breath, exhaling very slowly. "I only saw it once, but I heard it happened many times. Matthew was probably twelve at the time. He forgot to feed the sourdough starts, delaying everything for the day. Sam went crazy. It was like he was drunk with anger. He slapped Matthew across the face and said some pretty awful things to him—the kind of things you can't ever take back. I watched as Matthew cowered around him for many weeks after that, always flinching whenever Sam raised his voice—or his hand."

Amy shook her head. "Thomas, we've heard that Sam's dad was pretty tough on him. Do you know anything about that."

"Old Man Gottlieb had been dead for a long time when I got here, but from what I've heard, he was a very tough man. I heard he used to

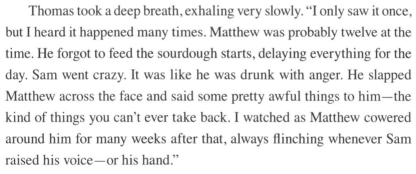

get into fights all the time with the lumberjacks who came to town. Sam said he had hands the size of loaves of bread from being broken so many times on the heads of those men. Sam got slapped around a lot growing up. That's how he lost his first few teeth. You may have heard that Sam's dad and Lily's father never got along?"

"No, I never heard that."

"Yeah, Old Man Gottlieb refused to sell bread to the Engelharts after he took Sam in one night. He'd been beat up pretty bad. I never got the details on that one, but Sam was just a kid—probably only thirteen or fourteen. The Gottliebs have a long line of anger management issues. I have no idea what has happened to Matthew, but I know Sam has tried to reach out to him. The last time I was in the cellar over at the bakery, I saw a whole box of letters Sam had written to him. They'd all been sent back."

"How long ago was that?" asked Jake.

"Two, maybe three months ago."

"They were in a box?"

"Yes. A black shoe box. I knew it wasn't any of my business, but the lid was off and the top letters all had recent postmarks. There must have been a hundred letters in there. The box was more than full."

Jake nodded. "Thanks, Thomas. I'm sorry to bring up painful memories, but this helps us to know more about the situation. We'd better be going."

Jake and Amy stood to go, thanking Thomas for his time. He reminded them of Eric Schmelding's travel presentation and suggested they bring folding chairs, or at least a blanket to sit on.

They were silent as they walked through the churchyard, holding hands. They both felt the weight of the things they'd heard. Until yesterday, Sam had been a saint, the one who had fed them both. He'd loved Jake and had encouraged his relationship with Amy. But his secret past was heavy and dark and had splintered his family. They walked down the familiar steps that lead to Hauptstrasse and took a seat on the bench at the upper fountain. Several groups of tourists walked the otherwise quiet street, taking pictures and commenting on the flowers hanging from the lampposts and cascading out of the window boxes. Jake and Amy watched the tourists, but the silence between them continued for several minutes.

"What are you thinking?" Amy finally asked.

"I'm thinking about those letters Sam wrote."

"What about them?"

"I'm wondering how I might get them out of the cellar without Sam finding out."

"What? Why?"

"I feel like I need to send them with Charlie."

"But, Jake, he already sent them back. Why do you think he'd look at them now?"

"I don't know, but I keep thinking about them. I don't know if it's just because I'm jealous that I've never had a letter from my own dad, or … I don't know. I just feel like I need to do it."

"But, Jake, how? It's not like you have an excuse to be in the cellar. Do you even know where the box is?

"No, I don't. Amy, I know it's a crazy idea, but it keeps coming back. If it's supposed to happen, it will. The more I think about it, the more I realize Thomas was right about at least one thing."

"What's that?"

"Things aren't always as they appear to be."

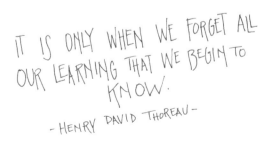

IT IS ONLY WHEN WE FORGET ALL OUR LEARNING THAT WE BEGIN TO KNOW.

– HENRY DAVID THOREAU –

HISTORY OF NIEDERBIPP 101

THE DOORSTEP TO THE TEMPLE OF WISDOM IS A KNOWLEDGE
OF OUR OWN IGNORANCE.
—BENJAMIN FRANKLIN—

U ncle Jerry, Aunt Bev is always telling us that you know a lot about history. Jake and I have been wondering what you can tell us about the Quakers who settled this town," Amy said after grace had been said over the dinner. Before they'd even arrived Jake and Amy had decided they didn't want to hear any more darkness, and this topic seemed safe, while also being interesting. They both had many questions that had surfaced in their discussions over the previous weeks, and this setting seemed as good a place as any to start working on the answers.

"What do you want to know?" Jerry asked, passing a bowl full of salad to Amy.

"I really don't know anything about my roots. My dad never even told me we were Quakers until just a few years ago."

"That figures," Bev said sarcastically. "Quakers are supposed to be peacemakers. That's not really your father's forte."

"Yeah, well," Amy started again after they'd had a good laugh. "I know that Quakers are supposed to be conscientious objectors and peacemakers, but it seems like this town has plenty of oxymorons."

"Well, thanks a lot," said Jerry. "We're all a little crazy, but you don't need to go calling us morons."

Amy shook her head, smiling. "Uncle Jerry, you know what I mean."

"Okay, what do you want to know exactly? I've learned, in my short life that there is an answer to every question," he said jokingly.

She looked at Jake. "Well, I've been to church services in many different places, but this is different than any of them. Jake and I both thought Thomas was a priest, but he's not—not really. The church isn't decorated, but then there's an elaborate pipe organ at the front with a statue of Jesus that was carved by a Jewish wood carver. Everywhere we turn, we discover something a little bit different than we'd expect. I guess we're just curious—just looking for answers."

Jerry nodded. "I told you there was an answer to every question, but I don't have them all."

"That's for ding-dang sure," said Beverly, pulling a funny face that caused them all to laugh again.

"I'll give it a try," Jake said, nodding to Amy. "Jerry, Bev, if I knew nothing about the Quakers, and wanted to know more, what would you tell me?"

"I'd tell you that if you don't know anything about the Quakers, then you don't know much about your country because a lot of what we love about America has been influenced by Quaker philosophies and by Quakers themselves."

"Like who?" asked Amy.

"Oh, more than you might suspect. William Penn was the founder of Pennsylvania, but there were more Quakers involved in the founding of this country than I can remember—signers of the Declaration of Independence and the Articles of Confederation, not to mention the Constitution. There were poets and abolitionists and patriots and even presidents."

"Presidents?" Amy asked. "Which ones?"

"Herbert Hoover and ... and Richard Nixon. Most of us aren't very proud of the latter. Nixon was raised a Quaker and might have done a little better if he'd stuck to his Quaker principles of pacifism and honesty."

"So, besides pacifism and high morals, what other philosophies did the Quakers believe in?" asked Jake.

"How long have you got?"

"How long do you need?" Jake responded.

"It's tough to put into a few words what ten generations have lived. William Penn and George Fox taught religious tolerance at a time in England when there was none. They both spent a lot of time in prison for preaching against the establishment and printing what they believed in pamphlets that they distributed throughout Europe. They were translated into many languages and found followers in small groups all over Western Europe.

"The Quakers came along at a good time. They had no staunch dogma, but taught that it was a time to return to an ancient faith, a faith where men and women were allowed to believe according to the dictates of their own consciences regardless of what the state or the church said. Penn taught that the

Holy Spirit itself should have more power over men's lives than priests or kings or even the Bible. Religion was used throughout the Old World to control people. William Penn and George Fox taught their followers that all people, regardless of gender, race, or economic status, were children of a loving God. They taught that all people not only had the opportunity but the responsibility to receive the whisperings of God in their own ears and hearts without the need for a middleman."

AMERICA IS GREAT BECAUSE AMERICA IS GOOD, AND IF AMERICA EVER CEASES TO BE GOOD AMERICA WILL CEASE TO BE GREAT. —ATTRIBUTED TO ALEXIS de TOCQUEVILLE (1805-1859)

"That sounds reasonable to me," said Amy.

"Yes, but you're a eighth-generation American. Those kind of ideas were considered very dangerous in William Penn's time. Ministers of the state-supported religions earned their livelihood from the tithes and offerings from their congregations, but they also had a lot of power that was given them by the kings. The Quakers questioned the morality and legality of such a system of government. They studied the Bible and saw that the apostles—those that were closest to Jesus, were not wealthy. They were simple people, mostly fishermen. Jesus himself was a carpenter. The early Christians didn't force burdensome taxes on their followers but lived the law of the tithe and cared for the poor and needy, encouraging those who followed them to have all things in common. The Quaker movement was a collection of ideas whose time had come."

"Is that how our ancestors became Quakers?" asked Amy.

"Yes. And the Quaker missionaries who traveled Europe looking for converts also helped. William Penn himself spent time as a missionary in Germany and probably Switzerland."

"That mural at the end of Zubergasse—and the stuff I read on the Internet—it made it sound like two whole villages just picked up and moved here. Is that really what happened?" Jake asked.

"More or less."

"That must have been pretty hard—packing up and heading off into the unknown," said Amy.

"Probably, but things weren't that great in Europe. Change was coming, but a lot of folks didn't have the patience to wait around for things to happen."

"What kind of change?" asked Amy.

"That was an exciting time in Europe. It was called the Age of Enlightenment."

"I remember hearing that in my history classes. Didn't that come about by people questioning the status quo?"

"You could say that. But one of the most important elements was who was asking the questions. *Common people* began questioning the traditions of religion and legislation that had been maintained for centuries, and from those questions, there arose a lot of new answers. It was as if a light turned on, and people all across Europe began seeing possibilities they'd never imagined before. The tyrannical powers of churches and government began to lose their control over the people. And as the people began to recognize the tarnish of the Old World, the need for a New World arose. It was in those circumstances that William Penn's Holy Experiment began to take root."

"And what was that exactly?" Jake asked. "I've heard the term before, but I don't know anything about it."

"The Holy Experiment was the seed of democracy as we know it. It was the answer to all the problems he believed were the decay of Europe."

"How did William Penn come up with it?" asked Jake.

"You know, I've wondered that many times and I believe it must have been pure inspiration. His ideas were new and radical, but they had the power to embolden men and women to make a difference in the world. It offered freedoms that had never been known before, and opportunities for common people to have a say in their future. If King Charles II had known what he was starting—if he could have known that sowing those seeds of freedom would inspire the rebellion it did—I don't think he ever would have done it."

"What did he do exactly?" asked Amy.

"He gave William Penn all the land that is now Pennsylvania."

"Why?"

"He wanted to get rid of the troublemaking Quakers, and he owed Penn's father a lot of money for his service to the Royal Navy."

"So he just gave him Pennsylvania?"

"Yep. I'm not sure if he really knew what he was doing. King Charles had never been to America before. He didn't know that this area included some of the most fertile ground in the New World. I really think the king was just trying to get rid of a menace and all of his followers. Sending them all to the New World was an easy solution."

"So, William Penn named a state after himself and invited everyone to come over?" Jake asked.

"Not exactly. Remember, this was 1680, give or take a few years. There were no states back then, just British colonies. The gift of that much land made William Penn the biggest landowner in the New World—besides the king himself. But Penn was a pretty humble guy. He wanted to name the place Sylvania, which means 'forest' or 'woods', but the king insisted they name the colony after Penn's father, so the name became 'The Woods of Penn.'

"Part of the Holy Experiment called for religious toleration. In the first years, it was mostly Quakers, but their dominance was short-lived as people of all faiths poured into the colony from all over Europe. Most people don't realize that for the better part of a century, Pennsylvania was the only place in the English speaking world where the Catholic Church could legally hold mass."

"I thought that was what America was all about—religious freedom." Amy said.

"It was, as long as your religion in those early years was Puritanism, or if you shared the same religion as the colony. The colonies were broken up along many lines, but religion was a major divider. The religious toleration for all religions that Penn and his followers adopted encouraged Philadelphia to quickly become the biggest city in the New World."

"The City of Brotherly Love," Jake mused.

"That's exactly right, but it was more than just love that brought people to Philadelphia. It was the New World's first planned city. After watching disease and fire wreak havoc in London, Penn designed the city on a grid pattern with wide streets, parks and open spaces. The Quaker beliefs of caring for the earth inspired them to work with the land rather than conquer it. But the colony offered much more than good planning and friendly neighbors."

"Like what?" asked Amy.

"Like free public education for all children, both boys and girls."

"That's pretty big," admitted Amy.

"That's huge, but that was just the beginning. With all the time Penn spent in English prisons, he championed prison reform. At that time, British law assigned the death penalty to over two hundred crimes. Under Penn's laws, only murder and treason were punishable by death. His pacifism dictated that all people be treated with respect. While the other colonies were cheating and murdering the Indians, Penn was making treaties with them, buying their land fairly, trading with them and honoring their rights as equal human beings and fellow children of God. He encouraged his followers to do the same and punished anyone who was caught mistreating them.

"A lot of things would be different if the Quakers had had more influence on this nation. I often think about the greatness of Penn's vision for America and for the world. He had a vision of utopia that he didn't just profess—he walked the walk, and encouraged everyone else to do the same."

"So, what happened? Why aren't their more Quakers now?" asked Amy.

"Penn was a man of peace when the world was in turmoil, and he died too early."

"But didn't anyone take up his cause when he died?" asked Jake.

"Sure, but no one had the same power and authority that he had. His sons inherited their father's land, but they didn't share his vision on many things, including religion. Penn's station in life gave him opportunities that working class folks seldom have. His father's wealth gave him the best education, and the time to use it in developing ideas and philosophies. Many of his best ideas helped frame America and the world we know today."

"Then why isn't he better remembered? I don't think I ever remember hearing about him when I was in school," said Jake.

"His birthday is observed around the world as a day of peace."

"It is?" Jake asked, surprised.

"Yep, October 24."

"I don't remember ever celebrating that day."

"One of his peace plans called for arbitration instead of war. That plan later laid the foundation for the United Nations which honors Penn's contributions by celebrating UN Day on his birthday, October 24."

"Why don't we learn stuff like this in school?" asked Amy.

Jerry shrugged his shoulders. "No one wants to admit that in our struggle for progress, a lot of good stuff gets swept under the rug and forgotten. Penn died a poor man, his wealth and health spent on building his dream for a better world."

"Uncle Jerry, I obviously don't know that much about Pennsylvania history, but it seems like most people settled along the coast, at least in the beginning. Why did our relatives come all the way out here?"

"That's a good question. From what I've been able to piece together, the people who settled Niederbipp felt like they needed to separate themselves from the world."

"Why?" asked Amy. "How were the Niederbipp Quakers different from the other Quakers?"

"Oh, there were more similarities than differences. They were idealists. They'd read the pamphlets that William Penn and other Quakers had produced, and they had wholeheartedly aligned themselves with their teachings. By the time they arrived in the New World in 1716, Philadelphia was already a busy city. Our ancestors and the people who came with them were mostly farmers and craftsmen, and city life didn't appeal to them. Your seventh great-grandfather, Johann Eckstein, and my sixth great-grandfather, Peter Seiler, were in that group. After spending the winter near Germantown, they decided they needed to find a place to put down roots. I think their faith was one of the biggest reasons they kept moving west. They felt like the people of the city had largely lost the ideals of simplicity and charity. They decided to remove themselves from that environment in an effort to preserve their faith and their families.

"At the time, this plot of ground was a hundred miles away from the nearest settlement. When they reached the Allegheny River, many in the group were tired and wanted to stay on the eastern banks, but the leaders of the group ordered that a ferry be built to take everyone to the other side and give the town one more layer of defense against the outside world. The ferry was in operation while the town was being built, but it was washed away one spring about ten years after they'd arrived. Before that, there was some trade that took place with the settlements further to the east, but things changed after the ferry was gone."

"Thomas told us that traveling salesmen came through here from time to time," Jake said, thinking of the potter's journals.

"They did for a while. The original window glass was brought in during that time. You can still find the bubbled glass in some of the window sections in the church and some of the old houses too."

"Why didn't they build a new ferry?" asked Amy.

"I think they might have, but the village elders saw how the love of material things was distracting for some of the young people. They predicted it would be a downfall for the community, and when a wagon filled with whiskey came traveling through a few months later, the villagers recognized the prediction as prophesy. When the ferry washed away a few months later, instead of rebuilding it, they decided to turn their backs toward Babylon with a goal of becoming completely self-reliant. They cleared the land for farms, raising their families and building up their own version of the utopia that William Penn had inspired. In relative isolation, the community grew and expanded. They purchased this land from the Indians, and they carved this town out of the wilderness."

"That last part sounds familiar. Did you have anything to do with the town website, Jerry?" Jake asked.

Jerry looked at Bev. "I've never seen it myself, but Bev asked me to put something together for the Travel Council."

"I had no idea you knew so much about this stuff, Uncle Jerry," Amy said.

"Are you kidding, your uncle is a walking encyclopedia of history. His old books have gotten more attention than I have for years," Bev laughed.

Jerry shrugged his shoulders, looking guilty. "I've always been interested in history. If I'd had any money when I was younger, I would have gone to college to study it, but I think I've done a pretty good job learning all I can along the way. I've never let my lack of money get in the way of my education. When you've got a passion, you've got to feed it, even if you are just a small-town barber."

Jake looked at Jerry and wondered what else he might have missed about the older man. "I wish I would have known you knew all this. I've learned more about history in the last fifteen minutes than I have in the last eight years in school. Have you ever considered being a teacher?"

Jerry laughed. "That would be a joke. I'm terrified of speaking to groups, other than family. There's no way I could ever do something like that."

"Thomas has tried to get him to teach on Sunday for the past twenty years. He even talked him into it once, but Jerry worked himself into a knot and got sick all over the church steps," Bev reported.

"But you talk to people everyday at the barber shop. That doesn't make you nervous, does it?" asked Amy.

"Of course not, but that's never more than five guys at a time. I just don't have it in me to stand in front of a group of people and say anything worth listening to."

"But ..."

"No way," he said, cutting Amy off. "I could never do that. I'm the kind of Quaker who likes my religious contribution to be silent, the way all of our meetings used to be."

"What do you mean?" asked Amy.

Jerry looked at Bev, then back at Amy. "Didn't your father tell you anything about the Quakers?"

"No, never. The only time I ever attended a Quaker church was when I came here in the summers, and I don't know if I ever really knew what it meant to be Quaker until just a few years ago."

Jerry shook his head. "So he never talked about the kind of meetings we used to have?"

"No, why?"

"Don't get me wrong, I really enjoy the meetings we have now, but the meetings we used to have were really ..."

"Really quiet," Bev interjected.

"What do you mean?" asked Jake.

"Traditionally speaking, there is no leader in a Quaker congregation, so there is no sermon, at least not the way we have them now," explained Jerry. "Some people speak when moved upon by the spirit, but I've attended lots of meetings where nothing was ever said—where we just sat in quiet meditation. I miss those quiet meetings. They were some of the most meaningful I've ever attended."

"So ... you just hang out waiting for someone to talk?" asked Jake, trying to imagine a silent church service.

"Well, Jake, it's a little more romantic than that!" Beverly said.

"I don't know about *romantic*," Jerry responded, "but we believe there is a piece of every man and woman that is sacred. Some people call it the spirit or the soul. Most Quakers refer to it as the 'Inner Light.' We believe that part of us is best understood when we can commune with it in quiet reflection."

"I'm not sure I understand." Jake said.

"Not many people do. That's probably why we don't do it anymore—at least not in an organized way on Sundays."

"Is that why Isaac spent so much time at the cemetery—and down at the river?" Jake asked, trying to piece together the things he knew about Isaac.

"I'm sure that was a big part of it," Jerry said. "Isaac didn't talk much about those things, but when he did, he often said it was the only way he knew to cope with the world. I think he missed those quieter meetings more than most. In many ways, he was probably more of a Quaker than any of us who grew up Quaker. The Psalm that says, 'be still and know that I am God'[1] was something he took seriously."

Jake looked at Amy, thinking about the weeping willow and the words that had been carved on the branch.

Amy caught Jake's glance and nodded knowingly before turning back to her uncle. "Why did the services change? Did Thomas change them?"

"No, Thomas participated in our meetings for many years before we learned that he was a priest. Things had already begun to change—out of necessity—before he started dressing like a priest again. We love the

[1] Psalm 46 :10

tourists because they keep our community alive, but when we began getting more and more attending our meetings we knew we needed to do something else."

"They didn't like it?" asked Jake.

Jerry shook his head. "It wasn't so much that they didn't like it as it was their misunderstanding of what we were doing. Silence is a foreign concept to most people today. Somehow people think they have to fill every second with sound. In a Quaker town—in a Quaker meeting, you have to be okay with silence. We had visitors jumping up, trying to fill what they perceived as a *void* with all sorts of nonsense."

"I'll never forget that one lady who went on for twenty minutes about her miracle hemorrhoid cure—shouting and hollering and screaming hallelujah," Bev said, shaking her head.

"We old-timers got together shortly after that and decided to have a more *normal* meeting. Things have just kind of evolved over the years to what we have today. We still have no paid ministry, which gives lots of people a chance to share their stories and Thomas is always willing to step in and help out. For a while, we tried to do a traditional Quaker meeting on Wednesday nights, but fewer and fewer people came, so we decided to let it go. It's been many years, but I still miss those quiet meetings."

Amy shook her head, looking frustrated. "I never knew anything about this, but I think I can understand why it didn't work for my dad. He's never been the quiet type."

"No, he hasn't," Jerry said. "That's why we were always surprised when you showed so much interest in going to church whenever you were here over a weekend."

She smiled. "There's something special about that church. I've always felt somehow connected to it."

"You should! It was our relatives who built it," Bev said with pride.

"Yeah, Thomas told us when he took us on the tour."

"Did he show you the Eckstein mark?" asked Bev.

"No, what mark?" asked Amy.

"I'm talking about the square with the E in the bottom corner."

"No." Amy looked at Jake, confused. "Where is it?"

"It's carved on one of the cornerstones at the church—and at least one of the cornerstones on nearly every building in Niederbipp," Bev reported.

"It is?"

"Sure! Your great-great … seventh great-grandfather, Johann Eckstein, his brother Josef and their sons set the cornerstones all over town. They were stonemasons, you know."

"Yeah, Thomas told us that too. Are there still a lot of the original families here in Niederbipp?"

"Fewer and fewer all the time," said Jerry. "Some families wandered off to start their own towns, but others have stayed to give life to the next generation. Each subsequent generation has brought an end to some of the original family lines. The Gottliebs, and Ecksteins and a handful of others are the only names that have remained since the beginning, and many of those are nearing extinction too. My mother was a Seiler, but she married a Sproodle. Her brothers were the last of the Seiler clan to live in Niederbipp."

Amy looked thoughtful. "I guess I never considered that. What will happen to Niederbipp when the older folks are gone? You guys have carried on a lot of traditions. What will happen when …" She trailed off, not wanting to finish.

"That depends a lot on your generation," Bev said. "That's why Isaac wanted to make sure we found a potter to replace him. More than most folks of our generation, Isaac worked to make sure Niederbipp was around for people to learn from."

"What do you mean by that?" Jake asked.

"Oh, that was a crazy old idea, one that the Engelharts perpetuated from the beginning," said Jerry.

"What was the idea?" Jake asked.

"It was an idea that came from the Bible—that a city which was built on a hill could not be hid from the world.[1] Despite the fact that they believed the city folk had lost track of the pure principles of Quakerism, the founders of Niederbipp saw the influence for good that Philadelphia had on the other colonies—the influence Quakers and other good-hearted people had on America in general. They believed there would come a time when the world would be hungry for what we have here—that people would want to return to the basic and simple truths that inspired the Enlightenment and the exodus from Europe," explained Jerry

"That was the main reason Isaac created the Niederbipp Travel Council," added Bev.

"Isaac was trying to make Niederbipp into an example for the world?" asked Jake, looking dubious.

"Yes. Isaac was always an optimist," Bev continued. "After Lily and Henry died, Isaac spent a lot of time doing what he called his 'homework.' He read everything he could find about William Penn's vision for America, and he often talked about the journals that Lily's family had left behind. And then one day he woke up and decided he was going to dedicate the rest of his life to carrying out the ideas that the Engelhart family promoted. I still remember when he first told me that he hoped people would come here, experience Niederbipp, and go home better people for it. I thought he might be nuts. But Isaac had a fire inside of him that made us all want to believe he knew what he was talking about. He hoped that the ideals of Niederbipp would spread throughout the world, encouraging people to become more peaceful and thoughtful and kind."

"How did it go?" asked Jake.

Bev took a deep breath. "Better than any of us ever imagined. I'll be the first to admit I was doubtful anyone would want to come here. Lots of people, including me, thought his efforts were a waste of time and money. Many of the old-timers still don't understand why people

[1] Matthew 5:14

come here, but every year, tourism increases as the word spreads. People come, poke around town for a few days and then go back to wherever they came from and tell everyone they know about the Shangri-La out in the middle of Pennsylvania. You can't pay for advertising like that. Those of us who have lived here our whole lives can't figure out what people get so excited about. I think Isaac's vision for Niederbipp has caused all of us to look a little closer at what we've taken for granted."

"Like what?" asked Jake.

"All sorts of stuff. I remember the first time I saw a tourist kneeling down on the cobblestone in the middle of Hauptstrasse. I thought he must have lost a contact lens, but he was examining how the stones had been cut and laid in place. I'd walked over those stones thousands of times and never *really* noticed them. Having tourists around has made me realize how blind I've been to my own world."

"Isaac made us all think a little deeper about who we are," Jerry added. "My interest in history centered mostly on Egypt before Isaac started asking questions about the founders of Niederbipp, and I realized I knew more about the other side of the world than I did about my own family. I would have missed out on a lot of history if I  hadn't started asking questions when I did. Many of the most important things I learned came from my grandparents who died just a few years after I'd begun taking a closer look at my own ties to this town. That might have all been lost with their generation."

"So, do you know much about the Ecksteins?" asked Amy.

"No. The Ecksteins are tough nuts to crack." Jerry said with a smile.

Beverly responded by softly punching his shoulder.

"See what I mean?" Jerry said, rubbing his shoulder and feigning pain.

"What do mean by that, Uncle Jerry?"

"He means the family has been fractured for years," Bev said.

"We heard that," Amy said, nodding to Jake, "But the person who told us said he wasn't supposed to talk about it."

Beverly pulled a funny face. "Who have you been talking to?"

"Does it matter?" Amy asked.

"Of course it does. There are always at least two sides to every story."

"All I know is that whatever it was, it happened a long time ago and people still aren't talking about it. What happened?"

Beverly shook her head. "We're not supposed to talk about it."

"Says who?" Amy persisted.

"My dad—your grandpa."

"Aunt Bev, I never even met my grandpa. He died at least ten years before I was born. I don't know why I should be bound by something that happened fifty years ago."

"More like a hundred years ago," Jerry piped in.

"What? Are you serious?" Amy said, shaking her head and getting worked up. "I don't know anything about my family because of something that happened a hundred years ago. I could be related to half the people in this town and I'd never know about it. Am I the only one who thinks this stinks? Bev, your dad isn't around any more to stop you from talking about it."

Jerry nodded his head slowly. "You probably are."

"I probably am what?" Amy said, her voice full of frustration.

"You probably are related to half the town, at least through marriage," he responded.

"Now how would you know that?" Bev asked, bristling and sitting back from the table.

"Bev, it's not hard to figure that out. This town was isolated from the outside world for long enough that *everyone* is related, at least through marriage."

"What are you saying, Jerry?" Bev asked.

"I'm saying Amy has a right to know the truth. If she'd fallen in love with one of the local boys instead of Jake, she might be marrying her second or third cousin without even knowing about it. I'm saying the Eckstein feud has gone on long enough. I'm saying its time to let the truth be told."

Amy smiled, folding her arms over her chest. "So what's the truth?"

TOUGH NUTS

CIVIL WAR? WHAT DOES THAT MEAN? IS THERE ANY FOREIGN WAR?
ISN'T EVERY WAR FOUGHT BETWEEN MEN, BETWEEN BROTHERS?
—VICTOR HUGO—

 don't know if anyone knows for sure, at least not any more," Bev said, looking directly at Amy. "It was never anything we were allowed to discuss. We were just always told we could never trust anyone from the Oliver Eckstein side of the family."

"Why?" asked Amy, anxious to get to the bottom of this.

"Because they are all thieves and liars."

"I don't even know who Oliver Eckstein was. Can we start there?"

Beverly looked thoughtful. "Oliver Eckstein would have been your ... your great-uncle, the younger brother of your great-grandfather, Gerhardt."

"And what exactly did he or his family steal?" asked Amy.

"It depends on who you ask. Some of my relatives said they were horse thieves, but I also heard they were witches and worshipped the devil."

"And you believe them?" Amy asked, surprised that she even needed to voice the question.

"I don't know. I used to believe a lot of things my older cousins told me, but then I met some of my second cousins and they seemed pretty normal to me."

"Where did you meet them? Do they still live around here?"

"I don't know. I met them here in Niederbipp years ago. If they're still alive, they'd have to be really old by now. They were probably in their twenties when they came by our home. I was just a girl at the time, probably only ten or eleven. My father invited them in but threw them out when he found out who they were related to. I'd never seen my father treat anyone like that before."

"Aunt Bev, what happened? If Johann and Josef worked together in the beginning to build all these houses and buildings, what happened to change things?"

Bev shook her head. "I don't know."

"You never asked?"

"No, I did a couple of times when I was younger, but I was always told not to talk about it. I was told to shun anyone who came from *that* family."

Amy shook her head, not able to comprehend the ignorance or reasoning behind the history. "So, let me get this straight. You're telling me that you and I have relatives out there—maybe even in this county who we're not allowed to talk to because of something that happened a hundred years ago?"

Bev looked sheepish. "I didn't make the rules," she said lamely. "We just did what we were told."

"Aunt Bev, I'm sorry, but I can't understand this. Did you know that we're somehow related to Mr. Allan?"

"Yes, but he's part of *that* family. He's a nice enough man, but you never know."

"Never know what?" Amy asked.

Bev looked flustered. "Amy, this is complicated. Mr. Allan and I ... we're cousins. We've been cordial with each other since we discovered our shared genealogy, but we were both raised in families that were supposed to loathe each other."

"So, wait a minute. If you and Mr. Allan are cousins, what does that make me?"

"Technically, Bev and Mr. Allan are second cousins," Jerry said, jumping in. "That would make you his second-cousin-once-removed. And his kids would be your third cousins."

Amy shook her head. "I guess that's why my parents stayed with him and his family on their honeymoon."

"What?" asked Bev. "I don't think so. Your parents went to California on their honeymoon."

Amy stood from the table and left the kitchen, returning seconds later with her sketchbook. She opened it and pulled the black-and-white picture of her parents from its pages, handing it to Bev.

"Yes, see, this is Lake Tahoe, that's where they went on their honeymoon. Lake Tahoe is in California," Bev said, handing the photo back to Amy.

"Yes, Lake Tahoe is in California, but this picture was taken in Vail, Colorado."

"How do you know that?"

"Because Mr. Allan gave it to me. Did you know he was the mayor of Vail for several years."

"Yes, I heard that, but Mr. Allan is old and he comes from that side of the family. You can't believe everything he says."

Amy looked upset. "Bev, why would he lie to me? I understand that he is old and a little senile, but he had a picture of my parents and told us they'd stayed with his family. My parents used to go out there to ski all the time before I was born. Why is this so hard for you to believe?"

"Because we weren't supposed to have anything to do with them."

"Oh, Bev, Robert Allan has been coming to me to cut his hair for years now. You might be the only one who still believes the old stories," Jerry inserted.

"Hah! What would you know about those stories? Most of them are true," Bev retorted.

"Bev, I've kept my mouth shut for years and let you believe whatever you wanted, because any talk to the contrary only got you upset. But having heard the other side of the story, it sounds like stubbornness is part of the family legacy on both sides."

Bev folded her arms across her chest and fumed.

"Aunt Bev, I'm not trying to ruffle your feathers, but don't you think this has gone on long enough? You don't even know the real reason why our families stopped talking and I can't imagine we have many more years to figure it out. Mr. Allan is getting old. As you said, every story has at least two sides. Don't you think it would be fair to figure it out before it's too late?"

Bev huffed. "I don't see why it really matters that much. Like you said, it's old stuff. Can't we just let it die?"

"No, we can't! I like Mr. Allan. He's a funny old man, but I feel like there's something inside his head that maybe only he knows. I don't want to wait for another generation to die before we start fixing things."

Bev shook her head but broke into a smile after a moment. "You might be more of a Quaker than I am, Amy. I can't figure out how a girl who grew up under my brother's roof could be such a peacemaker."

Amy looked thoughtful. "What's the point of keeping the grudges going, Aunt Bev? Have they ever brought anyone any happiness? My lack of contact with extended family never bothered me until recently, but discovering another side of the family has opened up a whole new world."

"Okay," Bev said resignedly, "but I have to warn you … you go digging in the past and you're bound to turn over some pretty weird stuff—and meet some very weird people."

"Bring it on," Amy said, taking Jake's hand. "I think we've had some good experience to prepare us for whatever lies ahead."

Jake laughed. "Yeah, you might even find out you're related to the Mancinis."

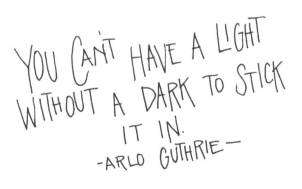

YOU CAN'T HAVE A LIGHT
WITHOUT A DARK TO STICK
IT IN.
-ARLO GUTHRIE-

SEEDS OF WANDERLUST

I HAVE LEARNED, THAT IF ONE ADVANCES CONFIDENTLY IN THE DIRECTION OF
HIS DREAMS, AND ENDEAVORS TO LIVE THE LIFE HE HAS IMAGINED,
HE WILL MEET WITH A SUCCESS UNEXPECTED IN COMMON HOURS.
—HENRY DAVID THOREAU—

Where in the world did you get those?" Amy asked, as Jerry passed the four old lawn chairs out of the small storage room door.

Bev laughed. "They don't make them like they used to."

"I've never seen lawn chairs like that either," said Jake.

"These?" Jerry said, holding one chair in each of his hands and raising them high above his head. A smile spread across his face as he looked at Jake and Amy. "We made these years ago with the kids as part of the 4-H requirements for the Eager Beaver Badge. Lawn chair re-webbing was kind of a stretch for the requirements, but we figured it couldn't hurt. We had such a blast making them that one of the boys later opened a business up in Erie that gives new life to old lawn chairs. That was before it was hip to recycle. All those tree-hugger types would really appreciate chairs like these."

He lowered the chairs, handing them to Amy and Jake.

Jake lifted the chair to examine it more closely. Interwoven with the few normal strips of lawn chair webbing was an unusual conglomerate of various materials: pieces of wool sweater, strips of a rubber inner tube, a section of garden hose, pieces of denim and other fabric, leather, rope and several other items that were unrecognizable. "These are cool!" Jake said, turning his attention to Amy's chair which was similar, but more colorful, hosting in addition to the other items, a collection of terrycloth strips that looked as though it might have once been a beach towel.

"Are you two coming?" Jerry asked.

They turned to see Jerry and Bev several paces ahead with their own colorful chairs hanging from their shoulders. They followed them through the narrow alleyway that ran next to Thomas' house and into the churchyard that was already filling with locals and tourists who were sitting on blankets and folding chairs. Jake turned and smiled at Amy as they walked past Eric Schmelding dressed in a long, colorful robe and sporting a pale-yellow, triangular-shaped hat that looked like a giant piece of Swiss cheese. He was engaged in an animated conversation with a middle-aged couple as a pimple-faced teenager adjusted the projector that sat on a rusty card table behind them. He turned and nodded his cheese-head hat as they walked past.

Out of courtesy for those without chairs, Jerry and Bev unfolded theirs on the back half of the courtyard, behind those who'd already set up in the best places. An image of a craggy mountain pass was being projected on a white sheet hanging on the church's front doors. The evening air was warm and comfortable as they mingled with the old folks of Niederbipp. They kept their eyes open for Joseph and Gloria but couldn't see them. Sandy, dressed in her scrubs, waved to them as she and her fiancé, Andrew, walked past, carrying a blanket. When he felt the stares from Clea Faber and Betty Finkel, the nice ladies who'd tried to line him up with their granddaughters, Jake put his arm around Amy and pulled her close so there would be no misunderstanding. Kai and Molly arrived later and sat on the side of the churchyard where they could make a quick escape if Baby Zane got cranky.

After another twenty minutes, the churchyard was filled with people of all ages and the sun had finally dipped low enough that the projected image was bright and colorful.

The Mayor stood from his chair and walked toward Eric. "My friends of Niederbipp, and those of you who are visiting with us tonight, welcome."

The Mayor's wife began clapping and a few others joined in before the mayor raised his hands to silence the crowd.

"We have the rare privilege tonight to hear from one of Niederbipp's most traveled citizens, Eric Schmelding."

Applause broke out through the whole crowd as Eric removed his cheese-head hat and bowed low with great pageantry.

"Eric has just returned to us from the Himalayas where he has spent the winter and spring months traipsing around in search of a rather elusive cheese made from the milk of alpine yaks."

A few young people laughed softly, but stopped when they saw the Mayor was serious.

"Many years ago, Mr. Schmelding began his travels in search of the rare, the exotic, and the delectable. When a few of us became curious about his travels and his unique profession, he began sharing his photos with us. I believe this is the twelfth summer in which we have hosted Eric and his travel show. As Niederbipp's one and only *Fromage bon vivant*, he has brought us photos from around the world and the stories to go with them. So, without any further ado, I give you Eric Schmelding."

The crowd applauded loudly as Eric removed his hat again and waved it over his head. "Goooood evening, Niederbipp! Or as they say in Tibet, *Tashi Delek*."

The crowd erupted again in applause.

"As the Mayor said, I have just returned from the Himalayas where I visited the countries of Tibet, Nepal and Rajasthan mostly, but being landlocked as those countries are, I also spent time in China, India and Pakistan. This first image is a view from the highest monastery on earth, the Rongbuk Monastery, located just shy of seventeen thousand feet above sea level and home to several dozen priests and nuns."

Eric pointed his remote at the projector, and the image changed to a different view of the monastery with multicolored prayer flags strung from rooftop to rooftop. A huge, imposing mountain looked down on the monastery. "Mount Everest, or as the Tibetans call it, 'Qomolangma Peak', the tallest mountain in the world and one of the most sacred and esteemed places on earth." The image changed again to a heap of rubble. Corrugated steel roofing panels, rocks and splinters of wood were tangled together. "This monastery was once home to more than five hundred monks but was destroyed by the Chinese in the early eighties. The people who live there now are constantly trying to rebuild what once was."

"This next image is a picture of two sisters—the daughters of one of the cheesemakers in Qinghai." The image was colorful, showing the two girls with high cheekbones, their windswept hair flowing across their colorful dresses. Another image showed the vats of milk and curd that would become the wheels of cheese in the next image. After that, there was little rhyme or reason to the order of Eric's photos, but nearly every one of them included a man or woman, a boy or a girl, neatly dressed in a rainbow of colors. The people were beautiful, their smiles endearing. There were several images of women, sitting together at giant looms, weaving rugs as they talked and sang together. Another group of pictures showcased beautiful children herding sheep, goats and yaks. Dancing monks dressed in scarlet robes followed images of prayer

wheels, nomad tents and pictures of crowded markets selling exotic clothing, bangles and food. Other images showed men and women dwarfed by the baskets and bags they carried on their backs or heads, filled with everything imaginable. There were palaces and pictures of vast, empty landscapes, old folks smoking from ornate hookahs and faces with far more wrinkles than teeth. But through all the images, there were smiles on the faces of beautiful people.

The presentation lasted more than an hour and a half and was coupled with commentary from Eric, explaining each of the images. They left Jake inspired. He'd never had the money to get into photography. He'd never owned a camera of any kind. But he was inspired by the way the images evoked thought and emotion in ways his pottery never had. The last image which Eric left on the makeshift screen was of a old woman, her face lined with age, her hair pulled back in a silver braid, smiling with every muscle in her sagging face and showcasing her single tooth.

Following applause from the crowd, Eric thanked everyone for coming and announced that his next presentation, "The Cheesemakers of Southern France," would be shown in three weeks. Jake and Amy continued sitting as they watched people stand and stretch before picking up their things and wandering off into the night.

"Are you two coming?" Bev asked. "We've got dessert back at the ranch—homemade carrot cake!"

Amy nodded. "Yeah, thanks, we'll see you there. We won't be long."

"What are you thinking?" Amy asked after Jerry and Bev were out of earshot.

Jake looked thoughtful as he stared at the image of the old woman projected on the screen. "Part of me wants to pack my bags and head off to Tibet, and another part of me feels like I just came from there. This was so cool."

"I'm glad you liked it," came a voice from behind them.

They turned to see Eric Schmelding.

Jake got to his feet and extended his hand to the man. "Thanks for doing this. It sounds like you've had an amazing life."

Eric nodded and smiled. "I have. I love sharing it with others. It gives my life meaning when others connect with the images from my travels."

"Didn't you tell us when we saw you down by the river that you give your presentations while you're traveling?" Jake asked.

A smile spread across Eric's face again. "Yes, it depends on where I am, but in most places, people like to see my presentations every night. Technology these days makes it easy. The hard drive on my laptop is only half-full but I have almost forty different presentations stored on it, and that little projector weighs only a few pounds. Even the most remote villages usually have generators or solar cells that can power my equipment for long enough to give the presentations. I've found that no matter where I go, people like to connect somehow with the world beyond their own village."

"And you can afford to do it for months at a time?" Jake asked, enviously.

"Yes, well, I'm a bachelor and I'm as cheap as they come."

Amy slid her arm around Jake's back and cozied up next to him.

He looked down at her. "Don't worry," he said. "I'm not getting any ideas. I'm just curious."

"It sounds like a good life, and much of it is, but I can't tell you how many times over the years that I have wished for what you two seem to have. True love and companionship have eluded me my whole life, and though I love my work and my hobby and have learned to love the people wherever I go, I have always missed out on what really matters."

"Mr. Schmelding, I took down the sheet. Do you want some help with your equipment?"

They turned to see the pimple-faced boy standing at the card table.

"That would be nice, Richard, as long as you don't need to get home."

"No, I'm fine."

Eric turned back to them. "Sorry, I'd better go, but I was hoping I might be able to get some pictures of you working on the wheel, Jake, and maybe some of you painting, Amy. Are you going to be around tomorrow?"

Jake nodded. "I've got some work to catch up on. I'll be around until four or so, and then I'll be over at the bakery helping Sam with a project."

"And I'll be with him," Amy said.

"Excellent. I should probably act like I own a business and be open during business hours, so I'll see you during my lunch break, sometime between noon and three."

Jake smiled, thinking of the cushy hour. He nodded, watching Eric Schmelding walk back to his equipment. They folded up the chairs and walked back to Bev and Jerry's, exhausted from their travels and the events of the day.

A WHOLE MARZIPAN TORTE

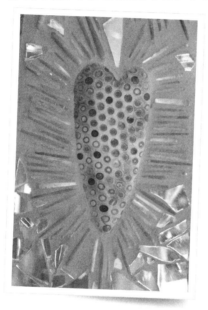

SOMEDAY, AFTER MASTERING WINDS, WAVES, TIDES AND GRAVITY,
WE SHALL HARNESS FOR GOD THE ENERGY OF LOVE;
AND FOR THE SECOND TIME IN THE HISTORY OF THE WORLD,
MAN WILL HAVE DISCOVERED FIRE.
—PIERRE TEILHARD DE CHARDIN—

ow long has the kiln been going?" Amy asked as she strolled through the open back door.

Jake looked up and smiled. He walked to her and took her in his arms, lifting her off the ground and spinning around a couple of times before setting her back down. Then he kissed her gently on the lips.

"Wow, what's gotten into you?" asked Amy, smiling from ear to ear.

Jake shook his head. "I had a crazy dream last night … that I was at that old monastery in the Himalayas. It was awesome. I was totally stoked to be there until I realized you weren't with me and the awesomeness faded into misery."

"So you're not going to take off without me?" she asked.

He leaned over and kissed her again, as though he meant it this time.

"I'll take that as a 'no'," she said, catching her breath.

"Amy," he said, dropping to his knees, "I don't want to put this off any longer. When I woke up last night after my dream, I wanted to wake up Thomas and come over to your aunt's house and marry you right there in the living room. We hardly talked about marriage at all last week and it's making me crazy. Please tell me you'll marry me."

She laughed, running her fingers through his hair. "You're crazy, Jake."

He looked serious. "I was hoping for at least a definite maybe. I'm not sure how to take, 'you're crazy, Jake.' Is that more like a 'yes' or more like a 'no'?"

She shook her head and began to laugh. "It's an absolutely 'YES'!"

"Really?" Jake said, scrambling to his feet. "You're not just teasing me, are you?"

She pulled him close 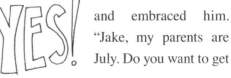 and embraced him. Then she kissed him again. "Jake, my parents are coming for the Fourth of July. Do you want to get married that weekend?"

"Amy, I sure hope you're talking about *this* Fourth of July."

She laughed, pulling him close again and held on for a long time. "I love you, Jake Kimball," she said softly as her chin rested on his shoulder.

"I know. I love you too. Do you think we can pull it off? We only have thirteen days."

"I've already been making plans for a week," she said, pulling back to look at him.

"You have?" he asked, incredulously.

"Yeah. I thought for sure you were going to ask me on our scooter ride last Monday. I kept expecting it all week, but this is as good a place as any."

"Promise me something," he said, looking around the old studio.

"What's that?"

"When our kids asked how I proposed to you, promise me you'll tell them it was more romantic than I just made it."

"On one condition."

"Sure, name your price."

She looked over his shoulder. "I need a big slice of that marzipan torte over there."

He smiled, turning to look at the torte. "When I was at the bakery this morning before they even opened the doors, Sam asked me what was going on. When I told him I was planning on proposing this morning, he suggested we celebrate with a whole torte instead of just a slice. I thought that was a really good idea. If you said yes, I figured we could share it, or …"

"Or what?"

"Or I figured I'd eat the whole thing by myself if you told me to take a hike."

Amy laughed, digging her fingers into Jake's ribs and causing him to squirm with laughter. "You think you can get rid of me that easily?" she joked.

"No, I just figured I would need some serious marzipan therapy if you told me you didn't want me."

She looked up into his eyes again and smiled. "I've never wanted anything more in my life?"

"Are you talking about the torte?"

She laughed, poking him in the ribs.

Sam had told Jake earlier that morning that marzipan slice, at a time of struggle or hardship, was wonderful, but that having a whole marzipan torte to share with someone you love, especially on the occasion of great happiness, was something all together different. Jake and Amy took their breakfast outside, sitting on the bench under the chestnut tree in the courtyard. The glass jar that had been sitting on the back steps was still half-full of Isaac's tea which they used to toast their future together as they made plans for the coming weeks.

With the Fourth of July landing on Saturday, they decided they'd try to plan the wedding for Sunday at noon, so those who'd have to travel would be able to be back to work on Monday morning. It was too late to send announcements in the mail. They would have to make phone calls or send emails in order to notify family and friends. Amy decided she'd leave most of that to her mom to notify her brothers and their families. She'd email her college roommates. Jake would send an email to his professor, Eric Lewis, and his college roommates, just to let them know, but he knew they probably wouldn't come. Niederbipp was not a crossroads to *anyone's* summer vacation. As they counted the number of people who might come from out of town, most of whom were Amy's brothers and their families, they both realized how Niederbipp had become their home and family in such a short period of time. Joseph and Gloria. Kai and Molly and Molly's dad, Bob Braun. Thomas. Bev and Jerry. Sam and his wife. Mr. Allan. Dr. Sandy and her fiancé, Andrew. Hildegard. David and Nancy Garber. Mayor Jim and his wife. As he thought about it, these people had become the brothers and sisters, the aunts and uncles that he'd never had. No one could replace his own mother. She would be terribly missed. But having Gloria around to love him like a son had already been a great comfort to him.

"Do you think we should have Thomas marry us?" Jake asked.

"Do you think he can?" asked Amy. "I'm not sure if his status as a priest is valid and neither of us are Catholic."

"Maybe we should just ask. There have to be people getting married in Niederbipp from time to time. Do you know anything about Quaker weddings?"

"Not very much. I think Bev and Jerry had a Quaker wedding, but I don't know anything about it. I just heard they're pretty simple."

"That sounds like the right kind of wedding to me, especially considering that we only have thirteen days."

Amy shook her head, smiling.

"What are you thinking?" asked Jake.

"I'm thinking this is perfect."

"In what way?"

"In almost every way. One of my roommates, Andrea, got married last spring at the end of the school year. She'd spent six months planning and fretting over her wedding. She came from a lot of money. I heard that her father budgeted sixty thousand dollars for the wedding and that she and her mother actually spent more than that."

"Are you serious?" Jake asked. "That's more than most people make in a year. How could you possibly spend that much money on a wedding?"

"Pride knows no limits."

"What do you mean?"

"I'm pretty sure she would have had a much simpler wedding if it weren't for her mom. Between her wedding gown and dresses for her twelve bridesmaids, catering, renting the country club on Cape Cod, flowers, pictures, announcements, flying people in from near and far, Champagne and party favors—it was beyond belief. As I watched her making plans, I found myself trying to figure out if I was jealous or just totally disgusted by the grandiose excess."

Jake shook his head. "Amy, I don't think I'll ever understand that kind of money. Sixty thousand dollars for a wedding!"

"No, that was only what the bride spent. The groom's family spent a mint, too, on tuxedos, flowers and hotel rooms for the guests. Between the two families, I bet they probably spent over a hundred thousand dollars before the weekend was over."

"Am I the only one who thinks that's crazy?" asked Jake.

"No way. The sad thing is—the last I heard, Andrea and her husband were separated and looking at a divorce."

Jake shook his head, feeling once again like a boy from the wrong side of the tracks. "Amy, I don't have … I can't …" He looked away, frustrated.

"I know Jake," she said, putting her hand on his chin and turning his face back to look at her. "That's what I meant when I said this is perfect. My mom won't be here to make any decisions, and I think my dad realizes—especially after last weekend—that his money has no clout here."

Jake smiled shyly. "So, are you telling me that you *really* want to keep it simple?"

"That's exactly what I'm saying."

Jake leaned over and kissed her. "I can't tell you how big of a relief that is. I was just thinking about how much money I have, and I don't even think I have enough to … there's that money Charlie gave me, but I don't feel good spending it on a wedding."

"Neither do I, but I don't think it will cost very much. I'd like to get a dress, and you probably ought to get a tie and a pair of pants that don't have glaze stains on them," she said under her breath. But Jake caught the not-so-subtle hint that she expected him to clean up, at least a little for their wedding.

"I've never shopped for a wedding dress before, but Molly says there's a place up in Warren that has dresses for under two hundred bucks. We probably ought to have some food for the people who come, but we could probably get away with a big cake and Sam could make that. I forgot about photos until last night, but I wonder if Eric would be willing to do our wedding photos. And flowers—I … I already talked to Gloria about the possibility of an upcoming wedding. She said she'd make me a bouquet."

Jake shook his head again, but looked at her, smiling. "It sounds like you've been thinking a lot about this."

Amy smiled. "Considering that marriage was the last thing on my mind when I came here for the summer, I'd say I've made some pretty big changes. I've already committed us to help with a birthday party for Mr. Allan on that same weekend, and I don't want to make this any more complicated than it needs to be."

"Amy, what planet are you from?"

She laughed. "Why?"

"I was just thinking there would probably be a lot of guys who would like to go there to see if they could find another girl like you."

AMy's PLANET

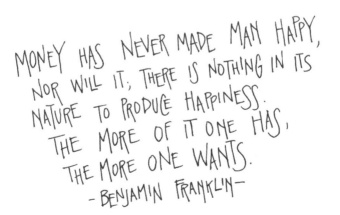

MONEY HAS NEVER MADE MAN HAPPY, NOR WILL IT; THERE IS NOTHING IN ITS NATURE TO PRODUCE HAPPINESS. THE MORE OF IT ONE HAS, THE MORE ONE WANTS.
- BENJAMIN FRANKLIN -

CONFESSIONS

CONTENT MAKES POOR MEN RICH; DISCONTENT MAKES RICH MEN POOR.
—BENJAMIN FRANKLIN—

I understand congratulations are in order," Albert, the town tailor said as he walked through the open door, interrupting Jake's work.

"Hey, Albert," Jake said, wiping his slip-covered hands on his apron and standing to take the tailor's outstretched hand. "I guess word travels quickly."

"That's what they say. Sam said you just got engaged today. Who's the lucky girl?"

"Oh, I thought you knew. Her name is Amy Eckstein, Jerry and Beverly Sproodle's niece." Jake watched as Albert's face registered the connection. "You just missed her, actually. She just ran home to pick up a couple of frames. She's a painter. She should be back soon if you'd like to meet her. Would you like some tea?"

"No thanks," he said, waving his hands. "I … I was really just stopping in to make sure what I heard was true. I was under the impression that you and Alice had something going on. I guess I must have been misinformed."

Jake squirmed, surprised by Albert's words, unsure of how to answer. "Umm, yeah … uh … you know, Albert, Alice is a great girl, but … uh, I don't really know what to say. I fell in love with Amy and as it turns out, we have a lot in common. Um, Alice and I … uh … no … I uh …"

"Yeah, I guess I was misinformed," Albert said again, looking disappointed. He wiped the sweat from his brow and took a deep breath. "Did you say you have some tea?"

"Yeah, sure. We have some in the jar on the back steps. I'll get it." Jake wiped his hands again on his apron as he walked out the back door, returning with the tall glass jar. Albert was unhitching his mug from the overhead beam and held it out to Jake for a fill-up.

"Do you mind if I sit down for a minute?" Albert asked.

"No, of course not, please," Jake said, offering Albert a stool even though his presence and conversation had made him intensely uncomfortable. "Hey, um, Albert, I really want to thank you for helping me with all the hospital stuff. They told me I probably wouldn't have made it to the hospital alive if it hadn't been for you. I also appreciate you doing all the fundraising."

Albert took a big gulp of the tea and nodded but didn't look at Jake, making him feel even more uncomfortable. For nearly a minute, nothing was said.

"I guess it was a lot to hope for," Albert finally spoke.

Jake wasn't sure what he was talking about and definitely wasn't going to guess, not after already feeling like he'd been put on the spot.

Albert looked into the bottom of his mug and shook his head. "I'm a tailor, Jake. I've worked with fabric for more than half my life, turning it into beautiful clothes for people who can afford my services. It has been a very fulfilling life. I have a great marriage and three beautiful children who are now grown and busy building lives of their own. Being involved in 'Jake Watch' was a big thing for me. Before you came here, I don't remember the last time I was really involved in helping anyone."

"But you help people every day, don't you—making clothes and stuff."

Albert nodded. "Yes, but I'm not so sure it really counts if you get paid to do it. Making clothes is my job. When I saw you bleeding all over Hauptstrasse that day, I remember thinking that I had an opportunity to be a hero. That doesn't happen every day, at least not for me, in my line of work. It felt pretty good to be the center of attention—to have people swarming around me, asking me for the latest update or news about you. I tell you, it felt pretty good."

"Albert, thank you for doing all that. You and so many others have helped me recognize the value of having good neighbors."

He took a deep breath, then shook his head. "I wish it were true, Jake. I wish it were true."

For the third time in as many minutes, Jake didn't know how to respond.

"I need to ask you to forgive me," Albert said, turning to look Jake in the eye.

Jake swallowed hard. "For what?"

"For taking advantage of you and your situation."

"I don't understand."

Albert shook his head. "I didn't think about it in the beginning, but once it started, I really took advantage of it—all those people coming into my shop to get their updates. It started out innocently enough, but I couldn't believe how business picked up during those days you were in the hospital."

"Sounds like karma to me." said Jake. "You helped me—your business got better. Isn't that the way karma works?"

Albert took a deep breath. "I don't think karma really applies if you're thinking about how you can personally benefit from a sad situation. I … when I saw how much my business was picking up, I realized I needed a steady source of new information to keep people coming to my shop. A crowd draws a crowd, and soon I had tourists flocking in to find out what the hullabaloo was all about. I sold seven custom suits in three days. I haven't done that kind of business in … never, actually."

"That's great! Isn't it?"

"It would be, but when people dropped in to see what I knew, if I didn't have any news, I'd make it up. I got as much real information as I could, but the HIPAA laws kept me from learning more. When Thomas said he was coming here to look for clues, I tagged along. I'm ashamed to admit I even coaxed Alice into visiting you. That wasn't very hard. She'd already expressed interest in you."

Jake nodded, putting the pieces together. "So the Twinkies were your idea?" he asked, laughing.

Albert closed his eyes and nodded. "Yep. I've been feeling guilty for the last two weeks as business has faded back to normal. It was fun to be in the middle of it while it was happening—fun to be connected to a celebrity, but now that it's over, I'm realizing what a jerk I was. I used you and your accident to put myself in the middle of something where I had no business being. After peeling back the layers of my justifications, I realized I was thinking too much about me, and not enough about truly helping a neighbor. I'm really sorry, Jake. I know my daughter has a reputation for breaking hearts. She's a beautiful girl. I got her involved, thinking … well, thinking it might keep you around if you fell in love with her and got married. I figured it would also help her settle down. But when I overheard Sam talking about your engagement this morning, I knew I owed you an apology."

Jake shook his head, smiling. "Albert, Alice's advances got me into some pretty chilly water with Amy. I almost lost her, but what you did for me, helping to raise money to pay for my treatment—that was amazing."

"Jake, the truth is—*that* was the Mayor's idea. Sure, I put the jar on my counter and collected money—I even encouraged my customers to donate to your cause, but the idea wasn't mine. I patted myself on the back and let others do the same, but it was mostly self-serving and selfish. I'm sorry."

"Albert, don't beat yourself up about this. A lot of good things have come of it. My medical bills have been paid and I just got engaged to the most beautiful, wonderful, amazing woman in the world. Things have worked out for all of us. Because of you, I've gotten to know Isaac through all the people you sent to try to talk me into staying. The things I learned—his words of wisdom and lessons of life—those things have helped me to understand who he was, and who I am."

Jake took a breath as his eyes scanned the studio. "Albert, the longer I'm here, the more I realize that my detour here was no accident. It seems the universe has been preparing me for this my whole life. I fought it for a while, but the time I spent in the hospital—it opened my eyes. I'm sure there are lots of things I still have to learn, but I feel like I can learn whatever I need to right here. I was thinking about that the other day. I feel like being in this shop is kind of like sitting on a beach where everything I need in life gets washed up on the sand, waiting for me to discover it. As I've thought about it, I think maybe my whole life has been that way, but I never noticed those things until I came here. In the silence of my thoughts and from the visits I've had from Isaac's friends, I've discovered the truths that lead to real happiness—to love and joy.

"You may feel guilty for benefiting from my accident, but I honestly have nothing to be upset about. I am in your debt for all you have done. Everything has worked out far better than I ever imagined. If you feel you need to apologize, then I accept it, but please, put it behind you and don't think about it again. We're going to be neighbors for a long time, and I have no reason to harbor any bad feelings. If it weren't for you, I might have already jumped ship and be floundering somewhere in the Mediterranean Sea. Instead, I'm right where I'm supposed to be."

Albert looked into his mug again and was silent for a long moment. The discomfort Jake had felt before returned with the silence as he wondered what Albert was thinking.

"I have another confession to make, Jake."

"Okay, bring it on."

"When I heard the committee to replace Isaac had chosen a young kid, I was pretty upset. I figured you'd be gone in a couple of weeks."

"So ... why'd you send people to meet me—to tell me their stories and talk me into staying?"

"Because I changed my mind after I met you. I never thought anyone could fill Isaac's shoes, but after I spent some time talking to you, I decided I'd reserve my judgment for later. I still don't believe anyone could fill Isaac's shoes, but you've got a good head on your shoulders and I don't worry about you figuring it out. It seems like you've already made better sense of your journey than most people twice your age."

Jake shook his head. "Then I've got you fooled. I'm not sure what I'm doing or where I'm going, but I feel like I'm finally on the right path to get wherever I'm supposed to be, thanks in large part to you and the people who've dropped in to visit and tell me their stories. It may take me a lifetime to fully understand who Isaac was, but I feel compelled to walk the same roads he walked."

Jake looked around the studio again, remembering his first

impressions of this place. "Ya know, when I came here, I was a very independent kid, but I feel like I've traded that all in for something much better."

"You mean a bunch of crazy old ducks who don't mind their own business?"

Jake smiled. "I guess that's part of it, but I traded in my independence to become part of the hive, to be part of a community who knows how to extract the nectar from the flowers of life and make something sweeter than honey. You can't do that alone. I tried—for the last couple of years I tried, but I'm supposed to be here and I know it."

Albert nodded slowly. "Sometimes I guess I forget why I stayed here—why I came home and set up shop here. Sometimes, when I watch the tourists wandering slowly around town, taking it all in, I realize how much I take this community—this town for granted. Isaac used to talk about his scooter rides—exploring the neighboring towns and countryside and coming home with new eyes. I guess we all need to do that sometimes, don't we—go away for just long enough to be able to return and see the place with a new perspective."

"Yep," Albert continued, getting to his feet and hanging his mug back on its nail. "I'm glad you're here, Jake. And again, I'm sorry for … for not being a better neighbor … a better member of the hive."

Jake shook his head. "Albert, thank you. No real damage has been done, and, like I said before, a lot of good has come of all this."

The sound of a bicycle made them both turn to the back door where Amy was dismounting the old bike, her right arm threaded through a half-dozen wooden frames.

"Come and meet my fiancée," Jake said, motioning

toward the door. Jake rushed toward her, helping her with the frames. "Amy, there is someone here I want you to meet," he said, nodding to the tailor.

Amy wiped her forehead on the sleeve of her shirt and turned to the doorway.

"This is Albert, the town tailor and Alice's dad. He came by to congratulate us. I guess the word's getting out already."

Amy looked at Jake and then at the tall man in the doorway and timidly extended her hand. "Nice to meet you," she said.

"I was just apologizing to Jake for encouraging my daughter to ... for. Jake was just telling me he'd fallen in love with an amazing girl. I congratulate you both and I'm truly sorry for doing anything to get in your way."

Amy blushed slightly, but smiled. "It's okay. I probably wouldn't feel the same way if ... well if things were different, but somehow things worked out and we're both the better for it."

Albert nodded. "So, when are you getting married?"

"July fifth," Jake said.

"*This* July fifth?" Albert asked.

"Yeah," Jake said, laughing at the surprised look on Albert's face. "We have some family coming into town that weekend and we decided that was as good a time as any."

"Wow, that's only like ..."

"Thirteen days away," Jake said, smiling at Amy. "We're planning on keeping it pretty simple."

"Have you made plans for a gown?" Albert asked Amy.

"No, not really. I heard there was a place in Warren that has gowns."

Albert shook his head. "You're not talking about Loretta's, are you?"

"Uh, I'm not really sure. I ... we just got engaged this morning. I haven't had a chance to check into anything."

"Do you make wedding gowns?" Jake asked.

"Heavens no, but my wife has made hundreds over the years.

I ... I feel like I owe you two. I know it might seem a little awkward, especially after ... but Lin is the finest dressmaker in the all the neighboring counties. I'd like to invite you to at least talk to her."

Amy looked at Jake, then back to Albert. "My aunt just suggested the same thing, except she said your wife is the best dressmaker in the state. Like Jake said, we're planning on keeping it simple, but I'd love to talk to her."

"I'm on my way there now," Albert said, stepping through the doorway. "I'd be happy to make introductions."

Amy looked at Jake again as if she were waiting for approval.

He nodded. "It's your decision, but it's not every day you get to visit with the best dressmaker in the state."

She smiled, handing him the frame that was hanging from the handlebars. "I'll be back before lunch," she said, as she kissed him.

Jake watched from the doorway as Amy and Albert crossed the courtyard and turned toward Hauptstrasse, disappearing from his view. As he sat back down to continue his work, he thought again about how everything he needed seemed to wash up on his shore.

OUR DUTY, AS MEN & WOMEN, IS TO PROCEED AS IF LIMITS TO OUR ABILITY DO NOT EXIST. WE ARE COLLABORATORS IN CREATION.

— PIERRE TEILHARD DeCHARDIN —

LIGHT AND TRUTH

GIVE LIGHT, AND THE DARKNESS WILL DISAPPEAR OF ITSELF.
—DESIDERIUS ERASMUS—

Wedding gown, accomplished," Amy said standing in the doorway with a broad smile across her face.

"You found one?" Jake asked, looking up from his place at the wheel where he sat sweating from the heat of the kiln at his back.

She dropped the bag she was carrying before walking to him. She ran her fingers through his hair, then leaning over, she kissed him. "Lin is amazing. She must have twenty dresses in lots of different styles."

"Did you try them on?"

"A couple, but they were all pretty fancy and most of them were too bare. I've never felt comfortable in that kind of a dress. I told her I wanted to keep it simple and she showed me a picture of a dress she made a few years ago that I really liked. It reminded me a lot of my sister-in-law's dress and we have about the same body type."

"So, she's going to make your dress?"

"Yeah, I don't want to waste any time looking around, and I'm sure I'll love it. It's also the right price. That roommate of mine that I was telling you about, she spent over three thousand dollars on a dress she'll never wear again. This will be the most expensive dress I've ever bought, but I realized it's only going to cost the same amount as one of my paintings. I figured we could handle that."

"That's awesome."

"Yeah, but it gets better. On my way home, I dropped by the grocery store to tell Kai and Molly. Kai told me Bob bought him a suit for their wedding that he hasn't worn since and offered it to you if you want to borrow it."

"Sweet. I don't think I'd ever wear one again either."

Amy smiled and shook her head. "He said his tie got ruined when Molly smeared frosting on it, so we'd probably have to find a tie for you, but that shouldn't cost us more than fifty bucks."

"Man, if I'd known it was going to be this easy, I'd have proposed a month ago."

Amy laughed as Jake pushed back from the wheel. Pulling her down to sit on his lap, he tried to kiss her, but she was smiling so broadly that he kissed her teeth, causing them both to laugh out loud.

"So, that's the way it works around here!"

They turned, startled, to see Eric Schmelding standing at the counter.

He laughed as Amy jumped off Jake's lap. "I'm sorry, I would have knocked, but the front door was wide open."

"You're fine," said Jake. "Come on in. Amy was just teaching me that kisses are a little better when they land on the lips rather than the teeth."

Amy blushed when Eric looked at her with raised eyebrows.

Jake stood to properly welcome him. "You'll have to excuse us. We just got engaged this morning."

"Well, that's wonderful. Congratulations. I could come back another day if it would be more convenient."

"No," said Amy. "We were actually talking about you earlier. We don't want to insult you and your art, but we wondered if you might consider photographing our wedding."

Eric smiled with his whole face. "I'd be honored. I haven't shot a wedding—at least not an American wedding in more than a decade. I'm probably a little rusty. The last wedding I shot was a Maori wedding in New Zealand a couple of years ago when I went down to give my stamp of approval to the Te Mata Cheesemakers and their unusual goat cheese called Pakipaki. Definitely one of the finest goat cheeses in the southern hemisphere. It was a real privilege to give them my stamp of approval," he said, standing a little taller and looking quite discriminating. "So, when's the big day?"

"Two weeks from yesterday," Amy responded. "At least that's what we're hoping for. We just started making plans this morning. We still have a lot of things to figure out."

"Well, again I congratulate you. I have many regrets in my life, but not taking the time to get married is my biggest regret to date. It's hard to find a woman who can appreciate my rather peculiar passions and travel schedule."

Jake shuddered inside, thinking about how his passions and this summer's travel schedule would certainly have cost him the happiness he'd found here with Amy.

"Have you eaten lunch yet?" Amy asked. "I was planning on making some sandwiches. I'd be happy to make one for you."

"I'd like that," Eric said, removing a large backpack from his shoulders and laying it on the counter. He unzipped his back pack and pulled out a black Cannon camera, attaching a lens before sliding the

strap over his neck. Jake walked past him to
lock the front door. As he turned around and
climbed the steps, he nearly burst out laughing.
Eric had looked so normal as he spoke to them
across the counter, but the counter had hidden his apparel below the
waist—a pair of bright, blue and orange, plaid pants and his two-toned
saddle shoes.

"Those are some great pants," Jake said.

"Yeah, they don't make them like they used to. I bought these to
wear to my college graduation. Hundred percent polyester. They look
as good today as they did in the early seventies. And the great thing is,
they still fit."

"I'll get started on the sandwiches," Amy said, smiling as she picked
up the grocery bag and turned to leave.

"Did you graduate in photography?" Jake asked, picking up the tea
jar on the back stairs.

"Heavens no. Political Science. Duke, class of 1971."

"Political Science?" Jake asked, surprised.

"Yes, I was planning on being a lobbyist. I was hell-bent
on changing the world."

"So what happened?" asked Jake as he welcomed Eric inside
the apartment.

"I tried it for a while, but I never liked the games I had to play
to have my voice heard. Washington was a mess, even back then.
Three years and twenty-four days after I moved to D.C., Nixon was
impeached over the Watergate scandal and I left three days later,
totally disenchanted with America."

"So you just packed up and left your dreams and your education to
travel the world?"

"Oh no, the travel came later. No, ... I did what a lot of disenchanted
folks were doing back then."

"Drugs?" Jake asked.

"Well, there was that, but I don't think anyone ever really found any answers in drugs. I know I didn't, and when the buzz wore off, my country was still a mess and my headaches had only gotten worse. No—drugs weren't really my cup of tea. We were all looking for something to help us make sense of the world. Some of my friends got into Eastern religions. Others went back to school. One of my buddies started a microbrewery. I scraped together all the money I could find and helped buy a commune in Vermont."

"Are you serious? I'm from Vermont—from Burlington."

"Ah, yes, been there hundreds of times. We used to sell our produce at the farmer's market down on the waterfront. The commune was just outside of Winooski."

"That's crazy," said Jake, "I think my dad grew up in Winooski."

"Yeah, it was a nice town."

"So what happened to the commune? Why'd you leave?" asked Jake.

Eric shook his head. "Everyone likes the idea of living in a utopian society, but the reality is, it takes a lot of work. I'm pretty sure the mortal man was never meant to live in paradise. We get bored after a while and start tweaking things and pretty soon the paradise begins looking a lot like the same mess on the outside of the fence. It was a good experiment and a lot of good came of it, but in the end we all parted ways while we were still friends. That's actually where I learned to make cheese."

"So, what brought you to Niederbipp?" Amy asked.

"Inheritance. My father grew up here but left when he was in his early twenties. My grandfather, Rudi Schmelding, left his watch shop and house to my family, but I was the only one of my siblings or cousins who didn't think Niederbipp was a total bore. I felt as though there was something different about this town—the way people knew and cared about each other—the way people accepted those from beyond the river and the hills with a unique form of brotherly love and acceptance."

"My uncle Jerry told us that has a lot to do with the Quaker roots," Amy said.

"Yes, I've spent a lot of time talking to your uncle over the years about the history of this town. You're lucky to have his knowledge at your fingertips. William Penn had some great ideas. I think more than anything else, the thing that has impressed me most about Niederbipp is that people here haven't strayed far from the basics."

"The basics?" Jake asked.

"Thank you," Eric said, as Amy handed him his sandwich. "Yes, the basics. Sitting down to break bread with your neighbors, looking past the end of your own nose, reaching out to the lonely, the fatherless and the poor. You wouldn't know it if you're from here, but lots of folks around the world don't even know who their neighbors are!"

Amy handed Jake a sandwich and joined them at the table. "My aunt and uncle said Isaac tried to make Niederbipp into an example for the world to follow."

"He did, but he never would have taken credit for that idea. It was an idea that came from some of Niederbipp's earliest settlers."

"Yeah, I think Jerry said something about their idea that people would come to Niederbipp in search of peace and direction and would go home and try to make their own towns a better place," Jake reported.

"Yes. Isaac was always excited to talk about that idea with anyone who'd listen. He was always inviting the tourists, the strangers, and the outcasts into his studio and home. Over the years, he often spoke of the debt he had to Providence for bringing him here—that the gifts he'd received obligated him to give back. Somehow, more than anyone I've ever met, Isaac found a balance between faith and works."

"Hey, we just carved that into a tile for Isaac's bench," Jake reported. "Faith without works is dead." [1]

"I'm glad you did. That was one of the truths Isaac lived by. He always said that answers came only to those who asked and then moved

[1] James 2:20

their feet forward. He empowered me to believe that answers to all of life's questions would come if I would move forward with faith and try to love the people I met along the way."

"I like that idea," Amy said. "How's it been for you?"

"In one word—awesome."

Jake and Amy smiled.

"We've done a lot of cool things for Isaac's bench," Jake added. "Thomas suggested we might better understand Isaac if we studied the parables of Jesus. I … I mean we … we designed Isaac's bench with a candle in the middle. In fact, his name and dates are on that candle with many of the things Isaac did and said radiating out from the light of that candle."

"It sounds like Thomas gave you some great direction. Isaac's whole life was a parable. You could learn something from nearly everything he did. He inspired many of us to become Candlelighters."

Jake and Amy looked at each other, then back at Eric.

"Candlelighters?" Jake asked.

"Thomas hasn't spoken to you about that?"

"No, why?" asked Jake.

"I … I just figured he would have if he talked to you about candles."

"I don't know if he ever really talked *specifically* about candles," Jake said, looking at Amy with questioning eyes.

"I don't remember him saying anything either, but he did seem pleased we used the candle in the design," she said.

"Huh, I guess I'm surprised he …" He trailed off, looking thoughtful.

"Eric, you can't bring this up and just leave us hanging," Jake said.

He nodded. "You're right. I give pause only because it sounds like Thomas must have also."

"Is it some kind of secret?" Jake asked.

"No, not a secret, but something we all feel is a kind of sacred calling." He looked out the window as if he was lost in a distant memory.

"Eric, this is obviously very important to you. Amy and I don't want to talk about anything we shouldn't, but can you tell us more about it?"

Eric nodded, closing his eyes. "I am telling you this only because I sense you are ready to hear it and because I know that you already know many Candlelighters."

"We do?" asked Amy.

"Yes. There are still at least a dozen around town and probably millions by now around the world. I bump into them from time to time in my travels."

"So what exactly is a Candlelighter?" Jake asked again, his interest piqued.

Eric looked them both in the eyes as if to emphasize the importance of what he was about to say. "Truth and light are often used synonymously in the Bible. Isaac once told me that he believed everyone in this world was like a candle. He said he'd stumbled into Niederbipp in search of answers and in return was given light in the form of love, and truth, and for the first time in his life, his candle was lit. If you included a candle on Isaac's bench, surely you've read the fifth chapter of Matthew."

"Yeah, that's where the idea came from," Jake said.

"Very good. In that parable, it talks about the importance of not hiding your light, but putting it on a candlestick so everyone in the house can benefit from it."

Jake and Amy nodded.

"And I'm sure you've heard, Isaac always made a point to share his light and truth with others."

They nodded again.

"Truth is an amazing thing," Eric continued. "It chases away the darkness of despair and leaves hope and joy in its place. He helped me recognize that there is no influence with greater power in this universe than light and truth. With love, patience and kindness, truth shatters the shackles of fear and inspires all people to reach higher. Isaac shared his light with everyone he knew, but he d i d much more than that. For those who listened and tuned their ears to hear, he bent down and lit their candles."

Jake nodded thoughtfully. "He was a Candlelighter."

"Yes. Do you see it now?"

Jake and Amy nodded.

"So, is that what you do when you travel the world?" Amy asked. "Are you lighting candles?"

"I hope so. My passion for cheese pays my way, but I've found that the world is hungry for light and truth. People who are searching are always eager to embrace it when they find it."

"You said there are many Candlelighters. How do you become one?" asked Amy.

"First, you must be committed to seeking truth. Then you must be committed to sharing it, however your gifts and talents may enable you to do so. It's not an easy thing to do and it always requires great sacrifice."

"Does it require that you be single?" Jake asked, thinking of the three Candlelighters he was sure he knew: Isaac, Thomas and Eric.

"No," Eric said, shaking his head with a little laugh. "Many of us are single, but usually not by choice. Gloria and Joseph are both Candlelighters, so are your aunt and uncle, Amy."

"Really? They've never said anything about that."

"No, I expect they wouldn't. It's not something you brag about. Remember the last part of the parable about the candlestick?"

Jake looked up at Amy. "We talked about this, remember? That it's not about you. It's about glorifying God."

"That's right!" she responded.

"One of the properties of truth is that it can only be maintained by gentleness, meekness and humility. There are some Candlelighters who have fallen away over the years because they become consumed with themselves, believing the light they have been given is all about them. You may be familiar with another one of Isaac's mantras. That joy in all its glory ..."

"... Can only be obtained through unselfishness." Jake said, completing Eric's words.

"That's right. The interesting thing is that when love or truth is substituted for joy in that formula, the mantra remains equally true. Isn't it amazing that selfishness can keep us away from all three? The only other force that comes close to the damning power of selfishness is fear."

"I think I understand that well," Amy said. "I almost let fear rob me of my desire to be a real artist."

Eric nodded. "I've noticed over the years that fear tries to break us down with its greatest force when we're working on improving our talents or taking a new step in a positive direction. It tries to attack our confidence and inhibit our growth."

"Why does it have to be that way?" Amy asked.

"Because the forces of fear hate the light. John talks about this in the Bible—that perfect love casteth out all fear.(Footnote John 4:18.) Isaac taught me that love's companions, namely truth and light, have the same power over fear. All these things shatter fear's darkness which exists only in the absence of light. When even the faintest light is present, there is hope."

"So, how long have the Candlelighters been around? Is it something Isaac made up?" asked Jake.

"Oh no, they've been around since the beginning of time, at least in one form or another."

"So, how did Isaac learn about it?" he asked.

"From his father-in-law and his wife, Lily, at least that's what he told me. Isaac said it was a tradition that had been passed down from long before the beginning of this town. You might have noticed the candle that is held by the captain of the ship in that old mural at the end of Zubergasse."

"Are you serious?" Jake asked. "I've walked past that mural a hundred times. I don't think I ever saw it."

"I'm sure you're not the only one. We miss details like that all the time, especially when we're not looking for them."

"You said you bump into other Candlelighters in your travels. How do you know one when you see one?" asked Amy.

"It takes a little while to develop an eye for recognizing them, but it's really not very difficult. It comes down to observing and discerning the fruits."

"Thomas talked about that on the symbols tour of the church," Amy said.

"That's right. Isn't that from Matthew somewhere?"

"Yes, Christ taught his followers that many wolves would come dressed in sheep's clothing, but that we could know the difference by observing a persons fruits." [1]

"So can you tell a Candlelighter just by looking at them?" Amy asked.

"Generally, yes. Some people are so full of light, you can tell immediately who they are. They're usually the people who have so much goodness in them that you just have to stand next to them or even look at them and you can feel their goodness oozing out of them."

"That sounds like Gloria," Amy said.

Jake nodded. "But Gloria's from Florida, isn't she? How did she become a Candlelighter?"

"I'm not for certain about Gloria specifically, but of the hundreds of Candlelighters I know personally, no one becomes one without making a sacrifice—without a change of heart—without experiencing a hardship."

"Yeah, you may have heard that I just went through a pretty crappy

[1] Matthew 7:15-20

experience in order to discover the truth about myself—and a lot of other things," Jake said, as he reached for Amy's hand.

Eric nodded with a smile. "Yes, Joseph and Gloria told me about your accident."

"I hope I never have to go through anything like that again," Jake added.

"Oh, are you done learning?" Eric asked wryly.

"I hope not. I just hope I don't have to learn that again, at least not the same way."

"You can take comfort in knowing that things like that rarely happen the same way twice, but life moves on and we often forget the lessons we learned and the progress we've made. Each day is a new day with its own challenges and heartache, but every day also brings with it the opportunity for learning and greatness."

Jake looked down at his plate with a furrowed brow, but said nothing and silence fell between them for a moment. He slowly lifted his head and spoke again. "So this humility stuff doesn't save you from pain and sorrow?"

Eric smiled with kind eyes. "I'm afraid not. Following the path of truth will never exempt us from trial and heartache, but it does give purpose and understanding to our hardships if we allow ourselves to be taught and if we seek for answers. I have often wished that things were different—that we could learn every lesson we need to learn from our first mistake, but life never works out that way." He turned and looked at the shelves behind him, overflowing with pottery. "Isaac taught me some very insightful lessons about life over the years."

"We've uncovered some of the lessons these pots have to teach," said Jake, "but we've both wondered why they needed so many reminders."

Eric nodded. "Jake, how many potter's works are displayed here?"

"Uh, seven, I think."

"Try thirty or more."

"But I thought Isaac was the seventh potter of Niederbipp," Jake said.

"He was the seventh *full-time* potter of Niederbipp, but many of those potters had sons and daughters, wives and apprentices, who participated in making pottery. Most of these pots were made by the full-timers, but the lessons that are to be learned from this collection extend far beyond the seven potters whose benches decorate the graveyard."

"Like what?" asked Amy.

"Isaac said they taught him that absolutely *everyone* makes a mess of something every now and then. We mess up our own lives and the lives of those we love the most by being impatient and selfish and unkind. From time to time, he shared with me his theory that there is a great potter in the heavens who stands ready and anxious to help us reach our potential if we invite Him to mold and shape our lives."

Jake stood and walked to the bedroom, returning with his sketchbook. He flipped it open and turned several pages before looking up. "We found this on Joseph's bench at the cemetery. "But now O Lord, thou art our father; we are the clay, and thou our potter; and we are all the works of thy hands."

"Ahh, yes, Isaiah 64: 8." Eric said with a smile. "It sounds so simple, doesn't it? The idea of allowing a wise and knowing Father to shape our lives as a potter does with clay. One of the most valuable truths Isaac taught me is the truth that God stands at the door and knocks, waiting to for us to invite Him in to shape our lives.[1] What a foolish thing pride is. It keeps us from understanding who we can become by separating us from the One who knows our potential, far beyond our own limited understanding. To a skilled potter, a block of clay is the embryo of beautiful and functional vessels. To everyone else, clay is merely dirt—without purpose or potential. So many lives are lost and so much potential is wasted by allowing fear and pride to dam-up our progression. I believe in a God with infinite goodness, infinite vision and infinite understanding. But God never forces that power and wisdom upon us. He waits for us to invite him in."

[1] Revelation 3:20

LEARNING FROM TROY

LOVE IS A PORTION OF THE SOUL ITSELF, AND IT IS OF THE SAME NATURE AS
THE CELESTIAL BREATHING OF THE ATMOSPHERE OF PARADISE.
—VICTOR HUGO—

Jake looked at Amy and nodded as Eric's words danced around in his brain. "I have to say, you're not anything like I expected you to be," he said, as he stood to clear the plates from the table.

"Is that good?" asked Eric, smiling.

"I think so. I figured you were just an eccentric cheese collector who wears funny clothes."

"And now?" Eric asked, eyebrows raised, as if he was trying to determine if he should be offended or not.

"And now I realize there's a lot more to see than your plaid pants or your cheese-head hat."

Eric smiled, nodding. "So the Trojan horse still works."

"What do you mean?" Amy asked, trying to hold back her laughter.

"I've learned that people are rarely as they appear to be. I've found that my talents and my apparel get me into places where I probably would never be welcome otherwise."

"So, you're saying you dress this way because it gets you past the guards at the gate?"

"Something like that."

"So once you get in, what do you do?" asked Jake.

"Well, I try to learn all I can about the people and the places I visit. If I were dressed as a National Geographic photographer or a priest of some sort, they might not trust me or give me the time of day, but if I show up as a famous cheese expert, dressed in silly clothes, I am a bit of a curiosity. People are disarmed and they invite me to warm myself at their fire. That is something we miss in our modern-day, Western society—the opportunity to sit down together at the end of the day and swap stories with the rest of the village. They inevitably want to hear from me, want to hear about my village and my people. That's when I get to tell them about Niederbipp."

Jake smiled. "So, you go all around the world telling people about Niederbipp?"

"That's part of it. They always want to see the Power Point too."

"How do people respond?" asked Amy.

"Oh, it really depends on the people. We forget sometimes that

America is the envy of the world. Hollywood reaches into the deepest of jungles and highest of mountains, and I've found that people throughout the world have a skewed understanding of who we really are because of it. Many people think we are all rich, that we live in mansions and that our fast cars are rivaled only by our fast women. Other people think we're violent, egotistical and wasteful. And though all those things are sometimes true, people around the world still look to America as a place of hope, as a place where dreams come true.

"I give presentations with the pictures I've taken from all around the world, but the presentation I show about Niederbipp is always the most requested. In some villages, I show the Niederbipp pictures night after night and tell them the stories of the people here who have helped me make sense of my life."

"Tell us what you mean—about the people who have helped you make sense of your life," Amy said.

Eric looked down at his hands and was silent for a long moment. When he spoke again, his voice was soft. "Remember how I mentioned that no one becomes a Candlelighter without experiencing a change of heart?"

Jake and Amy nodded.

"Well, my change of heart took place shortly after I moved here. I had a major weakness that challenged me and my state of happiness throughout the first thirty-something years of my life—impatience. I think I must have been impatient from birth. I couldn't wait to grow up to be like my older siblings. I couldn't wait to get my driver's license. I couldn't wait to graduate from high school. Then I couldn't wait to graduate from college and get to work. I was impatient with the women I dated. I was impatient with myself. I was impatient with my family. After I went off to the commune, I was impatient with my work there." He shook his head. "I used to measure the plants every day with a ruler and scream at the peas and the corn if they weren't growing fast enough."

"Did it work?" Amy asked, smiling.

"No. It gave me a way to vent for a while, but it wore off over time and left me even more impatient." He shook his head again. "My friends made me leave the garden permanently when they caught me pulling up the carrots to see if they were ready yet."

Jake and Amy looked at each other and laughed. "So, what happened?" asked Jake. "How did you overcome your impatience?"

"I think it started with the cheese. We started a fromagerie at the commune to use the extra milk from our cows and goats."

"But doesn't it take a long time to make cheese?" Amy asked.

"Forever!" Eric responded. "It nearly killed me. I never considered my impatience a weakness until that point. Do you realize there are nearly twenty steps in the cheesemaking process?"

Jake and Amy shook their heads.

"Yep, and each step requires time and patience. I quickly learned that the only process I could be fast about was the milking  of the cows and goats. I was the fastest milker in the commune. But after the milking was done, the process moved at a snail's pace. In the beginning, I ruined a lot of milk, trying to skip steps or do three of them at the same time. It was a joke, really. In the year that I ran the fromagerie, I made less than a hundred pounds of cheese."

"Was it any good?" asked Jake.

"I don't know. We sold the commune before the cheese was ready and I was so eager to get on the next thing in my life that I walked away from a year's worth of work without ever tasting it."

"Is that when you came here?" Amy asked.

"Yes. I received word that my grandfather had passed away just a few days before we sold the commune. My siblings and cousins came in for the funeral, but none of them had any desire to keep the shop going. I was thirty-three years old, single, and ready for a new start, so I took over the shop that had been in my family for five generations."

"No offense," Jake said, "but it seems kind of ironic that a man with no patience would become the owner of a watch shop."

"Yeah, hilarious, isn't it."

"How's it been?" asked Amy.

"Well, since the heart attack, it's been pretty good."

"What?" Jake and Amy asked in unison.

"Yeah, about three weeks after I moved in." He unbuttoned the top of his shirt and held it open to reveal a long, purple scar running down the length of his sternum, easily visible through his thick, white chest hair.

"How'd that happen?" Amy asked. "You were so young."

"Age has very little to do with it. Being around those clocks and watches all day long made my impatience run wild. I didn't notice until it was too late, that it had started a chain reaction, running my blood pressure through the roof. A lot of things go through your mind when you're thirty-three years old, lying in the hospital after nearly dying. Unlike you Jake, I was in the hospital for nearly a month, and the whole time I was there, I had only one visitor."

"Was it Isaac?" Amy asked.

Eric smiled, but shook his head. "No, I didn't get to know Isaac until later. It was my mother who came to be with me. My dad had been gone for several years by then, but my mom kept a vigil, spending every day for a month, sitting in a chair next to my bed, willing me to heal, telling me if I didn't get better, she'd kill me." Eric laughed. "Those were important days for me—days that brought healing to both my body and my soul as I listened to my mother pray for me.

"I hadn't had anything to do with my mother in years," Eric continued. "Since I'd graduated from college, I'd been home to visit only once—for my father's funeral, but my impatience and anxiousness to get back to my work kept me from connecting with anyone in my family. As I lay in my bed at the hospital with my loving mother watching over me, I began to wake up and realize what a fool I'd been. I'd been so anxious to get on to the next big thing in my life that I'd forgotten about what mattered most. That time gave me a chance to recognize that I'd filled my life with counterfeits and decoys of the real thing. After I recovered

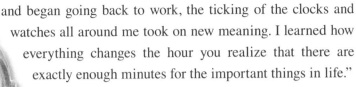

and began going back to work, the ticking of the clocks and watches all around me took on new meaning. I learned how everything changes the hour you realize that there are exactly enough minutes for the important things in life."

He lifted his wrist and held out his watch for both of them to see. "That realization caused me make a lot of changes in my life. Soon after, I removed the minute and second hands from my watch."

Jake and Amy smiled as they looked at Eric's watch, its single hand marking the hour.

"Ya know, minutes are important but never more important than people. I began learning those lessons in the hospital, and my learning continued when I became acquainted with Isaac."

"So, how did *that* happen?" asked Amy.

"There's an old Buddhist proverb that says 'when the student is ready, the teacher will appear.' "

Jake nodded, remembering his own experience with that truth.

"I was introduced to Isaac one Sunday. It had been years since I'd been to church. I hadn't had much time for God before my heart attack, but afterwards, I found myself with questions that I couldn't answer. Isaac invited me to dinner that night, along with several other people, and I remember watching him as he interacted with each of us—listening, laughing and sharing. I remember leaving this apartment, feeling as though a light in the basement of my soul had been turned on. That was all it took, at least to get me started down this path."

"So you spent a lot of time with Isaac?" asked Jake.

"Every chance I got. I started traveling with the Fromage bon vivants about five years after I came here, but for many years I spent as much time as I could with Isaac and the old men of Niederbipp. I never gave old folks much of a chance before then. Knowing what I know now, I wonder what I missed."

After they'd cleaned up and Eric had taken all the shots he wanted of the old pots, they went back to the studio. The kiln had reached temperature, so Jake donned the old leather gloves to protect his hands and arms as he slid the damper shut after turning off the gas. It was strange for Jake to have someone shadowing his every move with the black eye of the camera. It made him nervous, and he was happy when Eric moved on to take pictures of Amy who was working on the painting of the rocks she'd started on Saturday. Jake followed Eric, looking over his shoulder as his camera's shutter clicked repeatedly.

"Can I ask you something?" Jake asked after he'd watched Eric work for several minutes.

"Of course," Eric said, looking over his camera.

"You said something earlier—that when you graduated, you were determined to change the world."

Eric nodded.

"Do you feel like your dreams have come true?"

"I ask myself that question several times a year as I come and go. I'm not sure there is an easy answer. If I have changed the world, it's definitely not the way I believed I would."

"What does that mean exactly?" Jake asked.

Eric pinched the end of his mustache with his thumb and forefinger, looking very thoughtful. "I guess it means I've learned perspective. When I graduated from college and took that job in D.C., my ego played a big part of what I was and who I was planning on becoming. I don't think you can live in that world without an oversized ego. Sometimes, the noise and chaos gets so loud and out of hand in Washington that no one can hear the whisper of truth on the wind. For a long time after I left, I became so cynical that I completely gave up my dreams of changing anything."

"You don't seem very cynical anymore," Amy said, turning from her canvas to look at Eric. "How did you change your attitude?"

"Well, there really aren't any answers in pessimism or cynicism, are there? I'd been cynical for so many years that it took me a while to begin to see the truth that was right in front of me all my life."

"What truth are you referring to?" asked Amy.

"That change has to happen at a molecular level before it can have any effect on a larger scale. A lot of things changed in my life when I had my heart attack. It was during that time, when my heart was softened, that I began to think on a smaller scale. You know, it's funny that most of us believe that we have to leave home in order to change the world. I spent the first thirty-three years of my life thinking that—wanting so badly to have my name associated with some great thing or event. It was Isaac who taught me that changing the world begins with a change of heart."

He turned and looked at the row of mugs hanging from the overhead beam. "I've often thought that if every man could focus on the people all around him—like Isaac did, the whole world could be like Niederbipp."

"So, is that why you show people your pictures?" Amy asked. "Are you trying to help spread Niederbipp around the world?"

Eric smiled. "It's a crazy idea, isn't it? I thought it was when Isaac first told me about his idea, and maybe it is, but you know what? It works. Throughout the history of the world, the strong have conquered the weak with shock-and-awe campaigns, bringing them into submission with tactics rooted in fear. When Isaac first suggested to me that love could have at least equal power in its ability to change the world, I wondered if he might be crazy. But I watched him for a couple of years. I watched how his love and kindness created a chain that linked people together in a most amazing way, spanning age, gender, race and even economic status.

"It's so simple—that love can change the world, but I've seen it. I've fallen in love with people all over the world as I've shared my stories of Niederbipp. I was raised a Christian, but I don't think I ever really understood what it means to be one until I watched Isaac. Christianity is more than just a set of beliefs that we visit on Sunday. It's a way of living and breathing and loving."

"But how do you share your message with people who are hostile to Christianity?" Jake asked. "Is what you share welcome in Muslim or Buddhist countries?"

"Jake, the world has many different names for God, but I've found in my travels that with love and understanding, there is always more that makes men brothers than anything that makes them foes. Focusing on differences erects walls between neighbors—walls that dam us and our progression as members of the human family."

"That's beautiful," Amy said, looking very thoughtful. "But tell me, how do you get in—how do you even get a chance to share your message?"

"Remember the Trojan horse?"

She nodded.

"Well, try to imagine a Trojan horse with giant ears. I learned from watching Isaac that the sense of speech is the least important of our five senses, and though most of us have the gift of hearing, the ability to listen is something that has to be developed and learned. The customs of most of the places I travel are usually at least somewhat unfamiliar to me, but I've learned that if I watch and listen, I am usually given understanding. If there is a country or a people in this world without a portion of God's light within them, I have yet to visit that place. It is that light that makes us kin. It is recognizing that light in others that keeps me going."

"So, how do you share anything with people if they're not interested— or if they're satisfied with the amount of light they already have?" asked Jake.

"I learned a lot from watching Isaac. He often reminded me that light and truth come according to our ability to receive. If we use what we've been given and continue to petition the universe for more, more will be given to us."

"But if the people you visit already have some of that light that you're talking about, what makes them interested in getting more?" Jake continued.

"Most people don't know what they're missing until they recognize in someone else a brighter portion of light."

"Is that what Candlelighters do?" Amy asked excitedly. "Do they try to make the world hungry for more truth?"

"In so many words, yes."

"That sounds just like Gloria and Joseph," Jake offered. "I always feel so much love oozing out of them—so much warmth and kindness. I felt a strange connection to them from the first time I met them."

"They said the same thing about you," Eric said with a smile. "They're good people—some of the best folks I've ever known. I've learned a lot from them over the years."

"Like what?" Amy asked.

"I've learned that humility plays an essential role in one's ability to share anything. I've learned that light loses its power if you ever begin to believe you're a rock star—that it can never be about you. In the very moment we begin to believe that we deserve a portion of the glory for the light we've been given, that light begins to fade. We may be able to maintain the counterfeits of light—popularity or wealth, for example, but though those counterfeits sometimes  share a semblance of real light, they are usually only polished brass that may glow on the outside, but within, are tarnished and corrupt."

Jake shook his head. "Isn't that really hard?" he asked, turning to each of them. "Am I the only one who thinks it's difficult not to get excited about personal triumphs and achievements?"

"Of course not, Jake. We all want to be successful—we all want to be noticed for our hard work, endurance and success. But there's a big difference between glorying in ones own achievements and giving credit to God and everyone else who helped you get there. If people aren't careful, they begin to believe they are *self-made*. And when that happens … well, pride creates a slippery slope from there. Over the years, I have met a lot of people across the world, but I have yet to meet even one person who can embrace pride without it going to his head.

Pride is such a divider. It robs us all of the brotherly love God intended us to have, making us believe we are somehow better than our neighbor, and lifting us up on self-inflated foundations filled with hot air.

"People across the globe are looking for the light and are kept from it only because they either don't know where to find it or because some people are selfish with the light they've been given."

"So if this life is about finding light and strengthening our own, why does there have to be darkness?" Amy asked.

"Could we have any appreciation for light *without* darkness?" Eric responded.

The question caught Amy off guard and she paused to think.

"Having the contrast offers us a decision, doesn't it?" Eric continued. "And it seems to me that with each decision, there comes with it the potential for growth and understanding as we move either further into the light—or further into the darkness."

Amy nodded, a look of excitement spreading across her face. "I feel like this is part of the light I'm supposed to be sharing," she said, pointing her paintbrush at her painting. "I first discovered the light and the reality of God's love for me through painting."

Eric smiled and his face radiated kindness. "Isaac taught me that each of us is given a portion of God's light to share with the world in the form of our talents and passions."

"That's a powerful idea," Amy responded.

"I thought so too. The hard thing is—the darkness of this world knows the power of light. It does all it can to try to snuff it out—to discourage us from developing the talents with which we've been entrusted. It aims to keep us from nurturing that light before it has the power to shatter that darkness."

Amy nodded knowingly, turning to Jake. "Thanks for not letting me give up."

Jake nodded. "It's easy to support you in doing what you were obviously created to do."

"It's important to have good friends," Eric said, pointing to the mugs

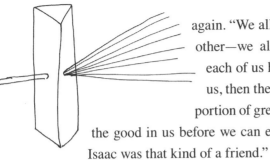

again. "We all have light to share with each other—we all have something to give. If each of us has a seed of godliness within us, then there must be within each of us a portion of greatness. Good friends often see the good in us before we can even recognize it in ourselves. Isaac was that kind of a friend."

"How did he do that?" Jake asked. "How did he do that for so many people?"

"Isaac once told me that most of us have the answers within us. Sometimes, we just need help deciphering the inspiration we receive."

"But that's just it—that deciphering. Isn't that the hard part?" Jake asked.

Eric nodded. "Probably not as hard as it sometimes feels. I once met a Candlelighter while I was on assignment in Switzerland. She was a physicist who'd helped in the pioneering development of fiber optic communications, but her expertise was in the area of dividing light into its range of colors. She invited me to her home one afternoon  and as we entered her office, I was astounded by the light and color that danced on the walls. She had a set of prisms hanging from an open window which divided the light into the full spectrum of colors. I learned from that visit that light is colorful and exciting. Although each of us responds to light, we each do it a different way. She reminded me that God's light, with its full spectrum of color, enters every human heart, customized to the person who receives it. Deciphering, more than anything, is about tuning your heart to the frequency of the light you receive. It requires practice and patience, but I believe in a God who is anxious to speak to *all* his children—who is waiting for us to listen."

"I don't suppose you have any secret formulas that would make that listening part a bit easier?" Jake queried.

LISTEN

Eric raised one eyebrow. "There is a formula, but I'm certain you already know what it is."

Jake looked at Amy, then back at Eric. "I'm not sure I do," he said sheepishly.

Eric nodded. "It's an easy thing to forget. That's why Isaac wrote it down in many places—even commissioned an old woodcarver to carve it into the limb of a special old tree down by the river." He smiled at Jake and Amy as their expressions registered their understanding.

"Be still and know that I am God," Amy said softly.

"Exactly."

"Thomas called that the eleventh commandment," she added.

"That's what Isaac called it too. He told me he figured it was one of the very most important of the commandments—that all the other commandments made more sense if you could recognize that there is a God. I remember him saying many times that if more people would take the time to be still, our world would be a more gentle and peaceful place. He suggested that in order to receive light and truth, taking the time to be still was the first step—the minimum price to pay."

Jake looked up. "What do you mean by that—the minimum price to pay?"

Eric looked at his watch before looking back at Jake. "That is probably a lesson for another day, but it's a good place to end. It should give you something to think about. The best answers in life are the ones the universe whispers in our ears after we've asked the right questions and made our investment."

THE CONSPIRACY

TRUE GODLINESS DOESN'T TURN MEN OUT OF THE WORLD BUT ENABLES
THEM TO LIVE BETTER IN IT AND EXCITES THEIR ENDEAVORS TO MEND IT.
—WILLIAM PENN—

ake and Amy spent the early afternoon working in the studio. While Amy made progress on her painting for the Garbers, Jake worked on Mr. Allan's Journey Jars. He decided he should make a few extra to be certain he'd have enough in case any of them were damaged in the firings. With July Fourth just twelve days away, he was nervous that they would not be done in time. He tried not to think about the deadline as he worked.

His sketchbook had many pages filled with doodles of Journey Jars—tall ones, fat ones, some with feet, and several with two openings as Mr. Allan had requested. As Jake drew those with two openings, he was reminded of the double-necked wedding vases he'd seen in the small giftshop just outside of the Acoma Pueblo in New Mexico three summers earlier. A small card attached to the vase explained how the vases were traditionally used by the people of the Hopi mesas to symbolize the coming together of two people and two families to form a new union. The bride and groom would each drink from the vase as part of the marriage ceremony, and then it would be kept in a place of honor in the couple's home to remind them of their union and covenant.

It really hadn't meant much to Jake at the time. It was an interesting idea, but as he thought about it now, he was surprised by the depth of meaning behind the vases. He even remembered the interlocking swirl pattern on one of the vases, colored with black and white on the front, a symbol, he'd learned, signifying a coming-together.

Turning from his sketchbook, he began cutting and altering the forms he'd thrown on the wheel earlier that morning. The work was different from anything he'd done before, but it was creative and fun and opened his mind to new possibilities. Like the teapots he'd made in college, the Journey Jars were complicated, having multiple pieces—lids, handles and feet.

As they worked, they talked about Eric and his visit and the "minimum investment" of taking the time to be still. Amy asked if Jake had had any more thoughts about Sam's letters to his son Matthew. He admitted he had, but wasn't any more confident about how he might get them out of the bakery than he was when he came up with the idea. Amy confessed that she still didn't understand but agreed to be his accomplice if Jake believed they might help.

Gloria stopped by just before five to congratulate them and announce that Mr. Allan's daughter, Cindy, had agreed to come to town for the party and was working on her brothers. Jake left the women alone to talk and made his escape to the bakery to begin the grout work on the new mosaic. As if on cue, Sam met him at the front door and locked the big glass doors behind him.

"So, how'd it go this morning?" Sam asked, expectantly. "Did you share the torte or eat it alone?"

Jake laughed. "I shared it. We're getting married on July fifth if all goes as we hope."

"You know, Jake, you had me worried there for a while, but you're really not as dumb as you look."

"Gee, thanks," said Jake, trying to keep a straight face. "I appreciate that. And thanks for the torte. I think it helped her make the decision."

Sam smirked. "You've already earned three years' worth of bread. You don't need to butter me up."

"Okay," Jake said, smiling. "But thanks." He looked down at the tiles at his feet. "Are you ready to get started?"

"In a minute. I picked up a grout trowel this afternoon over at the hardware store, and I think we have plenty of grout. I've got some chocolate milk in the cooler. Do you want to relax a minute before we get started?"

Jake was more interested in just getting done so he could get on with whatever the evening would bring, but as he looked at Sam's face, the memory of his conversation with Eric told him to relax and take his time. He agreed, and soon they were sitting together at the table in the back room, enjoying the day's leftover pastries and tall mugs filled with chocolate milk. Jake just let Sam talk, trying to be patient as he surveyed the room. Against the far wall, high on a shelf next to a stack of dusty baskets, he saw two mugs. They, too, were covered with a thin layer

of white dust, but he could still make out the words carved deep in the mugs' sides—"Prez" and "Vice."

Trying hard not to stare, Jake glanced at the mugs again and again. He knew it had been at least eight years since those mugs had been used by their owners, yet there they sat, ready and waiting to be filled once again. As Sam spoke, Jake's mind wandered to the eclectic set of mugs hanging in The Pottery. He'd already met most of the mug owners, yet there were still a few that hung there, covered in unknown years' worth of dust. The two collections of mugs were different in many ways, but Jake wondered if Isaac had ever awaited the visit of any of the mug owners in the same way he knew Sam longed for the return of his estranged son. These thoughts filled Jake with a melancholy feeling. Before Saturday, Sam had always seemed like a happy and jovial person. Learning of his past and current heartache had surprised Jake, yet he knew it was the truth. Lost in his thoughts, he didn't notice that Sam had gotten to his feet until he set down the new trowel in front of him.

"Do you think this will work?" Sam asked.

Jake took the handle. Closing his hand around it, he felt the pain of the blisters he'd acquired two days before when they'd laid the mosaic. "This looks like a good one," he finally said. "Are you ready to get started?"

As Jake mixed the grout in the same bucket he used for the mortar, he continued to think about the mugs on Sam's shelf. He wondered how Matthew might respond to seeing his old mug. He knew it would be easier to get the mug out of the shop than it would to get a shoe box full of letters out of a cellar he had never seen. He'd never stolen anything in his life, unless you counted the pack of gum he stole from the drugstore when he was five. When his mother discovered the stolen gum, she'd marched him right back to the store to apologize and pay for the contraband. But this was different. This was much bigger—eight years' worth of heartfelt letters and a mug that held untold sentimental

value. Could he do it? Could he essentially steal these items from the man who'd fed him and befriended him and trusted him?

As Jake knelt on the tile to begin the grouting, he winced at the pain in his knees, kneeling on the bruises he'd acquired on Saturday. He tried in vain to find a way to kneel that didn't hurt, and finally gave up, deciding instead to try to hurry. He scooped up a huge dollop of the soft grout with the rubber trowel and plopped it onto the mosaic, spreading it quickly into the crevices. Sam stood with his hands on his hips, watching Jake work in silence. Using the edge of the trowel like a squeegee, Jake went over the tile again and again, cleaning off the excess grout and exposing the tiles he and Amy had made. The grout made it look so much better, clean and finished. He scooped another dollop of grout from the bucket and was spreading it when a shadow crossed over his work. He turned to see Amy standing at the locked bakery doors. She winked at him and then waved at Sam who motioned for her to go around to the back door.

As Jake worked, waiting for them to come back, he said a silent prayer, petitioning the heavens for direction. He knew the relationship between Sam and his son was none of his business, but he couldn't dismiss the feelings he'd had. He had no idea what would come of his idea, even if he were able somehow to pull it off, but as he prayed, he knew he had to try. He considered just asking Sam for the letters. Surely it would be easier than trying to sneak them out—trying to steal them like a thief in the night, but he knew somehow he couldn't do that. Sam would have too many questions he couldn't answer without betraying the trust Charlie had given him. With the realization of what he had to do, his prayers changed, praying that Sam would understand, for surely he would find out. Though the idea was flawed, it was the only idea he had—the only idea he'd been given. His adrenaline was already flowing. He knew what he had to do.

STEPPING INTO THE DARK

THERE ARE ONLY TWO MISTAKES ONE CAN MAKE ALONG THE ROAD TO
TRUTH; NOT GOING ALL THE WAY, AND NOT STARTING.
—BUDDHA—

"Are you done yet?" Amy asked playfully as she strolled into the bakery's showroom, alone.

Jake tried to smile, but instead, his face showed signs of both stress and pain. "Where's Sam?"

"He's tied up."

"What?" Jake asked, laughing. "You tied him up?"

"Well, so to speak. I enlisted some help."

"From whom?"

"Nancy. She stopped by to check on the painting right after Gloria left. She heard we got engaged and offered to help. That's when I got the idea." She smiled mischeviously.

"And what idea was that?"

"I told her we needed her to distract Sam for a few minutes while we worked on a surprise for him. She suggested she could talk to him about our wedding cake, but she said she could probably only guarantee us about ten minutes."

Jake laughed, rolling over to sit on his rear end to alleviate the pain in his knees. "You're brilliant. Now we just have to figure out where the cellar is."

"Are you kidding?" Amy asked.

"No, why? Do you know where it is?"

"Yeah, I just walked past it on my way in. The door is wide open."

Jake shook his head, reaching up for Amy to take his hand. She pulled him up and they hurried into the back room where the trap door to the cellar was up, exposing the dark hole in the floor. Seven old wooden treads descended into the darkness. Jake looked at Amy and smiled timidly as he stepped onto the top stair. He knew he didn't have time to waste, but the darkness slowed his  progress until his eyes began to adjust. The cellar was dusty and full of junk. He stumbled over a dozen old broom handles before he found his footing on the earthen floor. The ceiling was low and Jake crouched, moving further in, unsure of where he should be looking. He bumped into a stack of rusty loaf tins, knocking them over against the wall with a loud clang that scared him so badly he jolted upwards, hitting his head on the rafters and causing him to bite his tongue. He tasted blood and spit on the floor.

"Are you okay?" Amy asked, sitting down on the top step, peering into the darkness.

"Yeah, I'm fine," Jake said, rubbing his head. "Didn't Thomas say they were just inside here somewhere?"

"Yeah, I thought so." She looked from side to side, hoping the shoe box had just been overlooked, but there was no sign of it. Jake groped his way to the back of the cellar, but returned to the stairs empty-handed. He looked very disappointed.

"Well, so much for that idea," he said, stretching as he stood to his full height at the stairs.

"Where do you think they are?" Amy asked.

"Who knows? It's been a few months since Thomas said he saw them. Sam must have moved them."

"So, what are we going to do?"

Jake shook his head. "I don't know. I guess it was just a dumb idea." He looked up at the two mugs on the edge of the shelf. "There's still that," Jake said, pointing toward them.

Amy turned to look. "Are those the mugs Thomas told us about?"

"I'm sure they are. I feel like we need to borrow one," Jake said, gently nudging Amy, encouraging her to stand so he could climb out.

He walked to the shelf and pulled the dusty mug from its resting place, putting the mug he'd used earlier in its position. "Do you mind taking this back to The Pottery?"

"No. Should I come back and look for the letters?"

Jake looked around the room. There was no sign of the letters anywhere. "I don't think so. I don't think we have any time. Sam will be back and Charlie and Jodi are going to be leaving soon. This mug will have to do."

Amy nodded. She quickly washed the mug off and dried it before kissing Jake and hurrying out the back door.

Jake got back to work and was nearly finished with the grout when Sam returned fifteen minutes later. Sam watched in silence as Jake went over the floor one more time with a big sponge, cleaning the excess grout off the tiles.

"How's it look?" Jake asked as he stood and straightened himself.

"It's beautiful," Sam said, but his voice trailed off without another word.

Jake looked at his work, proud of the way it had turned out and feeling an unexpected sense of relief that the project was finally done.

"I started this project a couple of years ago, hoping to leave it a better place for whoever took over. Now that it's done, I guess I ..." Sam trailed off, and silence fell as he stared at the finished floor.

"I'd better get these buckets cleaned out," Jake said as he picked up the grout and water buckets and headed for the back room. He was just rinsing them when Sam walked in and leaned his backside against the counter. "Thank you, Jake. It really is beautiful—far better than I could have hoped for."

Jake nodded, smiling. "Can I put these away for you?" Jake asked, motioning to the tools and buckets.

"If you don't mind, they go down in the cellar."

"Not at all," Jake said, picking up the buckets and heading toward the stairs, hoping another look in the cellar might expose a hidden shoe box somewhere. He returned a minute later, disappointed.

Sam thanked him again and as Jake wandered back to The Pottery, he wondered why he'd felt so strongly about the letters. It was a letdown. Everything had fallen into place in an amazing way—everything, except for the letters. Where were they? Had Sam moved them to another place? Had he given up hope and finally thrown them away? As Jake walked through the back door of the studio, his answer came. Charlie was there with Jodi, their backs toward him. They were talking to Amy, and under Charlie's arm was a black shoe box, the word "Florsheim", printed on all sides."

THE WAY OF PEACE IS THE WAY OF LOVE
-PEACE PILGRIM-

REAL NIEDERBIPPIANS

WE MUST LEARN TO REAWAKEN AND KEEP OURSELVES AWAKE,
NOT BY MECHANICAL AID, BUT BY AN INFINITE EXPECTATION OF THE DAWN.
—HENRY DAVID THOREAU—

lease tell me that's the box we've been looking for," Jake said, surprised by the relief he felt at seeing it.

Amy smiled as Charlie and Jodi turned.

"We were just telling Amy about this," Charlie said, handing Jake the black shoe box.

As he took it in his hands, Jake was surprised by how heavy it was. The twine that kept it shut was pulled tight, compressing the letters into a solid bundle, forcing the lid to bulge.

"I guess Thomas beat you to it. He dropped that box off at my mom's place an hour ago. He said he tried bringing it here but remembered that you'd be at the bakery and didn't want to go looking for you there and arouse any suspicion, especially since he knows Sam will to eventually notice the letters are missing."

"I knew this had to happen," Jake said, looking up to smile at Amy, but his expression quickly changed. "Wait, how did Thomas know we wanted them. We didn't tell him anything, did we?" He looked at Amy, confused.

"We probably had something to do with that," Charlie admitted. "When you told us yesterday about the letters and your idea of getting them to Matt, it got us thinking."

"Yeah, we both thought it was worth a try to take them to Matt, like you said," Jodi added. "We tried to put ourselves in Matt's shoes. I obviously don't know him, but if it were me, I'd love to have eight years' worth of letters from my dad, even if I had sent them back unopened. We talked to Thomas this morning about your idea, figuring he might know where the letters were kept."

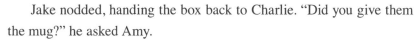

"He was more than willing to help," Charlie said. "He only asked that we keep it quiet that he had anything to do with it."

Jake nodded, handing the box back to Charlie. "Did you give them the mug?" he asked Amy.

"We've got it right here," Jodi said, holding up a brown paper bag.

"We actually need to be on our way," Charlie said. "I called Matt this morning to let him know we were in the neighborhood and asked if we might stop by to see him this evening. They're expecting us around eight and we figure it's about an hour away."

Jake nodded, extending his hand. "Then may the force be with you," he said with a grin.

Charlie set the box down and took Jake's hand, pulling him in for a man hug. "I'm glad you're here, Jake." He patted his back a few times before letting him go. "I'm not sure what it is, but this shop still feels like home." He turned and gave Amy a hug, too, as Jodi slipped past to embrace Jake.

"Can we take you two to dinner next time we're in town?" Charlie asked as he picked up the shoe box.

"No," Jake said, "But you can come to dinner at our house. You guys are always welcome here."

Charlie took a deep breath and nodded, choking back his emotion.

Jodi gave Amy a hug before they slipped out of The Pottery's back door and got into their car, the words, "Just Married," scrawled on the back window in pink lipstick. Jake leaned against the door frame and waved as they pulled away.

"What are you thinking?" Amy asked as they watched the car drive out of the courtyard.

"I was just hoping we made the right decision—about the letters and the mug. It's really none of our business, you know."

Amy lifted his arm and draped it around her shoulders, cuddling up against him. "I know," she said softly. "I have no idea what may come of this. We might have just forfeited three years' worth of bread, but … but my intuition tells me we made the right decision."

Jake nodded, taking a deep breath. "I guess maybe it is our business," he said after a long silence.

"What do you mean?"

"I suppose it's time we start acting like real Niederbippians."

Amy smiled, snuggling closer. "Let's go for a walk."

"Okay. Where do you want to go?"

"I think we'd better figure out what kind of a wedding we're going to have. I thought we could talk to my aunt and uncle. Besides, I'm hungry and I'm not in the mood to cook. I'm sure we could bum some food from them."

As they walked up Hauptstrasse, hand in hand, the reality of what they were doing began to sink in. He'd proposed to Amy. They were getting married in thirteen days. They were on their way to talk to her aunt and uncle about their plans. It was a strange feeling—a strange realization. He was excited, but he couldn't deny that part of him was also nervous. He'd never been engaged before. He looked at their reflection in the shop windows. He was holding Amy's hand—the hand he'd held so many times before—the hand he would hold for the rest of their life together. As he watched the evening light dance on her amber hair, a jolt went through his body. This was the girl he was going to spend the rest of his life with! He loved her and he knew that she loved him. They had already shared so much together and his excitement for the future increased when he thought of all they would share in the future.

"Jake, Amy," came a voice from the trellis covered stairs that led to the churchyard. They turned to see Sandy, dressed in her blue scrubs, and Andrew, her fiancé.

"Hey, what are you guys doing?" Jake asked, veering off to the right to meet them.

"We were just out for a walk. It's such a beautiful evening. I understand congratulations are in order," Sandy said with a broad grin. "I guess you didn't need to worry after all," she added, looking at Amy.

"How'd you find out?" Jake asked. "I just proposed this morning."

"Oh, I overheard one of the phlebotomists talking about it this afternoon," Sandy said, reaching for Amy's left hand. "I think you better get a ring on this girl's hand, Jake." She winked at Amy, and Jake watched out of the corner of his eye as Amy smiled.

"Are there any good jewelers around here?" Jake asked. "We haven't gotten that far yet."

"Yeah, there's a nice little shop, just this side of Warren on Highway 66," Andrew replied. "It's a small, family-run business, but they have a nice selection. It's called Castleton's."

Jake looked at Amy. "Maybe we could go up tomorrow during lunch."

"Sure," she answered.

"So, when's your big day?" Sandy asked.

"My family will all be here for the Fourth of July weekend, so we're hoping to get married on Sunday, the fifth."

"That's great," Andrew said. "We'll be getting married just the week after."

"Where are you getting married?" Amy asked.

"Here, at the church," Sandy said. "My family is Catholic and Andrew's is Lutheran, so we figured a Quaker church would be the perfect neutral ground."

"Is Thomas going to marry you?" Jake asked.

"No, we thought about it. We even talked to Thomas about it, but the more we learned about the Quaker wedding ceremony, we decided it would be better in keeping with our desire for neutrality," said Sandy. "What are you guys going to do?"

"We're trying to figure that out. We were actually just on our way to talk to my aunt and uncle about it. I've got Quaker roots and I think we're both kind of leaning that way."

"Well, after that showdown you had last weekend with your dad, Amy, you might be careful," said Sandy. "From what I understand, anyone who attends a Quaker wedding has the opportunity to give advice or share their thoughts and feelings."

Amy nodded, but she wore a worried look on her face.

"We've been meaning to stop by and talk to you about that," Andrew added. "Sandy and I were both impressed with how you handled that situation, Jake. I didn't even really know you guys, and no offense, Amy, but I really wanted to punch your dad in the face."

"We all did," said Sandy. "How's that working out?"

"I don't know. They're coming here for a marriage workshop the same weekend we're getting married. I'm trying not to worry about it."

Sandy nodded. "Good for you."

"Do you guys come from normal families?" asked Amy.

"Is there any such thing?" Andrew responded, stifling a laugh. "I think the only normal families are the ones you don't know very well."

"We were actually just discussing how we're going to keep my aunt, who is a very outspoken nun, away from Andrew's brother and his rather flamboyant partner. This is definitely going to be interesting."

"Did you ever consider eloping?" asked Amy.

Sandy and Andrew looked at each other and laughed. "Yes, we did," said Andrew.

"We still do," added Sandy. "But this is our home and our wedding. Our families may have their differences—and more than their share of strange personalities, but we plan to make this the only time we ever get married. We've talked about not inviting some of our family that we thought might cause problems, but we decided that since our wedding would link two families together for the rest of our lives, we'll invite everybody and let them make the decision whether they'll attend or not. So far, everyone is planning on being here, and though we're still a little worried, we feel like we made the right choice to include everyone. It seems like we have enough to worry about without spending our time imagining potential catastrophes."

Jake and Amy smiled.

"Well, we'd better not keep you. It sounds like you guys have a lot to figure out in the next few days," said Andrew. "To be honest, I'm a little bit jealous of the way you're doing it. We've spent the last six months making plans and we thought we were keeping it pretty simple."

"I've been trying to tell Andrew that nothing is simple with a Type A woman involved, especially when it's her wedding. Maybe we could take some pointers in simplicity from you guys."

Jake laughed and looked over at Amy. "We'd love to have you guys come to our wedding," he said, turning back to them. "We're not sure when it will be exactly, but we'll let you know when we find out."

"We'll be there," Sandy said enthusiastically. "We wouldn't miss it. Niederbippians have to stick together."

IN DEFENSE OF VIRTUE

THE REASON WHY THE WORLD LACKS UNITY, AND LIES BROKEN AND IN
HEAPS, IS BECAUSE MAN IS DISUNITED WITH HIMSELF.
—RALPH WALDO EMERSON—

"Well, to what do we owe this honor?" Jerry said, as he strolled into the kitchen. Bev had already dished them up large portions of her famous chicken broccoli casserole. "We've been wondering if we were going to hear from you two tonight at all. I don't like finding out from second-hand sources that my favorite niece is getting married."

"I'm sorry, Uncle Jerry," Amy said, standing to hug her uncle.

"You can't tell me you were surprised," Jake responded.

"No, I suppose you're right. I just thought I'd hear it from one of you first, not from Patrick Stevens and Stan Robertson and Jesse Thomas and a half dozen other guys who came in to get their hair cut. You two have been the talk of the town all day. Congratulations."

"Thanks," Jake said, offering Jerry his hand. "We're sorry we didn't let you know first. It's been a busy day."

"Yes, we heard that too. Have you called your folks yet?"

"No, I guess I ought to let them know," said Amy.

"Oh, you're too late for that," Bev responded.

"You called them?" asked Amy.

"No, your mother called here just after noon to see what we knew."

"How'd she find out?" Amy asked, surprised.

"Oh, Patrick Schneider, your father's old buddy, called him this morning to spread the news," reported Bev.

"What did my mom say?"

"She told me to tell you she loves you and is happy for you and asked me to make sure you call as soon as you can. She's called several times in the past couple of hours to see if we've seen you. We finally took the phone off the hook."

"I'm sorry. I'll call her after we eat."

Bev nodded. "So, tell us about your plans. We've had several people ask, and I don't have any answers."

"I'm not sure we do either," Amy responded. "We were actually hoping to ask for some advice."

"About what?" asked Bev.

"Jake and I have been talking about the wedding, and we wondered what you can tell us about a Quaker ceremony."

"What do you know?" Jerry asked.

"Not very much. We just spoke to Sandy and Andrew. They said they're having a Quaker wedding but warned us after the fiasco at Robintino's with my dad that everyone is allowed to share their thoughts at a Quaker wedding. I'm not sure I'm ready to hear everything that could come out of my father's mouth, or my brothers' for that matter."

"When you open things up like that for anyone to say what is on their mind," said Jerry, "there will always be the possibility of ugliness, but the probability of beauty should overshadow that fear. We've attended hundreds of Quaker weddings over the years, and every one of them has been a positive event."

"So, besides the fact that everyone can say something at a Quaker wedding, how are they different from any other wedding ceremony?" asked Jake.

"Well, to begin with, there is no priest or magistrate to conduct the ceremony."

"So, who performs the wedding then?" asked Jake.

"You have to think about it differently than you've imagined weddings or seen them portrayed in the movies," said Bev. "Remember that there is no paid ministry in the Quaker church, as we believe all people are equal in the sight of God. Because of that, everyone who attends the wedding is considered an officiant, and they all sign the marriage certificate as witnesses. We keep ours in our bedroom." She stood and walked out of the kitchen, returning seconds later with a large wooden frame, setting it on an empty chair. The certificate, written in fine calligraphy, was beautifully embellished with ornate flowers, hand-painted with watercolor.

"I always joke around with your uncle that this is my certificate of ownership."

"Who made this?" Amy asked, moving closer to examine it.

"My mother—your grandmother. She made the certificates for all the weddings from the time she was sixteen until she passed away."

"No one ever told me she was an artist," Amy said, running her finger over the glass covering the small flowers at the top of the certificate.

"Well, that doesn't surprise me too much. Your grandmother quietly did what she did without drawing any attention to herself. This was her wedding gift to us. I know she spent many hours working on it—she did for each of the certificates she made. She'd usually do her work on the kitchen table, late at night when the kids had gone to bed. I'm sure your father knew about it."

Jake moved closer as well. Amy rested the tip of her index finger at the top of the certificate where an eye was partially hidden within the vines. "Is this The All Seeing Eye of God?" she asked.

"Yes," replied Jerry. "Our brand of Quakerism believes that marriage is a covenant, not only between a husband and wife. We also invite God to be a partner in that covenant. I knew that, of course, when we got married, but I used to think that eye looked a lot like your grandfather's eye." Jerry smiled. "I wondered if it wasn't some way of suggesting that he was watching me to make sure I treated his daughter well. And maybe that was true either way."

"What do you mean, either way?" asked Jake.

Jerry looked thoughtful. "I suppose it's easy for me to imagine a loving God because of the way our fathers were with us. And because of that, I knew what would be expected of me long before I asked Bev's father for his daughter's hand in marriage. As I've thought about it over the years, I have recognized that God's expectations  are at least as high as the expectations held by her earthly father. I have forgotten these things from time to time over the years—I'm sure we both have," he said, reaching for Bev's hand. "But we've both recognized a direct correlation between a happy marriage, and remembering that through it all, God is our partner in this marriage. We can do a lot of things, but we can't do everything, and I don't believe we were ever meant to do it all on our own. Bev and I have tried to teach that to our children throughout their lives, but especially as they have prepared to marry.

"We talked about this a little when you came to get your haircut, Jake. If we believe there is a God in the heavens who cares about his children, we have to believe he cares a great deal about the unions that partner with Him in bringing those children into this world. Of course we all know that children can and often do come without a good union or without any union at all, but Bev and I were taught that marriage was established by God for the safekeeping of His children and to give order to our world. And we believe He wants to help us succeed."

He smiled at Bev and squeezed her hand before turning back to look at Jake and Amy. With his free hand, he pointed at the certificate. "Some people say that it's only a piece of paper, but to us it represents so much more than that—it represents a lifetime commitment and a covenant between two people and God and his angels. That's the meaning of the eye to me. There have been many nights over the last fifty-plus years that we have both gone to bed upset with the trials of the day, but without fail, that eye seems to find a way to look into my soul and remind me, both of my responsibilities, and of the help available to me if I'll ask. My father taught me that God expects us to do all we can to make our marriages work and succeed, but He never expected us to do it alone—without *His* help."

Jake forced a smile when Amy turned to look at him. "What's wrong?" she asked.

He shook his head. "I understand that this is the way it should be, but neither of us have great examples to follow. Everything I know about my dad—and my parents' marriage—and then what I've seen of your parents—I guess my feelings for God are obviously different than what I feel for my dad, but …"

Jerry nodded. "I'm sorry Jake. By saying those things, I didn't mean to get you thinking about painful memories."

"It's okay. You know, as I was listening to you talk about your fathers, a picture came into my mind of what I'd like my dad to be like, if I had a choice. I think I'd like him to be like Isaac."

Beverly smiled. "I know Isaac would be proud of you, Jake. He would have loved you like a son. I wish you could have come a year earlier—to have spent the last months with him. I wish you could have known him."

Jake swallowed hard, trying to keep his emotions under control. "I'm sorry I didn't get to know who he really was, but the things I've learned from all of you—the legacy he's left behind—hearing those stories has made me a better man. It has made be want to become like Isaac."

"You couldn't have a had better teacher," Jerry said. "You two may not have great examples within your families, but that can be a blessing too, if you let it."

"How do you figure?" asked Amy.

"Neither of you believes you came from a perfect home."

"And that's a blessing? I think it would be nice to have a normal family," Amy responded.

Jerry laughed out loud. "I invite you to search the whole world over, and I guarantee you'll never find a *normal* family—whatever that means. We're all broken, somehow. Being able to acknowledge that you're broken can be a great blessing as it fosters humility." Jerry stood from the table and walked away, returning a few moments later with another frame.

"*My* mother gave this to us for our wedding," he said, handing it to Jake and Amy. It was a cross-stitched design of a house with the words, "Except the Lord build the house, they labour in vain that build it." [1]

Amy read it aloud a second time before looking up. "She stitched an eye over the door," she said, pointing at the tiny stitches.

"Yes. She gave this to us after we returned from our honeymoon," said Jerry. "It was wrapped in a piece of fabric that turned out to be an apron for Bev."

"I remember thinking it was a rather odd-looking thing," Bev added. "The fabric for the ties didn't match the apron's fabric at all. But then I recognized the print on the material as the same fabric as the apron she wore every day. She had cut the apron strings from her apron and sewn them onto mine. It came with a

[1] Psalms 127:1

beautiful note that said she'd done her best to raise her son to be a man and it was up to me to finish the work she'd begun. She also told me she'd stay out of our business, which she did—for the most part. I didn't fully understand it at the time, but that was one of the most important and meaningful gifts I've ever received."

"Without examples in your own family that you want to follow, or pesky parents trying to make sure you do what they did, you'll be able to create your own nest with the principles that make the most sense to you," Jerry added. "You both have a good head on your shoulders, and from the sounds of it, enough faith and good sense to invite God's wisdom and influence into your lives."

Amy put her arm on Jake's shoulder. "My aunt and uncle have always been good at making lemonade out of lemons."

"What else is there to do?" Bev asked, matter of factly.

Amy leaned over the table, resting on her elbows. "Tell me something, why haven't you talked to me about this spiritual stuff before?"

"Because you haven't asked," Bev responded.

"But you guys are Candlelighters, aren't you?"

Jerry and Bev looked at each other and smiled. "Who told you that?" Jerry responded.

"Does it matter?"

"Not really. It's been more than thirty years since we learned about being a Candlelighter, but it still isn't easy for either of us to wear it on our sleeve—and we're not really supposed to. Each of us has to decide how we'll share the light and knowledge we've been entrusted with. Some are very good at sharing with large numbers of people. Your aunt and I have always felt more comfortable working one-on-one."

Amy looked surprised, but the look quickly changed to one of understanding. "Is that why you always made me feel like your daughter instead of just your niece."

"No, we did it because we love you," Jerry said with a wink and a smile.

"I know that, but you always treated me differently than you did any of my brothers."

"That's because what we saw in you from the time you were a child made us think you were different from your brothers, Amy." Bev reached across the table and squeezed Amy's hand. "You were born with a brighter light in your eyes than most kids have—brighter than all your brothers. We wondered for a while if it was just because you are a girl, but your uncle and I both knew you would grow up to be different from the rest of your family. We tried to nurture the light you came with without getting in your father's way."

Amy furrowed her brow. "So, why didn't you ever just tell me this stuff before?"

"We wanted to, Amy. We've tried to share it with you, a little here and a little there, to see how you'd respond. There are many who are given more light than they can handle, and turn away in fear because of it. We wanted you to discover the light that was within you," Jerry explained. "We all have a portion of God's light given to us that often lies dormant until it's nurtured and fed. Your aunt and I watched Isaac work with people for many years, helping them discover that light within their souls. We tried to do the same with you and whoever else we sensed was ready to hear."

"But I could have avoided a lot of pain if I understood these things earlier."

"Yes, and we're sorry about that, Amy." Jerry looked at Bev with sad eyes before turning to look at Amy again. "We wanted to reach out. We wanted to say more, but you need to understand that we were concerned that we'd lose you. We never stopped praying for you Amy—praying that something would happen that would allow you to see the truth of who you are. That's the main reason we encouraged you with your art."

"I don't understand."

Bev took a deep breath. "The talents and passions that we're born with are often directly connected to the light within us. If humility is present as we develop those talents, the light will also grow. You were born an artist, Amy. We still have the doodles you made for us and hung on the fridge when you were just a little girl. We both felt we needed to encourage that."

"Isaac helped us identify the talents in each of our boys," Jerry added. "Sometimes as parents, you get so busy you miss the obvious stuff with your kids. Bev and I have learned to recognize the light in people by looking for the talents they have. I've often wondered if Isaac's ability to recognize and nurture the light in others wasn't somehow connected to his work with clay."

"How do you mean?" Jake asked.

Jerry grinned broadly. "I've been in that clay cellar many times, and all I see is piles of uninspiring dirt. Isaac could see bowls and cups and plates that just hadn't been formed yet. He recognized the potential of what could be when I could only see what was. He was the same way with people. He was able to take the common man—the drunk, the thief and the beggar—and work with them until they became something extraordinary. I'm convinced that he was able to recognize the potential talents in others because he saw the light within them. He knew what they could become because he loved them. His love for each of us has made us all want to become something better."

"You sound like you speak from experience," said Jake.

"Yes, I do, and more than just because of the way he helped us as parents to understand our own children. He helped me too."

"He helped us both," added Bev.

"How?" asked Amy.

"Oh, in countless ways over the years. Somehow he always knew when I was about to murder my children," Bev said, cracking a smile.

"I think he spent more time fishing with my boys than I did," added Jerry.

"And then there was the time he saved our marriage when I was pregnant with Jack," said Bev.

Jerry looked coyly at Bev. "That's the story I promised to tell you sometime," he said, looking at Jake. "I was reminded of it by the way you defended Amy at the restaurant the other night. Isaac was always a great defender of virtue. He honored all women. He taught me to do the same."

"How?" asked Amy

Jerry shook his head, looking a little embarrassed. "Oh, I guess it all started rather innocently when someone left a girly magazine at the barbershop."

Amy looked very surprised.

"It was different back then," Bev said reassuringly. "The ads in the Sunday paper these days are usually more revealing than the girly magazines were back then. At that time though, they were considered very risqué, something no good Christian man would have in his possession."

"And that's why I threw the first one away," Jerry said defensively. "Especially after Bev saw it and loudly voiced her opinion. But the next month, another one showed up in the stack of magazines I kept on the table. I should have thrown that away too, but I didn't and before long, there were probably a half-dozen magazines in the stack. Bev was pregnant with our first son at the time this all took place. I'd convinced myself they were harmless," he said, shaking his head. "The only time I really ever looked at them was when the guys brought them to the chair when I cut their hair. It never really felt right, but I didn't do anything about it."

"I was feeling about as attractive as a big, fat mud fence," Bev said. "And I was already very sensitive and insecure. I stopped in one afternoon to say hi and when I saw those magazines, I was so upset, I almost gave birth to Jack right there on the barbershop floor. I picked one up and left without saying a word."

"What did you do?" asked Amy.

"I turned into a blubbering mess. I felt like I'd been betrayed, as though all the trust I'd had in Jerry was gone. I didn't have a body like the women in those magazines and I knew I never would. I felt like an old car that he'd just traded in for a new sleeker, sexier model. I don't know if there could ever be an easy time for you to discover your husband is involved with that kind of trash, but when you're eight months pregnant and feel and look like a tank ... I was devastated. I left the shop and just kept walking."

"Where did you go?" asked Amy.

"I only made it as far as the main fountain on Zubergasse before my swollen legs and feet were so sore I couldn't go any further. I sat down on the bench and fell apart. I know I wasn't thinking clearly, but I began imagining having to raise my child on my own. I was an emotional basket case, feeling completely overwhelmed, when I felt an arm around my shoulder."

"Was it Isaac?" Amy asked.

"No. It was Grover Braun."

"Molly's Grandfather," Jerry added. "I forgot about that. He was a great man."

"Yes, he handed me his handkerchief and sat with me while I cried. I'm sure he had no idea what to do with me and I knew I didn't want to get into anything with him. I was relieved when I heard my name and turned to see Isaac's face hidden behind a couple of big paper bags filled with groceries. Grover seemed equally relieved to have someone to pass me off to.

"Isaac walked me to his apartment and gave me a place to rest. I remember being such a mess that I couldn't talk for a long time. I finally handed him the magazine and continued to cry as I told him where I'd found it. I remember him looking at me as if he really understood what I was feeling."

"So what did you do?" asked Amy.

"They taught me one of the most powerful lessons I've ever learned," said Jerry.

"How?"

"It was Isaac's idea," Beverly said with a devious grin. "He went into the bedroom and pulled out a box of old keepsakes Lily had kept from our younger years. There were dozens of photographs of me. He handed me the scissors and we spent the next hour cutting and pasting my face over the faces of the women in the pictures. Very few of them looked right because a lot of the photos of me were black and white."

Amy laughed. "So, did you give the magazine to Uncle Jerry?"

"Nope. I took it to the barbershop and put it back in the stack. Jerry was already gone, so I went home and made dinner and pretended nothing happened."

Amy looked at Jake who was trying hard not to smile, anticipating what might happen.

"So, how did this end?" she asked.

"Very uncomfortably," said Jerry. "The next day was a very quiet day in the barbershop. Even the regulars who came in every day for their shaves were unusually quiet as they sat in the chairs and waited their turns. I didn't figure it out until the last hour of the day when a man sat down in the barber's chair and opened the magazine." Jerry shook his head. "I'll never forget the shock I had when I saw Bev's face attached to the body of the one of the scantily-clad models. I'm certain that was the worst haircut I ever gave anyone, as a huge range of emotions flooded my mind. At first I was angry, then embarrassed and finally, ashamed. As soon as the man left, I locked the door and sat down to look at what she'd done—at what *I'd* done. Before I left that day, I went through the magazines and threw them all away. Then I crawled back home and spent the next several hours apologizing."

"We kept that one magazine for several years," Bev added.

"That's right. I almost forgot about that."

"Yeah, I swapped it with a similar one I found under one of the boy's beds fifteen years later. It opened up a good discussion about the ingredients of respectful and healthy relationships."

"That magazine was one of the loudest lectures I ever heard," Jerry said. "I'm sure it was for our son, too. I don't think most men realize when they look at women like that that each one of them is somebody's sister or daughter or wife or even mother. When it was just a picture of an unfamiliar woman, it didn't seem like that big of a deal, but when it became my wife—the mother of my children—it became very serious. Respect is a river that flows in both directions. If a man wants respect from a woman, he has to respect her. I know that's why everyone who was there that night at the restaurant is proud of you Jake. You stood up for Amy. You were her champion."

"I've been disgusted by your father many times over the years, Amy, but that took the cake. I was ashamed to even be related to him that night," said Bev.

"Me too," Amy said, looking forlorn.

"Enough of that," Jerry said, trying to lighten the mood with a jolt of enthusiasm. "You've got an anxious mother to call and we've got some pictures to hang up."

"And I've got some pots to finish," Jake added.

It was only nine, but it had been a very long day. Amy knew she'd be on the phone for a while and hoped to start working on a marriage certificate after that, so she kissed Jake at the door and told him she'd see him in the morning.

As he walked home, he thought about the events of the day. It had started with one dream and ended with a very different one. He was getting married in twelve days to a girl whom he loved with a love deeper and wider than any love he'd ever known before. He went into the shop and turned on The Bluegrass Darlings. The music filled the room with excitement, and he danced as he worked, putting together the rest of the Journey Jars; adding feet and lids and handles to those that had been too wet earlier to work with.

He finished the jars just before midnight and was about to turn off the light and close the door on the day when 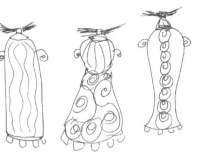 his eyes fell on the mugs hanging from the overhead beam. He had met most of their owners, but there were still three that hung there under a layer of thick dust. He wondered whose they were. Had they died? Had they moved so far away that they couldn't return? Would he ever meet them?

His questions about the mugs were soon eclipsed as the memory of what had taken place here that morning returned. He looked past the mugs to the front desk where Amy's easel was sitting in the shadows.

The reality of who he'd become fell upon him. This was more—much more than an inconvenient detour on his way to where he wanted to be. This was his life—the life he'd chosen with all his heart—the life the hand of Providence had been preparing him for since he was a child—maybe since the time he was born. As he looked at Amy's easel again, a rush of excitement hit him. This life that he'd chosen was a life that he would share.

And so Jacob Henry Kimball, the eighth potter of Niederbipp, who'd just proposed that morning to the woman he planned to spend the rest of his life with, changed his course. Instead of climbing the stairs to his bed, he stepped back into the studio and put on his apron. He wedged up a ball of buff-colored clay and filled the old, chipped batter bowl with warm water. He knew his proposal had been a romantic flop, but with Amy in mind, he sat down at the wheel to create a very special mug.

DISCERNING FRUITS

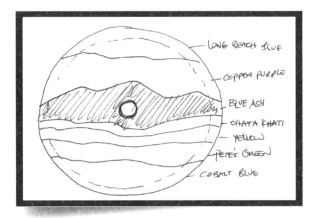

I MET IN THE STREET A VERY POOR YOUNG MAN WHO WAS IN LOVE.
HIS HAT WAS OLD, HIS COAT WORN, HIS CLOAK WAS OUT AT THE ELBOWS,
THE WATER PASSED THROUGH HIS SHOES,
-AND THE STARS THROUGH HIS SOUL.
—VICTOR HUGO—

aving opened the kiln's damper before he went to bed, the internal temperature had fallen to six hundred degrees by the next morning. Jake paced the floor, feeling anxious. The Journey Jars were drying nicely, but as he looked at the calendar that hung behind the front counter, his anxiety increased. Inside the kiln were the sinks he'd promised to the Parkins. They needed to be glazed and fired again. He hoped he would be able to glaze them today and get them back in the kiln for the glaze firing. He knew the timing would be tight if he was to get everything done in time. Working backwards on the calendar, he plotted out the firings. Three more would be needed to complete all that he had to do. Because the hard-brick kiln took so long to cool down after the glaze firing, Jake knew he would be unloading the kiln with gloves in order to get everything done.

It was still early in the morning. The sun was just touching the top branches of the chestnut tree in the courtyard behind The Pottery as Jake had made his way down the stairs. He'd awoken with thoughts of the mug he'd made for Amy the night before, and though he'd tried to get back to sleep, he knew he needed to get moving if he wanted to keep it a secret.

Near the warm kiln, the mug had dried sufficiently to be turned over and trimmed on the wheel. Trimming was always something Jake had enjoyed. It carved off the unnecessary clay on the bottom of the pot and created a ringed foot for it to stand on. After trimming, he held the mug at eye level, trying to imagine the handle that would perfectly fit Amy's hand and her long, narrow fingers. He  pulled a piece of clay from the bag on the table and worked it with his fingers until it was smooth, forming a wedge like a small carrot. After determining where the handle would begin, he scratched many small lines into the shoulder of the mug with his needle tool before doing the same to the wider end of the wedge. Reaching his hand into the bottom of the batter bowl, he scooped up a bit of slip with his finger tips and spread it over the scratched end of the clay wedge. Then, gripping it in his hand, he pressed the wedge onto the scratched area of the mug, smoothing the clay with his fingertips where the two pieces joined.

With the wedge secured, Jake picked up the mug in his left hand and tilted it ninety degrees, cradling it gently by its belly, the wedge pointing down toward the batter bowl he'd moved onto the wheel head. After dipping his right hand into the water, he loosely pinched the clay between his thumb and forefinger and pulled downward. He repeated this motion again and again, each pull forming and elongating the handle into a beautiful, graceful ribbon. Pleased with its shape and length, Jake tilted the mug upwards, the soft handle forming a graceful arc. He pinched off the excess clay and attached the bottom of the handle to the side of the mug, smoothing the two surfaces until it looked as though the handle had naturally grown out of the side of the mug.

He set the mug on his knee, and with the soft clay he'd pinched off the bottom of the handle, he formed a teardrop the size of a grape. Placing the teardrop on the top of the handle with the small end pointing down, he gingerly melded them together, forming his signature thumb-rest that he'd developed in college. He set the mug on the wedging table before standing to retrieve his sketchbook.

Jake had been thinking about Amy's mug for at least two weeks, and several of his ideas had been recorded in his sketchbook. He'd wanted to make something that had meaning to both of them—something that spoke love without words. After multiple sketches, he'd settled on a forget-me-not to symbolize that love. When the idea had come to him, he'd originally considered carving a band of the small flowers around the lip, but as the ideas developed, he settled on carving a single flower that would fill the side of the mug. It was a simple design really—a five-petaled flower that would be glazed after the bisque firing in a way that would highlight the flower. After making a light outline with a pencil, he used a small, metal loop tool he'd found among Isaac's tools to carve the simple line-drawing.

He was just finishing when he heard a knock at the open back door that startled him so badly he nearly dropped the mug. He looked over his shoulder, hoping it wasn't Amy and was relieved to see Thomas' face looking around the corner.

"Thomas! What's going on?" Jake said, relieved.

"I was just on my way home from the bakery and saw your light on. Is everything okay?"

"Yeah, I'm just finishing up some work before Amy gets here. I made her a mug and wanted to keep it a surprise until it's done."

Thomas walked closer, his eyes looking tired.

"Are you okay?" Jake asked, turning away from the mug to give him his full attention.

"I'm exhausted," he said, taking a seat on the stool across from Jake.

"Early morning?"

"That too. I didn't sleep last night, wondering if I'd have a friend once Sam figured out I was involved in stealing all those letters. I hope we did the right thing."

"I do too. You obviously know Sam a lot better than I do. How do you think he's going to handle it?"

Thomas shook his head. "I honestly don't know. I know our intentions were good, Jake. I just hope Sam sees it that way."

"Yeah. How long do you think it will take before he realizes the letters are gone?"

"Not more than a month. I'm not sure how often he writes, but for as many letters as there were in that box, he'd have to write fairly often."

Jake took a deep breath. "Thomas, I sent something else with Charlie."

"What?"

"When we couldn't find the letters in the cellar, I ... I took a mug from the shelf above the table and sent it with Charlie and Jodi."

Thomas' tired face looked suddenly ill. "Please tell me it wasn't the one that said, 'Vice.' "

Jake was slow to answer, surprised by Thomas' change in appearance. "What if it was," he asked timidly.

Thomas ran his fingers through his hair. "Oh boy."

"What, Thomas? What does that mean? What are you thinking?"

Thomas shook his head. "Well, between you and me, I think we probably got rid of every sentimental object that Sam had left in the bakery. I just hope something good comes of this or I'll be looking for a new job and you'll be looking for another place to get your bread, and we'll both be looking for a new friend."

"Do you really think it's that bad?"

"It's hard to say. I've never been involved in anything like this before. To be honest, it scares me."

"Don't you think Sam would see that our intentions were good, even if nothing good came of it?"

"I don't know, Jake. I hope so. There are lots of things that don't make sense in this world. I just hope that Sam will understand. I was worried about the letters, but hearing that the mug is gone too—I don't know. Sam is a passionate person. It's difficult to know how he'll respond. I guess we just have to wait and see."

"Well, is there anything I can do? There has to be something?"

"I think we've done plenty, Jake."

He didn't say anything more for several seconds, causing Jake to worry.

"All that's left to do is to pray, Jake. Charlie dropped all that stuff off last night. That means Matt has had it in his possession for close to twelve hours. There are probably hundreds of ways he could respond. I just pray he'll have an open mind." Thomas stood from the stool and nodded. "Well, what's done is done. I need to get some rest before I fall over. I'll check in later to see if you've heard anything."

Alone again, Jake considered what else he might do. He'd held Matt's old mug in his hands for only a short time, but he was confident he'd be able to make one that looked similar, at least similar enough that Sam wouldn't know the difference if he could put it back on the shelf where the original one had been. It would be at least ten days before he could get such a mug finished. It had been covered in a thick layer of white dust. Could he duplicate that? After considering a few different potential solutions, he stopped himself, realizing all the solutions he was coming up with had to do with deceiving Sam. Jake knew Sam might not be ready for the truth of what they'd conspired to do, but he knew he couldn't lie to Sam, not after all Sam had done for him. He couldn't. He wouldn't. If asked, he'd tell the truth and deal with the consequences, whatever they were.

Jake was making an omelette when Amy arrived just after eight. As they sat and ate one of the first meals he'd had since arriving in Niederbipp that didn't include Sam's bread, Jake told Amy about Thomas' visit. They spent the rest of the morning talking, hoping and praying that things would work out, wondering if they really should have involved themselves in the mess that had been going on for years. Just after noon, the bells on the front door jingled, bringing an abrupt and welcome change to the somber mood.

"Hello," Amy said, turning from her painting.

"You must be the lovely and talented Amy who we've been hearing so much about."

Jake recognized the voice but couldn't place it. Curious, he stood up from the wheel and walked around the counter to see Tom and Emma Parkin.

"David and Nancy Garber have been raving about you and your paintings," Emma said, as she extended her hand to Amy. "We're the Parkin's. This is my husband Tom and I'm Emma."

Tom looked up and nodded to Jake. "Hey, we were in the neighborhood and thought we'd drop by to check on your progress with the sinks."

Jake smiled, taking Tom's hand. "They should be done on Friday. I'm planning on glazing them this afternoon."

"That's great. We just finished the last of the tiling yesterday and were hoping things were coming along. How do they look?"

Jake turned and looked at the kiln. "I'd show you, but they're still too hot to touch. I was planning on glazing them after we get back from ring shopping."

Emma smiled. "So, it's true then. You're engaged?"

"Yes," Jake said, putting his arm around Amy's shoulder. "Amy's parents are signed up for your marriage workshop over the Fourth. We thought we'd kill two birds with one stone and get married the same weekend."

"That's right," said Tom. "We have your parents booked in one of our newest rooms. They'll be breaking in one of your new sinks, Jake."

"I don't know anything about your program," sdaid Amy, "but I'm glad my parents are getting some help. To be honest, I'm surprised they've been able to stick it out as long as they have. If you can help them, I'll be convinced that you're miracle workers."

Tom looked at Emma and smiled. "Well, we've seen some pretty amazing changes with hundreds of couples over the past ten years. But the success or failure of the program has more to do with the attitude of the couple than it does with anything we say or try to teach. People usually don't seek help until their marriages are so broken that they can't see straight. Unfortunately, many of us have to hit bottom before we recognize how broken we are."

Amy let out a long breath, setting down her paintbrush. "I think you probably have your work cut out for you with my parents. They've been struggling for a long time."

"Sometimes that's a good sign," Emma said, looking positive.

"Really?" asked Amy.

"Sure. It suggests they're not quitters. There are huge numbers of people we can't help because they give up on their marriages before they ever seek help. Most of the people we see are folks, like your parents, who once had a good marriage, but over time have grown apart. We find that they are often fighting for what they once had, wanting things to be as they once were—before they built walls around their hearts."

"The fact that they're still together after thirty-nine years of marriage—that's a good sign. It usually means they want to make things work. They may have just forgotten how," added Tom.

"How did you know they've been married thirty-nine years," asked Amy, looking surprised.

"It's our job to know," Tom responded with a wink.

Emma smiled and shook her head. "Your mom told us when she made reservations last week. They'll be one of the oldest couples in our group for that week, but we've had lots of clients who have been much older. It seems every marriage goes through a bumpy spot or two. Some of bumps just last a lot longer."

"How old are most of your clients?" asked Jake.

"Mid-forties to mid-fifties—usually after about twenty-to-twenty-five years of marriage," answered Emma.

"Why do you think that is?" asked Jake.

"Oh, lots of reasons," responded Tom. "It's a time of flux. The kids are starting to leave the house, midlife crisis takes its toll, menopause and other chemical changes in the brain kick in. It's a time when people look at their lives and wonder what else there is. A lot of folks,  after spending twenty-plus years raising their kids, find themselves asking questions about self-fulfillment. And as the kids leave the house, both husbands and wives find themselves asking what's in it for them. It can be a very selfish time—at least that's what we find. After twenty-five years of marriage, you tend to collect a lot of stones."

"Tell us about that," Jake said. "I noticed on your business card that it says something about stones. What does that mean?"

"Oh yeah," Tom said. " 'Creating oneness, one stone at a time.' Its part of an exercise we do with the couples. We use it as an object lesson about forgiveness."

"I think David and Nancy Garber said they were some of your clients?" Jake said.

"That's right. One of the first couples, back when we only had four rooms," responded Tom.

"They sure are excited about your paintings," added Emma. "They've been trying to get us to stop by and see your work for the past ten days. We've been so busy working, trying to get things ready for our reopening that we haven't had time."

"I'm just finishing a commission for them," Amy said, turning her easel around to face them. "I've never done a painting of rocks before, but I'm pretty happy with the way things have turned out."

Emma gasped audibly. "Amy, this is beautiful."

"Thanks. I still have to finish up the background there in the corner. It's been a fun challenge."

"Would you be interested in doing another one?" asked Tom, putting his arm around his wife's shoulder.

"Uh, sure. What did you have in mind?"

"I think you've pretty much captured what we're looking for," Tom said. "I don't know if we need the basket or not. I think I could be happy with just a small pile of rocks."

"No, I like the basket," said Emma. "I think there's a good tie-in with the workshop and the basket."

Tom nodded. "I can see that. I was thinking this would be great over the mantel in the dining room."

"I was thinking the same thing," responded Emma, "but do you think it's big enough?"

"I don't know. What kind of a frame did you imagine for this?" asked Tom.

Amy smiled. "I was thinking this would look best with an antique gold frame, but David and Nancy didn't say anything about a frame. I think they were going to handle that themselves."

"That sounds like Nancy," Emma said. "She's very particular. How big is this canvas?"

"Twenty by thirty," answered Amy.

"Can you go any bigger?" asked David

Amy looked at Jake before responding. "Uh, sure. How big are you talking?"

"How big do you have?"

"Not anything bigger than this. I'd probably feel better painting on Masonite if it were bigger than this. If we use Masonite, we could go as big as forty-eight by ninety-six."

"That would definitely be too big," Tom said, grinning. "How about thirty by thirty? The space above the mantel is actually square."

"Sure. When do you need it?"

Tom looked at Emma, then back again. "We'd love to have it for our grand re-opening next week, but we wouldn't want to stress you out, especially with your wedding coming up."

"We've always loved original artwork, but I'm sure we really have no idea what goes into it. Please tell us if that is completely impractical," Emma said, sounding almost apologetic.

Amy looked at Jake again before responding. "I can at least get started and see how it goes. Would my parents see it when they come?"

"Of course. It will be in the main dining room. The mantel over which it would hang is right next to the table where most meals are served."

Amy nodded. "Then I'd like to try."

Jake watched her quietly as she quickly drew up a small sketch for the Parkins to approve. He knew this was important for her—a painting that her parents would see and hopefully appreciate. He knew she'd spent parts of several days on the painting for the Garbers but somehow knew this new painting would take longer, and not just because it was bigger. As he watched them interact, Jake was reminded of the first time he'd met Tom and Emma. They'd arrived just moments after Mr. and Mrs. Crankypants, Amy's parents, had left the shop. With them, they'd brought a breath of fresh air. Jake had admired them and their relationship at that first meeting, and as he watched them now, he found himself wondering what they had—what they knew—that gave them their positive aura. There was something familiar about that aura— something lovely and endearing and optimistic. As he considered the familiarity of that feeling, another couple came to mind—Joseph and Gloria. His mind wondered as he compared the two couples. He knew Gloria and Joseph far better, but both couples shared a companionship that he admired. Like the interlocking rings pictured on the business card Tom had given him at their first meeting, their marriage seemed to be one of unity.

Suddenly, another image flashed in his mind. With the Parkins engaged in conversation with Amy, Jake walked to his sketchbook near the wheel and flipped through it until he found the business card. After reading the slogan about stones, he flipped it over to see the rings. And there in the middle of the rings was the forget-me-not, the flower that had meant so much to Isaac—the flower that had come to mean so much to Jake. He looked up and watched them in silence for a long moment. They had to know what this meant—they had to have an understanding of what this was. His mind raced as he considered all he'd learned about Isaac and the love he had shared with Lily. He knew they had shared a magic that was unusual—that had sustained Isaac long after her death.

Another thought hit him as he watched Tom put his arm lovingly on Emma's shoulder. In that moment, he knew they were much more than just a happy couple who ran a marriage retreat program. In their own way, with the talents and passions they'd developed, they were holding up their lights in a way that made others hungry for more light—hungry for the light they had. Like Thomas, Eric, Gloria, Joseph, Bev and Jerry, they were Candlelighters. A rush of excitement pulsed through his veins as the truth of what he'd just discovered settled in. And in that moment, Jake knew they had something he needed to learn—something that would change his own marriage—something that might enable him and Amy to know the kind of love that Isaac had shared with Lily.

He walked back to the counter and listened to the silence as the Parkins watched Amy finish her preliminary sketch. He watched as

Tom looked at his wife with a smile across his face. He watched as Emma nodded her approval.

"We love it," Tom said exuberantly. "It's going to be the perfect finishing touch to our home."

Amy grinned in response. "I could probably get started on it this afternoon."

"Are you sure?" asked Emma. "We really don't want to put any undo stress on you."

"No, it will be fine," Amy said. "We decided to keep our wedding simple, and I think this project will help me focus."

"You're sure?" asked David, turning to Jake as if to make sure he was okay with it as well.

Jake took a step closer to Amy, putting his arm around her shoulder. He smiled at the Parkins before laying their business card down on top of Amy's sketchbook. "If it's not too late, I'd like to throw one request into the negotiations."

"Sure," responded Tom without hesitation.

Amy looked at him with questioning eyes.

"We'd like to hear what you can tell us about this," he said, pointing to the small blue flower on the front of the business card.

Emma looked up smiling. "It sounds like you may already know."

Amy looked at the card, then back at Jake, surprise registering on her face.

"I thought we did, but maybe we only know half of it. I have a feeling that you might know something about Isaac that very few other people do."

Without a word, Tom licked the middle knuckle on his left ring finger and removed his gold wedding band, drying it on his shirt before handing it to Jake. "Look on the inside," he said.

Jake held the ring close to his eyes, but the light was blocked by Amy's head when she also leaned in close to see. "It's a forget-me-not," she said, looking up with excitement.

Emma handed Amy her ring, pointing to another forget-me-not engraved on the inside.

"We've had the same business cards for almost ten years," said Tom. "You two are some of just a handful of people who have ever recognized what it is."

"I think I can probably tell you the names of at least two others who would have recognized it," said Jake.

Tom raised one eyebrow, smiling.

"Gloria and Joseph," Jake responded confidently.

"Impressive. Most people don't pay much attention to such a little flower. How did you ..."

"We're artists," Amy said, cutting him off with a smile of her own. "Details are important to people like ..." She stopped mid-sentence and stared at them as if she'd suddenly seen something she hadn't recognized before. She turned to Jake with wide eyes. "They're ..."

Jake nodded. "I think they must be."

They turned back to find Tom and Emma smiling broadly.

"I'm guessing you must have spent some time talking to our friend, Eric Schmelding," Tom said.

"We have," Jake admitted, "but he didn't tell us anything about you. He just mentioned that there were other Candlelighters in the area. I didn't think much about it until I remembered seeing that forget-me-not on your card."

"That little flower and the potter who told us about it are the reasons we turned our home into a marriage retreat," said Emma. She looked at Tom with emotion in her eyes. "I feel as though there's a reason we needed to be here today. We needed to see this painting."

"I was thinking the same thing," Tom said. "It's obviously something we're never supposed to forget."

A friendly knock came from the back door, and they all turned to see Molly with a colorful sling draped across her front. "Am I interrupting anything?" she asked cheerfully, stepping over the threshold.

"Come on in," Amy said.

"Well, Molly Braun, what a pleasant surprise," Emma said, walking toward her. "We were just asking about you. Kai told us your little guy is getting big. How are you feeling?"

"Pretty good," Molly said peeling back the woven cloth of the sling to expose Zane's tiny sleeping face, his mouth full of his own fist. "I was just out on my walk and thought I better stop by to officially congratulate these two lovebirds."

Jake thanked her, but he wondered what might have been said had the interruption not come. After cooing over the baby for a minute, Emma and Tom expressed their own congratulations to Molly. While Amy and Molly spoke animatedly, Tom and Emma explained to Jake that they needed to get back to their work at the house and promised to stop by on Friday or Saturday to pick up the sinks. As Tom shook Jake's hand, he leaned closer to his ear and promised that their conversation would continue.

Ten minutes later, with the wind whipping Amy's hair across the back of Jake's neck, they rode out of town on the old Honda scooter. Jake smiled at his reflection in the mirror, the bug-eyed glasses he wore shining in the sun, and the bubble-headed Amy behind him, clinging tightly to his chest. He was getting married. He smiled to himself as they drove past the Bungee Bipp. He smiled to himself as they passed Yoder's workshop. And he smiled to himself as they pulled off the highway and parked the bike in front of Castleton's Fine Jewelry.

SIMPLE GIFTS

AS YOU SIMPLIFY YOUR LIFE, THE LAWS OF THE UNIVERSE WILL BE SIMPLER;
SOLITUDE WILL NOT BE SOLITUDE, POVERTY WILL NOT BE POVERTY,
NOR WEAKNESS WEAKNESS.
—HENRY DAVID THOREAU—

ood afternoon," said a very tall, thin, middle-aged man as they walked into the bright shop.

Jake nodded while Amy tried to tame her wind-blown hair.

"Is there anything we can help you with today?" the tall man asked, resting his hands on his hips, one hand holding a bright pink, feather duster.

"Uh, yeah, probably. We just got engaged

and we're looking for a ring," Jake said. "Some friends of ours suggested we check you out."

"Oh really, who?"

"Andrew and Sandy."

"Oh, yes. The nurse and the architect, right? You must be from Niederbipp."

"Yes, we are," said Jake.

"Well, do you know what you're looking for?"

"Uh, not really," Jake said, turning to Amy for help.

"Are you looking for a ring like your friends purchased?" the man asked.

"No," said Amy, speaking up. "We were looking for something a little more simple."

"Does that mean … what shall we say … smaller?"

"Uh," said Jake with a shrug, turning to Amy again for direction.

"Can you show us what you have?" she asked.

The man laid his duster down on the glass countertop and pointed to three long glass cabinets that ran parallel to the wall. Jake and Amy walked toward them as the

man took his place behind the cabinets. "My name is Paul Castleton," the man said, extending his large hand. Jake and Amy quickly introduced themselves, but their eyes were distracted by the glitz and bling on the other side of the glass.

"Why don't you pull up a stool there and make yourselves comfortable," Paul said, pointing to the vinyl-covered stools on wheels.

"What do you think?" Jake asked. "Do any of these look right?"

The rings in the first case all had large solitaire diamonds, but Amy looked past all of them and scooted her stool down to the next cabinet. Jake followed her. Rings had only really come up once between them— that night at Taufer's Pond when Amy had told him about the jock who proposed to her with a football shaped diamond. Since then, the subject had never really come up, and Jake had no idea what to expect.

"Can I see that one there?" Jake asked, pointing to a ring he knew was well beyond his price range but wanting to get some idea of what he should expect.

"Nice choice," said Paul, handing Jake the small white ring box.

He stared down into the box. A large square diamond was surrounded by gaudy clusters of smaller diamonds that spilled onto the band. He pulled the ring from the box, hoping a price tag might be attached. A tiny, white sticker was wrapped around the bottom of the ring with a half dozen numbers written on it that didn't make any sense to him. He looked up at Paul, clueless. If he understood clueless, Paul didn't let on. Instead, he handed Jake a black jeweler's loupe. Not wanting to openly admit his complete ignorance about such things, Jake responded by handing the ring and the loupe back to Paul.

Paul held the loupe to his eye and the ring just in front of it, squinting. "Beautiful diamond, GIA certified, princess cut, VS, J in color, three-quarters of a carat." He handed Jake the ring and loupe.

Jake shook his head and smiled. "I got carat and princess, but I have no idea what the rest of that means. You can tell me all that just by looking at it?"

"I'm sorry. I just assumed that since you were friends with Andrew and Sandy that you might know the terminology."

Jake tried not to laugh. "Sorry to disappoint you. I've never done this before. Can you just tell me how much?"

Paul looked down at the small sticker on the ring. "This is sixty-three hundred."

"Dollars?" Jake whispered.

Paul nodded. "Perhaps you'd like to take a look at some of our *smaller* rings?"

Jake took a deep breath and nodded.

"I'd like to take a look at this one," Amy said from the other side of the room.

Jake looked up, not having noticed she'd moved so far away. He walked to her side and looked into the cabinet while Paul put the other ring away.

"You know those don't have diamonds on them," Paul said, as he rounded the corner behind the cases, fumbling with a large ring of keys.

Amy nodded, smiling. "I really don't want a diamond."

"We have financing available if money is the issue," Paul said, causing Jake to bristle.

"Thank you," Amy said politely. "I'm an artist. A diamond would get in the way of my work. Besides, I know too much about diamonds to have one on my hand."

Paul nodded. "We also have Canadian diamonds if you want to stay away from the African sort."

Amy looked at Jake and smiled before looking Paul in the eyes. "Thank you, but I honestly would feel most comfortable with a ring like that," she said, pointing to the simple bands beneath the glass.

"Very well," said Paul. "What size are you looking for?"

"Seven, I think."

"Good." He sat down on a stool and pulled out a velvet tray with around thirty gold bands, each with a slightly different width and shape.

Amy tried the first one on, holding her hand out to see how it looked. As Jake watched her, his mind was met with mixed emotions. He remembered the things he'd learned about love from Gloria, how Joseph had parked his van and walked for a whole year to save enough money to buy her simple gold band with the microscopic diamond. Jake had money. It wasn't much, but it was enough to buy more than a plain gold band. He was grateful for Amy's simple tastes, but he worried that her simplicity might be unnatural, based on his financial circumstances. Either way, he loved her for it, but still he worried.

He sat down on one of the stools and watched as Amy tried on the different rings, trying to figure out what kept him from engaging more in the selection of the ring. He worried that it might be pride. Lots of people would be looking at her ring in the coming weeks and months—even years. They would look for a diamond, and not seeing one, would look at him like a poor loser. They wouldn't understand. But did it matter? Did it really matter what anyone else thought? As he looked away, deep in thought, his eyes fell on the rings inside the cabinet at his right. Intrigued by their shape and design, he looked closer. These were different from any ring he'd ever seen before. Two tiny hands came together to hold a heart. On top of the heart was a small crown. Each ring had a different band ranging from very plain to ornately carved with Celtic knotwork.

"What can you tell me about these rings?" Jake asked, pointing to the black velvet tray.

Paul looked over. "Those are Claddagh rings. They're Irish wedding rings. I've had them for a couple of years. They're really not very popular."

"What do they symbolize?"

"Oh, its been a few years, but if I remember right, the heart symbolizes love, the hands mean friendship and the crown is loyalty, I think. I'd have to look it up for sure. My wife liked them so we tried a few. They sold well so we ordered a bunch more, but those have just been sitting there for a couple of years."

Amy set down the rings she'd been looking at and scooted her stool next to Jake. "I like those," she said, looking over his shoulder.

"I do too. There has to be some cool history behind them. Do you know anything else about them?" he asked Paul.

"No, not really. They came with a little storybook, but I haven't seen that in a long time.

"May I try them on?" asked Amy.

"Of course." He pulled out the tray of rings. It was divided down the middle with men's and women's styles and sizes. They each picked one up and tried them on. After trying on three different rings, Jake finally found one that fit—a silver ring with oxidized highlights. After sorting through all of the ladies' rings, Amy also found one, very similar to Jake's, that fit nicely.

"Can we really do this?" Jake asked. "We're not Irish."

Amy laughed. "Does it matter if we like them?"

"I guess not. Are you sure you don't want a diamond?"

"When I can have love, friendship and loyalty for a fraction of the price? Are you kidding? Everything else is just a counterfeit, remember," she said with a wink.

Jake smiled, remembering similar words that he'd heard on Sunday from Jodi. "We'll take these," Jake said, turning back to Paul.

"Would you like them engraved?"

Jake looked at Amy and smiled. "Yes. Can you engrave a small, five-petaled flower on the inside of each of them?"

"A five-petaled flower?"

"Yes," Amy said.

"If you can draw it, my engraver can carve it, but it will take a couple of days."

"That's fine," said Jake. "We won't need them till the end of next week."

Amy grabbed a piece of notepaper and quickly sketched the simple design, sliding the paper across the counter to Paul.

"What do we owe you?" asked Jake, reaching for his wallet.

Paul looked at the sketch, then reached for a calculator with enormous buttons. "A hundred and twenty-five dollars," he said, getting to his feet. "Cash or charge?"

"Cash," Jake said, smiling at Amy.

As they started back to town, the smile that had accompanied him on the way out returned. He was getting married and in their effort to keep things simple, everything seemed to be working out beautifully.

IF THOU WOULDST BE HAPPY...
HAVE AN INDIFFERENCE FOR MORE
THAN WHAT IS SUFFICIENT.
— WILLIAM PENN —

SACRIFICE

FORGIVENESS DOES NOT CHANGE THE PAST,
BUT IT DOES ENLARGE THE FUTURE.
—PAUL BOESE—

o you mind if we stop by the Yoders?" Amy asked as they crested the hill just above the Amish workshop.

"Do you need more frames?" Jake asked.

"Yeah, I think I ought to order some more."

As they neared the workshop, they saw the Yoder family sitting at a picnic table under an old oak tree on the north side of the shop. They parked the scooter next to the buggy and dismounted, shedding the goggles and helmet.

"I hope you came to join us for lunch," John Yoder yelled from the table, waving his straw hat in greeting.

"No, that's okay," replied Jake. "We just stopped by to order some frames. We can wait."

"Nonsense," said Mrs. Yoder, getting to her feet and wiping her hands on her apron.

John smiled, shaking his head. "If you know what's good for you, you won't argue." A few of the boys and two daughters dressed in pastel dresses turned to look at them. "Benjamin and Jonah, please bring us two more chairs."

Jake and Amy walked through the short grass and into the shade of the oak.

"I know you already met my wife, Anna, but these are my daughters, Mary and Ruth, and my sons, Samuel, Eli, Benjamin, Ephraim and Jonah." Each of them nodded as their names were said, the youngest of whom, Ruth, looked as if she couldn't be more than  twelve. The boys returned with the chairs and Jake and Amy sat down at the end of the table. Mary handed each of them blue enameled plates with thick slices of bread covered in apple butter.

"My wife is the finest baker this side of Niederbipp," John said, pouring an amber colored liquid from a glass pitcher into two blue enameled mugs that matched the plates. These were passed down the line to Jake and Amy along with a bowl filled with pickles and carrots. "If we'd known you were coming, we would have saved some sauerkraut for you," he said apologetically.

"Thank you," Jake said, raising his mug.

John nodded as his children continued eating. "So, tell us, what brings you two from the north?"

"We just went up to Castleton's to pick out our wedding rings," Amy said. "We're getting married on July fifth."

"Woondershurn!" John exclaimed. "Anna returned from her stay with Kai and Molly with reports that you two were spending a lot of time together. Congratulations."

"Yes, our best to you," Anna said softly. "I was hoping to get over to speak with you while I was in town, Jake. I missed you a couple of times at The Pottery, but now I see why." A kind and approving smile spread across her face.

"I'm sorry I missed you," Jake said. "It seems like we're there all the time. Molly said something about you wanting to talk to me?"

"Yes. I wanted to thank you personally for coming to Niederbipp. My husband said he already told you about Isaac helping us rebuild our shop after the fire. He refused to accept any money in return. He sat at our table many times over the years." She pursed her lips, reaching for her husband's hand before she continued. "He was a dear friend to all of us. All of my children admired him. There aren't many English who gain the kind of respect Isaac had among the Amish. You may have heard that half of our community attended his funeral."

Jake shook his head.

"Yes, John was even asked to be one of Isaac's pallbearers."

Jake looked up, surprised, realizing what had just been said—that Charlie Smith and Matthew Gottlieb, the boys who had set fire to the Yoder's workshop, had been invited to share the honor of carrying Isaac's casket with John Yoder himself. Even in death, it seemed, Isaac was hopeful.

"I understand you spent some time on Sunday afternoon with a man and his wife," John said, speaking as discreetly as he could with the listening ears of his children all around him.

Jake and Amy nodded.

"They visited us yesterday for the first time. I remembered seeing that young man at Isaac's funeral, but before yesterday, I'd never met him. I would have gone my whole life and never known the truth of what happened that terrible night, but as he told me his story and asked for my forgiveness, I felt compelled to embrace him as my brother." John stopped to wipe away a tear from his eye. "The debt had been paid. The wrong had long been righted. We had forgiven the stranger who had hurt us. But after eight years, the sweetness of forgiveness had new power. My father taught me that forgiveness and joy are drawn together from the sweetest wells of God's mercy. I thought I understood that, but I think I learned yesterday that that well has no bottom. To drink from that water again and again over the years has taught me things I never could have learned—never could have learned without knowing the sorrow."

Jake turned to see Amy wiping tears from her eyes. John's words had touched them both—knowing the story from all angles now. All that is, except one. As he watched Amy try to regain control of her emotions, Jake knew that this story had far broader implications than the Yoders' and Charlie's alone. Somehow, it might have application to everyone, even him.

"As Isaac worked with us to rebuild our shop, we became good friends," John continued. "Over time, we learned he had no family, so we adopted him as a member of ours. When we learned he had no apprentice, Anna and I felt like we needed to offer Isaac one of our sons. Ephraim, the oldest, was already becoming a skilled craftsman. We considered offering Isaac one of the younger boys, but remembering what he'd done for us, we knew we couldn't offer him less than the best we had, even if it hurt our business."

John looked across the table at his oldest son who wore a surprised look on his thinly-bearded face. Jake guessed he was probably about his own age, maybe even a little older. John smiled through his tears as he nodded. "None of you have ever heard this before, have you?"

The children shook their heads.

"Your mother and I agreed to keep it quiet until we could talk to Isaac about it."

"You wanted me to become a potter, Father?" Ephraim asked respectfully.

"No, I wanted you to become a just and honorable man, and I felt that Isaac could teach you at least as well as I could."

Ephraim looked thoughtful, then nodded his head in understanding.

"Ephraim and his wife Rachel were just married last December,"

Anna offered. "They just returned from visiting family in Ohio."

Jake nodded, taking a drink from the mug. The taste surprised him. It was peppermint tea.

"So, why didn't Isaac want Ephraim to work with him?" one of the younger boys asked.

John tried to smile. "Because Isaac knew we needed him too." He shook his head, and closed his eyes, tears falling freely. "Your mother and I prepared ourselves for several days before we went to make arrangements with Isaac. We thought we'd be coming back the next day to drop Ephraim off, but ..." He trailed off.

"But Isaac told us that he knew that a potter would come," Anna said, picking up where her husband left off. "After crying with us over the sacrifice we were prepared to make, he told us he'd had many dreams of a young man who would come to Niederbipp to make pottery. We went home, relieved that Ephraim could stay with us, but we began that night to pray that a potter truly would come to work for Isaac."

"That's why we prayed for Isaac and his apprentice?" Ephraim asked.

John nodded. "Every day and night for eight years," he said, his voice cracking as he spoke.

"After a couple of years, we worried that our prayers had not been heard, and we went to visit him again to offer one of our sons as his apprentice," Anna continued.

"Was it me?" asked one of the boys who looked like he was about fifteen.

Anna smiled, running her hand over her son's hair. "Isaac assured us that someone would come and sent us home, feeling as though our prayers would be answered. We continued to pray. For eight years, we prayed as we watched Isaac grow older, but every time the subject came up, he promised us that someone would come."

"It seemed hopeless sometimes," admitted John. "I felt guilty as each of you boys got bigger and joined me in the shop, knowing that Isaac was still working alone. But he remained convinced someone would come, that our prayers would be answered."

Jake bit his bottom lip, reviewing in his mind how his life had been molded and shaped over the last eight years, preparing him to come here—preparing him to take Isaac's place.

He knew Isaac had dreamed about him—his words, written in the dedication of Volume 37 echoed through his mind. But hearing the words again from near strangers who had spent the last eight years hoping and praying that he would come, that Isaac's dream would become a reality—somehow brought it all home. Somehow, there was clarity and understanding and peace, knowing for certain that the hand of Providence truly had brought him here, answering every prayer he'd ever had and the prayers of unknown numbers of others.

Did God answer all prayers? For Jake, at that moment, the answer was a resounding yes. Nothing had happened exactly the way he'd imagined, the way he'd planned, or even the way he'd hoped. But as he looked at the Yoder s, his heart leapt within his chest. These faithful people had kept a prayer vigil for him, a stranger, for every one of the last eight years as he'd struggled to find his way in  life. There had been many painful days as he'd plowed his way through, bumping along the path of life. No part of it had been easy, and he knew in his heart that there would be many hard times to come. But today there was an emotion within his heart that was bigger than any emotion he'd ever experienced—gratitude. His heart and mind had already been softened by the feeling that he was where he was supposed to be. But as Mrs. Yoder reached over to take Jake's hand in hers, that *feeling* was gone, replaced with something real—*he knew*. Tingles raced through his body as he set his plate down on the table and embraced the woman. She was no longer a stranger. Maybe she never had been. In that moment, there was no line between Amish and English. They were fellow children of God who knew, having witnessed in person the touch of His hand.

PIECES

IF YOU WANT TO MAKE AN APPLE PIE FROM SCRATCH,
YOU MUST FIRST CREATE THE UNIVERSE.
—CARL SAGAN—

my held the pint jar of apple butter in her hand as they rolled onto the highway, the milk crate strapped to the back of the scooter, filled with hand-made frames. The time had gone quickly as they'd visited with the Yoders. Before anyone was

ready for the moment to end, a caravan of noisy tourists had pulled into the parking lot, squelching the reverence of their sanctuary. Mr. Yoder and his boys had put on their straw hats and excused themselves to walk back to the shop while Jake and Amy finished their lunch and Mrs. Yoder and her daughters put the picnic away.

Though it was already well past the time for The Pottery to be open, Jake accompanied Amy to the hardware store on Kaiserstrasse to help her carry the Masonite panel she needed for the Parkins' commission. He knew she was very capable of doing it alone, but he was glad for the excuse to be with her.

He stood back and watched as Amy interacted with the clerk. After cutting out the correct size for the new painting, Amy had the rest of the large panel cut into smaller pieces, including several dozen four and six inch squares that she explained would be used to create small portraits of Sam's pastries and other miniature paintings.

Back at The Pottery, Amy worked on the finishing touches for the Garbers' commission while Jake unloaded the kiln and glazed the sink basins. Despite the long candling process he'd given the sinks prior to the bisque firing, two of the basins were badly cracked, and he was grateful he'd made extras. The sinks were heavy and awkward, and while glazing the first one, it slipped from his fingers, landing loudly on the floor and sending shards across the studio. He slowed down after that and took his time, being extra careful.

The sinks filled more than half the kiln once they were glazed and stacked on the kiln shelves. Jake spent the rest of the afternoon glazing as many of the tiles for Isaac's bench as would fit, while Amy began her work on the Parkins' painting. For the most part, they worked in silence, each concentrating on their own work, lost in thought.

It was just after six when Jake sealed the kiln door before kneeling on the floor to light the burners. Firing through the night would mean he would have to get up several times to check on the kiln's progress, but he knew if he were to meet all his deadlines, this extra time would be needed.

He walked to the front counter where Amy was sitting on the tall stool. The Masonite board was no longer brown, but covered instead with a pale yellow paint surrounding the pile of stones that had been roughly outlined. Jake stood behind her, resting his hand on her shoulder. "How's it going?" he asked.

"Good. I've been thinking all afternoon what these rocks could have to do with forgiveness."

"Have you figured it out?"

"I don't know. I thought about that story in the Bible where Jesus saves that woman from being stoned to death by telling her accusers that whoever is without sin should throw the first stone. I like that story, but I don't know if it's reason enough for two separate couples to commission me to do a painting of rocks. I feel like there has to be something more, especially if the Parkins plan to hang theirs above their dining room table."

"When did David and Nancy say they were coming back? Maybe you could ask them."

"Yeah, that's what I was thinking too."

"So, what do you want to do tonight?" Jake asked.

Amy shrugged. "What do you want to do?"

"I remembered that I still need to email my professor and my roommates about our plans. Do you know how late the library's open?"

"Seven, I think."

"Do you want to go with me or should I leave you here to paint?"

Amy rolled her neck. "I'll go with you. I need a break." She quickly cleaned her brush in the cloudy liquid, drying it on a paper towel. She slid her palette into a thin plastic container and covered it with a lid to keep the paint from drying out. Then she grabbed the old leather-bound book that Thomas had given her and they headed out into the evening.

"So, have you learned anything about your family yet?" Jake asked, nodding at the old book.

She shook her head. "I'm still in the seventeen hundreds. I know I'm related to all these people, but I haven't read about anyone who sounds familiar. I guess there were four Eckstein brothers who originally came to Niederbipp. One died two years after they got here, but it's hard to make sense of how they all line up. I just found a pedigree chart when I was thumbing through the book yesterday. I think it might help make more sense. There are a lot of things I want to figure out before I meet Mr. Allan's kids. It's weird to think I have third cousins out there who I don't even know and have never heard of."

Both of the computers were available when they walked through the library doors. Roberta Mancini looked up over the top of a lusty romance novel that looked like it had been read many times. She scowled at them both when they said hello and pushed the timer across the counter without saying a word.

While Jake began the long process of accessing his email account on the dial-up connection, Amy opened her book to the pedigree chart. After four long minutes, the email opened. It had been more than a month since Jake had been on the computer, and he was surprised to find so many emails that had piled up since then. Most of them were junk. One from Hudson University inquired where he would like his diploma sent. Another, from Andreas, the Greek potter, called him a nincompoop and several less savory names in broken English for not showing up to the job he'd been offered. Several short emails followed from his roommates, wondering where he'd landed. Instead of responding to each one individually, he wrote one email and copied all of them, telling them where he was and what he was doing, along with an invitation to his wedding. He tried to imagine how they might respond to the news. He knew they wouldn't come. He knew they would probably all think he'd lost his mind. But for the first time since he'd met them, he knew he really didn't care what they thought. None of them had ever been good friends, not like the friends he'd gained since coming to Niederbipp.

The timer went off and Amy returned to the counter to have Roberta reset it. Jake smiled to himself as he listened to Amy trying to tame Roberta's sour attitude with kindness, but she gave up and returned to the computer table, rolling her eyes. Jake tried not to laugh as he worked quickly on an email to his professor. He told him about how happy he was and how he was enjoying living and working in Niederbipp. He talked briefly about his pots and finally, invited him to the wedding.

Jake had shared a friendship with Dr. Eric Lewis for the four years they'd worked side by side. Most of the formalities of a student/professor relationship had been gone for a couple of years, but as Jake clicked the send button, he realized how his perspective on that relationship had changed since coming to Niederbipp. Despite the lack of formalities, their friendship had never been very nurturing. It had been a working relationship, one that now seemed cold and rather empty, where before, Jake had considered Dr. Lewis one of his best friends. As he sorted through the rest the emails, mostly spam, he wondered to himself if he had ever really known friendship before coming to Niederbipp. The closeness he felt to everyone he'd met here already exceeded the closeness he'd felt with anyone at school. He wondered to himself what it was about this place that made things so much more meaningful.

When the timer went  off again, Jake got up this time to have Roberta reset it, while Amy jumped on the second computer to send an email to her girlfriends to announce her engagement and upcoming wedding. Jake closed out of his email and sat in front of the computer screen—thinking.

It had been at least a year since he had looked for his father. Part of him wanted to know if he was out there, but another part, maybe a bigger part, was fearful that he really might be. A memory unexpectedly flashed through his mind like a movie. He'd seen this same movie a hundred times before. It was the last memory he had of his father. It was a strange memory—one he'd struggled with every time he remembered it. He was only a child, not much older than three. He was crying as he watched his parents arguing in the kitchen of a home he barely remembered. The words they exchanged had been lost over the years, if he ever knew them, but he remembered the violence—his father pushing his mother against the wall—his mother collapsing on the floor. Then there was the twisted face of his father as he turned on him to yell loudly before turning and kicking his mother as she lay on the floor. And then he was gone, never to be seen again. Jake had never spoken to anyone about that memory. It was too painful—too ugly, and though the memory had returned many times, there were never any answers.

Jake stared at Google's home page for a long moment before his hands moved to the keyboard and typed in his father's name. John Henry Kimball. He hesitated for anther moment before clicking on the search button. The first ten of 23,100 links to Jake's search popped up after a short delay. The first several links were for genealogical research about two different men who shared his father's name but had died in 1931 and 1943. He scrolled down, looking at other links.

"Are you okay," Amy asked, startling Jake.

"Yeah, why?"

"Your hand is shaking the table."

He looked down at his hand. It was wrapped around the mouse, trembling like a leaf in a stiff autumn breeze.

"What's up?" she asked, looking concerned. She turned to Jake's computer screen and then slid her chair closer to his, putting her arm around him and resting her chin on his shoulder. "Did you find him?"

Jake shook his head. "Not the right one."

The timer went off for the third time, but they ignored it. Less than a minute later however, the cranky voice of Roberta Mancini sounded from the speaker directly above their heads: "The Niederbipp Public Library will be closing in five minutes. Please bring any books you wish to take with you to the front desk for checkout. The library will reopen tomorrow morning at ten. Thank you." There was a pause before she began again, sounding quite put out. "If you are using the computers, your time was up two minutes ago."

Jake might have laughed if the circumstances had been different, but her voice and attitude only made him angry.

"Should we go?" Amy asked, looking apologetic.

"I guess so." Jake was surprised by the sound of reluctance he heard in his voice. Like an elusive and reoccurring itch in the middle of his back that couldn't be reached, he turned away from the computer, resigning himself once again to the fact that he might never find his father. Still, there was relief that he hadn't.

They stood and were just beginning to walk out when a door opened at the back of the library and they turned to see Thomas locking the door to his small office. They stood near the front counter and waited for Thomas to see them.

"What are you two doing here?" he asked when he reached the end of the aisle and finally looked up.

"Sending wedding announcements," Jake said.

Thomas looked embarrassed. "I'm sorry I didn't congratulate you when I saw you earlier, Jake. I had a lot on my mind this morning."

"That's okay," Jake said, smiling.

"I'd like to talk to you both for a minute if you don't mind."

"I'd like it if you left so I could lock up," Roberta said, lifting her wrist and pointing to her watch, scowling.

"Have you eaten?" Thomas asked, as they walked through the narrow alleyway between his house and the library.

"No," Jake responded. "Not since we ate lunch."

"Then wait here," he said as they reached the stone pathway that lead to his cottage. "I'd invite you in, but it's a mess."

He returned a moment later with a brown paper bag. "This is my favorite bread that Sam bakes." He handed the bag to Amy. "It's Vollkornbrot—the polar opposite of Wünder Bread."

"Is it made out of bricks?" Amy teased, surprised by its weight and apparent density.

"Nope. Just a hundred percent whole grain, sourdough, rye bread with a bunch of seeds to boot." He struck out across the courtyard toward the cemetery and Jake and Amy hurried to keep up. "I received a disturbing phone call this afternoon," Thomas said, opening the  gate for Amy and Jake to pass through. "I came by The Pottery, hoping to catch you, but no one was home during business hours."

"I … we …" Jake said, stammering.

Thomas smiled. "Relax, I was just giving you a hard time. You two have a lot to organize if you're going to be ready for the fifth."

"So, tell us about the phone call," Amy said, a look of concern in her eyes.

Thomas waited until they were seated on the two benches closest to Lily's grave. "Charlie called. He said it didn't go well."

"What?" Jake said. "What happened?"

"He told me he put off talking to Matt about the letters until they were ready to leave—apparently they had a lot to catch up on. He told me the whole mood of the visit changed when he excused himself to go the car and returned with the box of letters and the mug. He said Matt became very quiet. Charlie tried to talk to him—tried to tell him what you and I had both told him about his dad, but he said Matt didn't say anything after that. He felt like it totally flopped, and when he and Jodi left shortly after that, Matt wouldn't even shake his hand."

Jake looked at Amy, then back at Thomas, concerned. "So what does this mean?"

"It means this may be one of my last loaves of bread," Thomas said, reaching for the bag. He pulled out the loaf and tore off three big pieces, handing one to each of them. "We'd better enjoy it while it lasts. I don't expect Sam is going to be very happy about this. We may have turned the rift into an abyss."

Jake leaned over, resting his elbows on his knees. He took a big bite of the dark bread, chewing slowly as he collected his thoughts. "Maybe it was a dumb idea," he finally said. "I just couldn't get it out of my head. I imagined Matt sitting down, looking at all those letters, and realizing that his father really did love him." He shook his head, looking away. "I don't understand."

"What part don't you understand?" Thomas asked.

Jake sat up and stretched. His emotions were near he surface and he was trying to find the right words. "I guess I just don't understand any of this. I've waited my whole life to hear from my father. I'd die to have some tangible evidence that he loves me or even cares if I exist." Jake shook his head. "If a shoe box full of letters doesn't faze him, I guess I don't know what will."

Thomas took a deep breath. "Well, you kids tried to help. Hell, we all did. That ought to count for something, right? I'm just afraid it won't be enough to keep Sam from tripping a fuse."

"So, Sam is down a mug and eight years' worth of letters that had all been sent back anyway. It obviously didn't go how any of us hoped it would, but *we did something*, didn't we? I'll take the fall for this," Jake said. "There's no reason for you to go down with me, Thomas. If you hadn't taken the letters, I would have." He turned and looked at Amy. "I've learned a couple things in the past few weeks. If we live our life based on fear, we'll either do nothing or we'll run away from the problem. I don't know if either of those options has ever produced anything good."

Jake looked Thomas in the eye. "It may have been a bad idea, but we did it out of love, didn't we? We did it out of love and I know that's better than not doing anything because of fear."

Thomas looked surprised, but then nodded. "You are right, Jake. You're absolutely right."

"I don't know why, but I still have a good feeling about this," Amy said. "It may take another eight years, but Matt is going to read those letters. I'm willing to wager my three years' worth of bread on it."

"I think you already did, didn't you?" asked Thomas.

"I guess we did," Amy responded.

As they ate what they knew might be their last of Sam's bread, the conversation turned to happier things as Jake and Amy talked about their plans for the wedding. Thomas had participated in far more Quaker weddings than Catholic weddings, and he encouraged them to move forward with their plans, offering his help. They  also told him about their lunch with the Yoders and the things they'd learned from them. While Jake recalled the Yoders story of praying that a potter would come, Thomas knelt on the ground in front of Lily's grave, scooping away the rich, brown dirt in front of her colorful headstone with his finger tips. They watched him carefully, trying to figure out what he was doing.

"Do you remember asking me how I knew that Isaac had a son?" Thomas asked.

"Yeah, you said you found out after Isaac died, right," Jake replied, his curiosity piqued.

"Yes. Do you remember what I told you—how I found out?"

Jake and Amy looked at each other. "Didn't you say something about the evidence always being there, but that you just needed to … dig a little deeper," Amy said, with wide eyes. They quickly knelt on either side of Thomas as he scooped away another handful of dirt, exposing a small, cobalt blue tile that was embedded in the side of the cement grave marker six inches below the surface of the dirt. It simply read,

Jakob Henry Bingham
March 14, 1955
May the light of love
shatter the darkness.

"It was here all along," Thomas said. "It was here all those years I sat and ate lunch on Henry's bench with him."

"How'd you find it?" asked Amy.

Thomas began pushing the dirt back into the hole he'd made before answering. "I helped move some of the dirt around after Isaac was buried. That's when I discovered it … when I saw the boy's name and date. It answered a lot of questions for me—about why Isaac always reached out to children—about why he understood loss." Thomas dusted off his knees and sat back down on Henry's bench to clean out the dirt from under his fingernails.

"Why do you think he hid the tile?" Jake asked, after he and Amy sat down next to him. "Why do you think he never told anyone about his son?"

"I don't know for sure, but you both read his journal. Nobody knew about this. Nobody knew Lily was pregnant when she died. After reading in his journal about that dream he had about Lily and Jakob … it was heartbreaking. I think it must have been too much. Things were different back then. Women often lost as many babies as they delivered. He may have thought that no one would understand him making a gravestone for a son before he breathed his first breath. That's one of the reasons I was so happy to finally read Volume 31."

"Did Isaac ever tell you about dreams he had?" Jake asked.

"Yes," he said, smiling warmly. "He told me you were coming,

Jake. He spoke many times about the potter who would come to take his place."

"What did he tell you?"

"He told me you'd be young and stubborn—that you would understand sadness, but that you would have a heart that could learn to love the people he loved."

Jake nodded thoughtfully. "Why didn't you tell me any of this before?"

Thomas shook his head and smiled. "Would you have believed me, Jake?"

"I don't know."

"I wanted to. I wanted to tell you the minute you walked through Isaac's door with that bouquet of flowers."

Jake smiled, memories of that night running through his mind.

"I didn't feel like you were ready to hear the full truth," Thomas continued.

Amy shook her head. "Thomas, you're a Candlelighter! Why couldn't you just tell him that he was supposed to be here—that this is his destiny?"

Thomas took a deep breath and sat up straight. "Because that has never been the way of truth," he said resolutely. "You have to *seek* truth—you have to *choose* it before it will reveal itself to you. It's never easy to watch people suffer because of the choices they make, but a Candlelighter cannot force the truth on anyone. We simply have to wait with patience for the time and condition that is right—for a person to ask. I don't believe the Father of Heaven and Earth is any different. He will never force us down a path where we do not want to go. Instead, He waits for us to ask for the direction we need. If we sincerely ask, He will feed us truth, one spoonful at a time. If we accept what we are given, He will wait for us to ask for more. But if we say we're full—that we don't want any more, He will leave us alone and wait for us to be humble enough to call on Him again.

"Jake, as I said, I knew who you were when you walked through the door, but I knew that your decision to stay had to be entirely yours—as it was for me—as it was for Isaac. If I had brought you to the cemetery and shown you this tile the first night you were here, what would you have done?"

"I probably would have freaked out and left as soon as I could," Jake said, laughing.

"That's exactly what I was afraid of. Most of us aren't ready to see the big picture until we've spent the time to put the puzzle together, piece by piece."

Jake and Amy nodded, each understanding that truth in their own way.

"So, what do you two propose we do about Sam's letters?" Thomas asked.

"Isn't it obvious?" Jake asked. "We wait and pray for the right pieces to fall into place."

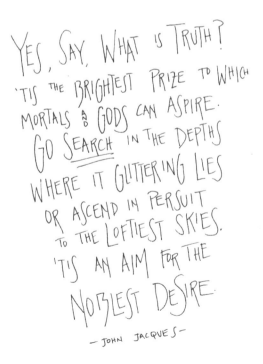

YES, SAY, WHAT IS TRUTH?
'TIS THE BRIGHTEST PRIZE TO WHICH
MORTALS & GODS CAN ASPIRE.
GO SEARCH IN THE DEPTHS
WHERE IT GLITTERING LIES
OR ASCEND IN PERSUIT
TO THE LOFTIEST SKIES.
'TIS AN AIM FOR THE
NOBLEST DESIRE.

— JOHN JACQUES —

SHAZZAM!

ONCE YOU MAKE A DECISION, THE UNIVERSE CONSPIRES TO MAKE IT HAPPEN.
—RALPH WALDO EMERSON—

he eastern horizon was glowing with the first light of dawn when Jake turned off the kiln and climbed back into bed. Despite his fatigue, he wrestled with his thoughts for over an hour before falling to sleep. But even then, his sleep was fitful and broken, filled with weird dreams about having to bake his own bread in the kiln. He finally got up and went to work.

Nancy and David Garber stopped by just after Amy arrived. They were thrilled with the painting and seemed pleased that Emma and Tom

Parkin had commissioned one for themselves as well. They explained that they had business in Pittsburgh and hoped to drop the painting off at the frame shop on their way. After writing a check and including a sizable tip, they left as quickly as they'd come, leaving any questions about the meaning of the rocks to be answered another day.

Jake spent the rest of the day working on the wheel and attending to customers while Amy painted. Hildegard dropped by late in the afternoon to congratulate them and order another cat bowl. She gave Amy a warm hug and expressed her condolences for having to have Doug Eckstein as a father. After laughing at her stories of Doug's younger years, they invited her to the wedding and promised her a seat within striking distance, joking that it might help keep him in line.

Molly stopped by with Zane just before closing, and they quickly made arrangements for dinner. While Amy took care of Zane, Molly ran back to the store to pick up some buttermilk and her husband. They returned a half-hour later to find the aroma of pancakes wafting out of the apartment's open door and down the stairs into the courtyard.

"Dudes, how'd you know I was totally craving pancakes?" Kai said, bounding into the kitchen with a garment bag swung over his shoulder. He handed the bag to Jake.

"What's this?" Jake asked.

"It's your suit, man," he said, giving him a congratulatory bear hug. "You can pass it on to the next chump who gets married. I'll never need it again."

"What about when Zane gets married?" Jake asked "He might want to wear it."

"Nah, that's like thirty years away. I don't want to hang on to it for that long. I would have tossed it a long time ago if Bob hadn't bought it for me."

Jake handed Kai the spatula and went into the bedroom to change, emerging a minute later looking like a businessman, except for his gray T-shirt.

"You clean up good for a red-neck potter," Molly said, clapping.

Amy smiled at him, but refrained from clapping as she was still holding the sleeping Zane in her arms.

"I can't believe it fits," Jake said, parading about like a runway model. "I don't know if I've ever worn a suit before."

"You'd remember it if you had," said Kai. "The only thing I like about wearing a suit is that you don't have to worry if your top matches your bottom."

The girls laughed and Jake went back into the room to change. When he returned, he put a saucepan on the stove, and added butter, sugar and buttermilk, stirring the ingredients together as the butter melted. When it began boiling, he took the pan off the stove and added a teaspoon of vanilla and teaspoon of baking soda, stirring it in until the concoction became frothy.

"What is that?" asked Kai as Jake poured the liquid into a small blue pitcher.

"It's called buttermilk syrup. It's an old family recipe. You're gonna love it."

After Amy said grace, they filled their plates with pancakes and Jake passed the syrup to Kai to get started. He sniffed it apprehensively before pouring the syrup over his pancakes. Without waiting for the others, Kai dug in with his fork, cutting off a huge piece of golden pancake and forking it into his mouth. Any hesitation he might have had was gone the minute the syrup touched his lips.

"Holy Cow!" he said, his mouth still full. "This is way good."

Jake laughed as Molly and then Amy took the pitcher, pouring the syrup over their pancakes.

"This would make dried grasshoppers taste good," Kai mumbled, his mouth full of his second bite.

The girls followed and soon they were all singing the praises of Jake's concoction.

"Dude, we could totally sell this stuff. We could be rich," Kai said.

Jake laughed. "My roommates used to tell me that all the time, but I don't think it would package very well. You'd have to keep it in the fridge and then you'd have separation issues. I don't know if it's worth the headache."

"No, man, we could totally figure this out. We'd have to come up with a cool name like "Happy Juice" or "Pancake Frosting" or ..." He smacked his lips and looked like he was concentrating hard. "*Shazzam!* That's it! *Shazzam!*"

They all laughed.

"I'll tell you what," Jake said. "You know how Isaac has all those mugs hanging on the beam down in the studio?"

They all nodded.

"Well, maybe we can start a similar thing up here with forks. You can pick your favorite fork and tape it to the ceiling, and every time you come over for some "Shazzam" you can use your favorite fork and we can sit down and talk about getting rich from selling my ancestral ..."

"No, I'm serious here," Kai continued. "We'd need a catchy slogan, like, um, 'Give your pancakes some passion with Shazzam!' or ..."

They laughed again and moved on while Kai continued to come up with silly slogans with each bite. The evening passed quickly as they talked about plans for the wedding. Molly asked about a honeymoon and upon discovering that Jake and Amy hadn't even talked about it, she opened an hour-long conversation about the countless places they could go, both near and far. But with tourist season in full swing, they knew they shouldn't be gone long enough to get to the other side of the world and back; at least not now. If they waited until fall, they could save enough money to spend three weeks or more in Europe, maybe Switzerland or Italy, where Amy could paint and Jake could visit other potteries.

It was after ten when Kai and Molly took Baby Zane home. As Jake and Amy washed the dishes and cleaned up the kitchen, they made a mental list of the things they still needed to do before the wedding. The list was short: cake for the guests, moving Amy's stuff into the apartment, checking on a marriage license, and making sure the church was available. Thomas knew of their plans, but they didn't want to make any assumptions they might be sorry about later. In less than three days, their marriage had been planned and organized without much pain or expense.

When the dishes were dried and put away, Jake took Amy's hand and they walked out into the night, following Hauptstrasse's lighted path.

"What are you thinking about?" Jake asked as they walked past Mancini's Ice Café.

"I was thinking about how right this feels," Amy replied. "It just feels like everything is as it's supposed to be."

Jake nodded, veering from the middle of the road to the old stone bench where they'd met for lunch so many times before. "I've been thinking about that, too. I find myself thinking that because things are going so well, something bad is going to happen."

"Like what?"

"I don't know. I keep thinking about Isaac's sketchbook, the one we found in the studio. Everything was wonderful for Isaac. He was happy and married to a wonderful woman. They were pregnant with their first child and Isaac was figuring out how to make a living as a village potter, and then, BANG! Everything changed. His whole life was turned upside down. I know our problems—I mean the ones we haven't seen yet—I know they're coming. Everybody has them—my parents, your parents, Gloria and Joseph. I can't think of anyone who doesn't have them. I guess I've just been wondering how long things are going to last the way they are."

Amy nodded, and leaned her head on Jake's shoulder. "I had a roommate, my freshman year, from Seattle. When she first got there, she used to get giddy every time the sun was shining." She stopped to laugh. "She'd wake us all up and get us moving so we wouldn't miss out on experiencing a sunny day. She told me once that in the winter months, she would often go sixty days in a row without seeing the sun—just rain and clouds every day. Her mom taught her to spend those cloudy days making plans for when the sun returned so they wouldn't waste a minute of sunshine."

Jake smiled to himself, remembering the time he spent with his mother on sunny days on the shores of Lake Champlain.

"It made me feel guilty for all the sunny days I'd wasted by sleeping in and then dragging myself around the house all day. I don't know Jake; maybe we need the clouds to help us appreciate the sunny days. Isn't that what Eric said the other day? Something about not being able to appreciate the light without experiencing the darkness."

"Okay, but doesn't it make you a little bit nervous about what might be coming. I mean, we've had it so good for so long."

"Aren't you forgetting that you were in the hospital just three weeks ago? That I had my bags packed and was on my way home?"

Jake squirmed. "I guess that's my point. That happened so fast. Everything changed so quickly. It just seems that there really aren't any guarantees in this life. It's always changing—always moving away from the things that are comfortable and normal."

Amy lifted her head and turned to face him. "Jake, I love you. I know we have no idea what might be coming, but I love you and I'm grateful that we're going to be facing whatever's coming together."

Jake nodded thoughtfully. "Promise me something, Amy."

"Okay."

"Promise me that when things change—that you'll remind me of this night—sitting here on this bench—talking about how happy we are."

She laughed. "I promise, Jake. But promise me something in return."

"Sure."

"Promise me that when things are good, we won't spend too much time talking about the hard times, or the bad times, or the times we made each other crazy. Promise we'll stay and play in the sunshine for as long as we can, and when the clouds pile up on the horizon, we'll do all we can to outrun them."

"It's a deal," Jake said, leaning over to kiss her.

BUTTERMILK SYRUP SHAZZAM

1 1/2 CUP BUTTERMILK
3 CUP SUGAR
2 STICKS BUTTER
2 TSP BAKING SODA
2 TSP VANILLA

MELT FIRST 3 INGREDIENTS UNTIL IT COMES TO A BOIL.
REMOVE FROM HEAT AND STIR IN BAKING SODA AND VANILLA

MIX IN DEEP SAUCE PAN AS THE SODA WILL CAUSE THE
MIXTURE TO TRIPLE IN VOLUME.
POUR OVER ALL THINGS BREAKFAST. YUMMY.

LOVE

AS I LIVED UP TO THE HIGHEST LIGHT I HAD,
HIGHER AND HIGHER LIGHT CAME TO ME.
—PEACE PILGRIM—

fter watching Amy tweak minor shadowing details on the Parkins' painting over and over again for several hours on Thursday afternoon, Jake walked to her side to take a closer look.

"It's beautiful," he said after a moment of observation.

"You don't think it's too dark in the corner there?"

"No. I think it looks great."

"I don't know. That one rock there seems a little flat, doesn't it?"

"Isn't it supposed to be a flat rock?"

"Well, yeah, but doesn't it ..."

Jake took her by the shoulders and turned her toward him, kissing her softly.

"What?" she asked, laughing.

"You remind me of me, the first time I made a mug. When it came time to make the handle, I messed with it over and over again until it was so screwed up, I threw it away. My teacher used to always tell me that the most important thing for any artist to learn is when to stop."

Amy smiled, blushing slightly. "My teachers used to tell me the same thing. Do you honestly think its okay?"

"Amy, I love it. I'm sure the Parkins are going to be really happy, too."

"Really?"

"This isn't about the painting, is it?"

"What do you mean?"

"Amy, this is the best painting you've ever done. This is about your parents, isn't it? Are you nervous about them seeing it?"

Amy let out a long breath. "Is it that obvious?"

Jake nodded, looking back to the painting.

"I've kind of resigned myself to the fact that my parents may never be happy about the direction I've chosen in life, but I guess a part of me still hopes they can open their eyes and see how happy I am ... that I am still a contributing member of society, even though I didn't choose the path they chose for me. Do you think that's too much to ask for?"

Jake shrugged. "I've wondered sometimes if my mom would still be worrying about me making a living in pottery if she were alive."

"I thought you said she was happy that you'd found something you loved to do."

"She was, but that was at the very end. She'd encouraged me when it was just a hobby, but I always sensed a lot of worry whenever I talked about making a living from it. I'm not sure she ever really understood what I was doing—what I was dreaming about."

"At least you had a chance to talk about it. I know my parents have never really understood what I wanted to do. It was always about making use of the education they paid for. It was always about the money I'd be making. I guess that's what it's always been about for my brothers too. I never fit that mold. I always felt there had to be more to life than that."

"Like what?" Jake asked, trying to hide a smile.

She poked him in the ribs before crossing her arms and leaning her back against the shelf to look at the painting. She tilted her head to one side. "Do you think it's crooked?" she asked.

"No, the floor is," Jake responded with a laugh. He leaned his back against the shelf, too, until their shoulders touched. "What do you think they'll say when they find out you've been painting pictures of rocks?"

Amy shook her head. "I don't know. I doubt they'll understand."

"Do you?"

"About the rocks?" she asked.

"Or about the painting?"

Amy took a deep breath, blowing her hair off her forehead as she exhaled. "I'm pretty sure I don't understand what the rocks mean, but these paintings have been good for me."

"In what way?"

"They've made me think. They've made me focus on the minutia. I've always tried to do that anyway, but this was the first time since I painted those bugs at the campus pond that I think I really saw the details. It's made me appreciate Mr. Allan and his treasures. It has also given me a chance to be still—to think about what Eric said about the minimum investment."

Jake nodded, encouraging her to continue.

"It makes me wonder how much I've missed along the way, trying to hurry through life. I knew I needed to come here this summer, but I feel as though I'm just beginning to understand why."

"Because you needed to meet me, right?" Jake said, nudging her with his elbow.

"You're a huge part of it, Jake, but being here has opened my eyes to a lot of other things too. It's made me think about who I am and what's really important in life. I felt that I had a pretty good idea about that when I came here, but I feel like maybe I only saw a small piece of the whole. It's like that tour Thomas gave us of the church. Those symbols were there all along, but we never really saw them until they were shown to us. I wonder what else I've been missing or misunderstanding. I guess I wonder if I've been like my dad."

"Amy, you're nothing like your dad."

"I don't know. I feel like I've also been blind to what is right in front of me."

"We all have that problem sometimes,  don't we?"

"Probably. I've been wondering, though, what it is about this place that seems to open all of my senses."

"What have you come up with?" Jake asked.

"Well, the first one would have to be love. It just seems like the river of love runs deeper here—like the current is stronger. Do you know what I mean?"

Jake nodded, thinking of the image her words had just conjured up in his mind. "I think so. It definitely seems like people care more about their neighbors here."

"Yeah, even when they're strangers or a couple of young kids like us. Everybody has accepted us and encouraged us. I realized this afternoon that not one person has asked us if we're not crazy to be thinking about making a living as artists."

Jake nodded thoughtfully. "I guess you're right. I can't say I've missed that kind of harassment."

"Neither have I. The only people I've heard it from since I got here is my family, and that's been easy to ignore if I can stay away from the phone."

"Easy?" Jake asked.

"Okay, not entirely, but I feel like the love I've felt from you, and Bev and Jerry, and everyone here has burned off the clouds of doubt and fear that my family has tried to put in my way. I feel that I'm beginning to understand what life could be like if I never had to deal with fear again."

"What if we didn't?" Jake responded. "What if we decided we wouldn't let fear into our lives or have any control over our decisions?"

"Do you think that's possible?" Amy asked.

"I don't know. From all we heard about Isaac, isn't that the way he lived his life? Can you think of anything you've heard that would suggest otherwise?"

Amy shook her head after a moment of thoughtful silence. "It was all about love, wasn't it?"

Jake nodded, his brow furrowed.

"What are you thinking?" Amy asked.

"About something Eric said the other day—that perfect love casteth out all fear. Do you think it's possible for people to have perfect love?"[1] "I'm not sure, but it doesn't seem that fear would have much power if perfect love were part of our natural make up." Her eyes widened suddenly. "Jake, have you ever seen the Broadway production of Les Miserables?"

"No, why?"

"I was thinking about my favorite line from that production when we were talking to Charlie and Jodi. It says, "To love another person is to see the face of God.""

Jake nodded. "I've heard that before."

"I don't think I ever thought about it this way before, but it doesn't seem like much of a stretch to say that love is a product of God."

"Go on," Jake said, encouraging her.

"Well, if perfect love casts out all fear, and if love comes from God,

[1] John 4:18

wouldn't it suggest that without perfect love—without God, there is only fear? That without God, fear has power? That without light there is only darkness?"

Jake let out a long breath. "Kind of sounds like our world sometimes, doesn't it?"

Amy nodded. "But it doesn't sound like anything we've experienced here. Maybe love, like that keystone in the arch at the church, is what holds it all together."

Jake walked back into the studio, returning with his sketchbook open to the notes he'd taken during the tour of the church.

"What did you remember?" Amy asked.

Jake pointed to his sketch of the archway, resting his finger under the keystone. He pulled out his pen and quickly sketched a similar archway underneath the first, but this time, instead of writing the symbols for Alpha and Omega on the top stone, he wrote the word "love." "Have you ever heard that God is love?" Jake asked.

"I was just thinking the same thing," Amy responded. "Remember what Eric said—how Isaac encouraged him to spread the idea of Niederbipp throughout the world through his slide shows? What if it was all about love? What if Isaac wasn't trying so much to spread Niederbipp as he was trying to spread the example of a town that was full of love?"

"A city that is set on a hill ..." Jake mused.

"What do you mean?" Amy asked.

Jake left the front desk and returned from the studio a moment later with the old bible from the shelf above the wedging table. He flipped it open, turning to the page where he'd first discovered the idea of the candle—Matthew 5, and read aloud, starting with verse 14.

Ye are the light of the world. A city that is set on a hill cannot be hid. Neither do men light a candle and put it under a bushel, but on a candlestick and it giveth light unto all that are in the house. Let your light so shine before men that they may see your good works, and glorify your Father which is in heaven.

"Sounds like Niederbipp."

"Yeah. I didn't see it before, but I guess I wasn't really looking. We missed it, didn't we? We missed the big picture," he said.

"Do you think we could have seen it before?" she asked.

"What do you mean?"

"Do you think we could have recognized any of this without all the stuff we've learned in the past few weeks?"

Jake looked away. "Maybe not," he said, his eyes wandering over the walls of the showroom, finally resting on Amy's painting. "What else do you think we've missed?"

"I don't know, but considering the things we've discovered in the past weeks, I'd guess we might have missed more than we've actually seen. I … I guess it makes me a little more sympathetic toward my dad."

Jake looked at her for a long moment before nodding, understanding what she was really saying. Her father had missed some of the most important things in his daughter's life. He really didn't even know her, his only daughter. But this realization of all the things they had missed right under their own noses gave Jake a different understanding of her father.

"So, how are we going to be different?" Jake asked after a long silence. "How are we going to be different with our own kids?"

She looked at Jake for a long time before answering. "We're going to have to always remember love, and do our best to listen and to see."

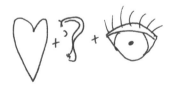

ONE STONE AT A TIME

WHO IS RICH? HE THAT REJOICES IN HIS PORTION.
—BENJAMIN FRANKLIN—

Where the heck have you two been all week?" Sam asked as he walked through The Pottery's open front door on Friday morning. "I was beginning to wonder if you eloped." He dropped a bag full of bread on the front counter next to Amy's easel. "I don't get you two. You were averaging a loaf a day when I was bribing you to get my floor done, and now that you've actually *earned it*, I don't see you all week."

"Maybe we're just trying to prolong our three years' worth of bread," Amy replied, setting down her brush to give Sam a hug. "Are you making house calls now?" she asked.

Jake came from around the corner, wiping his hands on his apron. "I guess we've been too busy to eat," he lied, trying to conceal the guilt he still felt at taking Sam's letters and mug. He shook Sam's hand but tried to avoid looking him in the eye.

"I've heard nothing but compliments about my new floor," Sam said, slapping Jake on the back. "I brought you your favorites, but thought I'd better stop by and find out more about this cake I'm supposed to be making for your wedding. Have you made any decisions yet?"

Jake looked at Amy, feeling relieved to change the subject. "Do you have any suggestions?" he asked.

"Of course, but I don't want to push anything on you. I was just thinking today that a carrot cake would be nice."

"With cream cheese frosting?" asked Amy.

"Naturally, though it's not bad with marzipan fondant too. How many guests do you expect to have?"

"Umm," Jake said, looking to Amy for the answer.

"Probably about sixty, if everyone comes."

"Good. And will three tiers be sufficient or would you like to have five?"

"No, three is enough," Amy said. "I don't want you to go to any more trouble than you already have."

"Nonsense! My wife always helps out with the wedding cakes. It's one of the few reasons that she spends time in the bakery. She's been hounding me to find out what you want ever since she heard you were engaged. She's a whiz at cream cheese frosting. What would you like on top? Some flowers, maybe?"

Amy looked at Jake this time. "Uh, sure, flowers would be nice," she said after she watched him shrug.

After Sam was gone, the angst Jake had felt about the letters returned with a vengeance. He was relieved at first when Thomas, their partner in crime, stopped by after lunch to check on them, but Thomas was cool and nervous and finally admitted that he, too, had been uneasy. After their discussion was interrupted several times by folks dropping in to buy pottery, he left, promising to return if he heard anything more from Charlie.

The kiln was finally cool enough to unload by two, but Jake still had to use the leather gloves to handle the pottery, especially the big sinks, with their thick walls, that retained more heat than the tiles. He examined each basin carefully, excited that each of them had turned out so well. Only one of them was warped slightly. With one having met its doom on the floor before it was even glazed and two more coming out of the bisque firing with cracks, he was grateful again that he'd made eight basins even though only four had been ordered.

As he stacked the finished basins on the rack behind the front desk, he looked up at Amy's painting drying on the top shelf. He touched the corner lightly to see if the paint was still wet. "Hey, it's almost dry," he reported. "It must be the warm day."

Amy turned around to look. "I used a lot more Liquin than I usually do. It makes it dry faster, but it probably won't be completely dry till Monday."

"It looks really good," Jake said, admiring the painting again. He turned to see Amy smiling.

"I like it too."

"What are you painting now?" Jake asked, turning to the small painting, mounted to the easel.

"That old trowel that Sam gave me. It's weird, but I feel somehow connected to these tools. I was attracted to them the first time I saw them, but knowing I'm somehow related to whoever it was who owned them is really cool."

Jake picked up the trowel that was sitting on the front counter and turned it over in his hand, rubbing his thumb over the Eckstein name that had been branded into the wood. "So you haven't figured out who G. M. Eckstein is yet?"

"No. The book from Mr. Allan is complicated and full of lots of stories, but with Mr. Allan's birthday coming up, I feel like I need to figure this out soon. What are you doing tomorrow?"

"Uh, working I guess. Why?"

"I was thinking I'd like to finish that book. I might stay home and read if you think you can handle things here."

"Sure," Jake responded. He knew she wasn't asking permission—she didn't need to—but he'd grown so accustomed to having her around all the time that he was surprised by the strange feeling of loneliness that her plans elicited within his mind. He shook it off, knowing he would have plenty of work to keep his mind occupied. He went back to the kiln and began loading the wares he'd made over the past several days: Mr. Allan's Journey Jars, bowls and the mugs, including Amy's very special mug that he tried to hide in the back so it couldn't accidentally be seen before it was done.

With the kiln and shelves still hot from the previous firing, Jake reasoned that any moisture that remained in the pots would evaporate quickly without any additional heat, negating the need for the overnight candling process. After a half-hour of letting the pots soak in the hot box, Jake lit the burners, mentally preparing himself to lose sleep, baby-sitting the kiln through the night. Then he busied himself, organizing and cleaning up the studio that had been left in disarray for several days as he'd glazed.

He was just finishing when he heard voices in the showroom over the purr of the kiln. He looked up to see the happy faces of Tom and Emma Parkin. Tom had a big gold frame draped over his shoulder.

"I hope we're not too late to invite you two to dinner," Tom said through a generous smile.

"No," Jake said, looking up at Amy. "We haven't made any plans yet. What did you have in mind?"

"A bribe," Emma responded. "We need your help."

Jake smiled. "What can we do?"

"We just picked up the countertops for our new bathrooms, but I've got a sore back and Tom can't do it alone. We were hoping, if you don't mind, that maybe you could come out to the house and help us. It shouldn't take more than an hour."

"Sure," Jake said, taking off his apron. "Your sinks just came out of the kiln this afternoon."

"Wonderful," Tom responded, lifting the frame off his shoulder. "Nancy and David called us from the frame shop several days ago to see if we wanted them to order one for us too. I hope we did the right thing. It didn't occur to me until we just picked it up that the dimensions might be off a little. Do you think your painting will fit?" he asked, turning to Amy.

"There's only one way to find out," she said, looking up at the painting.

"Oh, my gosh," Emma gasped. "Is that *our* painting?"

"Yes. Is it okay?" Amy asked, suddenly unsure.

"Oh, my gosh," Emma repeated, a broad smile spreading across her face. "It's beautiful! I can't believe all the texture in those rocks. Amy, you're amazing!"

"Thanks," Amy said, beaming.

"Wow," Tom added. "We both really liked the Garbers' painting, but this … this is amazing." He put his arm over his wife's shoulder and squeezed her as they both stared up at the painting. "Can we take it home?" he asked.

"It's still a little bit wet, but since you have the frame, I think it would probably be okay," Amy said. She slid her easel over to one side of the counter before taking the frame from Tom. She laid the front side down on the counter before leaning the painting out from the wall and reaching behind it, cautiously gripping the Masonite board with the palms of her hands. Then she carefully walked to the counter and lowered it into the groove of the frame. It was a perfect fit.

Amy secured the painting in place with the shiny hardware that came with the frame before lifting it up for them to see the finished product.

"It's perfect," Emma squealed with elation.

"It really is," said Tom. "Between Amy's painting and the Garbers' choice of frame, this is really going to class up our dining room."

Before pulling the scooter around so they could follow the Parkins to their home, they all made a couple of trips to the pickup, carefully carrying the basins and the painting. Just a mile out of town, they turned off the highway and onto a gravel road that led into a grove of trees before opening onto a beautiful clearing. There, in the middle of the clearing, stood one of the most magnificent house either of them had ever seen. Two turrets framed the front of the two-storey mansion, built entirely of colorful, round rocks that looked like they'd been gleaned from the riverbanks. Jake and Amy stared at the building, so taken by its beauty that they were unable to move.

"Are you two coming?" Tom asked over his shoulder as he walked up the cobblestone path to the big front door. Amy jumped off and Jake parked the scooter behind the pickup. They each hefted a basin and followed the Parkins into their home, their eyes darting back and forth, trying to take it all in.

Emma led them through the entryway, down a wide corridor and into the dining room where an enormous table was draped with a cream-colored cloth, heavily embroidered on the edges. A dozen candlesticks graced the center of the table. On one end of the room was a pass-through to the adjacent kitchen. On the other was a wall of windows that looked out on a bright and welcoming flower garden. On one wall, running half the length of the table was a huge fireplace the likes of which, Jake had only seen in the medieval castles of Europe. The thick, wooden mantel stood nearly six feet high, dwarfing Emma. Together, Jake and Tom lifted the painting onto the mantel, and leaned it against the thickly plastered wall.

Emma strained to lifet a large, ornate, lidded glass jar, half-filled with rocks, and Jake rushed to her side to help. Tom took the jar from Jake, thanking him and nodding to a second one on the table behind him.

With Amy's painting flanked by the two jars, they all stood back to look at the grouping. Tom walked to the wall and flipped a switch, bathing the painting in a soft light that gave it even more depth and texture than they had recognized before.

"Wow," Jake said, a shiver running through his spine. "This is awesome."

"It *is* beautiful," Tom replied. "We've been waiting a long time for this—for the perfect painting to hang there." He put his arm over his wife's shoulder again and they smiled at each other, looking very content.

"So ... can I help you with those countertops?" Jake asked, after a long silence, anxious to see the rest of the house.

As they followed the Parkins outside, their eyes, now more accustomed to the light, took in all that they had missed before: the ornate rugs, the fine woodwork, and the room just off the entryway that housed a vast library and enough comfy chairs to keep several people happy for hours. The Parkins had been so unassuming, yet they were obviously enormously wealthy. As they returned to the late-model Ford pickup, Jake couldn't help but admire them for their humility. He knew he never could have imagined that they would have a house like this, that they would have this kind of money. Taking one end of the granite countertop, Jake watched as the veins in Tom's arms bulged when he picked up the other end, and he knew Tom was no stranger to hard work. He knew they could probably afford to hire a whole crew of workers to do this work, yet they were working on it themselves. He was anxious to hear his story, to hear their story.

One after another, Jake and Tom carried the countertops up the stairs and into the area they referred to as the "new wing." Each of the rooms was elegant, with fine woodwork and Victorian wallpaper covering the walls, plush rugs that covered much of the hardwood flooring and delicate drapery hanging at the windows. The beds looked like something out of fairy tales, piled high with pillows and down comforters. The bathrooms tastefully matched the rooms in detail and design from the handcrafted, tile flooring, to the woodwork and linens. Every detail had been carefully thought out.

"I've never done countertops before," Jake said, as they placed the third one in its place. "How do you get them to match your walls and cabinets so closely? There's not even any wiggle room."

Tom smiled. "It helps when you do the work yourself. You get to know every nook and cranny."

"You made all of the cabinets yourself?" Jake asked incredulously.

"Yep. And every wall too."

"How long has this taken you?."

"Almost ten years."

"And you did it all by yourself?"

"No. Emma helped a lot. I couldn't have done it without her. We've worked together on it every day."

Jake nodded, picking up one end of the last countertop. His mind was reeling, trying to grasp what he'd just been told. Meticulous attention had been paid to every detail. Together, these two people had created something amazing with skill and expertise that he knew couldn't be duplicated, even by dozens of craftsmen.

"How did you do it?" Jake asked as they slid the last countertop into place.

"One stone at a time," Tom said, patting Jake on the back. "One stone at a time."

A PILE OF ROCKS

THE GREATEST HAPPINESS OF LIFE IS THE CONVICTION THAT WE ARE LOVED;
LOVED FOR OURSELVES, OR RATHER, LOVED IN SPITE OF OURSELVES.
—VICTOR HUGO—

Jake and Tom carried the basins into each of the new bathrooms, setting them on top of the new countertops. After washing their hands, they joined the women outside on the flagstone patio. Strips of gossamer fabric were strung overhead, suspended by thin wires that also supported strings of white lights, creating a dreamy ambiance under the shadow of the trees.

"We were hoping you'd join us," Emma said, handing each of them a plate with a gold-leaf rim. "Help yourself." She pointed to a silver tray filled with cold cuts and cheeses. "The kitchen staff won't be back from their vacation until next Tuesday, but Amy has just been telling me that the two of you have practically lived on sandwiches since you started dating. We'll have you back out when the Andrettis are here. They're amazing cooks."

Jake smiled at Amy who winked at him from where she sat, sipping her lemonade. This seemed like a dream world, so serene and beautiful. "How did you find this place?" Jake finally asked.

"We didn't really find it. It found us," Emma said.

"What does that mean?" asked Jake.

"Well, this wasn't much to look at twenty years ago. It had been abandoned for more than seventy years and everything was crumbling. Half the walls had fallen down with the roof, and a couple of generations of kids called this a haunted mansion." She nodded to Tom who stood and walked into the house, returning with a leather-bound album.

"This is the story of how our haunted mansion has become our home," Tom said, handing the book to Jake and Amy.

Jake opened the cover to the first page—a faded color photograph. It was the house, though barely recognizable. The turrets were really the only thing that looked at all familiar, and even they were damaged and falling apart, their conical roofs completely gone and a sizeable tree growing through the front window. Jake and Amy looked up at Emma and Tom, amazed.

"So how did you get from this to what you have now?" asked Amy.

"Deliberately," Emma and Tom said in unison.

"That's probably the most common question people have for us once they've seen where we started. It wasn't an easy thing to do. There were lots of times we wanted to give up and call it quits. Sometimes, when you're in the thick of a project like this, it's easy to lose sight of the big picture. But we had each other, and forty acres of silence all around us. You can learn a lot about yourself, and your spouse, in a setting like that."

"I don't mean to pry, but how much did this cost?" Amy asked, turning the page to see another shot of the dilapidated building that looked like it was beyond hope.

"A hundred and forty thousand dollars," Emma said. "That's all we had after we sold our home and paid off our debts."

"But, this must have cost millions," Jake said. "How did you get started?"

"By picking up the rocks that had fallen on the ground and deciding to build instead of throwing them at each other," Tom said, cryptically.

Emma put her hand on her husbands arm and smiled warmly. "We don't usually spill our guts to people who aren't part of our workshops, but with you getting married next week, we thought maybe we could share with you the secrets that we've discovered—that we've been given over the years. It's the stuff that makes our program work—the stuff that makes it real."

"We'd be honored," Amy said, looking at Jake who responded with a nod. "I'm guessing from Tom's comment and from the painting you commissioned that this might have something to do with rocks."

Emma smiled again and nodded. "Yes. Lots and lots of rocks."

"We've been curious about this all week as we've tried to figure out what the rocks are all about—as we've tried figure out why two couples would want paintings of rocks to hang in their homes," said Jake.

Tom turned to Emma and nodded, encouraging her to begin.

"Our story started more than forty

years ago. We met at Penn State in graduate school. We both came from broken homes and both of us were studying to become counselors."

"We wanted to fix families like ours," Tom added. "When you're a kid from a broken home, you grow up imaging solutions to the problems that your parents created. When we met, it felt like we already knew each other, almost like we'd grown up in the same home."

"In many ways, we had," said Emma. "Both of our parents divorced when we were ten years old and both of us spent the next eight years being pawns to our parents' schemes and games. We both learned manipulation and codependency and a new vocabulary that people who love each other shouldn't use. We learned in our early years that rocks can be used as weapons. We watched as our parents gathered up the sins of their ex-spouses and with hate and enmity, worked them over in their hands and minds until they became as solid as rocks. We watched as they collected these rocks, filling their backpacks and pockets with them so they could lob them at each other over and over again, hurting themselves and everyone who stood near them. Then they would gather them up, bind their wounds and start planning their next attack."

"That's some pretty intense imagery. I don't think I've ever heard it said like that before," said Jake.

"In all honesty, we hadn't either," Emma admitted. "It took us a long time to understand the truth of what we'd grown up watching—of what we'd become ourselves."

"You're not saying you've had marriage problems, are you?" asked Jake, looking surprised.

They laughed softly.

"History has an uncanny ability to repeat itself, even when two people from backgrounds like ours consciously try to make things better. Even with all the education and experience we'd gained along the way, I'm ashamed to admit that our marriage wasn't much better than our parents', at least not for the first twenty-five years," admitted Emma.

"That's hard to believe," Jake said. "I remember the first time I met you guys. I felt like you brought the sun into The Pottery with you, especially after ..." He paused, turning to look at Amy. "... especially after I'd met Amy's parents just a few minutes before."

"Thank you," Tom replied. "We feel like we've had a new light in our life since the day we bought this place. That was the same week we met your predecessor, Isaac. It was that week that we made the decision to work things out—to drop the rocks of enmity and start putting our life back together."

Jake shook his head. "You make it sound like it was really broken."

"In tatters," Emma said. "We'd been struggling for several years when Tom invited me to go with him for a drive one Sunday afternoon. I knew something dark was on his mind the minute I got in the car and we drove out of Pittsburgh. We used to go on Sunday drives all the time, but we'd never driven this far before."

"I figured I'd keep driving until I found the words to begin," Tom said, jumping in to explain. "I also knew how Emma would respond to what I had to tell her. So, like a coward, I went looking for a secluded place where I could take the tongue lashing I knew was coming."

Tom stopped and took a deep breath. "Experience is a harsh teacher. In our seminars, we spend a lot of time talking to our clients about how they can fix their marriages, but we rarely tell them the details about why we know so many of the answers. In the past forty years, between the two of us, I know we've probably heard and seen it all. You'd think that by watching others mess up their lives for years that we'd be less inclined to make the same mistakes, but even with all that information, we've experienced far more of our own mistakes than we should have. Some of us have to stick our hands in the fire before we recognize its power to hurt. I am one of those fools. I am one of those pots that Isaac kept on the shelf for others to learn from."

Jake and Amy looked at each other, surprised.

"Yes," Tom said with a little laugh. "We shared many meals with Isaac, surrounded by the lessons his predecessors had passed on to him. I'd like to think that this world would be a better place if all of us had lessons like that to learn from, but unfortunately, too many of us have to learn from our own sad experiences. After hearing a lifetime's worth of whisperings about my father's infidelity, I started down the same path and probably would have crashed the same way he had if it hadn't been for Emma's love and the light of truth."

Jake shook his head, not wanting it to be true. He'd admired the closeness of their marriage. This information seemed completely inconsistent with what he had observed.

"Those were the darkest days of my life," Tom continued. "For several years I'd been having an emotional affair with my secretary, and we both had made the decision to end our marriages and pursue the happiness we thought we deserved—together. It was against everything I knew … against everything I'd learned … against everything I'd been teaching to my clients and my children for twenty years.

"In the more-than-two decades that we'd been married, we'd seen our share of ups and downs. We had worked our way through the hard times and usually came out stronger, but after the twins left for college, our love for each other had grown lukewarm. We were busy with our careers, and the time we spent together became almost non-existent.

"I had spent more than a year thinking about a divorce, slowly peeling back any resistance I had, one layer at a time. I reasoned that Emma, with a successful counseling career of her own, could take care of herself. I didn't feel like she needed me. I'd convinced myself that with my children raised, my biggest responsibilities were taken care of, that we'd all be happier if we could pursue our happiness, independent of each other. I was that close," he said, holding his thumb and forefinger a quarter of an inch apart. "I was that close to hell."

"I had watched as so many of my clients had struggled in their marriages. Most of them had pulled through and were happier because of it, but I tried to ignore that. My secretary was young and beautiful and I was a fool. I'd created an imaginary happiness in my mind, and my wife was the only person who stood in the way." He reached over and took Emma's hand in his.

Jake watched as she smiled at her husband and squeezed his hand.

"I don't understand," Amy said, leaning forward. "How did you get from there to here?"

"You learn the true value of rocks," Emma responded with a wink. "Sometimes you have to see the darkness before you can appreciate the light."

JUST AS A CANDLE CANNOT BURN WITHOUT FIRE, MEN CANNOT LIVE WITHOUT A SPIRITUAL LIFE.
-BUDDAH

THE TRUE VALUE OF ROCKS

THE MAN WHO REMOVES A MOUNTAIN
BEGINS BY CARRYING AWAY SMALL STONES.
—WILLIAM FAULKNER—

 my shook her head. "I don't think I could deal with that," she said bluntly, sitting back in her chair.

"Neither could I," admitted Emma. "In fact, I didn't deal with it very well at all."

"So what happened?" Jake asked.

Tom took a deep breath, still visibly pained by the memory. "We were just on the other side of the highway. I knew I didn't want to be driving when I told her, so I pulled over and we walked down to the river."

"It was a good thing we were there," Emma said, breaking a smile. "I was rather loud. I've never taken bad news very well. For as cool as our marriage had become over the previous few years, I was hurt and angry. I had also had opportunities to step out on our marriage over the years, but I had turned them down, honoring the marriage vows that I had made.

"As Tom talked about how we should divide things up, I grew increasingly angry until I blew up. I know I slapped him a few times. I wanted to hurt him. I wanted him to feel the pain I was feeling. I was probably at the peak of my tantrum when out of nowhere, this man, dressed in overalls, walked up to us and interrupted me in a long string of words that I'm ashamed ever crossed my lips. His eyes stopped me cold.

"It was Isaac, wasn't it?" asked Amy.

"Yes," Emma said softly.

"Why was he there?" asked Jake.

"He told us we'd disturbed his meditation at his favorite tree and asked if he could either help our situation or show us a more suitable place to sow our words of anger. We held our ground, and I was about ready to tell  him where to go when he bent over and picked up a handful of pebbles. Handing several to each of us, he invited us to get it over with so he could get back to his meditation."

"What?" asked Jake. "Was he suggesting you stone each other with pebbles?"

"We wondered the same thing," said Tom, letting out a little laugh. "Whatever he meant, it seemed so outrageous that we both just stopped and looked at each other for a long time."

"What did Isaac do?" asked Amy.

"He stood about five feet away with his arms crossed over his chest, as if he were waiting for the fight to start. After a long and awkward silence, we both just dropped our rocks," reported Emma. "I was ashamed of the things I'd said. My anger at Tom was no less virulent, but as I stood in the silence, it was as if every awful word I'd said echoed off the hills and came back to me in an avalanche of slander and disgust."

"The silence offered me a similar reflection of what I'd just shared with my wife." Tom shook his head. "I was so ashamed of what I'd done to deserve the awful things she'd called me. It was such a strange moment—standing there—watching Emma as this old guy who we didn't even know stood a few feet away, waiting for something to happen."

"What *did* happen?" asked Jake.

"Isaac told us to follow him." Tom looked at his wife and patted her softly on the knee before he began again. "To be honest, I'm not sure why we did. I think we must have been in a state of shock. But we followed him up the same path we'd come down to the river. He led us across the highway, through a grove of trees and down an old dirt road that opened onto the clearing out front."

"That was the first time we saw the house," Emma said. "It was such a strange experience that I wondered for a moment if the man in overalls was some kind of a ghost who had escaped from the haunted mansion."

Jake and Amy snickered.

"He stopped for a minute at the edge of the clearing before he continued walking toward the old house. For some strange reason, we kept following him," Emma said.

"I've thought about that a thousand times over the past twenty years," Tom said. "If Emma hadn't experienced the same thing, I would have sworn it was a dream. I've heard about cases of post-traumatic stress disorder where people feel like they're walking around in dreams for days. That's the only practical reason I can think why we followed him all the way up to the walls of the house. Most of the windowpanes were broken and I remember how strange it was to have that tree growing out of the front window. A pile of rocks stood at the base of one of the turrets and Isaac invited us to sit down on the windowsill and rest our feet on the rubble."

"That was the first time we ever heard about the history of this house," said Emma. "I'm still not sure what is fact and what is fiction, but Isaac told us about the wealthy lumber baron, James Whitmore, who had this home built as a wedding gift for his young bride. The north wing was finished just before the wedding, and work continued for many years on the south wing as the family grew.

"According to the story, Mr. Whitmore was often gone on business for long periods of time, and on one particular trip, it was said that he became acquainted with a man who claimed he'd grown up with Mrs. Whitmore. Over drinks, it was divulged that she had lived a rather a riotous life before she'd become acquainted with Mr. Whitmore. Without any further provocation, Mr. Whitmore rode home as quickly as he could, incensed by the tale of his wife's supposed indiscretion. Drunk with anger, he dragged her out of bed by her hair and brutally rebuked her in front of her children and housemaids. In sorrow and humility, she admitted her transgressions that she'd long ago forsaken. But Mr. Whitmore refused to hear or forgive her. Enraged even further by her admission of guilt, he banished her to the unfinished south wing, dividing the children and staff between them and starting a civil war that raged for several years, fought with the sticks and stones that held the house together until both the family and the house were destroyed.

"When he was done with his story, Isaac bent over and picked up two of the rocks at our feet, handing one to each of us. Do you remember what he told us?" Emma asked, turning to her husband.

"I'll never forget it. He put his hand on each of our shoulders and looked us in the eye and said, "Each of you will have to decide what you'll do with these rocks, but I promise you that peace will only come if you use them to build something new to replace what is broken." Then he just wandered off the way we'd come, leaving us sitting there on the windowsill, alone.""

"That was it?" Jake asked. "That's all he said? He just left you there holding your rocks?"

"That's exactly what he did," Emma replied. "Most people probably would have accepted the figurative lessons those rocks were meant for us to learn, but something happened that afternoon that caused us both to stop mid-collision and realize we didn't like where we were headed. We spent the afternoon really talking to each other for the first time in years. We laughed and we cried and we gave ourselves permission to forgive each other. Like the old mansion, most of the things in our marriage were broken, but as we talked into the night, we found we both had a desire to repair things—to build something new. Instead of heading home, we drove into town and got a room at a bed and breakfast."

"I'm not sure we could have found our way home if we wanted to," said Tom with a hearty laugh. "We were so lost that we'd forgotten which way was up. I don't think we slept at all that night. We talked it out, clearing away the years of fog that had clouded our marriage. We both had successful careers and we were good at what we did. The whole experience that day helped us remember why we wanted to become counselors in the first place—to fix broken families. And so as the sun rose on the new day, we got up and set out to make it better than the day before."

"And we've tried to do that every day since," Emma added.

"I don't mean to sound skeptical," said Amy, "but help me understand this, Emma. I like to believe in happy endings, but this seems a little bit too ... ideal ... too simplistic. I mean, how do you forgive someone whom you've trusted with everything? It just seems like a bigger deal than what you're making of it."

"You're right, Amy. I'd be lying if I said it was easy to get through that. There were many days that I was frustrated, that I felt sorry for myself or was just plain angry, but every time I've felt a pang of anger, I've remembered the rocks, I remember this house. It was difficult to forgive. It certainly would have been easier to turn my back to Tom and say goodbye. I could have let his infractions destroy me and my family. Things like that destroy families every day around the world. I didn't want to be another statistic. I'm a fighter and I'm grateful I married one.

"Trust is a fragile thing, but it can be rebuilt, one stone at a time. It doesn't work for everybody, but we both wanted to change. We both wanted to find a way to be better—to be happy again. I know it wouldn't have worked if we both weren't willing to work on it. In the process, I discovered a lot of my own weaknesses. I don't know if we can fully appreciate the need for forgiveness until we recognize our own brokenness. I know we can't blame our spouses for the decisions we make, but we both decided to own the problems we'd created together. After more than twenty years of marriage, the line of delineation between my junk and Tom's junk was too fuzzy to recognize. It was *our* junk, and it required us both to go through the pile and discard the stuff we didn't need. In the end, it all comes back to the rocks, doesn't it? We could use them to rebuild a life together or we could use them to destroy ourselves and everyone around us."

"I still don't understand how you ended up buying this place," Jake said.

"That's a good story," said Tom. "We asked around and found out it had been deeded to the town of Niederbipp to pay for back taxes. When we spoke to the Mayor about it, he made us an offer we couldn't refuse—ten thousand dollars."

"For this?" Jake asked incredulously.

"No, for that," Tom said, pointing to the picture of the dilapidated house. "That was more than twenty years ago, and Niederbipp wasn't even on the maps back then. It was a good deal, if only for the land, but it was a lot of work. We emptied our wallets and shelled out our money for a down payment before we left that day. We were back up here the next weekend with our full payment. We came up every weekend for the first year, but after we had running water and electricity in one room, we moved up here so we could work on the house every night. That's when we decided to combine our practices and we started commuting to work together, spending our time in the car learning about masonry and woodwork and plumbing from books we found at the library. After three years, we were out of money, so we sold our house in Pittsburgh and bought tools and wood and mortar."

"But you guys had to have other people help you with this. There's no way you could have done this all by yourselves, even in twenty years," Jake said.

"We never said we did it alone," said Tom.

"Have you ever heard the story of Tom Sawyer whitewashing the old fence?" Emma asked.

"I think so. Didn't Tom trick a bunch of kids into … ?"

Tom raised his eyebrows, smiling. "What can we say? We have a lot of friends and grateful clients who wondered what we were doing out here in the country. Before long we had a full crew of helpers every weekend. We started small, one room at a time."

"But what about money?" Jake asked. "How did you keep things going?"

"Well, we were still working," Emma said matter-of-factly. "After ten years, enough people had heard about us and our project that we began hosting week-long marriage retreats. Using the house as a metaphor for marriage, we invited our participants to pitch in and lend a hand. There is something about *doing*, about getting your hands dirty that offers practicality and understanding to the theory of repairing a broken marriage. Most of the people who come to our retreats have very few skills that can be used on our home, but everyone can do something."

"I'll never forget the couple who spent three days straightening a five-gallon bucket full of rusty nails that we found in the cellar." Tom mused. "By the time they were done, they'd solved all their problems and remembered how to communicate with each other."

"Some weeks, we have to create work outside to keep couples from destroying our house. We send them out in the woods to dig post holes where they can work at the top of their lungs if they need without disturbing our other guests," explained Emma. "It usually only takes a couple of days of digging post holes before they figure it out—before they recognize the figurative fences they've built between themselves over the years."

"And over the course of a week, every couple gets to spend at least one day in the kitchen with the Andrettis," Tom said with excitement. "Learning to cook together is a great way to spice up your life, especially under the guidance of amazing chefs like Leo and Kim."

"The Andrettis were actually one of the first couples through our program," Emma added. "They fell in love with the house and did such a good job in the kitchen, we decided we could afford to hire them. They've been working for us ever since. Every couple has what it takes to make a meal together. But without a good recipe or an understanding of the spices of life, things can be pretty bland. Sometimes, by just taking away the fear of failing, couples come up with some of the most amazing dishes on their own. We've put together several recipe books over the years, full of new concoctions that couples invented by playing in the kitchen."

"That sounds fun, but my parents signed up for this?" Amy asked.

"Don't look so surprised," Emma responded, laughing at the quizzical look on Amy's face. "Lots of folks don't know exactly what they're getting into when they sign up, and maybe that's good. If people thought this was a work camp for folks with troubled marriages, we might have problems attracting clients, but each year, we have had to expand our workshops. They are always filled and we've never done any advertising. People come here, *remember* the reasons they fell in love in the first place, *discover* how to use the tools they already have to build a happy marriage, and in the process, they *become* something better, becoming the best advertising we could ever hope for.

"Even without knowing them, we can tell you that your parents will have at least one thing in common with the other eleven couples," Emma assured her.

"What's that?"

"They'll each show up with a backpack full of rocks that will have to be dealt with before we can go any further."

"I don't think I understand," she said.

"The rocks your parents will carry in their backpacks will be figurative rocks, of course. They might be pains or sorrows or disappointments that they've carried with them for years. As I said before, rocks are the baggage we carry when we are unable or unwilling to forgive. Instead of forgiving and letting the sorrow go, we allow it to fester and grow until it becomes hard and heavy and sometimes jagged."

"One of the first things we do when folks check in on Friday evening is hand each of them a bag of actual rocks and a black magic marker," said Tom. "We invite them to name their rocks— the things that they have used as weapons on each other or the things that have inhibited them from connecting with their spouse. Some people only have a few rocks while others come back to ask for another bag. When they have completed their assignment, we invite them to follow us down to the river."

"You throw the rocks in the river, don't you?" Jake said, sitting up in his chair.

"Yes, how did you know?"

"I've seen some of those rocks. Mr. Allan has a whole bunch of them in his bathroom."

"Yeah, I remember seeing them, now that you mention it," Amy said. "Those are the ones he says he has to scrub before he gives them away, right?"

"That's interesting," Tom said, looking at Emma with a surprised look on his face. "He's never mentioned that to us. We figured they all just washed off in the river."

"I guess not all of them," said Jake.

"We may have to think about using different pens," said Tom.

Emma nodded. "The thing of it is, forgiveness is sometimes such an abstract concept for people that this activity, though somewhat simplistic, offers each participant a form of release—an invitation and permission to let go of the hurt that each of the rocks has caused."

"Does it really work?" asked Jake.

"It's only a start," admitted Tom. "Each person has to decide if it will work or not, but talking about the rocks we've carried around with us, sometimes for years, helps us work through the pain. I remember one woman who wrote a whole story on her rock—something she had carried with her for way too long. It was the story of how her husband was studying for the bar exam and was under a lot of stress. One night, their baby was screaming and her husband came out of his study and yelled at her, that she needed to keep the baby quiet. The husband had long forgotten his insensitivity and impatience, but his wife had carried that event with her for nearly three decades, mulling it over in her mind, again and again until it had become a boulder.

"Most of the time, when a spouse watches their husband or wife toss the rocks into the river that have hindered love's natural tendency to grow and blossom, it becomes a very emotional experience. No one ever comes away from the river without experiencing at least three important things: sorrow for all the wasted time, a sense of freedom from the burdens of the rocks they've been carrying around, and a desire to spend the rest of their marriage building instead of destroying. Many people believe love is complicated. We've discovered over the years that we are the ones that make it so. Love is the simplest of all of God's gifts, but it can only remain simple if we forgive—if we can turn our weapons of war into building blocks. That's the lesson we've learned from this house as we put it back together, one rock at a time. That's the lesson we share with all who come here."

"So, now that you're done with the construction and finishes, how are you going to teach the couples who come here?" asked Jake.

Emma smiled. "We still have forty acres. A couple of years ago, when some of our clients were out digging post holes, they discovered a foundation for a carriage house that had been burned to the ground and buried under a foot of topsoil. As long as there are families who need help, this work will never be done. That is the charge Isaac gave to us as he shared his light with us over the years.

"We've never told anyone about this—he asked us not to, but a couple of weeks before he passed away, Isaac rode out here on his scooter to give us a gift. It was a ceramic candlestick that we keep on the mantel in our bedroom. It wasn't until after he left that we found a cashier's check for twenty thousand dollars rolled up inside, along with a note, asking that the money be put towards a scholarship fund for anyone who wants to attend our workshop but can't afford to pay for it."

"That's a lot of money," Jake said.

"Yes, it is. Emma and I cried about it for a whole week. It still makes me cry when I think about how he earned every one of those dollars with the same old, gnarled hands that have shaped so many of us over the years. He's the reason this all got started. I hate to think about where we might be if he hadn't stepped in and changed our course forever. But when I think about the all the people we've been able to help over the years, I realize the untold power that one Candlelighter can have to give light to the world."

"We asked him a few years ago if we could honor him by naming the new wing after him," Emma added. "He told us he'd think about it and then one day he brought us a small, two inch tile with a tiny blue flower glazed in the middle. He asked us to find a place for it in the new construction. He refused any other acknowledgment."

"A forget-me-not?" Jake asked.

"Yes. About the same time we began our workshops, Isaac entrusted us with a recipe for his very unique tea."

"No way! Isaac never told anyone, not even Thomas," said Jake. "The only other person I know who knows the secret is Hildegard, and she

said the only reason he told her was so the secret wouldn't die. We spent several days working on breaking that recipe. Why did he tell you?"

"Because we needed the medicine it had to offer," Emma said. "When Isaac heard what we planned to do with this old place, he was anxious to share everything he could. His peppermint tea has opened doors and hearts that have been sealed shut for years."

"So, that's why you put the forget-me-not on your business card?" asked Jake.

"No," replied Tom. "We put that on our business card, on our china, on our silverware, and everywhere else we can think of to help remind us that this isn't about us. Isaac warned us a long time ago that if we ever forgot the eternal source of the things he taught us, that we would lose its power and truth. The forget-me-not is a subtle reminder to us that all that we have comes from God and that it is meant to be shared. The house is always full of people who need our help. That old pickup truck is our only vehicle and after twenty years of hard work, we have yet to turn a financial profit."

"Are you serious?" asked Amy. "Are you saying you've never made any money?"

"Oh, no," Emma said with a smile, "we make lots of money, but every dime goes back into the next project. There is always a need for more lumber or mortar or tile. We pay the Andrettis and we get to live in a beautiful, ever-changing home. Twenty years ago, we made a commitment to God to pay a tithe on our income and somehow we always have enough."

Amy smiled and shook her head. "You might want to keep quiet about your financial status around my parents until my dad understands what you're all about—if he ever does. Money is always the bottom line with him."

"Isn't it that way with most of us?" asked Tom. "Its part of the makeup of every human being not only to want more than we have, but to want more than what our neighbor has, too. That's not an easy thing to overcome, but there is no room for greed or envy when you live your life based on love instead of fear."

"Jake and I were just talking about that yesterday. That's the way Isaac lived his life, isn't it? With love instead of fear?"

"Right there," Tom said, leaning forward to rest his elbows on the table, "that is the first truth of living your life in the light. To live by love is to live by the light of God. It is the answer to the darkness and emptiness this world knows all too well. If you can learn that, and then do it, your life will be blessed beyond belief."

TRUE LOVE DOES NOT COME BY
FINDING A PERFECT PERSON, BUT
BY LEARNING TO SEE AN IMPERFECT
PERSON PERFECTLY

−JASON JORDAN−

STONE WALLS

WE CAN EASILY FORGIVE A CHILD WHO IS AFRAID OF THE DARK;
THE REAL TRAGEDY OF LIFE IS WHEN MEN ARE AFRAID OF THE LIGHT.
—PLATO—

It was long past dark when they gathered up the remnants of their meal and carried them into the spacious kitchen. With the new information about the history of the house, they noticed something on their way out. Amy saw the first one, but as they moved from room to room, each took turns pointing them out—forget-me-nots—everywhere from the doorknobs to the carpets to the woodwork. Hundreds of them, some hidden, some in plain view, but each of them deliberately placed where they could be found if you were looking for them.

Before they left, Tom pulled a check from his pocket, written to Amy for three thousand dollars. She stared at the check for a long moment before trying to hand it back to Tom.

"Is it not enough?" Tom asked.

"It's not that. After hearing your story, I think I would rather give this back to you," Amy said. "Please, buy some lumber with it. Use it to keep your projects going."

"What, and deny you the opportunity to learn from it," Emma teased.

"We feel like we've gotten a great deal," Tom said. "If ever you decide you want more for it, please let us know."

Amy nodded slowly.

"Use it to help you learn the power of love," Emma said, giving her a hug before embracing Jake as well. Hugs from Tom followed.

"We know we're not your parents," Tom said, "but we're proud of you both. You have a bright future ahead of you, especially if you remember the things we've talked about tonight. If you ever have any questions or need any help, we'll be anxious to do what we can."

As they rode back into town, Amy held onto Jake a little tighter than she had before. Something had changed between them. Somehow, the understanding they'd gained from their visit with the Parkins had opened their mind to broader horizons.

Jake drove the scooter into the small parking lot at the barber shop and let Amy get off before he switched off the motor. He walked her to the door and kissed her before a word was said.

"What are you thinking about?" he asked.

"Sorry, I … I was thinking about tonight."

"Which part?"

They sat down on the steps and spoke for over an hour about the things they had learned from the Parkins and how they had put so many of Isaac's core values and lessons into practice. When Amy began to yawn, Jake stood and offered her his hand, pulling her to her feet.

"We haven't done very much to organize Mr. Allan's birthday party," Amy said, looking both tired and worried. "I was thinking I probably ought to get together with Gloria tomorrow and see who might be coming. I wish there were some way we could get his sons here, even if it was just for the day. I was thinking that maybe I could use some of that money from the Parkins to pay for some airline tickets. I'm guessing they would have to be pretty expensive this late in the game."

Jake nodded. "You're thinking about what Emma told you—about using your money to learn about love, aren't you?"

Amy nodded. "I just feel like I want to do something to … to earn this. I feel like everything that has happened in the past couple of months has been a total gift. I don't need this money. I feel as though I owe something to somebody. If it's not Mr. Allan's kids, maybe it's someone else."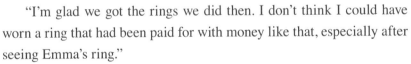

"I know what you mean. I've been thinking about that money Charlie gave me. In my mind, I've tried to spend it. I might have if you'd wanted a different ring, but …"

"I'm glad we got the rings we did then. I don't think I could have worn a ring that had been paid for with money like that, especially after seeing Emma's ring."

"What about it?"

"It was small—nothing I'd imagine a woman with a mansion would have. I think that's one of the things I like most about them. They're so unpretentious."

"That's cool. I guess it's all about perspective, isn't it?"

"Yeah, maybe," Amy said weakly, looking away.

"Are you okay?"

Amy crossed her arms, but didn't look back.

"Amy, what's up?"

"Oh, I was just thinking about some of that stuff about the rocks."

"You were thinking about your dad, weren't you?"

"How'd you know?"

"Because I was thinking about mine. It's not going to be easy, is it?" She shook her head, but Jake could see her tears.

"I know I have to forgive him for hurting me—for not being the dad I needed him to be. I've felt like I need to hang onto those stinkin' rocks for so long—to build up a wall and protect my heart from getting stepped on. I don't know if I can do this, Jake. I don't know if I can let it go. It seems different for someone you're married to—you have to be around them for the rest of your life. But I don't need my dad anymore. Can't I just try to forget him? Tell me the pain he's caused me will go away if I just forget him."

Her tears were coming freely now. Jake knew he didn't have any answers that would make it better so he said nothing, but he took her in his arms and held her close, letting her cry. He wanted to be strong for her. He wanted to keep it together. But as he thought of his father and the rocks he'd collected over the years to protect his own heart, his feelings rose within him until his tears mingled with hers.

They stood there for a long time, listening to the crickets and occasional sounds of sniffles.

"Will you help me?" Amy asked, finally breaking her silence.

"Yes, if you'll help me." Jake responded, lifting her feet off the ground in a bear hug. "I'll go get some rocks tomorrow morning. Maybe we could get started tomorrow night."

Amy nodded. "You probably shouldn't kiss me tonight."

"Why?"

"Haven't you heard the old saying?"

"Which one?"

She looked up at him and smiled, her eyes glistening in the pale light of the street lamp. "Don't kiss your honey when your nose is runny. You may think its funny, but its snot."

Jake burst out laughing and only stopped when Amy grabbed his ears and pulled him down till their noses touched. Then she kissed him—a long and gentle kiss. They both knew the monsters they faced, but they were going to face them together—with love.

WHEN THE POWER OF LOVE
OVERCOMES THE LOVE OF POWER,
THE WORLD WILL KNOW PEACE
-JIMI HENDRIX-

THE HAND OF PROVIDENCE

FOR LIGHT, I GO DIRECTLY TO THE SOURCE OF LIGHT,
NOT TO ANY OF THE REFLECTIONS.
—PEACE PILGRIM—

Jake was exhausted as he pulled the scooter into the shed behind The Pottery. He was halfway up the stairs before he heard the faint purr of the kiln and stopped in his tracks. He'd forgotten all about the firing. His mind raced, but quickly relaxed when he remembered what time he'd started it. It seemed like all the days had begun to roll together as one—the firings and the late nights numbing his brain. He walked back down the stairs and opened the door.

The peepholes were already glowing orange and he glanced at the clock, trying to orient himself. It was midnight. The kiln had been going for eight hours. The pyrometer registered just over fourteen hundred degrees. He knew the firing could have been done by now if he'd been there to turn up the gas a few hours before, but there was nothing he could do now beyond adjusting the gas pressure and waiting for the temperature to rise.

After adjusting the gas, he glanced at the clock again, guestimating that would take another two hours for the kiln to reach 1860 degrees. He was turning around when he saw the sketchbook, the one he'd been given just two weeks before, the one he'd been encouraged to fill with his thoughts and the things he was learning. He looked at the clock once again. He was really tired, but knew he wouldn't be sleeping well, anticipating the cruel sound of his alarm waking him to get up and baby-sit the kiln.

Jake plucked a pen from the handleless mug on the shelf and pulled the stool closer to the wedging table. He paused, wiping away several specks of glaze from the sketchbook's cover before opening it.

He looked down at the dedication Isaac had written in his own hand and swallowed hard. He and Amy had already read this, but he felt compelled to read it again.

To my friend, the eighth potter of Niederbipp—

There are so many things I would like to tell you, more probably than would fit in this volume and several others. Many of these things are written in the pages of the previous 36 volumes which I encourage you to study. I am sorry I do not know you personally, but I do not feel like I am writing this to a stranger. From the time of my dear Lily's passing, my nights have been filled with dreams that have comforted my soul, given me instruction, and offered me hope. I do not know your name, but I believe I know your heart. I have dreamt that my prayers for you have ascended to heaven on angel's wings. A merciful God has shown you to me and my soul rejoices in you. You, young potter, have been brought here by the hand of Providence.

A tear fell from Jake's cheek onto the open page, and he wiped it away quickly before it could be absorbed by the paper. He reread that last sentence. It was true. He knew it was true. How many times had he felt this before? He took a deep breath and read on.

You have already acquired many of the skills you will need to make it here. I encourage you to open your heart and mind to the truths all around you. There will be many willing to teach you, but I encourage you most of all to learn wisdom from that one source of all goodness and truth—the God of Abraham, Isaac and Jacob.

As you will know by now, I am the seventh potter of Niederbipp. Those who have passed on before me have created a tradition and a legacy that has been passed down through the generations, each one standing taller and wiser because of the understanding passed on to him from his predecessors. And so I give to you the same charges that were given to me. First, learn from the past that you may be a better husband, a better father, a better potter and a better man than the generations before you. And second, carve your path straight and wide for those that follow.

I pray that all of God's blessings will be with you now and forever,

Sincerely, your friend,

Isaac Aaron Bingham

Jake laid his hand on top of the dedication and wept for several minutes. These tears were much different from those he'd just cried with Amy. These were tears of happiness—tears that were accompanied with an overwhelming feeling of love. As they spilled from his eyes, soaking into his shirt, something happened—something he'd never felt before. Something touched his shoulder. He wanted to turn. He wanted to see who or what it was, but he couldn't. He felt paralyzed, but the rest of his senses were acutely alert as his whole being filled with a powerful energy. It seemed other-worldly, yet the calm that accompanied it felt strangely familiar. It lasted only seconds, but it left him so full of peace and happiness that it seemed as though his veins were filled with the very essence of a comforting fire.

And then it was gone, as quickly as it had come, leaving Jake unexplainably rejuvenated, as though he'd just awoken from a long and satisfying sleep. He turned to look over his shoulder, hoping to see some remnant of the being who had been there. But he was alone. He turned the page and put his pen to the paper. And the words came. They came quickly and clearly as he recounted the events of his evening with Amy and the Parkins. One page turned into two, and two to three, and still the words flowed from his pen as if they were anxious to leap onto the page and be given life.

After an hour, he stood to stretch and check the kiln. But when he sat down again, the words continued to come. For a long time, he avoided writing about his fears of giving up the rocks that had protected his heart, but as he finally began, he noticed how the feelings were different this time around. Somehow, as he wrote about the fears and the rocks, he knew he didn't want them any more. He knew he didn't need them. For the first time in his life, they seemed like a burden—a heavy, useless, hurtful burden.

He laid down his pen and listened to the gentle purr of the kiln. His thoughts turned to Amy, to the love he had for her, to the burdens he knew hung from her heart. Feeling as though he'd been released from the spell of his own heavy burdens, he wanted to help her. In that quiet moment, something changed his thoughts into prayer for the girl he loved. Having tasted the sweet fruit of forgiveness, his one desire was to share it with her and allow the wings of love to carry the burden away forever.

GOD ENTERS BY A PRIVATE DOOR INTO EVERY INDIVIDUAL.
— RALPH WALDO EMERSON —

FISHERS AND HUNTERS

IT IS BY SUFFERING THAT HUMAN BEINGS BECOME ANGELS.
—VICTOR HUGO—

ake was awake at first light. He wasn't certain he'd even slept after the firing was completed, but the surge of energy that had filled him the night before continued to sustain him. He arose from his bed and slipped on his clothes and shoes before walking out into the pale light of morning.

All was still. He considered taking the scooter but stopped in the courtyard, not wanting to pollute the beautiful silence with noise. So he walked. He cut through the abandoned streets, making his way quickly out of Old Town and across the highway where the grass grew chest high and rang out with the night's final cry of the crickets.

He scampered down the steep banks at the same place where Amy had first introduced him to the rickety old swing. Mist rose off the gray surface of the river and floated like clouds over the pebbled beach. Jake stopped to take in the beauty, the sound of his own heartbeat pulsing in his ears. After a minute, there was another sound, a swooshing sound. Jake turned just in time to see a huge bird soar over his shoulder and land at the water's edge less than twenty feet away. It looked at him quickly with his bright yellow eyes before darting its long neck out to catch a small water snake with its long, pointed beak.

Jake stood still, watching the huge bird skillfully eat its breakfast in one gulp with the flick of its neck. And then, as quickly as it had come, the beautiful bird beat its wings a couple of times and was gone, disappearing beyond the bend in the river. Jake smiled to himself, grateful for the show nature had rewarded him with for getting up so early.

He looked down at his feet at the thousands of beautiful rocks that covered the beach. Stooping over, he picked up a flat one and with a flick of his wrist, sent it skipping across the glassy surface until it disappeared, just shy of the opposite beach. He bent over and picked up another one and was about to skip it as well when he stopped. He only smiled at first, but then he began to laugh. He'd forgotten to bring something to carry the rocks.

He slipped the rock into his pocket and walked to the pile of debris wrapped around the roots of a tree a hundred feet away. There were lots of sticks and a collection of old plastic bottles and he was about to give up and move on when he noticed a piece of rusty metal hiding under a polished log. Upon closer inspection, he saw that it was a metal paint pail, its contents long ago forgotten. He freed it from the tangle. Its bottom was thin with several small holes, but it was good enough for his needs. He wandered back across the beach, picking up rocks as he went, filling the bucket well before he reached the steep banks.

Wildflowers dotted his trail back to town and Jake stopped to pick enough for a small bouquet, laying them gently on top of the rocks.

He was just setting the can down on Amy's front porch when the door opened. A groggy-looking Jerry stood in the doorway, wrapped loosely in a brown terrycloth robe.

"I sure hope you're not trying to steal my newspaper."

Jake laughed. "No."

"Did you sleep out here last night? Are you two lovebirds having a fight?"

"No," Jake said, laughing harder this time. "I'm just getting an early start. Can you see that Amy gets these?" he asked, lifting the bucket so Jerry could take hold of the rusty handle. Then he let go, throwing Jerry off balance with the weight of the bucket.

"What are you trying to do to me?" Jerry asked, catching himself.

"Sorry, I guess I should have told you they're rocks."

"Let me get this straight. It's not even seven in the morning on a Saturday when most of the world is sleeping in, and you show up with a bucket full of rocks and try to swap me for my newspaper and you think you can get away with it, because, what, you're getting married to my favorite niece?"

"Um," Jake said, trying not to smile.

Jerry waited for an answer.

"Umm," Jake repeated, trying to come up with something brilliant.

"Why don't you come in and have some toast while you think about it," Jerry said, turning around in the doorway. "And bring my paper with you."

Jake grabbed the newspaper and followed him into the kitchen.

"You should probably get these flowers in water if you want them to be alive by the time Amy wakes up," Jerry suggested, setting the pail down next to the sink.

Jake filled a Mason jar with water and stuffed the flower stems into its neck, arranging them the best he could.

"What's with the rocks?" Jerry said, pointing at the bucket.

"Oh, yeah, um, we visited with the Parkins last night. Amy did a painting for them and I made some sinks for their new addition. They shared some of their ideas about forgiveness. You didn't tell us they were Candlelighters too."

"Didn't we?"

"No."

Jerry nodded. "I guess we wanted you find out for yourself. Sometimes its better that way—to figure it out for yourselves."

"What do you mean?"

Jerry looked thoughtful. "You kids asked us about this the other night. Each of us has our own approach. I know we're all working for the same cause, but it's easier for some people than it is for us. The Parkins are of the same sort as Eric Schmelding."

"In what way?"

"They're fishers."

"Fishers?"

"Yes. They cast broad nets that have an effect on big groups of people. Bev and me, well, I guess we're more reserved. Kind of like the difference between Joseph and Gloria. I guess you could say that we're more like hunters, looking for the 'one.' It's more our style. Some of us haven't been able to get over our social phobias and be the kind of light we probably ought to be. Maybe we hide our light under a bushel a little too much, I don't know. The way I see it, all of us Candlelighters are doing the same thing, just in different ways."

The toast popped up, and Jerry put a piece on each of the plates before inserting two more slices into the toaster. He handed Jake one of the plates, and pointed to a jar of raspberry jam.

"So whgich way is better?" Jake asked. "Fishers or hunters?"

"I'm not sure any way is better. The world needs both kinds. That's what Isaac used to say. He was always more in our camp, the way he approached people."

"I guess you're right. I've never really thought about it that way, but now that you mention it, he did work with people one at a time."

"Isaac used to say that the work of sharing light with the world takes all types of people: some to sow the seeds, some to nurture the crops, some to harvest and some to glean the fields when the harvest is over. I guess there are plenty of metaphors for the work, but each of us is needed. Some of us are multi-taskers, and others are more specialized. And then some of us are still struggling with fear."

Jake nodded thoughtfully. "Is that why you didn't talk to Amy about this sooner? Were you afraid?"

Jerry took a big bite of toast, looking away.

Jake wondered if he'd asked too much.

"We were afraid," Jerry finally said, speaking softly. "We were afraid we'd lose her, the way we lost her brothers. They never wanted to have anything to do with what we had to share. We've wondered for years if we pushed them too hard. Of course, our realm of influence was limited to one week a year when they were here, but all of her brothers chose their father's path. When Amy came along, we wondered for a while if she'd been born into the wrong family. She was so different from her brothers, but I guess you already know that."

"I think so. I haven't met any of them yet, but from what Amy has told me, it sounds like it might be an interesting gathering next week."

Jerry smiled. "You can bet on it."

"So, Jerry, tell me, if you could do it over again, if you could roll back time with Amy and her brothers, what would you do differently?"

"I don't know, Jake. We never get more than one chance to swing at any single pitch, but for me, the answer would have to be more love. Truth is a scary thing sometimes, especially naked truth. Sometimes, it's so contrary to what we're doing or how we're living our lives, that when it shows up knocking on our front door, we send it away as we might a dangerous-looking stranger. We've made the mistake many times of jumping in too fast when we see people who need the truth we have. Instead of taking the time to love and understand them, we've become so anxious to share it that we try to nail it to their foreheads with a hammer, when what they really need is for it to land on their shoulder with the gentleness of a butterfly. Unfortunately, neither Bev nor I are very good butterflies."

"But at least you try," Jake said. "You've got to get some credit for that. I imagine there are probably lots of people who don't even care enough to try."

"That's rarely enough. There's an old story from the logging days about a couple of lumberjacks who were floating their logs down the river to the mill. One of them fell off the raft and began to drown. His buddy tried to help by tossing him a rope, but his friend couldn't catch it so he tossed a log, hit him on the head, and killed him. The worst part of that story was that the man was drowning in four feet of water. When the man was asked why he didn't just jump in and help his friend stand up, he responded that he didn't want to get his new boots wet.

"We all complicate things, Jake. We worry too much about our image. We let silly things get in the way. I know there's no love in fear, but I still let it win sometimes. I love Amy as much as I love any of my own kids. After trying unsuccessfully with her brothers, we let fear keep us from helping and loving her the way she needed. When she asked if she could come here for the summer to paint, we felt as though God was giving us another chance. We prayed that she would be able to learn the things we'd always wanted to share with her. I'm not sure she would have, Jake, if you hadn't been here. Our prayers have been answered, but not at all the way we'd imagined. I feel like we've not only gained a daughter, but a son as well."

"Thanks, Jerry. Thanks for making me part of your family."

"You're welcome." Jerry took a deep breath. "Promise me something, Jake."

"Sure, anything."

"Promise me you won't ever let fear keep you from loving Amy."

WE ARE UNLIMITED BEINGS. WE HAVE NO CEILING. THE CAPABILITIES AND THE TALENTS AND THE GIFTS AND THE POWER THAT IS WITHIN EVERY SINGLE INDIVIDUAL THAT IS ON THIS PLANET, IS UNLIMITED.
—MICHAEL BECKWITH—

T**OO**LS

IT IS IN PARD**O**NING THAT WE ARE PARD**O**NED.
—ST. FRANCIS **O**F ASSISI—

It was nearly three before Amy arrived at The Pottery. Jake's morning had been busy with tourists stopping in to buy pots, but still, he'd missed her. He was busy helping a customer when he heard her parking her bike at the back door and couldn't help but smile when he saw her. She carried the pail of rocks with her and waited patiently, watching as Jake fumbled with wrapping a bowl, seeming content to just observe.

"Gerhardt Michael," Amy said, when he finally turned to her after walking the customer to the door.

"Uh, gesundheit what?" Jake said, feeling lost.

"That's my great-grandfather's name. Gerhardt Michael Eckstein."

""That's quite a mouthful."

"Yeah, that's what I said. I found him this morning in that book. He's the guy who owned those tools we got from Sam—G.M. Eckstein."

"That's cool," Jake said, taking the bucket of rocks from her so he could give her a hug. "Did you find anything else?"

"Yeah. I found out why my side of the family thinks Mr. Allan's side of the family are all thieves and liars."

"Does it have anything to do with cattle rustling and a poker game?" Jake asked, trying to keep a straight face.

"No, it does not, Mr. Smarty Pants. But it does have a lot to do with those old tools." She reached into her back pocket and pulled out a piece of notepaper, unfolding it. "This book was actually pretty amazing." She pointed to the top of the page where she'd written her great-grandfather's name next to three other names, Oliver, Jens and Elsie.

"I've only figured out two of the family lines so far," Amy said, "but they're the important ones for this story. The problem started here, between Gerhardt and his older brother, Oliver." She pointed to the names. "The book was written by Rolf Eckstein who came through Jens's line, so I'm not sure which way he would have leaned. But according to Rolf, there was a dispute over some borrowed tools. Oliver apparently borrowed Gerhardt's toolbox to do some work at a neighbor's home. When the tools weren't returned, Gerhardt went to pick them up. An argument broke out when Oliver said he'd sent his son to return them on his way out of town a week before. Gerhardt didn't believe him, because according to the book, Oliver had always been jealous that Gerhardt had inherited the tools from Gerhardt *Mueller* Eckstein, their father. There was name-calling, and punches were thrown and by 1913, when this book was published, neither of the men had spoken to each other in more than seven years. Oh, and the book said the tools were never found."

"So let me get this straight," Jake said, counting on his fingers to try to keep things straight. "You don't know your second cousins because some crappy old tools got lost over a hundred years ago and nobody could get over it."

"Yep," Amy said, crossing her arms.

Jake shook his head. "Am I missing something here? Are those tools made of gold? I might be able to understand if they were good tools, but that old stuff? My hand still hasn't healed from that crappy handle on the trowel. Did you see anything in that box that was worth more than five bucks, even to an antique collector?"

Amy shook her head. "That's what I've been thinking about all morning. If I needed motivation to drop the rocks, I think I found it."

"Yeah, really. Who does stuff like that? I can't imagine splitting up a family over something so trivial."

"That might be because you're an only child."

"What does that have to do with it?"

"I thought it was crazy, too, at first, but then I started thinking about my own family. My brothers are already calling dibs on my parents' stuff. Mike has claimed my dad's Harley. Paul wants the cottage in Maine. All my other brothers have written their names on something, I'm sure. To you and me, they're just a bunch of rusty tools, but a hundred years ago, maybe it was a lot more than that."

"Did either of the brothers work as masons?"

"No, that's another thing. Gerhardt was a farmer and Oliver was a dairyman. They'd both need tools, but not masonry tools. The only thing I can figure is that they must have had sentimental value to each of them."

Jake nodded. He walked to the trap door in the floor and opened it, descending into the cellar. He returned with the box of dusty tools, setting them on a stool. "How old did you say these are?"

Amy looked down at her notes. "Well, the tools disappeared in 1906. My great-grandfather was born in 1878, so he was nearly thirty when the tools went missing. His father died in 1899, but I forgot when he was born. I don't know, I guess the tools could be as old as one hundred and fifty years."

Jake picked up one of the squares and turned it over, wiping the dust away on his pants. When he looked at the tool again, he was surprised by what he found. "Look at this," he said, pointing to the initials scratched into the surface.

"O. D. Eckstein?" Amy said, looking surprised.

"What was Oliver's middle name?

Amy looked at her notes again. "David."

"Huh, it kind of seems like we have a case of two brothers who didn't know how to keep track of their tools."

"What a dumb mess," Amy said, shaking her head.

"Yep, and there's not a lot we can do about it either. If we only could have found this box a little bit sooner, like a hundred years, we might have been able to save the family. What a shame," Jake said, his voice full of sarcasm.

"What if it isn't too late?"

"What do you mean?"

"I mean, it's too late for a couple of generations, but it's not too late for me. I don't know, Jake. I feel somehow responsible to set things straight. I've been thinking all day about Mr. Allan, wondering why he gave Thomas that book to give to me. It would have been worth it just for the motivation it's given me to forgive my own father, but there's more potential than just that. If we can figure out a way to get his kids here, I can meet my third cousins. Heck, we all can. My whole family will be here for the wedding anyway. How cool would that be if we could all get to know each other?"

"Amy, do you realize we have one week before our wedding?"

She laughed. "Yeah, I know, but everything's taken care of, isn't it? I still have to pick up my dress and find a tie for you, and we have to pick up our rings. I feel like we have the important things taken care of. I'm sure there are other details, but we could drive ourselves crazy worrying about them."

He knew he couldn't argue with her. There wasn't really anything pressing. In choosing to have a simple wedding they had certainly simplified their life. "Okay," he said after a moment of thought. "I'm in, but you know this is going to take some time to put together, right? We have to find phone numbers and figure out travel plans and organize food and lodging for everyone."

She smiled, pulling another piece of paper from her pocket. "I kind of already got started."

READ THE BEST BOOKS FIRST,
OR YOU MAY NOT GET TO
READ THEM AT ALL.
- HENRY DAVID THOREAU -

DANDELIONS AND FISH STICKS

INSIDE EVERY OLDER PERSON IS A YOUNGER PERSON
WONDERING WHAT THE HELL HAPPENED.
—CORA HARVEY ARMSTRONG—

By closing time, Jake had been fully briefed on the plans. Amy had been busy. Between her and Gloria, they had made contact with each of Mr. Allan's children and received commitments that they'd be there for a party on Saturday night. As an incentive, Amy had promised each of them an antique treasure from a recently discovered family time capsule. With all of the rooms booked in town for the July Fourth festivities, Amy would be moving her things into

Jake's apartment on Thursday to free up a bedroom at Bev and Jerry's for their kids who planned on coming in for the weekend. Jake would be sleeping in Gloria and Joseph's Volkswagen van with two of her nephews while the boys' parents would be in Gloria's spare bedroom. A cleaning crew would be dispatched Monday morning to clean up Mr. Allan's place and get it ready for all of his kids, their spouses and many of their grandchildren. Happy Huts, an outfit in Warren that rented miniature, portable log cabins would be delivering three of their deluxe huts to Mr. Allan's backyard for those in his family who wouldn't fit in the house and two more for Amy's brothers and their families. The spare bedroom in Jake's apartment would be used for another of Amy's brothers and his wife, and their kids would be sleeping in a tent they'd make by draping a quilt over the kitchen table. Her last brother, with his family of six, would be staying at Molly's dad's place who would be out of town for the weekend. Sam had already been alerted that the wedding cake would need to be made bigger and Bubba's Barbecue had been booked to cater a dinner on Saturday night at Mr. Allan's compound that would double as a wedding dinner before the fireworks show. The guests would have to take care of everything else on their own. It was perfect.

"So, should I be afraid to ask how much this is going to cost?" Jake asked as they walked out to the scooter after closing up shop.

"It's covered," Amy said with a wink.

Jake nodded. "Did you spend all the Parkins' money?"

"Nope. I have exactly enough left over to buy a new canvas and three tubes of oil paint."

"That sounds like a great deal," Jake said.

"Yeah, everything should work out fine as long as Mr. Allan is okay with picking up the tab for the airline tickets. Otherwise ..."

Jake rolled his eyes and kick-started the scooter.

They wondered at first if Mr. Allan had company, but as they rolled through the overgrown bushes that choked his driveway, they realized the man they'd seen as they pulled off the road was Mr. Allan himself. He had his back toward them and was swinging a golf club at an overgrown patch of dandelions growing up through the gravel. If he heard them, he gave no indication, so Jake turned off the motor and they watched as Mr. Allan decapitated the yellow-headed weeds, one at a time. Each time one went airborne, he lifted his hand to his brow and hollered, "Fore!"

They laughed to themselves quietly, watching the man at work. He'd dressed up for this occasion, a plaid set of knickers, argyle socks, and black-and-white, wingtip golf cleats. They quietly joked that even Eric Schmelding would be envious of this getup.

"Hey, what are you two doing here?" he asked, as he finally turned to notice them.

Amy jumped off the back of the bike. "We hope we're not disturbing you, Mr. Allan. I called you earlier to tell you we were coming. Would you like us to come back later?"

"Of course not. I've been waiting for you. I made us some dinner—fresh trout."

"Oh ... that sounds ... good. Did you catch them yourself?"

"Of course not. I forgot how to fish a long time ago, but I still like to eat fish on Friday. I've got some fish sticks in the oven. I'm just waiting for the timer to go off. I've got it right here in my pocket so I won't forget." He pulled the timer out of his pocket and handed it to Amy.

"Um, Mr. Allan," Amy said nervously. "Did the timer already go off?"

He scratched his head. "Come to think of it, I'm not sure if I set it."

Amy glanced at Jake before running to the house and he decided it probably wasn't worth the trouble to tell Mr. Allan that today was Saturday.

"You can be my caddy, if you'd like," Mr. Allan said, handing Jake his golf club after he'd parked the scooter. "I think I'd like to use my driver for this next hole. The dandelions are a little closer to the ground."

Jake nodded. Picking up the old vinyl golf bag, he handed Mr. Allan the only club in the bag, which happened to be a putter.

As Mr. Allan swung at the weeds, Jake looked up to see Amy, smiling.

"Take your time," she said under her breath. "He fortunately forgot to turn the oven on, too. They were still frozen. You boys have twenty-five minutes."

Jake smiled and nodded.

"I'm going to try and figure out how much work we're going to need to plan on for Monday. Can you keep him busy?"

"Of course, I'm his caddy and we have six holes to go. We'll catch you in the clubhouse."

Amy smiled again and returned to the house while Jake dropped the golf bag and joined Mr. Allan in the harvest.

"Was that your wife?" Mr. Allan asked after a moment.

"She will be next week."

"Good choice. She comes from good stock, you know. Did I tell you that she's my second cousin, once removed?"

"Yeah, I think I heard that," Jake said, surprised that he remembered.

"Yes sir, that means when you get married, I'll be related to my caddy. It's been years since I had a good one. I think you'll work out just fine."

"Thanks," Jake said, "I think it would be fun to work for you."

"Well, you can start just as soon as you finish my Journey Jars. I'm going to need them by next weekend you know. My whole family is coming into town for my surprise birthday party. That's why we need to clean up this place. I don't want to see any dandelions on my property."

Jake looked up at the overgrown yard, teaming with dandelions as far as they eye could see and he knew this was going to be a very long golf game.

Amy returned a half-hour later and invited them in to wash up. Jake was the first one into the bathroom and laughed to himself when he imagined what the Merry Maids would think on Monday when they discovered the bathtub full of rocks. He wished he could be a fly on the wall.

Amy was waiting for them on the veranda and Jake joined her, taking a seat in a high-backed chair with colorful rungs. They chatted as they waited for Mr. Allan to join them, but after ten minutes, she sent Jake in to find him. After looking in the kitchen and bathroom, Jake went searching and finally found him in his room, standing in front of the mirror, trying to make a very ugly toupee sit right on his head.

"Uh, Mr. Allan, can I help you," Jake asked, trying to determine the problem. He came closer and as his eyes adjusted to the light of the room, he noticed that a blue dress sock was hanging out from the back of the toupee, causing it to ride awkwardly high.

"Uh, Mr. Allan, I think you have a sock in your hair," Jake said, hardly believing that those words had just come out of his own mouth. He bit the inside of his cheeks, trying not to smile. He tugged softly on the sock to see if it would come lose and immediately regretted that he had even touched it as the whole toupee slid off his shiny scalp and into his hands.

"Oops," Jake said, feeling very awkward.

"Can you help me with that?" Mr. Allan asked.

"Uh, I think so," Jake lied. He tugged at the sock, trying to pull it away from the inside of the terrible rug, but it was definitely stuck. Then he realized there was not one sock, but two—two blue dress socks, folded creatively and scotch taped to the inside of the toupee.

"Mr. Allan, is there a reason these socks are taped inside your hair?"

"Yes, it needed some loft."

"Some loft?" Jake asked, continuing to tug on the socks.

"Yes, I forgot where I put it, but I found it in the sofa. It was kind of flat. My family is coming, you know. I was afraid they wouldn't recognize me without hair. I haven't seen them in a long time. I thought I better get used to wearing it again before they get here."

"Okay. Uh … Mr. Allan, did you staple a sock to your hair?"

"Maybe."

"Mr. Allan?"

"Okay, I did, but only because the tape wouldn't stick. I tried to hide the staples. How did I do?"

"Uh, pretty good considering that you stapled your socks to your hair." He looked up to see Amy's face reflected in the mirror. She was standing in the doorway with her hand over her mouth and nose, but she quickly left when Jake shook his head.

After another five minutes, they met Amy on the veranda. With Jake's help, Mr. Allan had decided that one sock was really plenty to accomplish the desired loft. But in the light of day, it might have looked better to have just stapled the sock to his head and forget the brown toupee that clashed against the long, gray, wispy hair that hung out underneath.

"Ahh, this is the life, eh? Fish sticks on the veranda with good friends," Mr. Allan said, clapping his hands.

Jake and Amy looked at each other and smiled, and they both knew that without a doubt, this was would be an evening that they wouldn't soon forget.

After dinner, Amy let Mr. Allan know what the plans were, writing careful notes that he could refer to later if he happened to forget. Jake would be picking Mr. Allan up on Monday morning at eight to get a haircut. Then he would spend the day with Thomas while the Merry Maids spruced up his place. Tuesday, the landscapers would arrive to trim the bushes and mow the lawn. Wednesday would be spent taking care of anything that the crews couldn't handle on Monday and Tuesday. On Thursday, the Happy Huts would be arriving in the afternoon, with the first guests arriving Friday morning. Saturday would be the birthday/ wedding party. Sunday would be the wedding and most of the guests would be gone by Monday morning. When the planning was over, Mr.

Allan stood from the table, walked into the house and returned with his checkbook, writing a large check to Gloria to reimburse her the airline tickets.

As they waved goodbye to Mr. Allan, Jake marveled at Amy and all the arrangements she had made. It had been several weeks since he had felt intimidated by her. Now, the intimidation had simply turned to awe. It was a wonderful thing to be in love with her, and he felt humbled that she had chosen to spend the rest of her life with him. Pulling onto the highway, Amy wrapped her arms tightly around his chest, and Jake knew that the road that lay ahead was going to be filled with magic.

BURDENS

FORGIVENESS IS THE FRAGRANCE THE VIOLET SHEDS ON THE HEEL
THAT HAS CRUSHED IT.
—MARK TWAIN—

id one of your neighbors get a new car?" Amy asked as they entered the courtyard after church on Sunday morning. A green Subaru Outback was parked in the shade of the chestnut tree.

"It's probably just a tourist trying to save some money on parking," Jake whispered when he noticed that the driver was sitting in the front seat with the windows down. Jake nodded to the man as they walked past. They had just started climbing the stairs to the apartment when they heard the car door shut.

"Excuse me, are you the potter?"

"Yes," Jake responded, squinting to look at the man wearing dark sunglasses and a yellow golf shirt.

"Can I help you?" Something made Jake felt tense, uncertain. "The Pottery is closed today, but I could make an exception if you're not going to be around tomorrow."

They watched as the man looked suspiciously from side to side.

"If you don't mind?"

"No. Come on in," Jake said, reaching into his pocket for his keys. "What part of Pennsylvania are you from?"

The man looked up nervously.

"I just saw your plates and figured you must be a tourist," Jake said.

"Oh, yeah, I guess I am," the man responded, looking somewhat less rigid.

"Well, welcome. I hope you don't mind walking through the studio."

"No, that's fine," the man said, nodding to Amy who was still standing on the second stair as he passed through the doorway.

"Are you after anything in particular?" Jake asked, leading the way to the showroom.

"As a matter of fact, I am. I'm looking for information."

Jake stopped, turning around slowly, a rush of adrenaline running through his veins. He looked past the man, grateful to see Amy standing at the open doorway, silhouetted by the daylight behind her.

"What would you like to know?"

"I'm a private investigator. I was hoping I might be able to ask you some questions."

"Uh . . . sure. About what?"

"I'd like to know about your association with a man named Sam Gottlieb. What can you tell me about him?" the man asked curtly.

Jake looked up at Amy who shrugged, looking nervous. "Uh, well, he's the baker here in town."

"And what's your association with him?"

"He's our friend," Amy said, cutting in. "I don't know much about private investigators, but aren't you supposed to tell us who you are before you start asking questions?" Her tone was firm.

"Actually, no I don't. Not according to the Pennsylvania law," the man replied, but there was hesitation in his voice that seemed off.

"Jake, I don't think this guy is really a private investigator."

"Why not?" the man asked, turning to face Amy.

She turned on the light. "Because you're driving a Subaru Outback with two car seats in the back. My sister-in-law has the same model. Do you want to tell us who you really are?" she asked, crossing her arms.

"Yeah," Jake said, surprised that the word had come out more gruff than he really intended. He walked past the man and stood next to Amy, trying to look as tall as he could.

M.G.
P.I.

The man took a deep breath and when he exhaled, he looked three inches shorter. He took off his sunglasses, exposing his bloodshot eyes.

"I guess I'm not really a tourist, either," the man whispered. "And I'm a really bad liar."

Suddenly, Jake recognized the man from the old photograph. He was older now, but without the sunglasses, his face still retained the same boyish look. Jake glanced at Amy and smiled, feeling a sense of relief. "We've been anxious to hear from you," he said, stepping forward. "Welcome home."

"You know who I am?" he asked, looking up.

"Let's just say that if your name is Matthew Gottlieb, we've been worried about you all week."

"Why?"

"We heard from Charlie that it didn't go very well. We've been worried about what Sam—I mean your dad—is going to do when he finds out that all his letters are missing, and that mug too."

"Before any more is said, can you answer one question for me?"

"Sure," Jake said. "What is it?"

"You don't know me. Why do you care?"

"Because we were jealous."

"Of what?" Matthew looked both surprised and disgusted.

"Of you."

"What in the world for? You don't even know me."

"No, we don't, but we were both jealous that someone loved you enough to write you a shoe box full of letters." Jake paused to watch his words sink in before he continued. "We were jealous that you have a dad who wants to have a relationship with his son more than he wants to breathe. We were jealous that you had someone who cared enough about you to not give up, to not stop trying to love you even though everything he did was rejected. Sam is *our* friend," Jake said, "but he *loves* you."

"He sure has a funny way of showing it. I was always a good kid. I never got into any real trouble . . . not until that night. He never saw that. The only thing he ever saw was the silly, little, insignificant crap that made him mad. Then he'd fly off the handle and slap me around. Every time I've looked at myself in the mirror over the past eight years, I've seen how much my dad *loves* me. If he'd only broken my nose, I think I might have healed, but that letter he  gave me . . . that damn letter . . . so full of hate . . . that broke my spirit."

"So why did you come?" asked Jake.

Matthew shook his head and looked down at his feet. "To bring back that stuff and tell you to mind your own business," he said softly. "I had to get them out of my house. They were making me crazy."

"Why didn't you just throw them away?" asked Amy.

"Because Charlie told me you and Thomas risked your necks to sneak them out. I didn't feel like it was right to leave you in the middle of this mess. Thomas was a good friend to me, and so was Isaac."

"Okay, if you really don't want them, we'll put them back," Jake said, trying to discover the man's real intent. "No harm done. You can just go back to Pittsburgh, and we all can forget that any of this happened."

Matthew stood where he was. "It's not that easy anymore," he finally muttered.

"Why not? We know where they go. I'm sure Thomas has a key. We can put them back today, before your dad even knows they're gone," Amy added.

He shook his head. "My wife read the letters. They've all been opened."

"Did you read them, too?" asked Jake.

"Not all of them . . . and not any of them until this morning while I waited for you." He shook his head before looking up at both of them. "You have no idea how hard I've tried to put this all behind me—to try to forget about it. I came home Monday night to discover my wife had spent the whole day reading those letters. At first, I hoped she'd discovered for herself what a jerk my father was so she could finally understand why I didn't want to have anything to do with him. I figured the letters would be full of the same hate and ridicule as the letter he'd given me the last time I saw him."

He sat down on a stool and ran his hands through his hair as he looked down at the floor, his elbows resting on his knees. "I didn't want to believe Charlie. I guess I didn't want to believe my dad was any different from the man who broke my nose and left me that hateful letter. I'm sorry I told you I was a private investigator. I just wanted to find out if he'd put you up to this . . . opening this old can of worms." He looked up at them with red and swollen eyes. "Did he?"

Jake shook his head. He opened one of the folding chairs for Amy and set another one down in front of Matthew before getting one for himself. As they sat together Jake told his story about coming to Niederbipp, about how Sam had fed him everyday since he'd arrived as part of a trade for work on a floor mosaic. Jake told him about the family picture hanging in the kitchen. He told him about Sam's lament over losing his only son, about how ashamed he was for the way he'd treated him. But it wasn't until Jake's story about discovering the mugs, about the chocolate milk and day-old pastries that Matthew's emotions spilled over. Somewhere, under the long-incubated pain and hurt, there was a happy memory. And like a gentle rain that puddles up until it fills the river, Jake and Amy listened as that one happy memory gave birth to another and another and another.

An hour passed before Jake invited Matthew up to his apartment to share some lunch, and the three of them sat at the table eating peanut butter and honey sandwiches on Sam's bread and drinking iced peppermint tea. As they ate, Jake and Amy both shared stories about their own fathers with Matthew, further defining their envy of the love Sam had for his son. Amy also shared what they'd learned about rocks and the Eckstein tools that had been the cause of a century-old familial chasm. The conversation was healing and enlightening for each of them in their own way. For Jake and Amy, it drove home the fact, if they needed any more, that the rocks of disappointment and neglect that they'd used to build fortresses around their hearts had only kept them cowering in fear rather than soaring with love.

After a couple of hours, Matthew confided in them that he really did want to find a way to repair the relationship he had with his father. He admitted that his heart had been softened by his father's letters and the friendship and conversation that Jake and Amy had shared with him. They offered to help facilitate a reunion as soon as he was ready, but Matthew seemed timid and noncommittal. So they backed off, leaving the offer on the table.

As they walked to his car, Jake asked if Matthew would mind parting with the old Florsheim shoe box in which the letters had been kept all these years, explaining his hope that the box could be put back in the cellar so as not to upset Sam.

Matthew sorted through the letters he'd already read, putting these back into the box and leaving the others on the front seat. He handed the box to Jake along with the mug before thanking them for their time and caring, promising that they would see him again.

Before he left, Jake handed him a piece of paper with his number written on it, inviting him to call anytime if there was anything they could do to help.

Jake and Amy returned to the apartment, picking up the bucket of rocks from the studio on their way. It was time. Over the past week, they had both experienced a gradual decline in the power of the demons they'd unintentionally held captive in their hearts. But they both knew from their experience with the natural ebb and flow of emotion and memory that the demons might return. And so, as they sat at the table, sorting through their rocks, they gave themselves and each other permission and encouragement to dismantle the ragged walls around their souls. One by one, they wrote upon the rocks, giving a name to each burden that had weighed them down. The exercise was surprisingly cathartic, and with the release of each additional burden, peace filled their souls.

With purpose and a united yearning for liberty, they rode their bikes south to the narrow bridge that crossed under the watchful eye of the pirate lookout. They parked their bikes and walked to the middle of the bridge where the water was deepest and the current, swiftest. And there, one by one, they surrendered their offerings to the river. As each stone disappeared beneath the water's mirrored surface, they resolutely released it from their care, freeing themselves of their fears. Then, with their pail empty, they rode back to town, lighter and freer, and ready to begin a very busy week.

THERE IS NO REVENGE SO COMPLETE AS FORGIVENESS.
—JOSH BILLINGS—

OVERTURE

LIFE IS THICKLY SOWN WITH THORNS,
AND I KNOW NO OTHER REMEDY THAN TO PASS QUICKLY THROUGH THEM.
THE LONGER WE DWELL ON OUR MISFORTUNES, THE GREATER IS THEIR
POWER TO HARM US.
—VOLTAIRE—

After hearing the church bells toll six times, Jake opened his eyes and stared at the ceiling. He'd gone to bed thinking about his father. Without the fear he'd always attached to him, new thoughts were allowed to take root. Jake was getting married in six days, and though he was grateful to have so many members of Amy's family coming, he felt a little sorry that no one from his own family would be there.

He didn't know what long-term role he hoped his father might play in his life, even if he could find him, but deep inside, he wondered what it might be like to stand shoulder to shoulder with the man who'd given him his name. A thought he'd had a hundred times before ran through his head. He wondered if he might have ever met him, ever passed him on the street, ever sat next to him in a bus or in a restaurant or a movie. He knew he wouldn't have recognized him if he had. The only memories that remained with him were nearly twenty-years old. For the same reason, he knew there was no way his father would ever recognize him.

He tossed and turned with these thoughts for nearly a half hour before an idea came to him. The only semi-accessible potential link to his father was the Internet. Fear had kept him from looking deeper before, but it was different now. He thought about his schedule, about when he might find some time to sit at the computer and really search. Mr. Allan would be expecting him at eight, and after that, his day was full trying to get the kiln unloaded and loaded again. And then there was the bother of Roberta Mancini and her ten-minute timer. He *knew* he didn't have time for that. There were so many things to do. Then another thought came to him. What if he could get into the library early? His mind raced, stopping when he thought of Thomas and his office there. Surely, Thomas would have a key.

Jake jumped out of bed and threw on his clothes. His first thought was the bakery. He didn't know Thomas' schedule, but he also knew he didn't have time to waste running all the way to his cottage only to discover he was working at Sam's.

Jake pounded impatiently on the back door of the bakery, out of breath from his run. After several long seconds, a tired looking woman whom Jake recognized as one of Sam's morning helpers opened the door. After asking about Thomas, she told Jake he had the day off.

Jake was completely winded by the time he reached the churchyard. He stopped for a minute to catch his breath at Thomas' door before he knocked. A moment later, the door opened. Thomas stood there in a bathrobe with shaving cream on his face. Jake didn't waste any time, telling Thomas he'd explain later, but that he really needed to get on the computer and asked for his keys to the library.

Minutes later, Jake took a seat at the computer and turned it on, trying to be patient as it warmed up. He glanced at the clock on the wall: 6:50. If he was lucky, he knew he could eke out one hour but no more. As the Internet connected, he said a silent prayer, and then he brainstormed, thinking of all the possible places he could search. Having already spent some time on Google without any success, he turned first to Facebook. com. There were three John Kimballs listed, but each of them were for guys at least three decades too young to be his father. He went next to MySpace.com, but the search produced similar results, John Kimballs that were all too young. He tried Classmates.com, narrowing his search to high schools in Vermont, but nothing turned up. Searches on LinkedIn. com and Blogger.com also produced zero results.

He took a deep breath before typing his father's full name into Google's search box. Twenty seconds later, the first ten of the 23,100 links popped up. Jake scrolled down the list. The first ten all looked familiar, so with no time to waste, he pulled up the next ten. He selected the first, then the fourth, then the sixth, reading through the headings as quickly as he could, clicking only on the ones that looked like they'd have a chance. After the first forty links, the headings for each link became more and more random and abstract, picking up anything and everything on the Internet that included those three names, but nothing leading to anything about his father.

Jake glanced up at the clock, trying to fight off his discouragement. He stared at the computer screen for a long moment before closing his eyes, trying to focus, trying to think of anything he hadn't already thought of. He thought of his mom, racing through memories that had any connection to his father. After a minute, a memory came to him. He was seven, maybe eight. He was in the car with his mother, driving to the woods to see the autumn leaves. They were on the highway as they passed an exit sign for Winooski. He had tried the word after sounding it

BECOMING ISAAC

out. He was laughing at the way it sounded and repeated it again. "That's where your father was born," she said, and he'd spent the next several minutes coming up with silly words that rhymed with Winooski.

On a whim, Jake added Winooski, VT, after his father's name in the search box, and hit enter. Twenty seconds later, one link popped up.

Jake stared at the screen for a second, reading the heading.

The Evening Telegram

Herkimer, New York, March 10, 1996 ... John Henry Kimball, formerly of Winooski, Vermont . . . intersection of Mohawk and Bellinger ...

With the click of the mouse, the link opened to *The Evening Telegram* website's archive page. Jake scrolled down several inches and read the headline.

Vermont Native Dies in Alcohol Related Crash

Jake took a deep breath as his heart began to race. He scrolled down further and continued to read.

John Henry Kimball, age 44, formerly of Winooski, Vermont, was pronounced dead at the scene of an accident that took place Friday evening at the corner of Mohawk and Bellinger. Police believe Kimball died instantly when the late model pickup truck he was driving lost control and flipped several times before coming to rest in a ditch. "Speed and alcohol most certainly played a significant role in this accident," reported Officer R. Williams of the Herkimer County Sheriff's Department. According to estimates, the accident took place about 11:30 p.m.

Kimball had a long history of DUI violations and was driving on a suspended license. "We should all be grateful this happened when it did," Officer Williams said. "This is a dangerous intersection, even under the best circumstances. If this had happened during the day, it's certain more people would have been injured or killed." Since January, this was the second fatal crash at this site, the fourth in the last eighteen months. Kimball worked as a machinist for Dempsy Brothers in Frankfort for the past eight years. Investigators spent time at Kimball's home at The Whistling Winds Trailer Park on Saturday morning. Neighbors described him as "reclusive" and "prone to the bottle." According to one neighbor, who wished to remain anonymous, Kimball supposedly has a son who lives in Vermont.

Funeral plans have been put on hold indefinitely while family members are located and the coroner has completed toxicological analyses.

Jake wiped a tear from his eye. He couldn't know for certain that this was his father, but in his heart he knew it was. How many other alcoholic men from Winooski named John Henry Kimball could there be? A surreal feeling passed over him as he stared at the screen for another minute before clicking the print button. He logged out before looking up at the clock. It was 7:45. He'd accomplished what he'd set out to do, but the answer he'd found offered him no comfort.

After locking the library door, Jake broke into a jog. As he ran down the quiet back streets, words from the article ran through his mind. *His father was dead.* He'd been dead for a long time. He wondered if investigators had made contact with his mother. She'd changed her name a few years after the divorce, taking back her maiden name, surely making it more difficult to find her. She'd never given any indication that she knew what had happened to him, and Jake couldn't think of any reason for her to keep him from finding out, if she had known. His father was dead. He had wondered about it so many times before, but now he knew. What angst might he have avoided had he known this sooner? He certainly wouldn't have wondered why his father never contacted him. Dead men don't write birthday cards or make phone calls. In many ways, his father had been dead to him for almost twenty years. It wasn't like this was completely new, and yet the definite recognition that he was, indeed, dead seemed strange. Jake had already cried his tears and waded through the disappointment of not knowing his father, but finding this now—now that he was getting married—now that he felt emotionally ready to look him in the eye—it all seemed more than a little cruel.

Jake was all the way home before he realized he'd forgotten to pick up the printout of the article on his way out of the library, but he knew he had no time to worry about it now. He rolled the scooter out of the shed and kick-started it, sending a flock of pigeons flying into the chestnut tree.

The house looked quiet as he rolled through the bushes that clogged Mr. Allan's drive. He knocked on the door several times, but when no answer came, he tried the door knob. It was unlocked. He turned the knob and pushed the door open a couple of inches, and called out to him, but there was no response. He started to worry. What if he'd died during the night? He couldn't. Not now. Not with all the plans they'd made for him.

Jake took a deep breath and let himself in. Again and again, he called Mr. Allan's name as he wandered from room to room, but was there no sign of him anywhere. His bed had been slept in, but he wasn't there now. Feeling somewhat relieved, though still worried, Jake walked back into the living room and was about to go out the way he'd come in when he heard it—singing coming from the veranda.

He walked to the sliding glass door and looked out. Mr. Allan was sitting there in his briefs and undershirt with his back toward the door. He had a huge set of headphones on and was singing, rather loudly and definitely off key.

Well I got me a fine wife, I got me old fiddle;
When the sun's comin' up I got cake on the griddle
Life ain't nothin' but a funny, funny riddle,
Thank God I'm a country boy.

Jake recognized the lyrics from a John Denver song, "Thank God I'm a Country Boy," and he was half-tempted to join him on the next verse. He pushed the door open and walked out onto the veranda until he stood just behind the old man. Jake smiled to himself when he saw what

Mr. Allan had in his hands—his dentures and a pink toothbrush. He watched as the old man dipped his teeth in a ceramic dish, then polished them again with the toothbrush, all the while continuing to belt out John Denver lyrics.

Jake tapped him on the shoulder, and the old man jerked violently, nearly catapulting himself out of his chair.

"Sorry, Mr. Allan, but we're supposed to be at the barber shop."

"What?" he yelled.

Jake laughed, reaching for the headphones. "Mr. Allan, I'm here to give you a ride to the barbershop," he said when he'd pried the headphones away from his ears.

"You're a day early. That's not till Monday."

"It is Monday, Mr. Allan. Yesterday was Sunday and tomorrow is Tuesday."

"Why didn't you say so?" he said loudly, scrambling to his feet. "Are you here for breakfast?"

"No," Jake said, trying to be patient and not laugh. "I'm here to take you to get your hair cut."

"Well, I ain't got much of that left anymore. I don't know why we even need to bother."

"Maybe Jerry could help you figure out that toupee of yours."

Mr. Allan nodded, slipping his teeth into his mouth. "Let's go then."

Jake followed Mr. Allan into the house, but instead of heading for his bedroom, he marched toward the front door. "Uh, Mr. Allan, do you think you should get some clothes on?"

He stopped in his tracks and looked down. "Oh dear, I think I must have left them down at the river when I was taking my bath. I knew I was forgettin' something. I must have gotten distracted by all those pretty rocks."

Jake waited on the veranda while Mr. Allan got dressed. As he sat down, he heard John Denver's words emanating from the headphones, and he reached over to switch the old tape player off. The dish that Mr. Allan had been using to rinse his dentures intrigued Jake. He dumped out the water so he could better examine it, turning it over. It looked like a miniature bundt pan, but it was made of gray stoneware and looked very old. The slightly bumpy texture on the outside of the dish caused Jake to look closer. He knew from his travels that this texture could only be achieved in a salt kiln, where, at high temperatures, rock salt was thrown into the flame. The flame would vaporize the salt and deposit it on the surface of the pots, forming a texture over the entire surface that looked and felt like half-melted glass beads.

Turning the dish over in his hands, he discovered a chop—the potter's stamp, pressed into the side near the bottom—a tiny crown. It had been several weeks since Thomas had spoken of Lamar Mancini's lost pudding mold, the prized jewel of his vast collection that had gone missing after an evening swim at the river. But it was this stamp that got Jake thinking, searching his memory for the details of that conversation. Had he not said something about the mold having been commissioned from a German potter for some king in England? Jake smiled to himself as he thought about it. He knew this had to be Lamar's mold. Salt glaze had been developed in Germany, but the crown—this had to be it!

After arranging to trade Mr. Allan a new bowl for his old one, Jake wrapped the dish in some newspapers and stowed it carefully in the milk crate strapped to the back of the scooter. With Mr. Allan's arms wrapped tightly around his chest, Jake pulled onto the highway and headed back to town. The sound of the wind and the engine muffled Jake's laughter that came freely when he imagined how silly they must look.

Mr. Allan was still wearing the bubblehead helmet and clutching his toupee like a dead squirrel when they walked through the barbershop door. Jerry jumped out of the barber's seat and set down his newspaper. After helping Jake remove the helmet from Mr. Allan's head, Jerry assured him that he had things under control and told Jake that he could leave.

He was walking back to his scooter when he remembered the library and the printout he'd forgotten to pick up on his way out. He hurried toward the library, but stopped running when he saw Roberta Mancini rounding the corner, pulling a two-wheeled cart behind her that was stuffed with books. He knew he didn't have time to deal with both her and her brother before he needed to be back at the shop, so he turned around and walked back to the scooter.

Motorized traffic was strictly forbidden on Hauptstrasse, but Jake figured the rules might not apply to a scooter whose engine wasn't turned on. He pushed the scooter across the pavement to where the cobblestones began and then he jumped on, coasting down the still-mostly-quiet street. He came to a stop next to a sign advertising the Grand Opening of the Mancini International Pudding Mold Museum slated for the coming weekend. The front door of the museum was open and lively piano music was pouring out onto the street, reminding Jake of an old-time saloon in a western movie.

The window display had a cardboard cutout of Lamar, his arms outstretched with a pudding mold in each of his hands. *The World's Largest Collection of Pudding Molds in the World* was scrawled across his cardboard chest, and Jake laughed at the redundancy. He followed the sound of the music past the ticket booth where the entrance fee was posted: $10 for adults, $5 for children and seniors. An annual family pass was also available for $100. The entryway opened into a cavernous room. On one wall, shelves held the ceramic, glass and plastic molds. Each mold was labeled with the name, make and model, along with the approximate year it was made and a number relating to the relative rareness of each of the pieces. Another wall displayed at least a hundred copper pudding molds in a variety of themes and shapes ranging from stars, to fish, to rings and grapes. Regardless of how quirky it was, Jake had to admire Lamar's passion.

MANCINI INTERNATIONAL MUSEUM OF PUDDING MOLDS

THE WORLD'S LARGEST COLLECTION OF PUDDING MOLDS IN THE WORLD!

Entrance Fees

Adults (18+)..................$10.00
Children and Seniors.........$5.00
Annual Family Pass.........$100.00

The music stopped, replaced by a whooshing sound, several clicks, and then the music started up again. Jake listened to the strangely familiar song while he wandered around, looking for its source. The music changed to a quick-paced rhythm that he recognized from his humanities class as Rossini's "William Tell Overture," otherwise known as "The Lone Ranger Theme Song." With no one watching, Jake gave in to the desire to gallop around in a circle, laughing while he did. He followed the music to the back room where he found Lamar sitting at an antique player piano, pumping his legs to keep the music going. Jake knocked on the door frame, and Lamar jumped up immediately.

The older man welcomed Jake to the museum as the first customer and informed him that he was welcome to look around after he'd paid the ten dollar entrance fee. Jake laughed and suggested they might work out a trade for an annual pass in exchange for a rare mold he had recently acquired. Lamar looked at him dubiously, but accepted the newspaper-wrapped bundle.

As the last piece of paper was pulled away, Jake watched as Lamar began to hyperventilate. Holding the mold against his chest, he turned to look at Jake, too filled with emotion to talk.

After graciously receiving the first-ever annual family pass issued by the Mancini International Museum of Pudding Molds, Jake walked back to his scooter with a smile from ear to ear. As he pushed the scooter back to the shed, Jake imagined Isaac being pleased that the object of so much contention over the past ten years was finally back in the hands of the man who owned the *world's largest collection of pudding molds in the world!*

MANCINI
INTERNATIONAL MUSEUM
OF PUDDING MOLDS
ANNUAL FAMILY PASS
EXPIRES
PASS HOLDERS SIGNATURE
This pass is valid only during regular operating hours.
Children must be accompanied by a responsible adult.
No outside food allowed.
0001

A HIGHER LAW

I EXPECT TO PASS THROUGH LIFE BUT ONCE.
IF THEREFORE, THERE BE ANY KINDNESS I CAN SHOW,
OR ANY GOOD THING I CAN DO TO ANY FELLOW BEING, LET ME DO IT NOW,
AND NOT DEFER OR NEGLECT IT, AS I SHALL NOT PASS THIS WAY AGAIN.
—WILLIAM PENN—

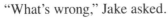

ake, I am so sorry," Amy said from the studio doorway. With tears in her eyes and a look of compassion on her face, she ran toward him, throwing her arms around his neck.

"What's wrong," Jake asked.

"I just went to check on Mr. Allan at the library and Thomas gave me the article about your dad."

Jake nodded. "I forgot to pick that up when I left."

"How are you feeling?"

"To be honest, I'm not really sure how I feel. I guess I'm disappointed, but he's been dead for a long time. I wish I would have known so I didn't wonder all those years why he never wanted anything to do with me. I don't know. I feel kind of numb."

"I'm sorry, Jake."

"Amy, there's nothing you could have done. I'm sad I'll never have the chance to talk to him—to ask him why he left—why he never tried to find me. But I guess we know why now, don't we?"

"It just seems like a really cruel way to find out," she said.

"Is there ever a good way to find out you'll never have a chance to talk to your parents again? Part of me wishes I could have found that article years ago. It's not exactly the closure I was looking for, but it's the only closure I've got. I guess I should be grateful I discovered the truth instead of holding on to some crazy, false hope for the rest of my life."

Amy agreed and the conversation continued for several minutes until Jake, having had enough sadness for one day, changed the subject, asking Amy about her morning. While he continued his work, glazing the Journey Jars, Amy updated him on the progress with Mr. Allan's house where she'd spent the morning supervising the cleaning crew. Overwhelmed by the mess, they had already made plans to return the following day to finish up.

While Amy helped a customer, Jake carefully slid the mug he'd made for her into the kiln and sealed the door before lighting the burners. He sat down with a pencil to figure out a schedule for the rest of his week. By firing overnight, he could turn the kiln off in the early morning. Then, if he left the damper open, he might be able to unload the pots by Thursday morning. If he could do that, he'd have the time to finish the Journey Jar handles for the Allan family gathering on Friday night. Somehow, it might all work out.

As Jake was briefing Amy on the schedule he needed to keep in order to make things work, Eric Schmelding walked through the front door and up the stairs to the showroom.

"Workin' late, are ya?"

Jake looked at the clock and then at Eric, smiling. It was only four forty-five. "Do we need to get a new clock?" Jake asked, pointing to the clock on the wall.

Eric looked at his watch, and then at the clock. "I guess sometimes the minute hand does matter." He dropped his bag on the counter and dug through it, producing three pint containers of Ben and Jerry's ice cream and three plastic spoons. He handed one to each of them and took a seat on an unoccupied stool. "At the end of a long day, there's nothing like sitting down for pints with friends," he said, raising his container in a toast. "After cheese, ice cream is the second best thing you can do with milk, and my friends Ben and Jerry, know how to do it right."

Jake and Amy laughed as they pulled off the lids and dug in.

"Kai and Molly said to say hi," Eric managed to mumble through a mouthful of Chocolate Fudge Brownie. "They wanted to join us for pints, too, but Molly had already made dinner."

"I'm glad you came," Amy said. "I've been thinking today that I need to commission you to do some photography before this weekend."

"What did you have in mind?"

Amy pulled out her great-grandfather's tool box and set it in front of Eric, explaining the history and the trouble that the tools had caused her extended family. She explained that she planned to give the tools away to each of the family members who came for the weekend, but that she hoped to take a picture of each tool to use as a reference for future paintings.

Without hesitation, Eric agreed, wolfing down his ice cream so he could get started. He began with the trowel, setting it up on the front counter, taking multiple shots from different angles.

"The purpose of my visit this evening was to compliment the two of you," Eric said as he pointed his lens at an old wooden plumb bob that looked like a top.

"For what?" Jake asked.

"For having a desire to learn—for looking past the end of your own nose—for learning to sacrifice. People have been talking, as they always do around here, but what they've been saying has intrigued me. I think it has intrigued all of us."

"Uh, oh. What did we do now?" asked Amy.

Eric moved the plumb bob and replaced it with a square, continuing to shoot without looking up. "Most people, when they're getting ready to get married, act as if they're the only two people in the world. Weddings, the world over, are one of the most expensive events in a person's life. People spend all sorts of money they don't have to make sure everything is perfect. Dowries and bride prices are exchanged with the hopes that everything will work out, that the bride and groom will live happily ever after. But for more than half of those people who got married today, and yesterday, and even for those who will marry tomorrow, their marriages will end unhappily."

"Thanks for the vote of confidence," Jake teased.

"Why do they fail?" Eric asked, looking up from his camera. "Why do so many marriages fail?"

"Because people forget that they love each other?" Amy said, sounding more like a question than an answer.

"I'm certain that's part of it. I am not a psychologist, but I think I have become a fairly good observer of people. I believe most marriages fail because too many people carry the attitudes they have on their wedding day into their marriages."

"I'm not sure I understand," said Amy.

"Selfishness," Eric responded. "You see it in every bride magazine and on the cover of every Hollywood tabloid. Behavior that would

seem greedy, selfish and irresponsible on any other day is not only condoned, but encouraged at the time of a wedding. We all complicate our lives with wanting the new, the bigger, and the more expensive. Unfortunately, this behavior often begins with a wedding and carries on throughout a marriage, robbing a union of simplicity, real substance and grace. There is nothing shameful about a simple wedding that offers a bride and groom a chance to actually listen to the words of the vows and covenants they are making, rather than being distracted by pomp and revelry. That is why the town is watching you. You are blessing your union with friendship and love and simplicity rather than complicating it with the weight and burdens of the world."

Eric moved the hammer and put an old chisel in its place. "I have been inspired by watching you kids over these last two weeks—your goodness, your humility, your willingness to learn and forgive and begin your lives together on a path of selflessness. I have admired your maturity. This week is the biggest week of your life, but instead of demanding attention with selfish behavior, you two are arranging to bring not only your family together, but also Mr. Allan's. Who does stuff like that? Who, when they're busy getting ready for a wedding, tries to change the future by healing the sorrows of the past? Who spends time learning all they can about forgiveness when the world gives them every reason to hold onto a grudge forever?"

They looked at each other and smiled. "We've had some great teachers."

"The world is full of truth and wisdom, but only those who are searching for it will find it. You have to be hungry before you look for food. I am convinced that if you two will stay the course you are on, your marriage will become a beacon, continuing to inspire the hope that your courtship has. Something wonderful happens when you learn to look past the end of your own nose. You begin to see that the world has need of the talents and light you have. And when you set aside your own desires to share what you've been given, for the good of the community, you have learned a higher law."

"A higher law?" Jake asked.

"Yes, the law of sacrifice. I talked to you about this the other day, but God has entrusted each of us with time and talents which, if used correctly, can be a healing ointment that can heal our aching world."

"That's what Isaac was trying to teach everyone, wasn't it?" Jake asked, struck with the truth of what he'd just been told. "He gave everyone a piece of himself ... and his time."

"Yes," Eric said, pointing to the mugs on the overhead beam. "I have learned that when sacrifice knocks on your door and asks if it can borrow a cup of sugar, it always returns with a ten pound bag of something even better. You may not be wealthy, but you will always have enough. You may not have fame, but you will always have peace. If we take the time to be still—if we offer that minimum investment—the universe will tell us where it needs our time and talents, just as it has told each of you. Answers will always come to those who seek them, and if we will listen, we can be part of the greatest work in the world."

IT IS THE EYE OF OTHER PEOPLE THAT RUIN US. IF I WERE BLIND I WOULD WANT NEITHER FINE CLOTHES, FINE HOUSES OR FINE FURNITURE.
— BENJAMIN FRANKLIN —

COUNTING BLESSINGS

THE MOST IMPORTANT PART OF PRAYER IS WHAT WE FEEL, NOT WHAT WE
SAY. WE SPEND A GREAT DEAL OF TIME TELLING GOD WHAT WE THINK
SHOULD BE DONE, AND NOT ENOUGH TIME WAITING IN THE STILLNESS
FOR GOD TO TELL US WHAT TO DO.
—PEACE PILGRIM—

What are you doing here so early?" Jake asked as he opened the
back door on Tuesday morning and found Amy already working.
"I couldn't sleep. I had an idea for a painting. I picked up
some breakfast," she said, nodding to a bag of pastries next to
her on the counter. "I hope I didn't wake you up."

"No, I couldn't get back to sleep after the firing finished up around four. I've been cleaning up the apartment, trying to get ready for this weekend."

"Do you need some help?"

"Yeah. It seems kind of strange, but I'd like your opinion on which bedroom you want to be ours, that is if you want to share a room with me after we get married."

Amy laughed. "I really hope you're joking."

Jake grabbed her, lifting her off the floor. "I was just checking. I didn't want you to think I was getting fresh if it wasn't welcome."

She kissed him on the nose, causing them both to laugh. "I don't care which room is ours. You can even snore if you don't mind if I leave my socks in the middle of the floor."

"It's a deal," Jake said, kissing her for real. "What are you painting?" he asked, turning to look at her easel.

She stopped him, grabbing his chin before he could turn his head all the way around. "It's a surprise—for our wedding. I knew you might see it if I painted it here, but it may take a little while and I want to be around you. Can you promise me that you won't peek?"

Jake turned his head slightly toward the easel.

"Jake!"

"Okay, I promise," he said, sounding like a little boy.

While they ate their breakfast on the bench in the courtyard, they made plans for the apartment. With Amy having found a happy place to work in the studio, they decided to keep the guest bedroom just as it was, though both of them expressed a hope that they'd have some time alone before opening their home to guests. The small kitchen and dining area could definitely use some TLC, but they decided they could put that off until the fall when they might have more time.

Before going back to the studio, they climbed the stairs to the apartment.

"It might be kind of small with two of us living here," Jake said, standing at the doorway.

"It will be perfect," Amy said, pulling him into the bedroom. She sat down on the bed, bouncing slightly to check the springs. "This looks cozy to me," she said, looking around the room at the blank walls. "There's lots of room for paintings."

Jake sat down next to her, staring through the shutters. "Is this really happening? Are we really getting married in five days?"

Amy laughed. "Yeah, are you okay with that?"

"No," Jake said sadly, looking very serious.

"What? What's wrong?" she asked, panic in her voice.

"I wish we were getting married tomorrow."

Amy pushed him over on the bed. Then she sat on top of him, bouncing him into the springs while hitting him in the face with a pillow.

"On second thought, maybe I could wait a little longer," Jake said, grabbing the pillow from her and returning the blows.

When they had stopped laughing, they went back to the studio to work. It had been a couple of weeks since the showroom had been dusted and organized, so Jake tackled that first, wanting to be as close to Amy as he could. While he worked, he opened up about the other thing he'd been thinking about all morning. While he was organizing the apartment, he'd stumbled upon Isaac's will and had sat down to reread it. He felt like Isaac would be pleased with what he was doing, but there were still two things he'd agreed to do, that still needed to be done.

"Amy, we haven't really talked about this, but I've been thinking about tithing. When I got here, I committed to pay a tithe on my income."

"So when are we going to pay it?" Amy asked.

"Wow, that was easy. I was worried I might have to talk you into it."

"I've been thinking about it since Thomas explained it when he gave us the tour at the church."

"I haven't done anything about it since I got here. It's kind of a lot of money. Are you sure you're okay with it?" asked Jake.

"Absolutely. I've kind of been setting it aside in my head since the tour."

"You have?"

"Yeah. There are still lot of things I don't understand about faith and about the Bible, especially the Old Testament, but the way I figure it, there are lots of things I won't know if I don't give it a shot. I remember Thomas said something about that last prophet in the Bible, Malachi, isn't it?"

"That sounds right."

"Yeah, remember how he said that for those who pay a tithe, that the windows of heaven will be opened and there won't be room enough to receive it? I have no idea how that works, or even if it does, but I think I'd like to try it. I've been wondering since yesterday if maybe that's part of the sacrifice that Isaac understood."

Jake nodded. "I feel like the windows of heaven have already been opened to me. I'm really grateful that you want to do this."

"I've never wanted to be rich, Jake. I've wanted to be happy. After our discussion with Eric last night, I think there is probably no such thing as true happiness without sacrifice."

Jake took a deep breath, feeling relieved by Amy's attitude.

"Do you think we'll have time to finish Isaac's bench before the wedding?"

"That was the other thing I was reminded of when I read Isaac's will. I don't know. The last of the tiles will be out of the kiln on Thursday. What's on the schedule for Thursday evening?"

"Nothing. I thought we could move most of my stuff down that night, but how long do you think the bench will take?"

"I don't know. It's not as big as Sam's floor, but there are more angles on the bench. Probably at least a few hours."

"Do you have everything you need?"

"No, but Sam does. He has at least half a bag of grout and almost a full bag of mortar. That should be enough."

By the time noon rolled around, Jake had organized the tiles that had come out of the kiln on Saturday and was anxious to get started. After gassing up the scooter, they rode up to Castleton's to pick up their rings. As promised, the rings were ready, a tiny, five-petaled flower engraved on the inside of each one. They thanked Mr. Castleton, but with no time to waste, Jake slid the ring boxes into his pocket and they hurried back to town. Passing the Yoders, they waved at the family picnicking in the shade of the oak tree. "We can't stop, but we'll see you Sunday," Jake yelled over his shoulder. Mr. Yoder waved his straw hat and grinned.

They rode past Niederbipp until they came to the turnoff for Mr. Allan's house. As they drove down the drive, they barely recognized the place. The landscaping crew had trimmed back the bushes, opening the path. A huge dump truck was parked near Mr. Allan's old cars, filled with all sorts of tree limbs and garbage. The overgrown lawn had been tamed, the weeds had been pulled, and the crew was planting pansies in the small flower beds that flanked the front steps.

Amy pointed to Mr. Allan, swinging a croquet mallet at a bright yellow ball near the far end of the yard. They parked the scooter and walked past the dump truck and the Merry Maids' minivan that was hidden on the other side. Jake nodded to the work crew and held the door open for a woman dressed in a white jumpsuit who was carrying two buckets of rocks that she dumped onto a large pile near the flower beds.

Jake followed Amy inside. They roamed from room to room, amazed at the transformation that had taken place. Every last one of Mr. Allan's pickle jars had been dusted and polished, making the hallway and living room look like a well-organized specimen closet in a science laboratory. The curtains were pulled back and the open windows

revealed a vacuumed carpet and dust-free furniture. Even the veranda was organized and devoid of the clutter that had clogged it before.

Another woman, dressed like the first, came from Mr. Allan's room wearing blue rubber gloves and toting a toilet brush. "Oh, Amy, how are you?" she asked, looking tired.

"Jean, you and your girls are amazing. This looks awesome."

"Thanks. This was a big one, but it's nice when a job like this comes together. You don't have to do much to feel like you've done a lot. We just have that front bathroom to finish before we're done. You know, in twenty years of cleaning houses, I thought I'd seen everything, but two bathtubs completely full of rocks? That's something I'll never forget."

"Two bathtubs? I just thought . . ." Amy said, pointing at the front bathroom.

"Nope, the master bath had even more than that one, and I've never seen so many toothbrushes in my life. We must have found five hundred of them throughout the house, most of them worn down to nothing. I think your cousin might have a bit of an obsession. Every time we turn around, he's trying to give us one of his favorite rocks or bottle caps. We finally asked the boys outside to set up the croquet set so we could get some work done. If he wasn't such a sweetheart..."

"I really appreciate it. How much more do we owe you for today?"

"Mr. Allan took care of it. He even gave us each a hundred bucks as a tip."

"He did?"

"Yep, best tipper I've had in . . . well, in *ever*, I guess. I would like to make a suggestion—for his safety."

"Okay."

Jean lowered her voice and stepped closer. "I know he's kind of old school, but storing his money in a shoe box under his bed is probably not the safest place."

Amy nodded, and thanked her for the advice.

Jake and Amy spoke to Mr. Allan briefly, taking a rain check on his offer for a game of croquet. He thanked them for helping him and gave them each a rock for their trouble.

With time running short on their lunch break, they zoomed back to town as fast as the scooter would go. Parking outside The Pottery, Jake ran inside and returned with a pea-green, vinyl bank bag, handing it to Amy. Together, they rode to the bank to add Amy to Jake's account. It had been a couple of weeks since a deposit had been made, and the classy looking woman who sat behind the desk gawked at them as they unloaded the contents of the bag onto her desk.

"What line of work are you two in?" she asked, staring at Jake's clay-encrusted pants and Amy's T-shirt, flecked with dabs of oil paint.

"We're artists," Amy said, smiling at Jake.

"Ahh, Jake Kimball, how are you, son?" a male voice said from behind them, causing them both to turn around.

"Hi, Mr. Smoot," Jake said.

"This must be the future Mrs. Kimball," he said, extending his hand to Amy.

"That's right. This is Amy. We're getting married Sunday."

"That's what I heard. Congratulations." He looked up at the woman behind the desk. "Georgia, make sure you take care of these kids, will you."

Georgia nodded, looking suddenly much more alert and attentive.

"Would you like any money back?" she asked, after the paperwork had been filled out and the money counted.

"Yes," Jake said. "If you don't mind, could we get all of the money back from that cashier's check, and then ten percent of the rest of the total deposit?"

"Uh, sure," Georgia said. "How would you like that?"

A few minutes later, they drove the scooter down the narrow alleyway between the library and Thomas' cottage. After parking in the shade of the churchyard trees, they climbed the stone steps together and pulled open the tall wooden doors. A rush of cool air chilled Amy's skin, causing goose bumps to rise on her arms as they walked down the center aisle to the beehive-emblazoned box that sat on an alcove in the wall. Jake pulled the bank-issued envelope out of his pocket, Benjamin  Franklin staring out through its oval window. Jake counted out twenty of the bills, sliding them back into the envelope. Then he handed Amy half of the remaining stack.

"I have an idea," Jake said with excitement.

"Okay?"

"How about, if every time we come here to do this, we think about the good things that have happened in our life."

"Can we say it out loud?" Amy asked, holding one of the bills over the top of the slot.

"Sounds good to me."

"All right. I became a painter," she said, letting the bill slide through her fingers and disappear in the box.

"I was given a pottery shop," Jake said, adding a bill of his own.

"I fell in love with a wonderful guy."

"I fell in love with the most amazing, beautiful and talented girl I've ever known."

"Do you think maybe we should limit the adjectives?"

"You can if you want. Maybe I'm just more grateful than you are."

She shook her head. "You're lucky we're in a church. I figured out who I am," she said turning back to the box.

"My girlfriend beats me up a lot less than she used to."

"Hey, are you going to take this seriously, or not?" she asked, trying both to look mean and keep herself from laughing at the same time.

"I learned how be still," Jake continued, with a wink.

"I learned to forgive."

"I've eaten amazing bread every day for two months."

"I've made new friends."

"I learned to remember the small stuff."

"I tasted six-year-old yak cheese."

"I decided to make Niederbipp my home for the rest of my life."

Amy paused, with her hand over the box. She looked into Jake's eyes as if she were staring into eternity. "I did, too."

One by one, they listed the good things they'd been given, and when the money was gone, they walked back down the aisle, continuing to count their blessings and making plans to pay their tithing next time in one-dollar bills.

ALL I HAVE TEACHES ME TO TRUST THE CREATOR FOR ALL I HAVE NOT SEEN.
-RALPH WALDO EMERSON-

MAKING THE MOVE

ONE SHOULD COUNT EACH DAY A SEPARATE LIFE.
—SENECA—

Jake and Amy spent Tuesday evening with Gloria and Joseph, finalizing plans for the weekend. While the girls were talking about flowers, Joseph pulled Jake aside to ask if he had made plans for their wedding night. Of course, he hadn't. He put his arm around Jake and handed him a piece of paper with the name of a bed and breakfast written on it—The Swaney Inn, just a few miles south of town. Joseph said he'd already checked on availability for Sunday night and reported that they could have their pick of three nice rooms. Jake thanked him for his help and thoughtfulness and slid the paper into his back pocket.

As they ate dessert, talking and laughing together, the feeling of belonging that Jake had experienced in Gloria and Joseph's home on several other occasions returned. Watching the other three interact—his future wife and two of the most loving and generous people he had ever known, Jake again experienced an affirmation that he was where he was supposed to be.

He thought back on his first day in Niederbipp, how he'd looked through the dusty windows of The Pottery and wondered why he had wasted his time coming all the way here. He remembered going to the old train station, looking for the next available bus out of town. He was embarrassed by the person he was back then—impetuous, bull-headed, self-absorbed. He'd been so busy trying to get to where he wanted to be that he hadn't opened his eyes and realized he was already there.

And then there was Amy. As his love for her had grown, it had caused him to stretch, to become less selfish, to become a better man. She had inspired him on so many levels and he was grateful to have a friend like her—a friend who would be his companion for the rest of his life.

As he walked home that night after dropping Amy off, his mind was once again filled with gratitude. Things weren't perfect. The Pottery was still old, the apartment was both old and small, the town was still full of quirky people, but this was life, his life, the one he had chosen, and the one he now embraced with everything that was good in his soul.

With Amy focusing on her painting, Jake filled his Wednesday by making more bowls for the showroom. The normal flux of weekend tourists arrived earlier this week, so in addition to working on her painting, Amy stayed busy wrapping pottery. Many of the tourists wandered through the showroom and loitered in the studio, watching

Jake work. One couple stayed for an hour, mesmerized by the art of creation.

With the warmth of the day working in his favor, Jake was able to trim the bowls in the late afternoon, filling the drying rack with stacks of fresh ware. He knew it would be at least two weeks before these would make it to the showroom floor. In college, the lag time from start to finish for his pottery projects was only a mild annoyance. But now, with tourists and locals stopping by every day to peruse the shelves, Jake felt pressure to be continually producing in order to keep the shelves full.

The kiln was still too hot to unload by Wednesday evening, so Jake and Amy adjusted their plans and decided to spend the evening moving Amy's stuff into the apartment. After separating what she would need for the next three days, most of her things fit into the two suitcases she'd brought with her to Niederbipp. After dinner with Bev and Jerry, they rolled the big suitcases to the apartment, one at a time, balanced on the seat of Aunt Bev's old bike.

The reality that his life would soon be intertwined with Amy's hit him harder than ever as she loaded her clothes and personals into the unused drawers in the dresser at the foot of the bed they would soon share. For four years, he had shared his apartment at school with roommates, but this was entirely different. This was new and exciting. They had already shared so much together, but sharing a bed and a dresser and a bathroom was a strange but welcome change. She had far more clothes than he did, but seeing his clothes hanging in the closet next to hers and her shoes lined up next to his offered a surprising feeling of comfort. Somehow, the old apartment felt more like home.

After Amy's clothes were put away and her suitcases stowed in the cellar, they sat down on the bed and talked about life and their dreams for the future. As Jake held Amy in his arms, she thanked him again for honoring her as a woman and treating her with respect. The discussion moved naturally to things of a more intimate nature, but the respect they shared for each other kept them from moving any further toward intimacy than what they had already enjoyed, saving the rest for after the wedding.

Walking Amy home was difficult that night, despite their resolve. Jake lingered longer than usual on Bev and Jerry's porch and when he finally left, he didn't go home. Instead, he went for a long walk, out past Mr. Allan's place, where the lights of town were no match for the stars in the dark sky.

He walked to the middle of the bridge where he and Amy had given their rocks back to the river just a few days before. He sat down, dangling his feet over the edge. After a minute of staring at the reflection of the stars in the dark water, he lay back on the narrow, wooden bridge, gazing into the night sky. From his vantage point, the Milky Way seemed to mimic the course of the river, lighting the heavens with its billions of stars.

In the silence of the night, with only the song of the crickets to keep time, Jake opened his mind to the universe. There had been many times since his mother's death that he'd wondered about heaven. On those occasions, as thoughts of her ran through his head, the distance between heaven and earth seemed very small. Over the past year and  a half, there had been many times when Jake had felt alone, but as he thought about it now, he had no feelings of loneliness. Though he was a newcomer, he felt like a native son of Niederbipp. So many had embraced him and loved him, opening his heart and mind again to the blessings of love.

After half an hour, he picked himself up and began walking home along the dark, deserted highway. Once again, his thoughts turned to Isaac—the potter who had died and given all of this to him—the potter who was continuing to shape lives from the grave. Isaac's legacy was marked by the thousands of pots he'd made over his lifetime. But more importantly, his legacy was graced by the people he'd loved and the lives he'd shaped and influenced with his generous heart and careful hand.

Back in the apartment, Jake opened his sketchbook and flipped through the pages until he found it—the low-resolution picture of the old potter he'd printed off at the campus library. Lying in bed, Jake stared at the blurry image, hoping that if Isaac were able to observe him from wherever he was, he would be pleased with the man and the potter his replacement was becoming.

NO ONE CAN FIND INNER PEACE EXCEPT BY WORKING, NOT IN A SELF-CENTERED WAY, BUT FOR THE WHOLE HUMAN FAMILY. - PEACE PILGRIM-

THE COMMUNITY BENCH

TOO OFTEN WE UNDERESTIMATE THE POWER OF A TOUCH,
A SMILE, A KIND WORD, A LISTENING EAR, AN HONEST COMPLIMENT,
OR THE SMALLEST ACT OF CARING, ALL OF WHICH HAVE THE POTENTIAL
TO TURN A LIFE AROUND.
—LEO BUSCAGLIA—

nxious to get started on Isaac's bench, Jake didn't waste any time on Thursday morning. Reaching into the still-hot kiln with his gloved hands, Jake burned his forearms several times before all the tiles could be unloaded. The colors were brilliant, even brighter than the tiles from the previous firing, and he was excited to see them all together on the bench.

Sam was happy to give Jake the rest of the mortar and grout when he heard that it was going to Isaac's bench. He also loaned him the tools and buckets they'd used to finish the bakery floor. Once he'd accumulated everything he thought he'd need, Jake began making trips to the graveyard. After schlepping the first load by hand, he wised up and employed the scooter with its milk crate strapped to the back to make the rest of the runs. Then, at three, Jake left Amy to tend the shop and went to the graveyard to begin his work.

Hildegard stopped by just as he was mixing the mortar and asked if she could be of any assistance, but before he even got started, she disappeared, returning with a shoe box full of Isaac's potshards, mostly broken cat bowls that she hadn't been able to bring herself to throw away. She offered them to Jake to use on the bench.

Thomas stopped by not long after the first tile was laid, offering his help. When he saw Hildegard's shards, he went to his house, returning with a few broken pieces of his own, including a handful of assorted shards he'd found near the old dump site by the river.

As a small crowd always draws a bigger one, more people began dropping by to see what was going on. Before long, it had become a party, each person anxious to see what Jake and Amy had come up with. With the heat of the day pounding down on the bench, the mortar dried in one area before he was ready and Jake had to scrape some of it off and reapply before setting the tiles in place. After watching this, two of the war widows left quietly, returning with several umbrellas to block the sun from shining directly on the bench along with a gallon of lemonade to share with the party.

Before Jake finished the top portion of the bench, new people began arriving every few minutes, many of them carrying broken pottery as a contribution to the project. They stood around the bench, looking over each other's shoulders, ooing and ahing as the design came together, one piece at a time. When Jake began applying the tiles to the vertical edges of the bench, the first tiles started sliding with the pull of gravity, but they didn't stray far before people began volunteering to hold the tiles in place until the mortar dried. Soon, ten people were kneeling on the dirt surrounding the bench, supporting the tiles as the mortar set up.

"What does it say? I can only see the words on this end," the Mayor asked.

"It says, 'Joy in all its' on this side," a woman answered.

"It says 'Be still and know that,' on this side," said another woman.

A tall man in a plaid leisure suit, who was not involved with holding the tiles in place, walked around the perimeter of the bench reading the carved tiles aloud. "It says, 'Joy, in all its glory, can only be obtained through unselfishness.' And these two sides say, 'Be still, and know that I am God.'" The crowd seemed to nod their heads in unison as if to give their approval.

"What are we going to do with all these shards?" Betty Finkel asked, pointing to the pile of potshards that had accumulated on Henry's bench.

"We still have the legs," someone suggested.

"We could help with that, couldn't we?" asked a man wearing a bright red bow tie whom Jake recognized from the Tourist Council.

"Uh, sure," Jake said. "But most of those are too big. We would need to break them up so they could lie flat."

Two men were dispatched to fetch hammers, while several others sorted through the shards to find the most colorful and attractive pieces. Someone had brought a chipped lid from a bean pot and while people sorted through the shards, Jake took the liberty of mortaring it onto the leg that faced the gate. Then, selecting several dozen triangular pieces, he made the lid look like a whimsical sun with multicolored rays expanding outward. As the mortar dried on the edges, those who had been holding the tiles in place also got involved in the process of selecting pieces for the mosaic.

Sam arrived with a few dozen day-old pastries just as Jake was finishing the first leg. When the second leg was nearing completion, the crowd talked Jake into doing the under side as well, even though only those who lay down on the ground would ever see it.

Finally, when every inch of the bench was covered and everyone satisfied that at least one of the pieces they'd contributed to the project had been included, they stood back to admire their work.

"What's everybody looking at?" Lamar Mancini asked as he climbed the stairs to the graveyard, but any answer that might have been given was drowned out by the shout of praise for Amy who followed just a second behind him. She blushed as she came closer and stood next to Jake, looking at the bench they had all created together.

"When can we sit on it?" a child's voice was heard over the din of the party.

"Let's give it a couple of days. You're welcome to sit on it as soon as it has been grouted," Jake said, looking at Amy. "I might not get to that till next week sometime. Amy and I are getting married on Sunday at noon and you're all invited."

The crowd erupted in cheers.

"What should we do with the extra shards?" Hildegard asked, pointing at the small pile of shards that remained on Henry's bench.

"You could take them home if you'd like. Maybe in sixty years, when my kids and grandkids make my bench, you could bring them back and we could do this again."

The crowd laughed. After a few minutes, most of them began filing past the bench, congratulating Jake and Amy on a job well done and thanking them for letting them all be a part of it. Many stopped at the pile of shards on Henry's bench to pick up a few of the pieces on their way out of the graveyard.

"You two outdid yourselves," Gloria said, once the crowd had thinned. "That was good of you to get so many of us involved. I know this was healing to many of us, including me." She knelt down next to the bench and ran her hand over the surface, scratching off a piece of rogue mortar. "You remembered," she said, stopping at the tiny blue flower on the candlestick.

"Yes. We also remembered the hearts," Jake said, pointing at the stylized jar of hearts that her story had inspired him to carve into one of the tiles.

Gloria smiled, looking over the details a little more closely. "It looks as if you thought of everything."

"Do you think Isaac would like it?" Amy asked.

Gloria nodded. "You have captured some of the greatest elements of his legacy. I'm sure he'd be happy to know he will be remembered for all these things."

"I had several people ask if you do commissions," Thomas said from behind, causing them all to turn around. "How'd you get the word out about this? The only time I've ever seen this many people here is on Memorial Day."

"And at Isaac's funeral," Sam added. "I thought three dozen pastries would be plenty, but I had to cut them in half and still some people didn't get any."

"I figured Sam must have told everyone," Jake responded. "People just started showing up out of nowhere."

"What did I miss?" asked Beverly as she reached them.

"A great party," the Mayor said, clapping Jake on the shoulder.

"It's done?" Bev asked, a look of excitement in her eyes. She stood next to Jake and Amy with her hands on her hips and looked over the finished product, speechless.

"I don't know about you folks," said the Mayor, putting his arm around Jake in a fatherly way, "but I think we chose the right guy."

ALLAN TOWN

IF YOU LOOK FOR TRUTH, YOU MAY FIND COMFORT IN THE END;
IF YOU LOOK FOR COMFORT YOU WILL NOT GET EITHER COMFORT OR TRUTH
ONLY SOFT SOAP AND WISHFUL THINKING TO BEGIN,
AND IN THE END, DESPAIR.
—C. S. LEWIS—

U m, Excuse me. We're looking for Amy Eckstein. We were told we might find her here."

Jake looked up from his work at the wedging table where he'd been working on the Journey Jar handles all morning. "She's not here right now, but I expect her back soon. Is there anything I can do for you?"

"Are you Jake?"

"Yes." He wiped his hands on his apron and approached the middle-aged couple. "What can I do for you?"

"I'm Karl Allan and this is my wife, Miriam," the man said extending his hand. "We just got in from Irvine, California."

"You're Mr. Allan's son," Jake said, smiling at the man who looked like a much younger version of Mr. Allan, even down to the sunspots on top of his bald head.

"Yes."

"It's nice to meet you. Your dad has been looking forward to seeing you for a long time. I'm glad you guys could come for his birthday."

Karl smiled and shook his head. "I probably should straighten you out about that."

"About what?"

"If you know my dad, you probably know he's become a little senile?"

"Yes."

"Well, after I got off the phone with Amy, I was talking to my brother and we remembered that our dad's birthday isn't until September."

Jake laughed. "Are you serious?"

"Yeah, September 22. He'll be eighty-six on September 22."

"To be completely honest, that sounds about right. He gets confused a lot. He told us his birthday was on July 4."

"Yes, that was my mother's birthday."

"It was very nice of you kids to plan a party," Miriam said.

"I can't take any credit for that. That was all Amy. We've both really enjoyed getting to know your dad. He's quite a character."

"Yeah, well, thank you," Karl said again, but his demeanor seemed a little cool.

"When was the last time you were here?" Jake asked, trying to keep the conversation going.

Karl looked at his wife, then back at Jake. "It's been a while."

"It's been nearly twenty years," Miriam jumped in. "The last time we were here was for Karl's mother's funeral."

"None of us really had a very strong relationship with our dad," Karl said.

"That's what I heard."

"From whom?"

"From your dad. Amy and I have spent a fair amount of time with him over the last few weeks. He has a lot of regrets about how he neglected his kids to pursue his career."

"He should."

"Karl, be nice. This may be the last chance you'll have to see your father," Miriam said.

"That's why I'm here. That's why you talked me into to coming—to spend some time with a man I hardly know before he dies."

"I'm sorry," Miriam said, turning to Jake. "We don't want to sound ungrateful for what you and Amy have put together. Each of the kids has dealt with this in their own way. It hasn't been easy for any of them to come to grips with who they are and their relationship with their father. Their mother was really the only glue that held this family together and now that she's gone . . ."

"You must be Karl and Miriam," Amy said from the back door, wearing a broad grin on her face.

They all turned to look at her.

"And you must be Amy," Miriam said, extending her hand.

Amy swept past her hand and embraced Miriam and then Karl. "I feel like I already know you. Your dad has told us a lot about you. I'm *so* glad you could come. Before I met Paul and Cindy, I had never met any of my third cousins. Did you just get in?"

"Yes," Miriam replied. "We arrived an hour ago. We stopped by Sam's to get some lunch. My mouth started watering for his pastries right after I got off the phone with you."

"So, you haven't been out to the house yet?"

"No, not yet. We weren't sure what we should do. Karl wasn't ready to see his dad without his siblings being there. We stopped by the flower shop and talked to Joseph, but he said you would probably have more details than he," said Miriam.

"Have your kids arrived yet?"

"Jamie flew in with us. We left him at the new pudding mold museum. Bert and Heather are coming in from San Diego a little later with their two sons. It must have taken you a long time to organize all of this," said Miriam.

"No, not really. It was actually kind of fun. Gloria helped a lot. We're just glad you were able to come on such short notice. I know it's been a while, right?"

"Yes," Karl muttered.

"Well, with all the family coming in, and my family, too, we made some unique arrangements. Paul and Cindy and their families already claimed two of the Happy Huts for themselves and their kids, so you two and Robert and Leslie get to sleep in the house. It's going to be a little bit tight, but I guess that's what reunions are all about, right?"

Amy's enthusiasm was contagious and before she could finish, even Karl's mood seemed to have lightened. Amy gave them each a copy of the agenda for the weekend and encouraged them to enjoy the afternoon in Niederbipp and head out to the house whenever they were ready.

When they were gone, Jake asked about Cindy and Paul who had arrived around noon with their spouses. Amy reported that Cindy was gracious, but that Paul wore the same sour expression that Karl had and admitted that this might take a little more energy than she originally thought it would.

While Jake finished the handles on the Journey Jars, Amy went through the weekend plans. Her parents had called that morning from the road to say they were running late and wouldn't be stopping by

before they checked in at the Parkins' as they had originally planned—
news that Jake and Amy both found comforting, considering everything
else in their plans.

Cindy and her husband Ed were planning on cooking breakfast
for everybody at Allan Town on both Saturday and Sunday mornings.
Paul, his wife Kirsten and their three teenagers were already setting up
a round-robin croquet tournament out at the house that would include
everyone. Since most of Amy's family wouldn't be arriving until the
morning, she had arranged with Mr. Allan to have a family gathering
that night, after Robert and Leslie arrived, so he could share the Journey
Jars with them.

With the parade kicking off at ten and festivities taking place all
day at the fairgrounds, Amy figured all the families could take care
of themselves on Saturday until the barbecue at five, where the Allans,
the Ecksteins, and the Sproodles would gather together to celebrate Mr.
Allan's faux birthday, open the "time capsule," and get to know each
other better. The fireworks would begin at ten back at the fairgrounds
and with any luck, everybody would get at least a few hours of sleep
before church services and the wedding.

With the Journey Jars secured safely in the milk crate on the back
of the scooter, and the old Eckstein toolbox held on Amy's lap, they rode
awkwardly out to the Allan compound just after seven. They found the
family congregated on the veranda, catching up and sharing memories.
Mr. Allan had never met several of his grandchildren, and many of the
cousins had only had very limited contact with each other over the years.
But as Jake and Amy watched the family happily interacting with each
other, they knew their efforts had been worth it.

Robert and Leslie arrived shortly before eight, and the sound of
the gathering became louder by several decibels as the siblings and the
cousins made up for lost time. All of them thanked Amy and Jake for
making the reunion happen while chiding each other for letting so much
water pass under the bridge since they had last been together.

After an hour, Mr. Allan asked Jake to bring him the Journey Jar that he had shown him and Amy weeks before. The family gathered around the table as Mr. Allan took off the lid and began removing the contents of the jar. He handed the pocketknife to Karl, and with sad eyes, asked him to forgive him for yelling at him when he lost it. He handed Cindy the pink button and told them all about his memory 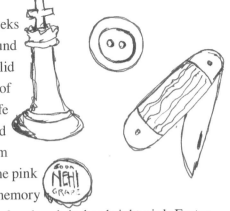 of a beautiful little girl dressed up for church in her bright pink Easter dress. To Paul, he gave the bottle cap and talked about his memory of drinking grape Nehi on a log down by the river while he fished with his red-headed son. For Robby, he sorted through the pile and pulled out the ivory-colored chess piece, setting it in the palm of his son's hand, reminding him of the nights they'd spent together playing chess on the veranda.

With unusual lucidity, Mr. Allan went through each of the items that came from the jar, telling his children and grandchildren about the memories he most cherished while pleading for their forgiveness for the way he'd neglected them. Before he was done, each of the children, their spouses and the grandchildren, had experienced emotions ranging from laughter to tears, but each of them knew of the love their father and grandfather had for them.

When he was finished sorting through the treasures, he asked Jake to bring out the Journey Jars he had commissioned for each of them, and line them up on the table. Then with great hope in his eyes, Mr. Allan handed one of the jars to each of his children and grandchildren before explaining the change of heart he'd had over the past years as he'd learned the true value of family and time and

treasure. He invited each of them to remember the small things in life so they wouldn't become the fool that he had been. With deep emotion choking his words, he spoke of how he would live his life if he had the chance to start over and apologized again and again for missing many of the most important events in his children's lives. After praising their mother for the fine job she had done to raise good and honorable children, he appealed to them to do all they could to be a better parent than he had been.

Jake and Amy watched as the sour faces they'd seen earlier faded away, becoming filled, instead, with sorrow, regret and humility. Then Mr. Allan, turned to Jake and thanked him for his handiwork. Reaching for Amy's hand, he pulled her close and gave her a hug, thanking her for giving him this treasured time with his family.

Before they left, Mr. Allan pulled them both aside and handed them one of the Journey Jars with two lids, similar to those he'd given to his children. "*Remember* what you heard tonight," he said softly. "As you *discover* your true treasure, I hope that each of you will *become* a better parent and a better spouse than I was. I may not be around to check up on you, but I hope that as you share your journey together, you will always remember to cherish the treasure that the journey of life will bring to you."

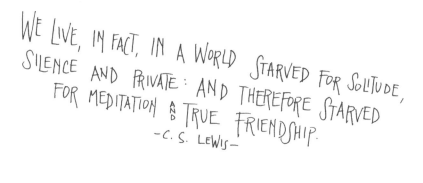

WE LIVE, IN FACT, IN A WORLD STARVED FOR SOLITUDE, SILENCE AND PRIVATE: AND THEREFORE STARVED FOR MEDITATION & TRUE FRIENDSHIP.
—C. S. LEWIS—

OF PIRATES AND PANSIES

TO BE YOURSELF IN A WORLD THAT IS CONSTANTLY TRYING TO MAKE YOU
SOMETHING ELSE IS THE GREATEST ACCOMPLISHMENT.
— RALPH WALDO EMERSON—

With the lessons Mr. Allan had shared with them still fresh in his mind, Jake decided to ignore the fact that the holiday weekend would definitely bring lots of pottery-hungry tourists with deep pockets. He and Amy had planned on keeping The Pottery open, at least until noon, but counting time as the treasure that it is, he got up early to post signs on the windows that the shop would be closed for the weekend.

Jake was just sitting down for breakfast when Amy knocked on the door, carrying the last of her personal items. Her cousin had just arrived from Erie with his family for the Fourth of July activities and was anxious to take over her bedroom at Bev and Jerry's. While she put away her things, Jake made some more toast, and they had just sat down to eat on the top step when a car pulled up at The Pottery's back door—a green Subaru Outback. Jake's heart raced as he remembered Matthew's promise to return soon, but as the driver stepped out of the car, Amy squealed and ran down the stairs to embrace him.

"Jake, this is my brother, John, my sister-in-law, Liz and their sons, Zach and Levi."

"I've been looking forward to meeting you," Jake said, extending his hand to each of them. He patted each of the boys on the head and was grateful he'd worn his steel-toed clogs when Zach decided to stomp on Jake's foot in response. "We were just eating breakfast. Would you like to join us?" he asked.

Jake pushed open the door and the boys walked in, each carrying a sleeping bag.

"I don't see a tent," Levi said impatiently as he stood in the small kitchen.

"That's cause it's a magic tent that only comes out after dark," Amy said as she walked past them, into the guest bedroom.

"Did you find these old pots in a treasure chest?" Levi asked, turning to Jake.

Jake looked up at John and nodded. "Yeah, I guess you could say that. Has your dad told you about the pirate lookout?"

"He sure did. When can we go there?" asked Zach.

"Maybe after the parade if you want. There are lots of fun things to explore around here," said Jake.

"Do you think we might find some treasure, too?" asked Levi.

"Definitely. The river is full of treasure."

The boys looked up at Jake with wide eyes. "You mean like gold and swords and stuff?" asked Levi.

"Well, maybe, but some of the other treasures are easier to find."

"Like what?" asked Zach, anxious to hear all about it.

"Like the best skipping rocks in the whole world and more sticks than you've ever seen."

The boys looked back at Jake in awe.

"Are you tellin' me you've never ridden on Blackbeard's swing before?" Jake asked, playing to their sense of wonder and awe.

"I might have. I'm two years older," said Zach. "But I think I forgot. I was really little back then."

"Then we'll have to go. Maybe your dad could come along to help fend off the pirates."

Jake didn't have to do anything else; the boys were completely won over. He made pancakes for the whole crew while the boys made snakes at the kitchen table with clay from the studio. When it was time to eat, they opened the kitchen window and hung the snakes out to dry on the clothes line. When the boys turned their noses up to the sound of buttermilk syrup, Jake told them about their friend Kai, a reformed pirate, who was test-marketing the syrup under the top-secret code name, "Shazzam!" He said they'd been looking for

a couple of lab rats for the experiment who were just about the same age and size as they were. Of course, the boys were anxious to show their courage by being a part of it.

By the time breakfast was over, Liz, who had been fighting with the kids since they'd left home at three in the morning, was convinced that Jake was either a snake charmer or a lion tamer. While the girls cleaned up breakfast, the boys went outside to climb the chestnut tree in the courtyard.

"I'm sorry to admit I judged you before I got here," John said as they stood underneath the tree and watched the boys climb. "We've all been very protective of our sister. When I heard she was marrying a potter, I have to admit I pictured a high school dropout dressed in dirty overalls."

"Yeah, I'm sorry to disappoint you. My overalls are in the wash today and they say my GED is in the mail."

"You know what I mean, right?"

"I'm not sure if I do, but I'll tell you what, I'll set aside my ignorant notions of your job if you set aside yours of mine."

John laughed and extended his hand. "It's a deal. It sounds like you've dealt with questions like that before."

Jake laughed this time. "Yeah, I have. Being a potter isn't an easy life, but I chose it very deliberately. I know your dad thinks I'm crazy. Has he cooled down since his last visit?"

"What do you mean?"

"Didn't he tell you that he came here three weeks ago to take Amy home?"

"No, he didn't, but we don't talk that often. Was my mom here, too?"

Jake nodded. "Yep. It was pretty ugly. Do you have any advice?

John shook his head. "Liz's father runs a carpet cleaning business. He basically disowned us when we told him we didn't want to be part of the business like my brothers-in-law and their wives. It's taken ten years, but he's finally coming around."

"So you think it might be the same way with your dad?"

"No, you probably ought to plan on twenty years for my dad to come around."

Jake laughed, feeling like he had a friend.

Amy and Liz joined them in the courtyard and they walked through the shortcut to Hauptstrasse where they found a place to stand against the shop windows next to the other revelers awaiting the commencement of the parade. A minute after they arrived, the ground beneath them shook as the sound of three cannons marked the beginning of the parade. A marching band was heard at the top of Hauptstrasse and everybody followed the sound as horns and drums blasted John Philip Sousa's "Stars and Stripes Forever." The band was followed by the Mayor who was sitting on a motorcycle side car while his driver, who was dressed like Uncle Sam, wove the motorcycle back and forth across the cobblestone street. The Niederbipp 4H Club followed, waving American flags. An old man rode past, dressed in overalls and riding in a tiny cart that was pulled by a team of flighty goats. Josh Adams, the apple man, followed behind at the front of a most unusual four-wheeled bike with nine seats and six sets of pedals. His whole family was on board, waving and ringing bells that were attached to the handlebars. A large group of children holding a banner that read, "Granny Ruth's Famous Cookies" came next, followed by Granny Ruth herself who was holding the arms of two young men as they walked. She waved at Jake and blew him a kiss.

Lamar Mancini followed after Ruth, wearing a pudding mold on his head, but instead of walking down the middle of the street like everyone else, he was running from side to side, handing out flyers for his new museum. He also waved at Jake, but was pushed along by a group of men dressed in Revolutionary War costumes and brandishing period muskets with shiny bayonets. Zach and Levi were fascinated by the weapons and probably would have followed after them if they hadn't been distracted by the man who was standing on the backs of two old mules painted to look like zebras. There  was a clown who drove a miniature car around in circles until he tipped over and had to be dragged out of the road so he wouldn't be trampled by an ostrich and a spitting llama advertising an exotic petting farm. The final group in the parade consisted of a bunch of teenagers and adults dressed up as nerds with glasses and pocket protectors. They held a banner that read, "Be Nice to Nerds—Niederbipp, PA, Original Home of Compute Corp." Jake recognized Brian as he led the way, dressed in a pair of plaid pants that were pulled up almost to his armpits.

The crowd fell in behind, following the parade to the fairgrounds where a carnival had been set up, complete with games and rides. Jake and Amy took the boys and left Liz and John to take a nap in Jake's apartment. On their way to the fairgrounds, Mike and Steve, two of Amy's brothers, caught up to them along with their wives and kids. Following a happy reunion filled with hugs and congratulations, they continued on toward the carnival where they cheered on a couple of Amy's nieces and nephews who were trying to catch a greased pig. They moved on to the Ferris wheel and the inflatable jump house before picking up hotdogs, lemonade and cotton candy, and then taking their lunch down to the river to relax in the shade of the trees. Zach and Levi both fell asleep on the beach with ketchup and mustard smeared on their faces, while Jake taught Amy's older nieces and nephews how to skip rocks.

John and Liz, accompanied by two of the Eckstein boys and their families finally caught up with the group around three. Together, they all walked past the Allan compound to the narrow footbridge that crossed the river to the pirate lookout. For many of them, it had been years since they had been here, but each of the children had fallen asleep to the stories their fathers had told them about the pirates and the swing that went so high it caused you to lose control of your bodily functions. Together, the men counted out the paces as they walked through the thick forest, and when they finally reached the base of the tree, they stared up at it like they were remembering a long-forgotten dream.

"What are you pansies waiting for?" Amy asked, halfway up the ladder.

Jake was the first to reach the top, but he stayed near the ladder to help others. To his surprise, none of the other adults accompanied the eight nieces and nephews who climbed nimbly to the top. Jake and Amy walked to the edge and sat down, dangling their feet above the forest floor.

"You let them climb up there?" they heard one of the mothers say.

"They're fine," one of the men responded.

"Then why aren't you up there?"

"I've been up there a million times. I don't need to go up again."

"That's got to be twenty feet off the ground."

"Relax, its only fifteen."

"This is the pirate lookout you told our kids about?"

"Yep."

"Did your mother ever see you up there?"

"Of course not. Moms aren't allowed here. Amy can take care of them."

"Hi, Mom," one of the kids said, looking over the edge.

"Oh honey, please come down."

"I'm fine, Mom. Jake and Amy are up here. We're looking for pirates."

"For crying out loud. Amy, will you watch him."

"Sure," she said. "Alex, come over here, its easier to see the pirates if you dangle your feet over the edge."

"Thanks a lot, Amy!"

"No problem. You heard the guys. Moms aren't allowed out here. Go back to the picnic table. You'll feel better there."

There was a long exasperated huff, followed by the sound of retreating footsteps.

"Where are the pirates?" Levi asked

"It might still be kind of early for river pirates. They usually don't come out until just before dark," Jake responded.

"Is that true, Aunt Amy?"

"That's what I heard," Amy whispered, "but sometimes you can catch them early if you're quiet. We made a lot of noise coming up here. They probably got spooked."

"Can you tell us about the family jewels?" one of the older nieces asked.

"Sure," said Amy. "When I was a little girl, your dads traded me to the pirates for a bunch of jewels."

"Why?" asked Zach, with wide eyes.

"Because I was too creative and I was too powerful. They'd try to lock me up so I wouldn't follow them here, but I always got out and found them. Then I'd make them play with my dolls."

The younger boys started laughing. "Dad played with dolls?"

"Well, not all the time. I usually gave them a choice. They could either play dolls with me or they could dress up like princesses."

Now all the kids were laughing.

"How did you make them do it?" asked one of the older girls.

"Well, most of the time I pushed them so high on the swing that they begged for mercy. I only let them get off if they would dress up as princesses."

"That's awesome," said one of the girls.

"So, how did they trade you to the pirates?"

"The pirates had been looking for a cook for a long time, so your dads tricked me into applying for the job and then sold me to the pirates for some of their treasures. By the time I figured out what was going on, I was in a cage and my brothers were running away with the jewels."

"So, how did you get away?" asked Levi.

"It was easy. I baked my famous Paprika Pie. The pirates loved it and ate all that I made, but when the night came, their skin started itching and burning and they all jumped in the river to cool off. That's when I escaped and came back up here to find your dads asleep. I took all the jewels they traded with the pirates and brought them up here. Then, one at a time, I tied them up in their sleeping bags and strung them up in the tree. Ever since then, they've been afraid of heights. They know the jewels are up here, but they never come up because they're too afraid."

"I don't believe you," one of the older nephews said. "Where are the jewels now?"

"Oh, I keep them over there on that rusty nail." She turned and pointed at the nail where the strings of carnival beads had been hanging for years.

"Wow, Aunt Amy," gasped one of the younger nieces. "Can you still make our dads dress up like princesses?"

"Probably, but your dads have all gotten fat. They'd probably wreck my dresses."

Jake couldn't hold it in any longer and he burst out laughing.

"You better watch it, Jake," Amy said, pointing her finger at him. "The dresses would still fit *you*."

Jake looked away, biting the insides of his cheeks. "Look, pirates!" he whispered, pointing down at the river where the passengers of three canoes were engaged in a water fight as they drifted lazily down the river. The kids watched quietly until the canoes floated around the bend and were gone from their view.

"I think it's almost time for dinner," Amy said, getting to her feet. But before she descended the ladder, she pulled her nieces and nephews together. "Promise me something," she said softly.

They all nodded.

"Promise me you'll always remember today, that you saw the river pirates and the family jewels, too."

"I promise," said Zach, and the others nodded seriously.

"Promise me one more thing. Promise me that if I ever get old and forget about the family jewels, that you'll tell my babies the stories."

They nodded again, feeling a sense of responsibility.

Jake was the last to climb down the ladder, but before he did, he reached up and removed one of the necklaces from the rusty nail and slid it quietly into his pocket.

BUBBA'S BARBECUE

KEEP AWAY FROM THOSE WHO TRY TO BELITTLE YOUR AMBITIONS.
SMALL PEOPLE ALWAYS DO THAT, BUT THE REALLY GREAT MAKE YOU BELIEVE
THAT YOU, TOO, CAN BECOME GREAT.
—MARK TWAIN—

The smoke from the barbecue tickled their noses before they were even halfway across the bridge. Amy and Jake led the pack of hungry pirate hunters across the river and over the trail until they came to Allan Town. Jake had never seen such a big smoker. It looked as though it might have been made out of a recycled submarine. As the aroma wafted across the yard and down to the river, everyone seemed to be salivating.

The front yard was set up with the most elaborate croquet course in the world, enabling eighteen players to play at once. A game of ultimate Frisbee was being played in the backyard while a bunch of kids played tag. Gloria and Joseph waved from the veranda where they were visiting with two of the Allan children, while Thomas and Sam had taken on two of Amy's brothers in a game of horseshoes. There were watermelons and sodas chilling in the river, while the chefs from Bubba's stood sweating near the barbecue. Eric was busy taking pictures of all the events.

"Who are you looking for?" Jake asked after watching Amy scan the crowd.

"My parents. Do you see them?"

"No," he said after a minute of searching. "I don't see the Parkins either. Maybe they're still tied up with the workshop."

Amy nodded, hoping he was right.

The food was ready by five-thirty, and the boys from Bubba's opened a double-sided buffet line, serving salad, watermelon, baked beans, corn-on-the-cob, coleslaw, pulled pork sandwiches and ribs. Introductions continued to be made throughout dinner as third and fourth cousins—Ecksteins, Allans and Sproodles—sat down next to each other to eat. Amy walked Jake through the crowd, introducing him to the rest of her family and her Sproodle cousins who had come into town for the holiday weekend and the wedding. They were surprised to find Bev and Jerry looking surprisingly comfortable as they ate dinner on the veranda surrounded by the cousins they were supposed to loathe.

Finally, just before seven, Doug and Cathy Eckstein arrived with Tom and Emma Parkin. Jake and Amy handed them the plates of food they'd been saving for them and invited them to take a seat at the largely abandoned table on the veranda. While Cathy and the Parkins were chatty, Doug remained fairly aloof, even chilly with a tone of discomfort. It had been three weeks since the fiasco at the restaurant, but Doug seemed to still harbor the same spirit he'd had when he wrote his letter to Amy.

"What's wrong?" Jake asked Amy as they walked inside the house to retrieve the time capsule from where they stowed it in the bathroom closet.

"I just feel like my dad is going to blow up and ruin everything."

"That sounds like fear talking."

Amy took a deep breath and then nodded. "It probably is. I thought I'd let it go, but this isn't as easy as I hoped."

"I know," Jake said, putting his arms around her. "I'm sorry."

"I just hope if he's going to blow that it happens tonight rather than during the ceremony tomorrow."

"It's not too late to elope," Jake said.

"Yes it is, and besides, that's fear talking."

Jake nodded. "I know."

Leaving the younger kids to play in the front yard, Jake and Amy invited anyone who cared to the backyard for the promised opening of the ancestral time capsule. With Mr. Allan, Aunt Bev, and her father sitting together at the table to her right, Amy pulled the old book she'd been given by Mr. Allan out from under the black garbage bag. She held it up in her hands, explaining the story of their common ancestor and the unfortunate loss of the tools that had produced years of mistrust and misunderstanding and several generations of people who didn't know their history or their relatives.

Offering a few plausible explanations for the disappearance of the tools, Amy explained that no one knew for sure what had happened or where they had been for nearly one hundred years. With Jake's help, she pulled off the garbage bag to reveal the old, rusty tools. She explained that the trowel had recently been used to complete a couple of mosaics around town, and though the tools were old, they were still functional. Laying each of the tools out on the table in front of her, she invited a representative from each of the families to come forward and choose a tool that was undoubtedly used to build some of the structures in

Niederbipp and were once owned by their great-great-great-grandfather, Gerhardt Mueller Eckstein.

"This is the reason we weren't allowed to talk to each other?" Bev asked Mr. Allan, as the family came forward to view and touch the antique tools. Bev reached across the table to pick up a handful of rusty nails and Amy watched as she shook her head. Then dropping the nails on the table in front of her, she put her arm around Mr. Allan, her second cousin, who she'd been taught was untrustworthy and contemptible. They cried and laughed together as their kids came forward as cousins and now friends to examine and inherit the seemingly innocuous tools that had separated their fathers and grandfathers for too many generations. To Amy's surprise, after viewing and handling the tools, only a few of her cousins and siblings took one with them, leaving the majority scattered across the table. Unlike the generations before hers, the tools and the legend behind them had lost their power of jealousy and division. As Jake watched them return to their blankets and chairs on the lawn, he considered how time and distance seemed to have healed the rift that probably never would have happened in the first place if brothers could have forgiven each other and moved on.

When everyone returned to their seats, Sam rolled a cart through the open doorway, stacked with a giant birthday cake and eighty-six blazing candles. After Mr. Allan invited his grandkids to come up and help him blow out the candles, Sam reached across the table to the trowel they'd used on his floor and Isaac's bench. He wiped it off on his apron and winked at Amy and Jake before using it to cut and serve the cake to the guests. Standing as straight and tall as he could, Mr. Allan thanked everyone for coming to his party and invited them to come back next year to do it again. Putting her arm on Mr. Allan's shoulder, Amy stood to thank them again and remind them that they were all invited to the wedding in the morning. As darkness began to fall and the cake disappeared, many of the younger families gathered up blankets and headed down the path to the grounds for the fireworks show.

"I know we're not family," Tom Parkin said, approaching Amy, "but do you mind if we took one of the tools to put on our mantle by the picture you painted. It's a pretty incredible story that Emma and I would like others to know about."

"Sure," said Amy. "Take your pick."

Tom selected one of the old squares and then he and Emma slipped away, thanking Amy and Jake and their neighbor, Mr. Allan, as they left.

Amy had seen fireworks in Niederbipp several times over the past twenty-two years, but they had usually been viewed from the hills above town or from the fairground lawn. Watching them from the river was even more spectacular as the water's glassy surface mirrored the colorful display.

Jake wrapped his arms around her as they sat on the bridge with a dozen of their relatives. He watched the reflection of the lights in Amy's eyes and marveled once again at her beauty. They were getting married—the culmination of an amazing weekend. He had enjoyed getting to know so many people, but he was definitely looking forward to the time when it could be just the two of them. Somehow he knew, however, those circumstances would probably never be, at least not for long. As the ribbons of lights faded from the river and the sky, the reality of his future hit him powerfully. They had learned the truths and properties of joy, and now that they knew them, they felt compelled to live their life selflessly. Somehow, he knew he would be sharing Amy for the rest of their life together. She would be his wife and lover, but many others would have need of a piece of her time. He knew that when children came to their marriage, she would have to divide her time and love even further. There would be customers and friends and extended family that would need her and the love she had to share.

As they walked back to the Allan compound, Jake's thoughts turned to Isaac and the things he'd learned about him since coming to Niederbipp. He wondered if he'd had a private life beyond the quiet moments he'd spent by the river or at the cemetery. His life, it seemed, had been consumed with loving others. As Jake thought about the differences between his life and Isaac's, he realized how so much of his previous life had been consumed with worrying solely about himself. He wasn't Isaac, and though he admired everything he knew about him, he knew he never could be. But a part of him—a big part of him, wanted to try—wanted to be the kind of man that Isaac was—wanted to live his life in such a way that would leave a legacy of influence that would last for generations.

From all the people who had come to visit The Pottery, the mug owners, Isaac's customers, and his friends, Jake had learned the lessons that lead to a joyful life. He had learned that fear loses its power when embraced by love. He had learned that selfishness has no claim to joy. He had learned that true love is a verb. He had learned that truth can be found wherever there is light. Jake knew that these and so many other truths he'd learned since coming to Niederbipp could help the world become brighter, kinder and gentler. He wasn't sure how, but he knew for sure that Isaac's legacy needed to live on, that others needed to benefit from the love, humility and wisdom he had shared with all who knew him. Jake figured it would take a lifetime, but he knew he wanted to become like Isaac.

The lights from the veranda cast an enchanting glow on Mr. Allan's yard. Even from a distance, they could see that Amy's parents were enjoying themselves as they sat around the table with the older man and his kids. A couple of big pickle jars sat empty in the middle of the table, their contents spread out for all to see. Jake and Amy stood in the shadows and watched for several minutes as those at the table took turns swapping tales.

"What are you thinking?" Jake asked after watching Amy stare at the gathering.

"I'd like to be a fly on that wall."

"Don't you think you could be? I'm sure you'd be welcome."

Amy shook her head. "Something tells me my dad needs this. I don't want to get in the way. Besides, I'm tired."

"Do you want to go home?"

Amy nodded.

They walked passed the veranda and were nearly beyond the glow of lights in the yard when they heard their names and turned to see Cathy running towards them. She hugged Amy before turning to do the same to Jake. "Amy," she said, holding her by her shoulders, "I've been looking forward to your wedding for as long as I can remember. After our last visit, I can't blame you for not involving me in your plans, but please—is there anything I can do? Any last minute details that need some attention?"

Amy smiled in the soft light, exposing her perfect teeth. "Thank you, Mom. We decided to keep our plans simple. I can't think of anything else we have to do."

Cathy nodded but looked disappointed, almost hurt.

"I love you, Mom," Amy said, reaching out to embrace her again.

Cathy held onto her daughter for a long time. Then, letting go, she smiled through her tears and said goodnight before turning to walk back to the gathering on the veranda. Jake and Amy watched until she was gone before they turned to go. Instead of walking home along the highway, they stuck to the trail along the river that was lit by the light of the moon and hundreds of fireflies flashing their yellow-green lamps. They stopped when they came to The Crying Place to watch as the waxy leaves of the willow shimmered like strings of silver coins in the moonlight. They continued on until they came to the place where they'd spent Mother's Day afternoon together with Bev and Jerry. They stopped briefly to admire the beauty of the town as they had on that first day they met.

They were nearly to Bev and Jerry's place when Amy reminded Jake that she was staying at the apartment and he was sleeping in Joseph's van. The lights were dim as they opened the door to the apartment. A blanket had been thrown over the kitchen table and a tiny, motionless hand was sticking out from under the makeshift tent. With the muffled sound of snoring coming from the guestroom, Jake gathered up his pillow and a blanket before kissing Amy goodnight, telling her he'd be back in time to help make breakfast.

The streets were quiet as he walked to Gloria and Joseph's. He'd only seen the van under its canvas cover, and it looked quite different than he imagined with its camper top open. Amy's nephews, Cameron and William, were still awake, telling ghost stories and casting shadow puppets with a flashlight onto the canvas pop top. The boys had taken the two smaller beds, saving the larger for Jake. They chatted for a while but soon faded off to sleep, leaving Jake alone with his thoughts and dreams of his future.

BUT THE PATH OF THE JUST IS AS THE SHINING LIGHT, THAT SHINETH MORE AND MORE UNTO THE PERFECT DAY.
-PROVERBS 4:18-

WELLS AND FIRES

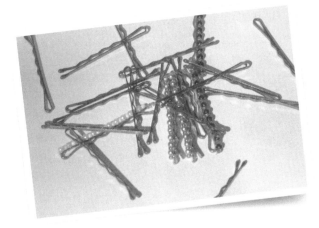

WHEN WE SEE GOD IN EACH OTHER,
WE WILL BE ABLE TO LIVE IN PEACE.
—MOTHER TERESA—

The sound of church bells woke Jake with a start. He sat up straight, fearing he'd slept through his wedding, but his heart rate slowed when he recognized that the van was still bathed in the shadows of morning light. He quietly got dressed and crept out of the van, trying not to wake Amy's nephews.

Zach and Levi were already up, eating their cereal on top of the tent when Jake walked into his apartment. With both bedroom doors closed and the sound of running water coming from the bathroom, Jake got busy making omelettes. The boys, of course, wanted to help, so Jake handed them the carton of eggs and a mixing bowl while he sliced and diced peppers and onions, ham and cheese. When he turned back to the boys, he found them quietly fishing for eggshells, straining the golden ooze with their fingers. After washing off four small hands, Jake mixed the eggs with milk and poured it all through a strainer into a frying pan to separate the eggs from the shells. When he turned around again, he found the boys stealthily chowing down on the grated cheese. He chased them into their tent where he wrestled them to the floor and tickled them until they begged for mercy.

Retreating back out of the tent, he found Amy and Liz smiling at him as they watched the circus. Jake had just enough time to pour the rest of the ingredients into the frying pan before the counterattack was launched in which he found both of his legs immobilized by the boy's boa constrictor-like death grip. He tried to walk out of it, but was tripped up and fell to the floor, defeated. The boys responded with war cries, followed by a litany of wrestling moves from Double Gutwrenches and Flying Headbutts to Jackhammers and Swandives from the kitchen furniture. By the time they were done  exacting their revenge, the omelette could no longer be an omelette and Jake reluctantly turned it into fancy scrambled eggs.

With his pride in shambles, Jake gave the boys an assignment to count all the pots on the shelves while the adults ate breakfast. Before the boys could finish, Jake tiptoed into the bathroom to shower and shave and lick his wounds.

The apartment was quiet when Jake opened the bathroom door. He stuck his head out slowly, waiting for a surprise attack, but it didn't come.

"Hello, I'm going to go in my room now. If you are going to jump out and attack me, now would be a good time," he announced, hoping the monsters would reveal themselves while he was ready.

Laughter came from the guest bedroom. "We sent the boys out to play so you could get ready," someone said from behind the closed door.

"I laid your suit out on the bed," Amy added.

"Uh, did you want me to put that on now?"

"Did you have something else in mind?"

"Umm, no, sure, that's great," Jake managed. "Sorry, I've never gotten married before. Are you going to wear your wedding gown to the church?"

"Yes. We won't have time to change after services. The wedding starts at noon, remember?"

"Right." Jake went into his room and got dressed. Kai's suit was nearly a perfect fit. He fumbled with the tie Amy had picked out for him for several minutes before he thought it looked right. He was sitting on a chair in the kitchen, tying his shoes, when he heard the guest room door open. He looked up to see Amy. Her ginger hair was swept up on top of her head and laced with tiny white flowers that complemented her simple but elegant gown that flowed down to within inches of the floor, revealing her bright red Mary Jane's.

"Isn't this supposed to be bad luck?" asked Jake.

"Not for the Quakers, at least not according to Bev," a voice said from behind, and Jake looked past Amy, surprised to see her mother standing in the doorway.

"You look very handsome," Cathy said as she walked to Jake. She gave him a hug before straightening his tie and picking a piece of lint off his shoulder. "Thank you for taking care of my daughter."

Jake smiled and nodded. "You're welcome. I hope I can do that."

Cathy nodded. "From what we've heard in the last two days, I feel like you two have learned some great things about life and love."

"I think we have," Amy said, stepping forward to give Jake a kiss.

"I wish you would have told me you needed some jewelry," Cathy said. "I would have brought my pearls. They would have looked so good with the neckline of your dress."

Cathy's words were lost to Jake and Amy who were admiring the way the other looked. Amy's dress was beautiful, fitting her tall, slender form like the custom dress that it was. Jake held onto her hands, lifting her arms and twirling her around to see how she looked all the way around. Devoid of lace, beads or bows, the dress was very much an expression of Amy and her natural, uncomplicated beauty. "You look amazing," he said, grinning from ear to ear.

Amy blushed but returned the smile.

"Are you nervous?" asked Jake.

"Only about what my dad is going to say today."

"Oh, I don't think you need to worry too much about that," said Cathy.

"Why not?" Amy asked, turning to look at her mother.

"Your father had a long talk with Mr. Allan last night. He gave your dad a letter he found down by the river."

"Oh, no, not another letter," Amy said, turning to face Jake, confused.

"It was your dad's letter to you—the one he wrote the last time we were here." Cathy responded.

"I thought you threw that into the river," Amy said, turning to Jake with a look of surprise written across her face.

"I was going to, but I couldn't. I put it inside a hole in the tree trunk instead," he admitted. "I . . . I didn't feel right throwing away the first letter you ever got from you father."

"I think that was the best thing you could have done with it," Cathy responded. "Mr. Allan gave it to Dad as we were leaving last night. He said he'd found it down by the river and suggested that your dad read it, keeping in mind the truths that had been revealed by that old tool box that ruined several generations of his family. Your dad spent most of the night talking to Tom Parkin. When I left to come over here, he was more mellow than I've seen him in years."

Amy took a deep breath and exhaled very slowly. "Do you think he'll change?" she asked softly.

Cathy smiled and nodded. "If he *can* change, it seems this is the place for that to happen. I feel like we've been immersed in truth and humbled by the mess we've made of the things that matter most. It seems as though the Parkins have something that we're badly in need of."

Amy smiled and embraced her mother. They held onto each other for a long time. "I'm so proud of you," Cathy said. "And Jake's right, you look amazing."

The chapel was already filling with guests and locals for church services when they arrived. Beverly met them at the door, along with several of Amy's sisters-in-law and a gaggle of her nieces. They whisked Amy away while Aunt Bev pulled Jake aside.

"Listen," she whispered, taking Jake's hand and slipping a string of pearls into it. "I've been holding onto these pearls for more than fifty-five years, hoping someday to give them to my daughter."

"Aunt Bev, I'm not going to take your necklace," Jake protested.

"Jake, they're not mine. They never were. I wore them on my wedding day, but only to honor my best friend. These were Lily's. Isaac bought them for her on their honeymoon and he gave them to me after she died. I know he'd want you to have them."

Jake opened his hand and looked at the beautiful, freshwater pearls. Each one was unique, ranging slightly in color from light grays and off-whites to orange and yellow. He remembered reading in Isaac's journal about them, how he'd bought them for Lily in Erie. He looked at Bev and saw she was crying.

"They were always meant to be for the potter's wife," she said, closing his fingers around them.

Jake nodded and thanked her, slipping the pearls into his pocket and swallowing hard to keep his emotions from coming to the surface.

They walked into the church and up to the front where Amy was sitting, surrounded by her nieces and nephews. One of her nieces moved, making room for Jake to sit down next to her, and they all packed in tightly as the last of the congregants continued to slide into their seats.

Mrs. Smith winked at them as she slid onto the organ bench to play the prelude music. It was a familiar tune, but it wasn't until the congregation stood to sing, that Jake recognized it, "Count Your Many Blessings." Jake smiled at Amy as he held the hymnbook open for them both, as her hands were busy holding one of her youngest nephews, a tow-headed youngster named Timmy.

As the congregation took their seats, Thomas walked to the lectern. When he turned to face them, he looked stressed. "I was up a little later than usual last night," Thomas said, forcing a smile, "and as luck would have it, I received a phone call early this morning from today's speaker. Apparently she got food poisoning last night from a bad potato salad, and isn't feeling up to snuff. She asked me to take over for her.

"As I've been thinking about what I might say to you, I keep coming back to a memory from the first year after I made Niederbipp my home. I'd gone walking with a few of my friends on a trail in the hills above town. We stopped at an old well to get a drink and as we sat in the shade of the ancient trees, my friends told me a story of the shepherd who'd once lived there. Brushing away the leaves from an old bench, they pointed to the words that had been carved deep into the wood. These words have given me much to think about as I have pondered them in quiet moments over the years. So I wouldn't forget them, I wrote them inside the cover of my Bible."

Thomas lifted the book closer to his face. "It said, "We drink from the wells we did not dig; we warm ourselves by the fires we did not kindle. We sit on benches hewn by other men's hands, while our lungs are filled with air we did not create." Thomas closed the book and looked up at the congregation.

"I'm certain I didn't fully understand what that meant then, but over time, as I have repeated this in my mind again and again, I believe I have begun to understand what this means. There have been times in my life when my pride gets the best of me—when I begin to believe that whatever light I have is of my own creation. It is at those times that I am most grateful for the truths written on that bench.

"After I received the phone call this morning, asking for my help, I went for a walk to clear my mind and to seek inspiration. Walking down the cobblestone streets, past the buildings and shops, I realized that everywhere I looked, I saw the mark of human hands that were not my own. Walking further, I came to the river and sat down on a log to sort through my thoughts, but I became distracted by the insects, the birds, the trees and the water itself—all of which would exist and continue without me there to enjoy it—all of which was created by another hand with unlimited power and creativity.

"Feeling small and weak, I walked home, wondering what benefit, if any, I was to this world. I walked again over the stones I did not set in place and through the churchyard where I sat in the shade of the tree I did not plant. After some time, I walked into the house I did not build, ate the oatmeal I did not grow from the bowl I did not create. Then I dressed in the cloth I did not weave before coming to the church I did not build so I could listen to the music I did not make.

"I am not a builder, nor a weaver, not a musician, nor a farmer, but God, in his infinite wisdom and goodness, has created only one of me in the whole world and has endowed me with a few good gifts. There have been times in my life when my selfishness has led me to become a net-consumer. Instead of sharing or exchanging the gifts I have been given, I have been content to drink from other men's wells and warm myself at other men's fires."

Jake looked around the congregation to see women fanning themselves with a variety of small folding fans they'd pulled from their purses. He loosened his tie and tried to think cooler thoughts as he felt his temperature rising inside his suit.

"Living in a small town has changed many of those ideas," Thomas continued. "Though I still have plenty of days where I wonder what value I have to this world, I have learned that though my talents are small and my gifts, limited, I have something to give—something to share. This morning, as I looked down at the cobblestones, I found myself wondering if the stonemasons who set each stone in place hundreds of years ago had any idea that their work would be around to inspire my thoughts. I wonder if the men and women who built this fine chapel ever imagined the generations of people who would pass through its door and be touched by the spirit as they sat in these pews.

"Those who dig wells and kindle fires rarely do so for themselves alone. Each of us, regardless of our age, our income, our gender or our station in life has at least one gift to give to this world. We each hold in our souls a link to a chain or a piece to a puzzle that is an essential part of the whole. God, in his wisdom and grace, plants a seed of greatness in every human heart. I am convinced that if we nurture that seed with faith and love, it will grow until it can provide fruit and shade and shelter to a world in need of every good gift.

"Yesterday, our country celebrated its independence. Across America, friends and families gathered together to watch parades and have barbecues, but few of us probably thought of those whose lives were cut short when their blood was spilt in defense of our liberties. Each and every day, we all benefit from the sacrifices of those who went before us. Few, if any of us in this congregation today, will be called upon to put our lives at risk for our freedoms. It is a hard thing to die for one's beliefs, but it seems that it may be at least equally difficult to live for one's beliefs without becoming complacent. Somehow, when the path is smooth and the living is easy, we tend to fall asleep and forget Luke's reminder in the twelfth chapter, forty-eighth verse, 'that to whomsoever much is given, of him shall much be required.' The wells have been dug and the trees have been planted, but if we do nothing but drink the water and dance around in the shade, we are dead and with us, our children and our children's children. To continue to live, we must give, we must share, we must open our hearts and minds and souls and bring forth the fruits of the tree that God has planted in each of our souls.

"I am reminded of one of my favorite hymns. It was written over a hundred and thirty years ago by a Christian song writer named Phillip Bliss. According to the story, Mr. Bliss was traveling with Reverend Dwight Moody. One night, the Reverend addressed a congregation, relating a story of a boat and its crew who met their doom against the rocks near Lake Erie's Cleveland harbor. There is a lighthouse that marks the channel to that harbor, and though it was shining brightly that night, and though the captain was brave and skilled, it was not enough to bring the boat safely out of the storm and into harbor. Why? Because the lower lights—the lights which captains use to align their boats with the lighthouse and the channel—those lights had been blown out by the storm. Reverend Moody concluded his sermon with a strong admonition to everyone in the congregation that night, saying that the Master will take care of the great lighthouse, but that it is our duty to keep the lower lights burning bright.

"After listening to that sermon, Mr. Bliss went home and wrote a beautiful song. "Let the Lower Lights Be Burning." There are many people in my life who have shared their light with me. Many of these good people have helped me to remember who I am and what I have to share with others. There have been many who have warmed my heart and stoked my fire. There have been many in my life, as I hope there have been in yours, who have marked with their light the way into the safe harbor."

Jake took Amy's hand. Her nephew had fallen asleep on her shoulder, but she managed to turn her head to look at him. "Thank you," he whispered.

Amy squeezed his hand tightly and turned back to Thomas, drawn by the sound of his voice. He opened the Bible and read several verses relating to light and truth in both the New and Old Testaments. Jake's mind was caught away by all the things he'd learned about light from the Candlelighters who'd been anxious to teach and share and answer questions. One after another, from the day he'd arrived, they had lined up in a row to lead Jake down this road. Distracted by his thoughts, he began looking around the congregation. Kai and Molly were sitting just across the aisle with their baby. Gloria and Joseph were just a few rows back. Eric Schmelding, dressed in the same knickers he'd worn on the day they'd met him, stood on the right side next to several other men who had either arrived late or offered their seats to the women when the congregants exceeded the seating capacity. Hildegard was in her usual place on the back row. Without having to search, he also spied Sam and his wife next to Bev and Jerry. The Mayor and his wife sat on the front row, not far from Sandy and Andrew. In a short period of time, these people had become his people. Each of them had loved him and helped to open his eyes and heart to truth and love.

"For our closing hymn, we will sing, "Let the Lower Lights Be Burning," hymn number 312," Thomas said, snapping Jake out of his thoughts. The organ started up and the congregation rose to its feet. Amy moved Timmy's head to her other shoulder so she could stand closer to Jake as they sang the words of the hymn.

Brightly beams our Father's mercy
From His lighthouse evermore,
But to us He gives the keeping
Of the lights along the shore.

Dark the night of sin has settled,
Loud the angry billows roar;
Eager eyes are watching, longing
For the lights along the shore.

Trim your feeble lamp, my brother!
Some poor sailor, tempest tossed,
Trying now to make the harbor,
In the darkness may be lost.

Let the lower lights be burning,
Send a gleam across the wave!
Some poor fainting, struggling seaman
You may rescue, you may save.

At the close of the benediction, the congregation stood. Timmy was peeled off Amy's shoulder by his mother, and well-wishers offered their congratulations as they walked past.

The crowd cleared, leaving Amy and Jake surrounded by Amy's adoring nieces who were charmed by the beauty and magic of their aunt's dress. Jake watched as Amy spoke lovingly to each of them.

"Don't you think Amy looks like a princess?" one of her nieces asked Jake.

"Absolutely," said Jake. "Don't you think she could use some jewelry?" he asked, playfully.

Several of the nieces nodded in response.

"Well, I happen to have brought some with me," Jake said. He put his hand into his breast pocket and withdrew the strand of carnival beads he'd taken from the pirate lookout the day before.

One little girl squealed with delight while the others reached out to touch the brightly colored beads.

"Those are the family jewels from the pirate lookout that I told you about last night," an older niece proudly announced to her younger cousins.

"Do you think you might be able to find your way back there?" Jake asked the older girl.

"Maybe . . . I mean probably," she said confidently.

"Do you think you could take your dad back there with you, say, maybe this afternoon, and hang these back on the nail?" asked Jake.

"Definitely. Why?"

"Because we're a little concerned about their safety. Valuable jewels like this, they really need to be kept in a safe place."

Amy looked at Jake with questioning eyes.

"I think it's time to pass the guardianship of the family jewels on to the next generation," Jake said, handing the necklace to Amy's oldest niece.

"Remember the secrets," Amy said softly. "And never let the pirates know you have them."

The girl looked down at the jewels as if she'd just been handed the world on a silver platter. She thanked them and led the new gang of guardians out into the sunlight to better examine their treasure.

"What are you up to?" Amy asked when they were gone.

"I like those beads, but they didn't match your dress very well. I thought these might be better." He reached into his pocket again and pulled out the string of pearls, clasping them around her neck.

"What is this?" she asked, touching the pearls.

"Just some old family jewels. Your aunt gave them to me on our way in. She said they were meant to belong to a potter's wife. They were Lily's," Jake said softly, trying to swallow the words as quickly as he could to keep his emotions under control.

Amy took a deep breath as she remembered the story from Isaac's sketchbook. "I love you," she said, wrapping her arms around his chest. "And I can't wait to be the potter's wife."

WHERESOEVER YOU GO,
GO WITH ALL YOUR
HEART!

-CONFUCIUS-

NEW BEGINNINGS

WE ARE TOO READY TO RETALIATE, RATHER THAN FORGIVE,
OR GAIN BY LOVE AND INFORMATION.
AND YET WE COULD HURT NO MAN THAT WE BELIEVE LOVES US.
LET US THEN TRY WHAT LOVE WILL DO:
FOR IF MEN DID ONCE SEE WE LOVE THEM, WE SHOULD SOON FIND THEY
WOULD NOT HARM US. FORCE MAY SUBDUE, BUT LOVE GAINS:
AND HE THAT FORGIVES FIRST, WINS THE LAUREL. IF I AM EVEN WITH MY
ENEMY, THE DEBT IS PAID; BUT IF I FORGIVE IT, I OBLIGE HIM FOREVER.
—WILLIAM PENN—

In an effort to keep with Quaker wedding traditions of guests sitting together in a circle, two chairs were set at the front of the chapel, just a few feet in front of the first pews. Many of the family and guests milled about while Gloria hung small bouquets of wild flowers from the ends of each pew. Jake and Amy tried to help but were sent out to mingle with their guests in the churchyard.

The Yoder family was there, resting in the shade and attracting the stares of all the out-of-towners. Jake and Amy brushed past the others to welcome them with warm handshakes and hugs. Out of the corner of his eye, Jake saw a man watching them. When he looked closer, he recognized the pudgy man as Dr. Eric Lewis, his professor from Hudson. Jake walked quickly to him, embracing him awkwardly before pulling him over to meet Amy. They chatted briefly before they were pulled away by other guests.

Amy's parents stood apart from the crowd, watching silently as their daughter and future son-in-law moved from friend to friend, all the while being followed by Eric Schmelding's camera.

Sam drove the bakery truck into the churchyard, parking next to Thomas' cottage. Enlisting the help of several of the men, they unloaded the wedding cake and carried it carefully up the stone stairs, setting it just inside the church doors to keep it from melting in the sun. On top of the cake was an unusual display that only those who'd frequented The Pottery would understand, two mugs—one that was rather tall and plain and another with an intricately carved blue flower on the side.

When the clock tolled twelve, Jerry stood at the top of the stairs and announced that the wedding would now begin. Jake and Amy walked back up the stairs and entered the chapel, followed by their friends and family. As they had been instructed, they walked to the front of the chapel and sat down next to each other on the two chairs, while Jerry ushered the guests into the first several pews. When everyone was settled and silence had fallen, Jerry stood and nervously welcomed those who had come to share this day with Jake and Amy. Then he turned to Jake and Amy, inviting them to stand and take each other by the right hand.

"Because few of us are familiar with Quaker weddings," Jerry said, "Jake and Amy have asked me to explain how things work. Quakers believe that all mankind is equal in the eyes of God; therefore, there is no priest or minister who will officiate in this marriage ceremony. In the state of Pennsylvania and according to Quaker tradition, you and I will be witnesses to the creation of this union. As the tradition goes, once they have exchanged their vows and taken their seats, you will have the opportunity to contribute to the ministry of this ceremony. If you feel so inclined, we invite you to share whatever you would like as directed by the light within your heart." Jerry nodded to Jake and Amy before taking his seat on the front row.

Jake took a deep breath and smiled at the guests before he began. "Friends, in the presence of the Lord and of this assembly, I take thee, my friend, Amy Eckstein, to be my wife, promising with, Divine Assistance, to be unto thee a loving and faithful husband until death shall separate us."

Amy looked at Jake and smiled sweetly before turning to look at her family and guests. "Friends, in the presence of the Lord and of this assembly, I take thee, my friend, Jacob Henry Kimball, to be my husband, promising, with Divine Assistance, to be unto thee a loving and faithful wife until death shall separate us."

After kissing each other, they sat down and silence fell, broken only by the giggles of the children whose joy could not be restrained. After a minute, Gloria stood. When she began, the words came out slowly as she tried to control her emotions, but soon, she gave up and let the tears mingle with her words of appreciation and love for her adopted son and daughter-in-law. She complimented them on the handsome couple they made and expressed her confidence in the love that she had witnessed growing between them, suggesting that love would continue to grow with each passing day if they would continue to act and live without selfishness.

Beverly stood next to congratulate Jake and Amy. She spoke of the same feelings of pride and happiness that Gloria shared, and suggested that they always remember that love is a daily decision and one that needed to be met with patience and kindness and understanding.

Eric Schmelding stood, and after explaining that he had little to offer by way of advice because of his status as a bachelor, he suggested that from his observations of couples all around the world, those who knew how to laugh together seemed to be the happiest. He encouraged them to continue in faith and love and selflessness, but never to forget the need to laugh. Before sitting down, he also encouraged them to continue to share their light through the talents they'd been given.

Kai and Molly stood together briefly to express their happiness with the union and their wishes for a lifetime of shared friendship.

Thomas stood, and pointing to the all-seeing eye carved into the beam high above their heads, suggested that God could be a member of their union if He were invited into their home through regular prayer and gentle words. He reminded them to pay attention to the small and simple things in life and always to look for fingerprints of the Creator.

Cathy stood from her place on the front row and turned to look at her family, her children and grandchildren. Through tears of happiness, she expressed her love for Amy and Jake and applauded the life they had chosen which had caused her to evaluate her own. Speaking to all of her children, she expressed her hope that each of them would learn from the mistakes she and their father had made in life and in marriage and be stronger partners and parents because of it. Before sitting down, she put her hand on Doug's shoulder and publicly expressed her love for the man she'd married, the father of her six children who had provided well for them. Then turning to Amy and Jake, she encouraged them to use the lessons they'd learned about forgiveness and share them with their children and their children's children forever.

One of Amy's nieces, a girl of about six or seven, stood and delighted everyone by telling Amy how pretty she looked and how happy she was to have a new uncle.

John Yoder, the Amish craftsman stood and on behalf of his family, thanked Jake once again for coming to Niederbipp. With a tremor in his voice, he offered a simple, beautiful prayer of hope and happiness for Jake and Amy. Before taking his seat, he told them that they were always welcome at his table and if Jake ever needed an apprentice, he would be happy to send one of his sons to learn the potter's art.

Amy's brother, John, stood. He admitted that he'd done a little research about Quaker weddings when he heard his baby sister had chosen such a wedding. He said he worried that it would be kind of weird, but that he was grateful for the experience that would allow him to express his love for his *favorite* sister in a public forum. He also welcomed Jake into the family and apologized for judging him before he'd ever met him. He said he spoke for all the brothers by saying that if Jake didn't take care of their sister, there would be hell to pay, but then, laughing, thanked Jake for loving his sister and encouraging her greatness and creativity. He closed his remarks by saying that if they ever were starving, they would be welcome to come and live in a makeshift tent under their kitchen table.

After John sat down, a long period of silence followed where only the sounds of restless children were heard. Finally, looking somewhat reluctant, Amy's father stood. He said nothing for a long moment, looking down at the floor. Cathy reached up and held his hand encouragingly. Finally, with emotion in his voice, he began to speak softly.

"I don't remember ever being afraid of anything in my life," he said, turning to look at his family and the other guests, "but coming here this weekend has caused me a great deal of anxiety. I am a proud man. I don't want to turn this wedding into a confessional, but . . . but I do need to apologize. I have been a jerk to all of you, or as my old schoolteacher more eloquently stated, I have been a stubborn animal akin to a donkey."

He forced a smile as he nodded at Hildegard. "Before this weekend, I don't know if I have ever truly apologized in my life. Apparently, that is a genetic flaw I inherited from my great-grandfather. I am beginning to realize how my inability to recognize and admit my mistakes has affected nearly everyone here today. It has been said that it takes a big man to admit when he is wrong. I have been a very little man, and I am sorry.

"Last night, as I sat in company with my second cousin and his children, I was struck by the reality of where my life might be if it weren't for a loving wife and forgiving children. I have tried to live my life without regrets, but the reality is, when I open my eyes, I have hundreds of them. In my pursuit of financial success, I have forgotten the faith of my youth. I have bullied and neglected my wife and children. I have burned hundreds of bridges and made a mess of most of my business associations. I have made lots of money over the years, but as I sat down and heard my cousin Robert Allan speak of his greatest treasures, I realized that Jake was right—I have missed everything that is important. My eyes have been blind to the things that matter most.

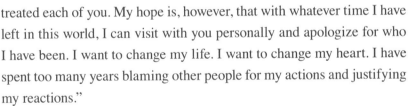

"As I have observed Jake and Amy yesterday and today and heard stories from everyone I know here about how they have loved and treated each of you, I have become increasingly ashamed of the person I am. I don't feel as though I can ask you to forgive me for how I have treated each of you. My hope is, however, that with whatever time I have left in this world, I can visit with you personally and apologize for who I have been. I want to change my life. I want to change my heart. I have spent too many years blaming other people for my actions and justifying my reactions."

Doug took a deep breath and turned to look at his daughter. She was crying and as he looked at her, he wept in front of his wife and children for the first time any of them could remember. "I'm sorry, Amy," he whispered through his sobs. "I'm sorry I have been blind to who you are. I am sorry for my insensitivity. I am sorry that the first letter I ever wrote you was such a disaster. I would like to say I am proud of you, but I know I deserve none of the credit for the beautiful woman you have become.

"Jake, I want to thank you for loving Amy. I am sorry for judging you and I congratulate you both. You are indeed a handsome couple. I would like to give you some sage advice, but I am not a sage and I am in no position to give any advice, so I will just say thank you for making me come to Niederbipp, *twice in three weeks*, to finally learn the things I wish I could have learned when I was much younger."

He sat down, but Amy stood from her chair and ran toward him, throwing her arms around his neck.

"I love you," he whispered through his sobs.

"I know that now, Dad. Thank you."

Doug held onto his daughter for a long time as all of her brothers looked at each other as if they were wondering what had just happened. For most of the people who had known Doug Eckstein for years, this apology was a good start. But for Amy, on the day of her wedding, to hear a simple apology and words of love from her father, it was enough. It was all she needed.

Amy returned to her seat where Jake stood, waiting to embrace her. They stood together, hand in hand, and thanked everyone for their love and friendship and for coming to support them.

Jerry stood once again and presented the marriage certificate that Amy had created. After Jake and Amy signed their names, they exchanged rings and with them, another kiss. Then Jerry took the certificate back and turned to face the gathering. He cleared his throat loudly and then began to read.

On this, the fifth day of July,
at the Niederbipp Chapel, in Niederbipp, Pennsylvania,
Jacob Henry Kimball and Amy Eckstein
mutually agreed to join their lives together
through the sanctity of marriage,
and promised before God, Angels and Friends
that they would honor and love each other,
practice unselfish kindness,
be quick to forgive,

and faithfully seek after the light of truth and joy.
As further confirmation of this covenant and its obligations,
they set their hands to this certificate:
Jacob Henry Kimball and Amy Eckstein
And we, having been present as witnesses, also set our hands
in support of their marriage.

Jerry looked up from the certificate and smiled at his niece and his new nephew before turning to their guests. "Jake and Amy would like to invite you to sign this certificate, and then we invite you to the yard to enjoy some cake, and from what I've been told, a very special blend of iced peppermint tea."

As Jake and Amy cut the cake, Sam plucked the mugs from the top tier and filled them with peppermint tea. Jake winked at Amy as she was handed her new mug. Then he raised his mug high. "To joy!" he said, smiling at his new bride.

"To joy!" she repeated, and cheers rose up as they clinked their mugs together and then drank deeply.

After an hour of mingling with their family and friends, Amy climbed to the top step and tossed her bouquet into a small but jubilant crowd made up of her nieces and the daughters and granddaughters of her cousins. As the crowd cheered, Joseph drove into the churchyard in his vintage Volkswagen bus and tossed Jake the keys.

Amidst the cheers and well-wishes of all the people they knew and loved, the eighth potter of Niederbipp and the most amazing, beautiful and talented girl he had ever known, drove out of the churchyard, anxious to begin the next chapter in The Book of JOY.

THE SPIRIT OF MAN
IS THE CANDLE OF THE
LORD.
PROVERBS 20:27

THE STORY BEHIND THE STORY

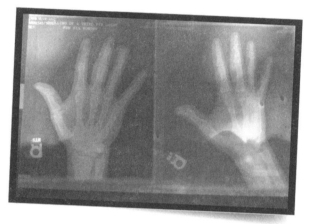

A TRULY GOOD BOOK TEACHES ME BETTER THAN TO READ IT. I MUST SOON
LAY IT DOWN, AND COMMENCE LIVING ON ITS HINT. WHAT I BEGAN BY
READING, I MUST FINISH BY ACTING.
—HENRY DAVID THOREAU—

I suppose this is a strange way to begin an afterword, but since I am an artist and not really a writer, I am going to try to get away with it. Why? Because this is part of the story and I don't want it to be lost as simply the junk at the end of the book that no one reads.

There are two questions I am most often asked by people who have read my books. "Does Niederbipp really exist, and if so, how do I get there?"

One woman came up to me at a book signing, and after telling me how much she'd enjoyed my first two books, declared that she *absolutely* had to move to Niederbipp. Her neighbors and community were a bore to her. The people were ignorant, self-righteous and mean. But she was convinced that if she could live in Niederbipp, eat Sam's bread, drink Isaac's tea, and walked down streets filled with happy people, she would be happy.

"Can you tell me where it is?" she persisted. "I've looked on every map and atlas and spent a lot of time searching for it on the Internet. Please, you've got to tell me where it is?"

I looked at this woman and sadly told her that she would never find it.

Does Niederbipp really exist? Yes, it does! But unless you carry the lessons of Niederbipp in your heart, you will never find it. If, however, you take these things to heart—if you will live your life unselfishly—if you will face life's decisions with love instead of fear—if you will learn to know and love your neighbors—if you will learn to forget yourself, then Niederbipp will never be far away, and these books will give you the road map you need to get there.

During the last few weeks, while I was finishing this book, I struggled to know how to wrap things up with Matthew and Sam. I played out dozens of scenarios in my mind. Everyone loves a happy ending, right? But one night as I went to bed, I had a dream. As much as I would have liked to wrap up their story in a neat bundle, I couldn't. I wasn't supposed to. I believe there is in each of us both a Sam and a Matthew. We have each been hurt or broken by someone we love, and before this life is over, we will each hurt or damage someone we love. And so, I felt inspired that I must leave it up to you to decide how their story will end. Each holds in his or her hands and hearts the key to unlocking the truth, but you each must decide how to use that key.

There is at least one more bit of unfinished business that I have intentionally left as is. It seems sometimes that our world is driven by money. Jake held onto two thousand dollars from the money he received from Charlie. Knowing what you know about Niederbipp, and having watched Jake and Amy learn the true value of money, I leave this for you to decide what Jake will do with it. What would you do? That's a lot money. I might be tempted to spend it on cheese, but if I did, I'm afraid I would have to deny the things I have learned from Isaac about the true value of money.

As I finish this book, and with it, this series, my mind and heart are filled with mixed emotions. Part of me is really going to miss Niederbipp, but another part of me is excited to learn how to live my life post-Niederbipp. For the past twelve years, my life has been influenced by Isaac and the people of a charming town on the banks of the Allegheny River. I have never really felt as though this is my story, that is, that I own it. Part of the story *is* my story. I am a potter and this is loosely based on my experience as a potter's apprentice in a little town in Germany about fifteen years ago, but that is where my story ends and where the lives of the people of Niederbipp begin to take shape. I would love to claim the wisdom of this book as my own wisdom, but it is not. By saying that, no one should assume it was plagiarized either. The experience of writing this book was for me, more than anything, the experience of learning to listen to a voice that told me these things as I sat at my wheel and made mud pies.

In 1881, my third great grandfather, Isaac Behunin passed away. He was born in Oswego County, New York, in 1803. He married Elmina Tyler in 1834 in Erie, Pennsylvania, and spent the rest of his life settling the West. He was a man of character and courage. When I was in the sixth grade, I did a school report on Isaac, and from that time, I felt a closeness to him that to this day I cannot explain. Twelve years ago, when I began "hearing voices," it was Isaac's voice who was talking to me, telling me these stories.

From the beginning, I felt compelled to record the things I was hearing, even though I was just a potter, not a writer. At first, I doodled in my journals and sketchbooks, but when the things I was learning began keeping me up at night, I knew I needed to take it more seriously.

I started getting up in the middle of the night and recording what I had learned that day from Isaac. It was very inconvenient. I had just gotten married, I was making pottery full time and going to school—*and I was not a writer.* But Isaac continued to come and talk to me as I sat at my wheel and created things out of mud. I wrote when I had time or when I felt more compelled to write than to sleep.

After a couple of years, I had accumulated a hundred pages. As luck would have it, my computer crashed and all was lost. At first, it was a bit of a relief. I wasn't a writer anyway, so I figured it was just the universe telling me to get real. But Isaac never really left. He kept coming. He kept finding me in the quiet moments in my studio. I felt compelled to start again.

My business continued to grow. I was doing a show every February in Philadelphia, selling my creations to galleries across the country. I was regularly having to work sixteen-hour days in order to keep up. In those days, I was going through ten tons of clay a year. I had a mortgage, a new son, bills, life, and writing fell by the wayside— something I would visit in the evenings and on weekends  if I didn't have anything better to do. I was busy trying to make a living, but all the while, Isaac continued to stand behind me and whisper in my ear. I knew there was medication for people like me, but the things I was learning were positive and motivating and lit up my life in a way that only truth can.

Then, my life began to change. In 2004, I was diagnosed, at age thirty, with arthritis—in my right hand of all places. Potters kind of need their hands to make stuff. I fought it with everything from meds, to chiropractic, to acupuncture, to all sorts of voodoo, but nothing worked. Finally, after six months of worry and pain, I received a couple of cortisone shots into the afflicted knuckles. A week later, I felt good again and got back to work. That very day, my left hand began to flare up, often making it impossible to do my work on the wheel.

I responded by changing the way I worked, choosing to hand-build my work rather than using the wheel which had been the cause of some of my worst pain and problems. But as much as I tried to run away from the pain, it kept catching up to me.

For several years, I continued to write whenever I could, but I knew it was never enough. I knew I was supposed to be writing more, but I was afraid.

Fear is a powerful force. I call it the Great Inhibitor that keeps us all from becoming what we are supposed to be. I was making a living as a potter—something that is nearly impossible—and I didn't want to give that up to take a big step down a dark and lonely hallway. A couple of years passed as I continued to write in my spare time, but felt inhibited by fear to give it any more time and energy.

In January of 2007, I was up late one night working at the wheel, making some teapot lids for the show in Philadelphia. Teapot lids require a huge amount of dexterity, and as I sat struggling with my hands, trying to make them do what they used to do, I realized I had lost all that dexterity. I was broken. I was humble. I felt like I had been swallowed by a whale. Finally, after struggling for several minutes to make my hands work, I began to weep, knowing that all I had worked so hard for could suddenly be lost. As my tears fell into my work, an audible voice spoke to me. The voice told me that I knew what it was I was supposed to be doing, that the experiences I had been given were meant to be shared, and that I needed to get on with it. 2007 was the last year I went to the show in Philadelphia.

Shortly after that experience in the studio, I stumbled upon a scripture in 2 Timothy 1:7: *For God hath not given us the spirit of fear, but of power, and of love, and of a sound mind.* I had been fearful. I had given into that fear. I had allowed it to win. But I knew that fear did not come from God. He gives us power and love and a sound mind—all of which I had forgotten in the face of my fear.

I took heart from that and other scriptures and began to take steps into the dark. It was hard at first, wondering how I was going to pay the bills without the Philadelphia show, which constituted about sixty percent of my annual income. But somehow, my family did not starve, and the work came, and I had time to write. I turned off my TV, and I jumped into writing and rewriting and bringing things together.

After a year of serious writing, I had accumulated what would have equaled an 850-page book. It was long and detailed and needed some help. An acquaintance, who had had some experience with the publishing industry agreed to take a look at it, so I very reluctantly printed a copy and gave it to her to peruse. She called me six weeks later to tell me she had finished and we set a day to meet.

The morning of our meeting, I woke with a dream. People were flipping through my book, watching the hands of a potter make a pot. I knew that needed to be part of the book. But when I told this woman about my plans, she very quickly told me that she was certain no publisher would ever want to spend the time and money to put a book like I had envisioned together. Strike one.

Then she proceeded to hand me my manuscript, dripping with red ink. After ripping the story apart for the next half hour, she told me she thought it was a decent first draft and that if I ever decided to re-write the book, I might consider some changes—like punctuation. Isn't that what editors are for? Strike two.

I was devastated. This was my baby, and no one likes to be told they have an ugly baby. I set the manuscript on top of my kiln with the full intent of throwing it into the kiln during the next firing and be done with it. I wasn't a writer, and it was time for me to finally face the music and give up the silly dream.

But something happened. For the next two weeks, every time I walked past the manuscript, it shouted out to me to finish it. So, after an arts festival, I swallowed my pride and went back to start over. I tore it all apart and began putting it back together, slowly, painfully, and deliberately. It took a full year, but I rewrote the book at least a dozen times, each time, learning something new about being a writer.

I knew what the book was supposed to look like—I had seen it in a dream—but having heard that no publisher would want to do what I had in mind, I again jumped in with both feet. I talked to a graphic designer friend, Bert Compton, and shared with him my ideas. He said he'd been waiting his whole life for a project like this. I hired him that day and soon we began staying up late, after our kids and wives were in bed, putting *Remembering Isaac* together. It was a lot of work, but after several weeks, we had a book.

My wife and I had been saving our money to build a new kitchen, but instead, we bought fifteen-hundred books. I had an art show coming up and anticipated I would be able to sell five hundred books at that show. I came home having sold fifty-five books. I walked out into the my studio, to the sea of books that clogged up my work space and wondered how anyone could be so dumb as me. I had spent ten thousand dollars and eleven years of my life chasing a silly dream. I figured that I would be stuck giving away my books as wedding gifts for the rest of eternity. I was really depressed, and faithless, and the old fear began boiling up again.

But something happened. People went home and started reading about Niederbipp and Isaac and Jake's adventures, and within a week, strangers began calling me to ask if I was the Ben Behunin who wrote a book about a potter.

"Yes, I am," I said.

"Well, can you tell me where I can get one? My friend read it and has been raving about it. I checked the bookstores, but they don't have it yet."

"Yeah, well it's kind of new."

"So, do you know where I can buy a copy or two?"

"Come on over to my garage!" I'd say excitedly. "I've got a whole bunch."

And so it began. After selling nearly a thousand books on my own, most of which, from my garage, I talked a distributor into carrying my book. In December, 2009, *Discovering Isaac* came out and now, seven months later, I am finishing the series with *Becoming Isaac*. It has been an interesting journey that I feel is probably only beginning.

There are many lessons I have learned along this strange and often turbulent path. Faith is a journey, one that has perhaps as many valleys as it does peaks. None of this has been easy. I feel like I have been taught and humbled every step of the way. I never intended to write a book, and when I did, I never intended to get rich by it, which is a good thing, because I think I might have just broken even.

I feel like I have learned a lot about myself over this journey. I have learned about sacrifice and love and the value of money. I have learned about God and fear and faith. I feel that the windows of heavens have opened and poured out understanding about life that I never had before. I learned the importance of being still and listening to the wind blow. I learned that the universe is anxious to speak to all of us if we will find a quiet place to sit and be still and tune our ears to listen to its small and gentle voice. I have learned that when the universe knows you're listening, it tends to pour out more than you can receive, filling your life with new abilities and expectations.

This is the end of one story, but the beginning of many more. We each have a story to share, whether it be with music or words or deeds. We all have a light to share with the world that has the ability to shatter the shackles of darkness. Your story may still be within you. With love and understanding, I encourage you to let it out. Share the light with which you've been entrusted and shine with every sunbeam in your soul.

Viva Niederbipp and cheers to the journey!

Ben Behunin August 2010

THE SOULS OF PEOPLE, ON THEIR WAY TO EARTH-LIFE, PASS THROUGH A
ROOM FULL OF LIGHTS; EACH TAKES A TAPER - OFTEN ONLY A SPARK - TO
GUIDE IT IN THE DIM COUNTRY OF THIS WORLD. BUT SOME SOULS, BY RARE
FORTUNE, ARE DETAINED LONGER - HAVE TIME TO GRASP A HANDFUL OF
TAPERS, WHICH THEY WEAVE INTO A TORCH. THESE ARE THE TORCH-BEARERS
OF HUMANITY - ITS POETS, SEERS AND SAINTS, WHO LEAD AND LIFT THE
RACE OUT OF DARKNESS, TOWARD THE LIGHT. THEY ARE THE LAW-GIVERS
AND SAVIORS, THE LIGHT-BRINGERS, WAY-SHOWERS AND TRUTH-TELLERS,
AND WITHOUT THEM, HUMANITY WOULD LOSE ITS WAY IN THE DARK.
-PLATO-

Thank you, Isaac!

GLOSSARY
FOR WEIRD WORDS YOU DON'T KNOW

Bat: In ceramics, a bat is a disc made of wood, plaster or plastic. It is attached to the wheel head, allowing a potter to make a pot and then remove the pot from the wheel by removing the bat on which it was made.

Bisque Firing: The primary reason for bisque firing is to prepare the ware to be glazed. Submerging a piece of greenware in glaze would cause it to break down and fall apart. A bisque firing, usually to about 1800°F, hardens the clay to a state where the glaze can be applied without the ware breaking down. Because ware in a bisque firing is not glazed, pieces can be stacked on top of or inside of other pots without fear of the pots fusing together. Because of this, many more pots can be fired in a bisque firing than in a glaze firing.

Candling: Also known as preheat. Candling refers to a small flame that is introduced to the kiln, warming it and drying out the pots inside. It is critical to make sure all the moisture is drawn out of the pots before the rapid temperature rise of the firing begins or the pots with be blown to pieces by the inability of the water vapor in the clay to escape quickly enough.

Damper: Similar to a damper on a fireplace. It allows the heat to escape from the kiln and is the primary way to regulate the amount of reduction present in the kiln. This is adjusted throughout the firing using a long iron pole.

Glaze: Glaze at Pottery Niederbipp is applied only in liquid form by pouring onto bisqueware or by dipping bisqueware into the buckets of glaze. Glaze is made of a variety of materials that when melted at high temperatures, form a surface like glass. Some common ingredients include feldspars, clays, silica and metallic oxides.

Greenware: Unfired pottery. Term can be used for pots that have just been made and are still wet or to pots that are bone-dry and ready for a bisque fire. At this state, the pots are very fragile and extreme care is taken when handling them.

Kiln: In the ceramics world, there are hundreds of different kinds of kilns. The kiln at Pottery Niederbipp is gas fired and made of firebrick. It is used to fire pottery, making it first into bisqueware and then after the ware is glazed, it is used to used to fire the pottery to about 2360° F where the glaze matures, making it functional and non-porous.

Pyrometer: A high temperature thermometer that uses a thermocouple, or probe, placed in the door of the kiln with leads that are attached to a reader that helps a potter determine temperature inside the kiln. The one used at Pottery Niederbipp is an old fashioned analogue pyrometer with questionable accuracy.

Wax Resist: A mixture of wax and other ingredients that remains liquid at room temperature and is applied to pots for a variety of reasons. The resist protects the areas where it was applied, shedding the second glaze, while the unprotected or unwaxed areas received a second layer of glaze.

Wedging, wedge: Similar to kneading bread dough. Its main purposes include getting rid of air bubbles, rounding the lumps of clay for use on the wheel and mixing the clay so there is consistency found throughout.

SOURCES

- Ben Behunin's Sketchbooks, volumes 3-22
- Erin Barrett's Sketchbook (all the really nice thumbnail sketches.)
- Photos by Ben Behunin, Bert Compton, Steven Seiko, Al Thelin and Irene Meier
- The Holy Bible, King James Translation
- Brainyquote.com
- Quotationspage.com
- ThinkExist.com
- Cover art-"The Joys of Niederbipp" by Erin W. Berrett, www. EWBpaintings.com

THANK YOU PAGE

To my wife, Lynnette, who never doubted, and sacrificed her new kitchen and innumerable other comforts for this series. I hope to make it up to you someday. Thank you for loving me, unconditionally.

To my children, Isaac and Eve, who gave up time with their old man so I could pursue this course. I hope you will always remember that I love you. I hope these books have made me a better father.

To those who have purchased my books and shared the good news with their friends. Thank you for your words of encouragement and kindness that have kept me going when I have doubted and feared.

To Bert Compton, my friend and co-creator, who shared my vision for this series from the beginning. Thank you for sharing your talents with all who open these pages.

To Marilyn Smolka, Rex Scott, Maxine Babalis and Lynnette for your generous gift of editing this book and making it easier to read.

To Alan and Patsy Johnson, who more than any other mortals, taught me the power of love. Thank you for sharing your light with us.

To my parents, who taught me that work is the answer to most of life's struggles.

To Isaac, for patiently teaching me these things and waiting for me to listen. Thank you for not giving up on a sometimes proud and stubborn potter.

To the God of Abraham, Isaac and Jacob, for entrusting me with this gift and revealing the secrets of joy.

BEN'S BI?

I was born in the hospital in 1973, when my mother, who had been carrying me in her belly for nine months, decided it was time was time for me to move on. I later became the oldest of eight children who provided me with ample opportunity to learn how to tease.

I began working with clay as a freshman in high school, erroneously believing it would be an "easy A". I was pitiful, but I kept working at it, and after making more than my share of dog bowls and ashtrays, I won a scholarship to a junior college where I continued my studies in art and business.

For two years, I served as a Fromage bon Vivant in Switzerland, Germany, Austria and Wisconsin, while spreading the good word of Niederbipp to all who would listen. I later returned to Germany to work as a potter's apprentice before continuing my studies in the Sandwich Islands.

In 1996, I became a full-time potter when my neighbor offered me the use of their backyard studio. After the first year of full-time potting, I scraped together all my money and bought a ring for very pretty girl, Lynnette, who later agreed to be my wife and the mother of our children. I am pleased to report that my wife still loves me, and that we share our life and home with our two children, Isaac and Eve.

I still consider myself a Fromage bon Vivant, but usually only on the weekends or when invited to parties. I own the world's largest collection of Ben Behunin pottery in the world. I like to make up silly songs, whistle while I work, and bust out crazy dance moves, which I teach to my children. I used to eat a lot of Ben and Jerry's ice cream, but have been forced to cut back in recent years as my metabolism continues to change, and I don't like to work out. I like to fly fish when I have the time. I am a virtuoso harmonica player, and have recently learned how to play Oh Susannah with my nose. I sleep when I am tired, eat when I am hungry, and get cranky if I don't hear the sound of the ocean at least once a year. I listen to Prairie Home Companion nearly every week. I wear bow ties on Sundays. I like to attend the funerals of strangers. Now that this series is finished, I will begin working on several other books that have been begging to be written.

Personalized books can be ordered at
www.benbehunin.com
where you can also request to
receive updates about Isaac and other publications.

Ben enjoys hearing from his readers. You can reach him at:

Abendmahl Press
P.O. Box 581083
Salt Lake City, Utah 84158-1083

Or by email to
benbehunin@comcast.net

More information on this book is available at
www.rememberingisaac.blogspot.com
www.benbehunin.com
And www.vivaniederbipp.com
and on Facebook
Ben's pottery is available at www.potterboy.com
and many fine galleries across the U.S.A.

If you would like to feature Remembering Isaac or Discovering Isaac
in your book club, please contact Ben for a group discount.

For speaking engagements including book clubs and inaugurations
please call (801)-883-0146

For design information, contact Bert Compton at bert@comptonds.com

MOST MEN LEAD LIVES OF
QUIET DESPERATION
AND GO TO THEIR GRAVES
WITH THEIR SONG STILL IN THEM.
-HENRY DAVID THOREAU-